THE
LAND
GIRLS

The daughter of a Durham miner, Annie Wilkinson now lives in Hull where she divides her time between supporting her father and helping with grandchildren.

Also by Annie Wilkinson

A Sovereign for a Song
Winning a Wife
No Price Too High
For King and Country
Sing Me Home
Angel of the North

THE LAND GIRLS

ANNIE WILKINSON

**SIMON &
SCHUSTER**

London · New York · Sydney · Toronto · New Delhi

A CBS COMPANY

First published in Great Britain by Simon & Schuster UK Ltd, 2014
A CBS COMPANY
Copyright © Annie Wilkinson, 2014

1 3 5 7 9 10 8 6 4 2

Simon & Schuster UK Ltd
1st Floor
222 Gray's Inn Road
London WC1X 8HB

www.simonandschuster.co.uk

Simon & Schuster Australia, Sydney
Simon & Schuster India, New Delhi

A CIP catalogue record for this book is available from the British Library

HB ISBN: 978-1-47111-539-4
EBOOK ISBN: 978-1-47111-541-7

Typeset by Hewer Text UK Ltd, Edinburgh
Printed and bound in Great Britain by CPI Group (UK) Ltd, Croydon, CR0 4YY

The real land girls

Acknowledgements

Madeleine McDonald–Ullyat and her friend Barbara Cierpka, for their help with translation of some text into German.

Doreen Wiles and her brother Bill for their kindness in sharing memories of their wartime childhood in East Hull.

My cousin Elizabeth Till for memories of life during the war.

Avril Taylor who helped me with my research into wartime farming methods.

Mrs Susan Butler, writer on local history, whose website is at: www.howdenshirehistory.co.uk.

Brian Pears, whose website, North-East Diary, is at: www.ne-diary.bpears.org.uk.

Numerous other websites dealing with life during the war.

Hull History Centre; Howden Library; Beverley Library; The Carnegie Centre in Hull.

Knighton Joyce, for her book *Land Army Days: Cinderellas of the Soil*, and the East Riding of Yorkshire Council's East Riding Rural Life Project for the pamphlet *The Women's Land Army*, both of which I drew on heavily for this novel.

Chapter 1

From her vantage point behind the polished oak counter of the Maypole grocer's and confectioner's in Holderness Road, young Muriel Dearlove was taking a moment to admire her own reflection in the plate-glass window, darkened by the billboard leaning up against it. Dark eyes, strongish nose, generous mouth. Abundant dark hair, tied back in a bun. Wispy corkscrew curls that always escaped the little cap she had to wear. Not bad-looking, as a matter of fact. She had to admit it herself. She breathed in, squeezing in a waist that measured just an inch or two more than she would have liked, and gave herself a smile of approval. The smile died as, beyond her reflection, Muriel spied old Mrs Musgrave looming out of the shadows of a January late afternoon.

'Four farthing buns,' Muriel muttered to herself.

At a minute before closing time, the bell above the shop door tinkled the alarm and Mrs Musgrave came out of the greyness and into the light – and presented herself at the counter.

'Four farthing buns,' she demanded.

One by one, Muriel carefully lifted four farthing buns with the tongs out of the glass-fronted display and put them in a paper bag, wondering how many times she must have served this self-same customer with these self-same bloody farthing buns. Must be fifty thousand, at least.

'You're a bit late,' she remarked. 'You're lucky we've got four left. It's only half a minute to closing time, and it's only five minutes to blackout time.'

Mrs Musgrave gave her a malevolent stare. 'You've got six left, and I don't want no rudeness,' she said.

Miss Chapman, the blonde, plump manageress of about fifty summers, looked up from her task of cashing up, glanced at the clock and went to lock the shop door.

'Don't be rude to the customers, Muriel,' she said, on her return to the till.

'No rudeness intended, I'm sure,' Muriel said, with a shrug and a pert toss of her head. For the fifty-thousandth time she held the two top corners of the paper bag and swung it round to twist the ends to hold the buns in. Her mild irritation gave the movement just enough added velocity to burst the bottom of the bag and send the buns bouncing across the tiled floor. The manageress looked, but said nothing.

With profuse and insincere apologies, Muriel emerged from behind the counter to pick them up, sauntering towards them with a careless, intensely feminine swing of the hips.

Mrs Musgrave glared at her. 'You've done that on

purpose! I'm not having them now. Don't think I'm having them, after they've been on the floor.'

Muriel put the offending buns at the back of the counter. 'Would you like the other two?'

'I suppose I'll have to, now.'

Muriel put the two remaining farthing buns into a clean bag and put them on the counter with a distinct lack of contrition. 'That'll be a halfpenny, please.'

'Have you got any ham?'

'No,' Muriel lied. She'd already put the ham back in the cold room, and a customer who habitually walked into the shop half a minute before closing time on a Friday afternoon didn't deserve to have it dragged out again.

For a fraction of a second Miss Chapman paused, and with an almost imperceptible twitch of her eyebrows she shot a fleeting glance in Muriel's direction. Muriel held her breath, expecting an order to fetch the ham, but Miss Chapman was quietly concentrating on her cashing up as if the pause, the twitch and the glance had never happened. Keeping her own counsel, like all the three wise monkeys rolled into one, Muriel thought.

'Any bacon?'

'No, and the cheese ration's down to an ounce a week,' Muriel cheerfully announced.

Mrs Musgrave gave her a baleful stare. 'An ounce of cheese, then, and don't drop it on the floor.'

'Have you got your ration book?'

Mrs Musgrave produced the book. 'Don't let your

hand slip, will you, and give me a crumb more than I'm due to.'

Muriel carefully clipped out one cheese coupon and put it in the cheese coupon box, then handed the book back and cut an ounce of cheese from the seven-pound block at the back of the counter to wrap it in greaseproof paper.

Mrs Musgrave picked it up, her displeasure evident from the way she threw it in her shopping bag.

'It's measured out to us, Mrs Musgrave. We have to account for it all.'

Mrs Musgrave's lip curled. 'It's a good job you're not made out of chocolate,' she sneered, 'you'd eat yourself. And don't sell them mucky buns to anybody else, either!'

'I don't think anybody else will be coming in, at this time. Anything else?' Muriel trilled, with a bright and glassy smile.

'I've a good mind to report you. That's what else!'

Muriel took the money and then unlocked the door and bowed her out with insulting obsequiousness. Mrs Musgrave went off with a resentful glance at the very preoccupied manageress and dark mutterings about not wanting no cheek from that little madam. And they'd better watch out, because she knew someone who knew the managing director.

Muriel closed and locked the door and mopped Mrs Musgrave's footprints off tiles which had been immaculate before her arrival.

Miss Chapman lowered the blackout blinds. 'I wouldn't put it past her to report you, either. Is it all back in the cold room?' she asked, meaning the bacon, cooked meats, butter, lard, cheese and eggs, which were kept on a large and icy stone slab to keep them from going off.

'All except the cheese.'

'How far have you got with the coupons?'

'All done, except the cheese.'

Muriel put the cheese in the cold room, emptied the mop bucket and got back to the coupons – butter coupons strictly for butter, bacon coupons for bacon, and never to be swapped for anything else. Every day they had to be counted and balanced up as if they were money, to be sent on to head office. Muriel noted the totals, then handed them over, wondering if she'd still be sane when she got to Miss Chapman's ripe old age or whether she'd have gone completely crackers from the constant snipping and counting of coupons in this freezing food shop, with its tiled floor in the public areas and concrete floors at the back of the counter, and no warmth anywhere except for one tiny gas fire in the staff room.

Coupons done, she got the bucket of sawdust and spread a generous covering over the floor, to be swept up as soon as they opened the shop tomorrow morning. It would leave the tiles nice and shiny. Miss Chapman took a pride in shiny tiles.

'There's your wages, Muriel,' said Miss Chapman, holding out ten shillings set aside from the day's takings before cashing up.

Muriel put the money in her pocket. 'Thanks. I'll be counting coupons in my sleep,' she said, pulling off her little white cap and shaking her dark hair loose.

They put on their coats. Miss Chapman switched off the light and they stepped out – out of the numbing cold of the Maypole Grocer's and Confectioner's and into the numbing cold of darkening, bomb-ravaged Holderness Road.

Miss Chapman locked the door. 'I wish they'd let us wear trousers, and warm socks,' she said. 'My legs and feet are frozen, and I've got bad circulation at the best of times. I could cry with my chilblains. And when I get home beside the fire, they'll feel even worse.'

'My circulation must be good. I don't get them.'

'Wait till you've stood about in food shops for thirty years! Well, thank goodness the nights are getting lighter. With British Summertime all year long now there's just enough daylight to see our way home.'

'And not enough to see our way back in the mornings,' Muriel said, lifting her small-boned, five-foot-and-a-peanut frame onto her bicycle. 'I hate the dark mornings even more than the dark nights.'

Miss Chapman heaved her rather heavier body onto her bike. 'Well, can't have it all ways. Good night, then.'

'Good night, Miss Chapman.'

Muriel rode up Holderness Road and along Sherburn Street to Morley Villas, a tiny side-street with its three houses either side separated only by a narrow footpath. Her mother had already drawn the blackout curtains. Not even to be able to peep through your curtains and see a friendly light from a neighbour's house felt depressing. For the rest of the evening they would feel holed up in some sort of underground existence cut off from light, air, wind and stars, and the rest of mankind. All right for moles and badgers, but Nature never intended people to live like that, Muriel thought. She put her wages on the mantelpiece, took off her coat and sat down by the fire with the *Hull Mail* while her mother got the evening meal ready. It was Friday, so it would be herrings fried in oatmeal, with spuds and turnip mashed together with pepper and salt. The ration didn't run to butter.

'I've just been reading the paper,' her mother called from the kitchen. 'The government's lowered the call-up age to nineteen now, for single girls. Thank goodness you're only eighteen next birthday. I hope the war's over before it's your turn. That lass of Broadheads' writes home telling them what she has to put up with in the Land Army. Out in the freezing cold every day, digging sugar beet up, working like a slave – and horrible sandwiches in her pack-up. They've got a Scotch matron at the hostel, and she's real tight with the food. She gave them cold mashed potatoes in their sandwiches! And they were that hungry, they ate 'em! Ugh! "I hope our Muriel never has to do anything like that," I told her mother. "That's a real nice job she's got at the Maypole. She'll probably be a manageress before long."'

Muriel rolled her eyes and shook her head. To be trapped for life in the Maypole grocery, never going anywhere else, with sour old customers like Mrs Musgrave and nobody new or interesting to meet – perish the thought. 'Freezing cold in the fields can't be any worse than freezing cold in the Maypole,' she said.

'You want to look after that job; they're few and far

between, jobs like that; you ought to think yourself lucky.
And that lass of Broadheads' is out in the wind and rain,
as well as the cold. Course it's worse.'

'They won't work when it's raining. And at least she's
got a chance of getting warm, if she's digging sugar beets
up. She probably gets a sweat on. We can't, stuck behind
that counter all day. The only chance we get to thaw out
a bit is when we wrap our hands round a cup of tea and
sit on top of the fire in the staff room.'

'Maybe, but you get home every night, and you don't
have to eat cold mash in a sandwich,' her mother said.

'I want a bit more out of life than being manageress at
the Maypole for donkey's years. I want a bit more out of
life than going to bed with a cat, and trotting off to the
spiritualist church for a regular séance.'

'You're talking about Doris Chapman. Who's asked
you to go to bed with a cat? Or go to the spiritualist
church?'

'Nobody.'

'Why don't you get yourself out dancing, like you
used to?'

'Because I've nobody to go with, now. Barnacle Bill's
in the middle of the Atlantic somewhere, and Irene
Reynolds has joined the WAAFs. Her dad gave his
permission. I've already told you.'

'Well, there's no chance of your dad giving permission,
nor me either! So you'll have to make the best of it. And
don't call him Barnacle Bill. What's wrong with Kathleen
Moss, anyway? Why don't you get out with her?'

'If he can call me "Podge" and sing "She's Too Fat for Me" – meaning me, every time he sees me, I can call him Barnacle Bill. And I've hardly seen Kathleen Moss since she started walking out with that fireman.'

'Oh well, you could find someone to go out with if you tried hard enough, I'm sure. Nip across to Bill's mother's and tell the bairns their tea's ready, will you?'

At ten past eight the sirens went. Muriel's mother squeezed under the stairs with Arni and Doreen, the two youngest, while Muriel went to take refuge with the widow at number three. They'd all long since stopped going to the public shelters, since experience had shown that people were no more immune from being bombed to bits in them than anywhere else. On the contrary, public shelters seemed to be the bombers' favourite targets – and they stank.

At around nine o'clock a couple of massive explosions gave them some nasty moments, but by half past nine the all-clear sounded, and Muriel crawled out from under the stairs and went home, thankfully stretching her cramped limbs.

Later on, curled round her hot water bottle in bed, she closed her eyes. There, dancing in front of them were – not bombs, but coupons. Stray bacon coupons jigging about among the egg coupons, and cheese coupons among the bacon.

What had Miss Chapman said? 'Wait till you've stood about in food shops for thirty years . . .'

That thought was more horrifying than any air raid

Muriel had ever experienced, and Hull had suffered plenty. The air raids were always terrifying, but she'd come out of them alive, and glad to be alive, along with everyone she cared about. But thirty years behind the counter in the Maypole seeing the same dreary old faces every day would be a living death. If she had to stand about in the Maypole counting coupons for the next thirty years, she'd have something a lot worse than chilblains – she'd be completely crazy. If life had nothing better to offer she might as well kill herself now.

She pictured herself thirty years hence, a finicky old spinster with precise, fussy little ways – like lonely, loveless Miss Chapman, who had been doomed to perpetual spinsterhood by the 'War to End all Wars'. That Great War had robbed her of her fiancé by robbing him of his sanity and landing him in De la Pole lunatic asylum. Miss Chapman had visited him for years and had never had the heart to take up with any other man, or so Muriel's mother always maintained. But even if she'd had the heart, other men were thin on the ground, after the Great War.

'I sleep with Stanley,' Miss Chapman had once jokingly admitted, referring to her neutered tom cat, the only male ever to have had the honour of sharing her bed. Muriel had sometimes wondered, but had never asked, whether Stanley had been her fiancé's name.

Either way, if you wanted an example of a fate worse than death, you wouldn't have to look much further than that, she thought.

Chapter 2

'Thank goodness it wasn't the shop,' Miss Chapman said, as she unlocked the door the following morning and stood scanning the place for damage.

Muriel wasn't so whole hearted. She was certainly glad there was none of the muck that often resulted from nearby explosions – windows smashed, ceilings down and tiles and plaster shaken off, making a mess that might take days of hard work to clean up. But would she have been sorry to see the place demolished beyond repair? Not really, she thought, with a smile – until the thought of being transferred to a branch further from home or missing the wages altogether wiped the smile off her face.

Miss Chapman locked the door behind them, took off her coat and handed it to Muriel. 'Only the sawdust to sweep up, I'm glad to say.'

'Bilton and Marfleet Lane, this time, according to our ARP warden,' Muriel said, taking the coat and going to the back of the shop to hang up both coats and fetch the sweeping brush.

They worked together swiftly, until the sawdust was

gone, the glass cleaned, counters polished, carving knives sharpened, coupon boxes at the ready and all the perishable food brought out of the cold room and placed conveniently at the back of the counter. At a quarter to nine, they opened for yet another day of slicing ham and bacon, cutting and weighing butter and cheese, counting coupons according to government regulations and all the other same-old, same-old jobs that added lustre to the days of manageress and assistant in the cold Maypole grocery.

After a busy Saturday morning Muriel was making a paper cone to contain an ounce of pepper she'd weighed for a customer when the shop bell tinkled and Gladys Broadhead herself walked in. Muriel knew her from school, but Gladys was a full two years older, so although they'd always been friendly, they'd never been friends. Muriel was struck by how fresh and vital she looked, how rosy-cheeked and glowing, as unlike her pallid, city-dwelling former self as cheese from chalk.

'Well, fancy seeing you here!'

'Yeah, a dozen incendiaries and a couple of high explosives to celebrate my homecoming – nearly as good as a twenty-one-gun salute! My dad says you hadn't had a raid for ages before I came home. But nobody hurt, thankfully.'

'Plenty of people's houses demolished, though.'

'Aye, and you can get back where you came from, if you're bringing raids with you!' the customer chimed in.

'Not until I've had my holiday. I'm due a rest.'

'You are. My mother's been telling me what a rotten time you're having, what with the sugar beet and the wurzels. You don't look bad on it, though,' Muriel remarked, putting the pepper into the customer's shopping bag with her other groceries. 'Anything else?'

'No, thanks.' The customer picked up her bag and her ration book and went, leaving Gladys the last customer in the shop at two minutes to lunchtime.

'Are you sorry you joined, then?' Muriel demanded.

'Well, I'd have had to do something, wouldn't I? I'd rather have gone into the forces, the Women's Auxiliary Air Force, or the Women's Royal Navy Service, where you're paid by the government and get all sorts of perks, like free rail travel. But I couldn't get my dad to give permission, so it was a toss-up between the Land Army and factory work, and I didn't fancy staying at home and going into factory work. So it had to be the Land Army – plenty of back-breaking work, no perks, and mean little wages paid out of the farmers' own pockets. We do all right for a social life, though, and the laugh of it is that the officers aren't allowed to fraternise with the women in the ranks in the Women's Services, but they can fraternise with us all right, so we have a whale of a time at their dances. I didn't even wait for them to send me the official form – I was ready for off. I'd had about as much as I could stand of the grumpy old sod in the armchair.'

'That would be your dad, I suppose,' Muriel said.

'You suppose right. I don't say much about the dances and outings in my letters. With a Victorian throwback like him for a dad I don't want them to think I'm having too much fun.'

'Time for your break, Muriel,' Miss Chapman said.

'Come round to our house. We can have a natter,' Gladys offered.

Muriel pulled a face. 'What, and eat my pack-up with the grumpy old sod in the armchair watching me? I don't fancy that.'

The doorbell jangled and Muriel's twelve-year-old brother Arni burst into the shop dragging a go-cart he'd made out of old pram wheels and wooden lats and looking as if he'd won the pools. In the cart lay a heavy green silk parachute tied into a bundle with its own rope.

'Why aren't you at school?'

'Been up to Bilton Grove, to make sure Grandma French was all right after the bombing. There was an unexploded parachute mine in one of the gardens, with the parachute still stuck to its rear end! So I beat it to my grandma's with my heart in my mouth, in case someone else nabbed it before I could get back with the carving knife to slice the rope off. You and our Doreen can have it for a skipping rope,' he said, magnanimously.

Miss Chapman looked horrified. 'Going near unexploded bombs! You'll get yourself killed one of these days, you silly boy.'

Muriel reiterated the warning. 'You will, so be careful. But I'm a bit too old for skipping, Arni. I wouldn't say no to the parachute, though. I could get a few pairs of French knickers and underskirts out of that,' she said, casting a covetous eye on the bundle of green silk. Clothing coupons were in short supply and she had few to spare for underwear.

Miss Chapman nodded thoughtfully. 'You could. I know a one or two who have.'

Arni's eyes locked with those of Miss Chapman. His nodding kept perfect time with hers, and he gave her a knowing smile. 'Aye, I know a lot of folk who wouldn't say no to that,' he said. 'They're worth some money on the black market, them. You can make all sorts from 'em: curtains, skirts, knickers, all sorts of stuff.'

'What do you want for it, then, Arni?' Gladys asked.

'Oooh, ten bob, maybe.'

'Ten bob! What about a price for pals?'

'Look in my eye,' Arni said, presenting his right eye for Gladys's inspection, with a forefinger directing her gaze towards the dark brown iris. 'See any green?'

'No, you cheeky pup. Only on the parachute.'

'I'll give you five shillings for it, Arni. You can have it this minute,' Miss Chapman offered, quietly. Muriel looked at her, aghast.

'Done,' said Arni.

Muriel recovered enough to round on him. 'You're heartless, you are. You've got no family loyalty at all.'

'Business is business,' Arni shrugged.

'I'll tell you what, Muriel,' Miss Chapman said. 'If you want to take Gladys for a cup of tea in the staff room, I'll turn a blind eye.'

'And we'll turn a blind eye to you trading on the black market. I'm surprised at you, Miss Chapman,' Gladys said, in mock reproach.

'I'd say I'm surprised at you, Arni, but I'd be lying.

You've always been a little Shylock,' Muriel said, and the reproach in her dark eyes was genuine. 'Come on, Gladys, I'll give you a cup of tea, and you can tell me all about the Women's Land Army.' Without another glance either at Miss Chapman or her brother, she led the way to the staff room, closely followed by Gladys.

'Did our Arni tell you he found a parachute?' Muriel demanded that evening, as she stood at the mirror over the fireplace, examining her face. It was a pretty face, but her social circle was so limited it was tragic. Her youth and good looks were going completely to waste, she told herself, while squeezing her juiciest spot.

'He never mentioned it.'

'That's because he sold it! For five bob, to Miss Chapman!' Muriel exclaimed, watching a little worm of thick yellow pus extrude itself from the spot. She wiped it off with a wisp of cotton wool damped in witch hazel, and viewed the result with satisfaction.

Her mother smiled. 'He's got his head screwed on right, our Arni,' she said, her voice laden with maternal pride.

'You could have had a pair of curtains out of that, or I could have had some decent underwear. You can get a few pairs of French knickers out of one of them. Instead of that he goes and sells it to Miss Chapman.'

'Well, it was his parachute,' her mother shrugged.

'Aye, well, it's her parachute now. I'm surprised at her, encouraging him to risk life and limb. And what does she want with silk French knickers?'

If she was looking for sympathy, Muriel quickly realised there was none forthcoming.

'What do you want with silk French knickers, come to that?' her mother rasped.

Muriel turned from the mirror and looked her in the eye. 'I haven't got enough underwear, that's what.'

'Maybe she hasn't, either.'

'I know, but she's old.'

Her mother's eyes took on a dangerous light. 'She's the same age as me.'

Muriel turned back to the mirror. Well, *you're* old, she thought, but she saw the wisdom of keeping that observation to herself. She changed the subject.

'Gladys said she hated it at first. She was billeted in a farm, and the farmer's wife never spoke a civil word to her. She likes it better in the hostel. And they got the rep from the War Ag to come and give the warden a good talking to, so the food's not that bad now, except they get too much beetroot. And like she says, you've got to do something. The ATS, or the Wrens or something, and her dad wouldn't stand for her going into the women's forces.'

'Neither would yours, so you can forget it,' her mother said.

Muriel paused for a moment. 'Gladys says she doesn't know why any farmer grows sugar beet, it's awful stuff to harvest, you have to dig it up, and bash two together to get as much muck off as you can, then lay them in rows, and then go along the rows cutting the tops off. She says it breaks your back, just about.'

'You think yourself lucky, then, and stay where you are.'

'But that's only one side of it! Gladys says they're near an airbase, and there's plenty going on in some of the villages as well. She's at a dance somewhere every week, with plenty of forces chaps to dance with. She says I should join them. I'd never be short of a partner.'

'You're never short of a partner at the dances here. There's all the servicemen.'

'Yes, but I've nobody to go with here. There, there's always the other Land Army girls. And you've got more chance of meeting a good lad, going to forces dances. Meetings with these foreign servicemen don't come to anything. They're here today and gone tomorrow, like sailors, with a girl in every port. The lads in the forces though, there's a fair proportion from round here. They understand us, we understand them, we know what we're playing at, Gladys says.'

'Hmph!' her mother snorted. 'Gladys has got a lot too much to say, if you ask me. But it's what me and your dad say that counts.'

'We're going dancing tonight, me and Gladys.'

'Well, that's all right. Enjoy yourself, and make sure you're back in this house for half past ten, and not a minute later.'

'All in together girls, never mind the weather, girls . . .'

Arni had given their little sister Doreen the parachute rope, impressing her with his generosity by telling her it was pure silk, and fit to hang a peer. With the ends knotted, it made a good skipping rope, long enough to stretch all the way across Sherburn Street. On Sunday morning Muriel found herself at one side of the rope with Gladys at the other, turning it so that ten-year-old Doreen and Bill's sister Betty could skip in it together, along with half a dozen other children who'd escaped evacuation.

'You ought to see us in the Land Army hostel, Muriel,' Gladys called across the street. 'It really is "all in together, girls" there. There's a rota for everything.'

'When I count twenty the rope's got to be empty!' the girls chanted. 'One! Two . . .' and one by one they dodged out between turns of the rope.

'I wouldn't mind being on that rota,' Muriel shouted, above their voices.

She was having the best weekend she'd had in weeks. Last night she and Gladys had been to the City Hall and danced their legs off, trying to do the 'jitterbug' with a couple of Canadian servicemen. This afternoon the Canadians were taking them to the pictures.

When they came out of the cinema, the Canadians walked with them to the station, carrying Gladys's luggage like the gentlemen they were.

'I'm glad I bumped into you,' Gladys said, after they'd gone. 'I'd have had nobody to go about with, otherwise, but I shan't be sorry to get back; they're a great bunch of girls in the hostel. I'll be dancing to the Coldstream Guards' band, doing their quicksteps and Military Two Steps next Saturday night.'

'I'd rather do the jitterbug,' Muriel said.

'Well, we haven't got round to that yet, in Malton. But we've got whist drives, and pictures – everything. And the best thing about it is there's no heavy-handed father laying the law down, telling you what you can do and what you can't do, and what time you've got to be in. I'm certainly glad to get away from that.'

Muriel listened, soaking it all up like a sponge. She waved Gladys off at the station for her journey back to Malton and the Coldstream Guards, and then set out on her own journey back home, more unsettled than ever. That welcome little flurry of dancing and pictures-going was over, and she had the prospect of another year of dreary routine facing her. She passed the Maypole at the railway crossing at the bottom of bomb-ravaged Holderness Road, despairing at the thought of another year filled with washing jam-jars and counting coupons and having to be in for 'half past ten at the latest'. That's if she ever went out – which she hadn't done for weeks previous to Gladys's arrival, and with Kathleen Moss walking out with a fireman, and Bill Peterson and Irene Reynolds gone, she would be staying in until someone like Gladys showed up again.

No! She could not, and would not stand another year working in the Maypole and sitting in the house with her mother every night while Gladys and almost everybody else she knew was off having a good time, Muriel thought. She would write her notice out as soon as she got home, and hand it in to Miss Chapman the minute she got to work on Monday morning. Then during her dinner break she would go straight into Hull and sign up for the Land Army. It might make her a bit late back, but what did that matter? She'd be leaving anyway.

The woman in the Land Army recruiting office told her they would need her parents' permission, and handed her the form for her mother to sign. Muriel gave her a confident smile and took it, very tempted to sign it herself and avoid the row she knew would be coming at home, but she wouldn't have put it past her mother to march straight down to the office and raise hell, so forging her signature would probably be going a step too far.

'You've done what?' her mother exploded, when Muriel presented her with the form. 'Given your notice in? Have you gone daft? Well, you can take your notice back again. You're keeping that job at the Maypole; it'll keep you out of harm's way for the duration. I'll be down to see Doris Chapman tomorrow morning.'

Muriel dug her heels in. 'It's not up to you, Mam, and I'm not taking my notice back. Anyway, Miss Chapman thinks I'm doing the right thing. They'll take me on in the Land Army, so I'll be leaving the Maypole on Saturday, and if you won't sign the form you look like having to keep me on what my dad sends, because the Land Army's the only job I'm having.'

Arni cheered her on. 'Good for you!'

'You just wait till your dad hears about this!' her mother threatened.

But Muriel had no fears about that. Her dad was well

out of the way in Wallsend, too far away to do anything, even if he'd wanted to.

As the sole remaining masculine presence in the house, twelve-year-old Arni squared up to their mother and added the weight of his opinion to the dispute. 'I think you should sign the form, and let her go,' he said.

Muriel saw her mother begin to weaken, and struck a patriotic note to push her argument further.

'Bill Peterson's off with the Merchant Navy, risking the U-boats to bring food into the country, and I'm going to help to feed us all by growing it on the home front,' she insisted. 'I'll be doing my bit for my country.'

Her mother capitulated and signed the form, handing it to her with a sour expression. 'You don't know when you're well off, but you'll learn the hard way,' she said. 'You'll have a rude awakening when you get to some of those farms, you silly little idiot, and don't say I didn't warn you. Don't come crying to me, that's all.'

Chapter 3

A week later, nothing daunted by her mother's dire prophecies Muriel tootled merrily off for Hull train station, rigged out in the full Land Army uniform of green V-necked knitted jumper, fawn shirt, a pair of cord breeches that were so stiff she could barely sit down, topped by a thick bum warmer coat and a felt hat and carrying the rest of her kit in a small suitcase. From Hull she embarked on the first train journey she'd ever taken alone in her life, bound for the remote East Riding village of Griswold.

It was standing room only on board. A young army recruit started chatting to her and left her with a cheeky: 'See you darling!' and a cheery wave when he got off the train in Beverley.

She laughingly gave him the routine riposte: 'Not if I see you first!' and made a mental note to think of something a bit more original for next time. Hearing peals of laughter further down the train she edged her way past the standing passengers and tracked the laughter to its source - a group of Land Girls, and some of them in uniforms as new as hers.

'Are any of you lot going to Griswold?' Muriel asked.

Three of them were, and they got off the train with Muriel at a stop called Griswold Halt, a mere platform with neither waiting room nor ticket collectors. Half an hour later they were walking up the sweeping drive to Elm Hall, and into its imposing entrance hall, part of which had been partitioned to make an office. As she led them up the grand staircase and into their dormitory, the warden, a skinny, sour-faced woman with greying dark hair who went by the name of Miss Hubbard, told them that the house had been the ancestral home of the local gentry until requisitioned as a Land Army hostel.

Having claimed bed and locker, Muriel and a girl called Audrey set out together to explore their new surroundings before the evening meal.

'The Yorkshire Wolds,' Muriel said, gazing at the countryside. 'Oh, wouldn't it be grand to live here all the time! What a difference from mucky, bombed-out Hull, except you wouldn't know, coming from Leeds.' She inhaled the crisp, cold air and surveyed the fields and hedgerows beyond her, still deep in their winter sleep. The low January sun shed its brilliant light on tall, leafless trees, casting their gaunt shadows across the land. Her spirits soared at the sight.

Audrey shivered, pulled her Land Army hat down more firmly over her fair hair, and thrust her hands into her pockets. 'Aye. And cold enough to freeze the balls off a brass monkey!'

A no-nonsense twenty-year-old, Audrey had joined

the Land Army after finding factory work not to her taste, and the foreman even less to her taste than the work.

'It's lovely, though,' Muriel said. 'This is what we're fighting for, Audrey. This. This is England!'

'Feast your eyes on it, then,' Audrey said. 'It's not costing us anything, is it? And it's a better outlook than bombed-out Hull and mucky Leeds, I'll grant you that. Although they were "England" as well, last I heard.'

Muriel was feasting her eyes on it, and breathing it in, and the feasting and breathing filled her with the sort of rapture that no amount of cynicism could spoil. Poor Hull, she thought. Poor battered, broken Hull. Poor mucky Leeds, and all the towns and cities like them. Coming out of Hull, away from cramped houses in close-packed streets and landing here in Griswold was like going to heaven without even having to die. She pitied the poor people who had to stay in those streets, who couldn't breathe this air and see this lovely, open countryside, and revel in all this light, and air, and space.

'Did you ever do any Shakespeare at school, Audrey? Do you remember the bit about "this precious gem, set in a silver sea"? Only it's better than a gem. Gems are hard and dead. This is a living, breathing thing!' She gave a self-conscious little laugh at her own flight of fancy.

'Maybe so,' Audrey conceded. 'Aye, I reckon you're right. But if we want something to eat tonight we'd better be getting back to the hostel. We must have walked for miles.'

There was nothing feminine about the way Audrey walked, Muriel noted. Shoulders back and arms swinging, she marched on, military style, with her eyes fixed determinedly on the horizon and her fair hair streaming in the wind. Muriel, a head shorter than Audrey, half-ran to keep up. Half an hour later, breathless, tired and footsore, she asked: 'Why is it that the walk back always seems twice as long as the walk out?'

'Probably because you're generally half knackered going back.'

'And you're out to enjoy the scenery at the start of a walk, and on the way back all you want to do is get there in time. I hope we're not too late for tea. I'm starving.'

'Me too.'

'My stomach thinks my throat's been cut. Feasting on scenery's all right when your stomach's full, but it's hard to keep your mind on it when you're famished,' Muriel said, brought down to practicalities by the stark prospect of going to bed hungry.

'Let's get a move on, then.'

An army Land Rover passed them and pulled up a few yards ahead. They ran to catch it up.

'Are you lasses from the Land Army hostel?' the 'Tommy' in the driving seat demanded.

'Yes!'

'Want a lift?'

'Not half!'

'Hop in the back, then. Anything for the Land Girls. We'll go the long way round, just for you.'

They had no sooner hopped in the back than the driver was off, and Muriel's heart almost stopped when she saw that the half-dozen men already sitting there were Germans – all dressed in prisoner-of-war uniforms. Looking at them, visions of demolished streets and people buried alive under the ruin of their houses arose before her. Trying to shield herself from all physical contact with them she sat down, horrified to be trapped in this confined space with men of the monstrous, goose-stepping race that had laid waste to her city.

The man facing them spoke to her in broken English, and tried to show her a photo of his family. Muriel felt her face turn to stone. She stared at him as if he had two heads and said nothing throughout the whole of the journey, leaving Audrey to say 'yes' and 'no' in all the right places. Muriel was never so relieved as when the Land Rover dropped them off outside the hostel.

'If I'd known they were Germans, I'd never have got in,' Audrey declared as they went inside and joined about twenty other girls.

'Huh,' Muriel snorted, still stony-faced. 'I feel as if I need a bath now – but a third-class ride's better than a first-class walk when you've got to get somewhere in a hurry, I suppose. So we're back in time for tea and I'm glad, because I'm starving. And at least we know what the buggers look like now.'

'Not much different to the folk round here, as far as I could see,' Audrey said. 'That young one nearest the driver couldn't take his eyes off you. Didn't you notice him?'

Muriel gave a short, sardonic laugh. 'I can see you're a comedian!'

'No, honestly,' Audrey nodded. 'Straight up! God's honest truth!'

Muriel shook her head. 'Hard luck for him, then. I've huddled under staircases while they dropped bombs on us too many times to be very fond of the Germans. And my dad certainly had enough of them during the Great War. He can't stand 'em – none of our family can – so they're not likely to get any encouragement from me. Anyway, they wouldn't even bother. They'd see I hated 'em, straightaway.'

'Are you talking about the German prisoners, like?' asked a cheerful, friendly girl with auburn hair and a Geordie accent. 'They're a surly-looking lot, aren't they?'

'They're evil. I hate them all. I'll be careful about taking lifts, in future, and make sure I don't bump into them again,' Muriel said.

'Why, that might take a bit of doing, like, if you end up working on the same farms. But they're few and far between, thank goodness. There are plenty of Italians, though. I'm Eileen, by the way.' Eileen smiled, exposing a row of white but crooked teeth.

'Oh well, rather them than the Germans, if we've got to have any at all. You should see what they've done to Hull. We had a city before they started on us.'

'And Coventry,' another said. 'If you saw Coventry you'd weep.'

'And Liverpool, and London,' other girls told them as they filed into the ornately decorated dining room and sat on long benches at the rough trestle tables that had replaced the old squire's mahogany, telling tales of death and devastation dealt by the Germans throughout the length and breadth of England.

'The Ities are all right, though,' their leader Laura Martin said. 'They'll sing opera to you and try to feel your backside while they're telling you what a *bella donna* you are and how they always hated Mussolini. You'll be glad of your thick corduroy breeches when they're about. Other than that, they're harmless. But they're absolutely bone idle.'

'Well, at least they never dropped bombs on us, did they?' said Muriel.

'If I hadn't been starving hungry,' Muriel said, 'I couldn't have eaten it.'

After a dismal meal of soggy, tasteless vegetables served under an equally soggy pie crust that went by the name of 'Woolton Pie' the girls had retired to the common room – formerly the squire's drawing room – to relax as near to the fire as they could get, on a battered old leather settee, and various armchairs. In the corner stood an upright piano.

'Why, no. It was as bad as food can get, man,' Eileen said. 'I've thrown better stuff to the pigs at home.'

'It couldn't get much bloody worse, could it? Unless she actually does start feeding us on pigswill,' Audrey snorted, her voice loud enough to reverberate round the building. 'Maybe she is feeding us on the pigswill, come to think. That bread had spots of mould on it.'

'Shush! She'll hear you.'

'I hope she does.'

'I'm nearly as hungry as before I sat down.'

'I hope it'll improve.'

'Don't bank on it,' one of the girls who had been there a while said. 'We've complained before, and it improves for a bit, and after a week or two it's just as bad again. A couple of women come up from the village every day to help her do the work, and we suggested she let one of them do the cooking, but no. She insists on doing it herself.'

'And after all the trouble I took to get here!' Muriel said. 'I'm a year under the age, and I was exempt, because I was working in an essential service – food – believe it or not. So I told them that I didn't want to be exempt. I insisted on doing my bit and when they gave in I had to chuck my job up, or else my mother would never have signed the form.'

'If tonight's muck is a fair example of what we're going to get to eat, you might be sorry you left both your job and your mother.'

'I was working in a munitions factory, until I had a stand-up fight with the foreman, and told him where to stuff his job,' Audrey said. 'Then the government were on my back, so I ended up here. It'll not be long before I'm having a stand-up fight with the warden, if this carries on.'

Muriel poured oil on troubled waters. 'Well, let's give her a chance. It ought to improve – now she's got all our ration books. What about you? What do they call you?' she called to a woman who was sitting on the piano stool attempting to play, but the piano was sadly out of tune. She gave it up, and turned to Muriel. A little older than the rest, she had a pale, perfectly symmetrical face, fine featured with calm grey eyes and short, softly curling mid-brown hair.

'Barbara. Barbara Barstow. I got my call-up papers shortly after my husband had been reported missing.'

That put even more of a damper on the group's spirits than the meal had, and a chorus of voices murmured sympathy. A few of the women knew from personal experience what war really meant, and told their own stories of loss and tragedy, of men killed or wounded in the forces, or of loved ones dead or injured in the air raids.

Muriel listened to their tales of disaster with great sympathy, but no real comprehension. None of it had really touched her. Her father had been called up at the start of the war, but was safe in Wallsend, training other soldiers. Bill Peterson – who she'd been walking out with until he sang Fats Waller's 'She's Too Fat for Me' in her ear just once too often – had joined the Merchant Navy and was on the convoys, with no mishap, so far. She lived near to the most bombed area in Hull, but not one person close to her had suffered any loss beyond broken windows or missing roof tiles.

She warmed to this group of young women, knowing they were going to be friends. In spite of the terrible food and the sad stories she was overjoyed to be among them, out in the world and free. Goodbye to the Maypole grocery and coupon-counting in bombed-out Hull. She was here, deep in the countryside, in this wonderful company, and loving it. Goodbye, kids' games and skipping ropes, and listening to her mother and grand-mother harping on about looking after that good job. Goodbye to having to be in by half past ten and not a minute later. Like Gladys, she would be at dances and do's everywhere, and never lack for company. She could hardly wait for the fun to begin.

At half past nine the warden appeared, and ordered them all to bed. They'd all better get to sleep, because they would have to be up by half past five in the morning to get breakfast and make their own sandwiches. And they'd have to get a move on because the lorry would be here at six o'clock, to drop them off at the farms.

Muriel had the bunk above Audrey's. Eileen was in the top bunk to her right, and Barbara top left. They had barely had the chance to undress and climb into them before the lights were snapped off. The bunk was ice cold, and they had no hot water bottles. It would take them ages to get warm enough to go to sleep.

'I wish I'd thought to put my socks on,' Muriel said.

'Me too!'

'And me! I'm bloody freezing.'

'No talking! Go to sleep!' the warden rasped.

Muriel's jaw tightened. That woman had fed them rotten food, and now she was ordering them about like kids. But there was no point arguing – in seven and a half hours she would be getting up in the cold and dark, just when her bed was nice and warm. But they were 'all in together, girls', in the glorious countryside, so Muriel was not downhearted. She closed her eyes, remembering the girls' names and their stories, where the laundry was, and the iron, where to find the lavatories, the bathrooms and the kitchen, and where to put her boots . . .

The silence was disturbed only by their rhythmic breathing. There would be no wailing sirens warning of air raids, no scrambling out of bed to hide under staircases here. There was nothing around here to bomb. And then Muriel heard the dull thrum-thrumming vibration of planes in the distance – not German planes, she could tell that by the sound. No, they must be RAF – not fighters but bombers, flying over to Germany to drop their loads. A few Germans might be scrambling under their own staircases before long, she thought.

Serve them right.

Chapter 4

'Come on, shake a leg! Rise and shine, if you want any breakfast. The lorry will be here in half an hour. Come on, up, up, up!' the leader, Laura Martin urged.

Curled up into a tight little ball beneath the bedclothes, Muriel raised one bleary eye above the covers to see Laura up and dressed. Girls were sitting up and yawning and stretching their limbs, others scrambling into their clothes. Muriel groaned, and sank beneath the bedclothes. How she hated cold, dark mornings. An instant later, the bedclothes were rudely whipped back, and she was exposed to the freezing air.

'Come on, Sleeping Beauty,' Laura insisted.

'It's still pitch black outside,' Barbara said. 'It's still the middle of the night. There's no sign of dawn.'

'There will be, before you get your sandwiches. And if you don't get a move on and get into the common room to make your own, you'll get none – and believe me, after a morning's work, you're going to be hungry,' Laura said. 'And remember to bring your oilskins. It's rained every day for weeks, and it'll probably rain again today.'

Washed, dressed and in the dining room, they were confronted with a breakfast of dry bread and thin slices of cold fatty bacon, all laid out on one of the trestle tables.

Muriel's stomach rebelled. 'Ugh! We'd have been ashamed to put that out in the Maypole, and the Maypole's the sort of shop that sells broken biscuits.'

'Bread and jam for me,' Audrey grimaced, lifting a spoonful of plum jam out of a stone jar.

'The tea's not bad,' Eileen called from a table further down the dining room.

'Thank the Lord for that,' Audrey said, and helped herself from a brown enamelled teapot that must have held two gallons.

After a hasty breakfast, they hurried after the other girls into the common room to find a table laden with piles of bread and plates of grated carrots and mashed prunes, the two options for sandwich fillings. Then, with sandwiches, a screw of tea and a screw of sugar they all piled out before it was light to an icy lorry waiting in the yard. Muriel's efforts to clamber into the back were not helped by breeches so stiff that she could barely bend her knees. She lost her footing on the floor of the lorry and, with arms and legs flailing, landed heavily on her back.

The driver burst out laughing. 'Oops! Watch out, girls! I forgot to mention, it is a bit slippy. I had to hose it out after carrying a load of something dirty yesterday, and the water's frozen to ice.'

Muriel had just enough breath to gasp: 'A bit slippy? It's like a bloody skating rink!'

Eileen clambered in after her. 'Are you all right?'

'Aye, if you call a broken back all right.'

The rest of the girls climbed in very cautiously. Still grinning the driver started the engine and set off, jerking Muriel off her seat.

'Is he trying to kill me before I get there?' she asked, struggling to her feet for the second time, to hysterical laughter from the other girls.

After six bumpy miles the driver stopped. 'Half a dozen wanted here.'

'Audrey, Eileen, Muriel, Barbara, Betty and Vera,' the leader said. 'On you go.'

The driver let the tailboard down and out they went, to stand beside a large field of something Muriel couldn't have identified to save her life.

A dour-looking man in his fifties provided them with implements. 'Wurzels,' he said, taking his cue from the vacant look on Muriel's face. 'You'll be pulling wurzels. We're late getting them up, and they're needed, so put your backs into it, lasses.'

'Well, it could be worse. It could be kale, or Brussels sprouts,' the leader called, from the back of the lorry. She gave them a wave as it carried her away with the rest.

A quick demonstration, and the pulling began in earnest. After an hour of it, Muriel stood up to see acres of still unpulled wurzels that looked as endless as the Siberian steppes.

'How will we ever get to the end of it?' she asked.

'Are we really expected to get to the end of it?' Barbara wanted to know.

'What are wurzels, anyway?' Muriel asked.

'Cattle feed.'

'I thought cattle ate grass.'

'Well, they eat grass when there's grass, and wurzels and silage when there's none.'

The farmer came and stood over them. 'Come on, lasses, less talking and more pulling,' he said. 'I'm paying you for this.'

'Why, I thought we were doing it for the country,' Eileen said.

'We're all doing it for the country – and it's costing me money, so put your back into it.'

Muriel bent to the work again.

'I think I've put too much of my back into it,' she said when it was time for lunch, and trying to straighten up again was agony.

Judging by the flood of groans and complaints coming from the other girls, she was not alone. Ravenous, gnawing hunger helped them to force down dry, curled-up-at-the-corners carrot sandwiches that would otherwise have been uneatable. Tea came up from the farmhouse in a greasy bucket, and it tasted good. They drank gratefully out of chipped enamel mugs with Muriel half wondering at the fact that they hadn't been expected to pass the bucket round and drink from that.

'I'm dying to go to the lavatory,' Audrey said when everything eatable and drinkable had been eaten and drunk.

'So am I!'

'Me too!' the rest of them chorused.

'Get behind the hedge,' the farmer said.

'I'm not getting behind a hedge. I want to GO,' Audrey insisted.

The farmer frowned. 'It's a mile to the farmhouse. Grab a handful of dock leaves and manure the field instead.'

'Ugh! That's disgusting,' Muriel protested.

Audrey evidently felt it beneath her dignity to reply. Instead she turned and began the walk to the farmhouse, followed by Muriel and the other girls.

'And don't be long about it,' the farmer shouted. 'There's plenty to do yet. You've hardly made a dent in it.'

When they arrived at the farmhouse the farmer's wife gave them a frown to match her husband's, and directed them to an earth closet outside the house.

Audrey went first. She emerged with a look of revulsion on her face such as Muriel had never seen in her life before.

'I wish I had gone behind the hedge, now,' she said, 'and that's what I would do, if I were you.'

'If it wasn't for the thought of him peering through the branches, and nettles stinging my backside, I might,' Eileen said.

Muriel shrugged. 'Any port in a storm, I suppose. I don't fancy baring my backside to the world either, whether anybody can see it or not.'

And since they'd made the trek to the farmhouse they all used the earth closet, and all came out nauseated.

'I am so very glad,' Barbara said, as they walked back, 'that we've already eaten our sandwiches.'

It started to sleet shortly after they resumed work. Muriel looked towards the farmer, fully expecting the wurzel-pulling to be called off, but no such thing. They donned oilskins and with water running down their necks they pulled until it was almost dark, when half a dozen German prisoners who had finished their own work came over to help them finish their quota. Most of the girls kept them-selves aloof, considering their men in the forces, but Eileen showed some appreciation. Audrey went even further, and treated the prisoners just as she'd have treated British lads, much to Muriel's disgust. Fraternising with the enemy, she thought. Whose side was Audrey on, anyway? But she was glad enough that the work was done and thankful to see the lorry arrive to take them back to the hostel. She straight-ened up as best she could and walked to the lorry like a crippled crab, desperately trying to avoid any strain on her lower back and hardly able to pick her feet up for the weight of the mud clinging to her boots. The other girls were almost as bad. After an agonising ride they arrived at the hostel to be presented with a meal that looked as if it had been made from the leftovers of the last one. There were feeble protests, but no mutiny, since they were too exhausted. Neither was there any thought of going to the village pub, or to the pictures, or even of socialising with each other, except to moan and complain. Bed and obliv-ion seemed to be the highest ambition of them all.

'This is not what I joined up for – a broken back, and blistered hands and feet,' Muriel said, examining the blisters and broken nails on hands that looked as if they would never scrub clean again. 'I joined up to dance with officers to military bands, and go card-playing, or to the pictures.'

'Did you see anything about dances and the pictures on the form you got signed? It wasn't on mine. But then, I didn't see anything about getting behind hedges and manuring fields, either,' Audrey said. 'I always knew fields had to be manured; I just never realised I'd be expected to do it personally.'

'I never read the form,' Muriel said, after the laugh was over.

'Why, I cannot stand much more of this, man,' Eileen said. 'It's killing.'

'You know what?' said Audrey. 'We'd better get used to it, because we've signed our lives away.'

'We have,' Muriel grimaced, 'and we haven't finished slaving yet. Come on, lasses. We're on the rota for the washing up.'

By half past nine Muriel lay in her cold bunk with her thick socks on, staring into the darkness and listening to Barbara's snuffles as she cried herself to sleep. It was excusable; Barbara had a lot more than backache to grieve over. And to tell the truth, Muriel felt like joining her. The Maypole now looked like a vision of Shangri-La. Dear old Maypole. Civilised, kindly Miss Chapman. Even Mrs Musgrave seemed tolerable. And her mother, who had a decent meal ready for them every night – she'd never appreciated her as she ought to have done. Her mother had been right, as usual – but to admit it would have choked Muriel. She wanted to go home but she couldn't, because her mother, her father with the army in Wallsend, her brother and sister, Miss Chapman, and the whole of Morley Villas including Barnacle Bill somewhere in the middle of the Atlantic – they would all pour scorn on her.

And she'd given her job up! The very job that had exempted her from this torture and would have exempted her for the duration. She'd signed up to meet lots of new friends and go out dancing with officers and playing cards in village halls, not to lie half-starved in a freezing bed with blistered hands, blistered feet, and a broken back – and no energy left to do anything but shiver. She'd thought it would be fun in the hostel, but everyone was too tired to talk, never mind to go out. She would have curled up to warm herself but she daren't move for the searing pain in her back. The slightest shift of position lit fires inside her spinal column.

She wanted to go home, but she had no job to go to, and the humiliation was not to be borne. 'All I can say,' she muttered, to anybody that cared to listen, 'is that the hostel and farms round Malton must be a lot different to what they are here.'

She dragged herself out of bed on command the following morning to face a day with nothing different in it, except that her back was already broken and her boots and coat were damp before she started out. She was very careful how she got in the lorry, though.

On the third night, Barbara did not weep alone. By the fourth, every new girl in the hostel was crying herself to sleep.

Chapter 5

On Saturday, just as they were finishing work for their
half day and looking forward to going into town to spend
their wages on fish and chips, a thunderstorm began, with
pelting rain – too bad to venture out of the hostel, even
for the desperate. Their faces brightened at midday, when
they saw trays full of nicely browned chips and Cornish
pasties, and fell again when they sat down to eat them.

'Aren't Cornish pasties supposed to have a filling?'
Muriel asked, after prising the thick, hard pastry apart and
finding very little inside.

'Well, I'm not Cornish, but I always thought so,'
Barbara said.

'Neither am I, but I could get a knife through all the
ones I've had before. I've had to break this with my bare
hands,' Audrey said. 'There ought to be some gravy with
them, as well.'

'No, that's not quite correct,' Barbara contradicted.
'They were taken to the tin mines by the miners. I don't
think they'd have had the gravy boat with them.'

'Bugger the gravy boat. We're not in the bloody tin

mines and I'm fed up with this. We've worked like navvies for a full week, and we've done it on empty stomachs. It's time we got some decent food,' Audrey said, her cheeks ruddy and blue eyes bulging with anger.

'Come on, Laura, you're the leader. Make her produce something fit to eat, or you'll have a mutiny on your hands,' Muriel said.

The clatter of knives and forks stopped, and all eyes turned to Muriel, Audrey and Laura.

Laura shrank back. 'I've got no authority over her,' she protested.

Muriel's lips compressed into an ironical little smile, and then she said, 'We're supposed to get double rations, working on the land. Well, I've worked in food, so I know what four ounces of bacon and two ounces of butter looks like, and I can tell you, we're not even getting single rations. So if you've got no authority over her, Laura, I'm for going to someone who has. I'm for complaining to the War Agricultural Committee.'

'Well, you do it then,' Laura said. 'I'm not reporting her. She's like a sadistic games mistress who once cracked my shins with a hockey stick. On purpose. I'm not crossing her. In the first place, she'd bear a grudge forever and she'd make damned sure she got her own back – and in the second place you won't get anywhere with it when you've done.'

'Won't I? I will, though!' Muriel promised, and the chorus of approval showed that eighteen other girls, at least, were right behind her. She looked out, as a flash of lightning lit up the leaden sky. She heard a roll of thunder, saw the rain sluicing down the window pane and shivered. 'I'll go down to the telephone box in the village and ring the representative as soon as the rain lets up,' she said.

The rain didn't let up, so Muriel and Audrey donned their oilskins and trekked to the telephone box in the Market Square. The rep seemed very reluctant to believe that there could be any fault to find with the warden's catering, but promised to 'look into the matter as soon as convenient'.

'We'll all have starved to bloody death by then, by the sound of it,' Audrey swore.

'Hmm! It didn't sound as if there'll be much help forthcoming from her!' Muriel agreed.

Audrey's expression became savage. 'There'll be one hell of a stink if there isn't,' she promised. 'There'll be a strike!'

On Sunday, their much-longed-for day off, the weather was worse. Freezing cold, sleet, and a severe gale kept them inside, but the day was not lost. They used it to get better acquainted, write letters, read, and listen to the wireless and the gramophone. Dinner, for once, was quite passable. Muriel reckoned that as well as the vegetables they must have had at least two ounces of beef apiece – and it was not too tough.

'Why, that wasn't bad, was it?' Eileen enthused. 'I feel set up till teatime now.'

There were favourable comments all round, and then

one of the girls asked: 'Anybody want to learn the jitterbug? Joan –' she yanked Joan's hand up, 'brought a few
records and she's offered to teach us after we've had a cup
of tea.'

'I can already do it – a bit,' Muriel said.

'Ah, but we live near an American airbase, and I learned
it from the GIs,' Joan said in a broad Norfolk accent, that
sounded very posh to Muriel's Northern ears.

Wonderful. Muriel was keen to join in everything –
what else had she left home for? After tea she helped them
push the table and chairs aside and, in spite of her sore
back, jitterbugged with the rest, learning a few new
moves. Wearing their thick socks, stout leather shoes and
breeches, they hopped and spun, slid under each other's
legs and were thrown over each other's backs all afternoon to records played on the gramophone, sometimes
falling but laughing and calling encouragement to each
other. The floorboards vibrated to their heavy footsteps
– until the few girls whose backs were still too sore to
attempt it, including Audrey and Barbara, were sick of
hearing the same tunes played over and over again. Then
they called a halt and replaced the furniture. The gale was
still howling outside, but inside there was laughter and
good humour, and the warmth of sheer exertion and
blossoming friendships.

Muriel had as much fun as she'd ever had in her life,
and a lot more than going dancing with Kathleen, Irene
or Gladys. Nearly as much, in fact, as she'd had with
Barnacle Bill Peterson at the height of their infatuation

with each other. Joining the Women's Land Army hadn't been such a bad idea, after all. They'd had some fun, and here, with their own ready-made social circle, they would have plenty more.

Flushed, exhausted, and happy, she was setting the table for tea with the other girls when the warden came in, accompanied by an ageing, rather aristocratic lady. To her astonishment, the Voluntary Representative of the War Agricultural Committee had braved the storm and announced her intention of eating with them, unless the warden had any objection.

The warden shrugged her shoulders. 'Who am I to object? I haven't had as much as a minute's notice, but you're from the Agricultural Committee, so you can turn up when you like. It's all in the kitchen, ready to put on the table.' After a pause and a sniff she added with a martyred expression: 'I don't want anybody to go short, so seeing as I've only catered for the twenty girls and myself, I'll go to my sister's in the village.'

'There's no necessity. I shan't want much.'

'No. I'll go. It will be nice to see my sister anyway,' the warden said, and with another sniff: 'Enjoy your tea.'

The other girls laid the tables and made the tea, while the rep took Muriel, Audrey and their reluctant leader Laura aside.

'We hadn't had a decent dinner all week, up to today,' Muriel said. 'The meals have been awful, and we haven't been getting our full rations, either.'

'I don't know how we've worked on it. Look at these

breeches,' Audrey said, pulling them away from her waist to demonstrate the gap. 'They were tight before I got here. They're hanging off me now.'

They both looked at Laura, demanding confirmation.

'Well, the food hasn't been very good all week, but today's was all right, wasn't it?' was all they got from her.

The others began to pour the tea and carry in plates of sandwiches. Muriel flushed as she watched the rep's eyebrows lift slightly at the sheer quantity of food. She sat down with them to a meal of potted meat or cheese sandwiches with pickled onions and beetroot, followed by apple pies and vinegar cake, with lashings of hot tea and enough milk and sugar for it. After a week on short rations, they all ate like gannets.

After they had finished, the rep rose to her feet. 'Does anyone else have any complaints about the food here?'

No one spoke up.

'Does anyone expect any more of hostel catering than this, after three and a half years of war and rationing?' the rep pressed them.

Another silence, then Muriel spoke up. 'That's just it. We don't expect any more than we've had in these last two meals, but the rest of the food's been awful. I wish you'd sat down to one or two of the others.'

Audrey backed her up. 'It's true,' she said, 'this is only the second decent meal we've had, and we've been here a week.'

The rep gave her a frosty stare, patently not believing it.

Barbara, Eileen and a couple of the other girls confirmed it, but nobody else spoke.

'I came here without notice, and in the worst gale of the winter so far,' the rep said, with an air of suppressed exasperation. 'Miss Hubbard can hardly have been expecting me. To imagine that she prepared this meal especially for my benefit is absurd. I shall now depart, in hopes of reaching my destination before the blackout. I have eaten the food Miss Hubbard provides, and I have found no fault with it. It's fresh, wholesome, and there's plenty of it. I won't discuss your complaint with her, as I feel it would do more harm than good. But please bear in mind that she has the sole responsibility for twenty of you and it's unreasonable to expect her to provide the same sort of home cooking and comfort that your mothers would provide. Some of you are quite young but you're not children, and you must learn to make the best of things, like the rest of us. We're fighting a war, and we all have to make sacrifices.'

With that, the rep rose to her feet and made a dignified and rather haughty exit. Muriel and Audrey went to the window of the common room with one or two others and saw the wind almost rip the door off her little car when she got in. She drove away with the gale howling, blowing leaves and branches all over the garden. A second or two after the car disappeared through the gates there was an almighty cracking sound, and the ancient elm that had given the Hall its name crashed to the ground, brought down by the hurricane. The other girls dashed to the window.

Muriel shivered with fear. 'My God, just look at it! She

only just got out of the way in time. I hope she gets back all right.'

'It's a good job she did. You'd have had it on your consciences if she hadn't,' Laura said.

'On our consciences?' Muriel echoed. 'What are you talking about?'

'We're not responsible for the bloody weather,' Audrey snapped. 'If she'd had any sense, she wouldn't have come out in it.'

'She wouldn't have, if it hadn't been for you.'

'The woman was quite old enough and competent to make her own decision as to whether she came out or not, Laura,' Barbara exclaimed. 'And I must say, I rather resent the way she spoke to us. We haven't all come here straight from our mothers, but she talks to us as if we're spoiled brats!'

'That's obviously what she thinks we are,' said Joan, in her drawling Norfolk accent. 'And liars, as well.'

Laura pulled a face, and shrugged. 'Anyway, I told you it wouldn't get you anywhere.'

Muriel rounded on her. 'It might have done, if you'd backed us up.'

'We've had two decent meals since we arrived, and we ate them both today,' one of the girls who'd kept silent during the rep's visit complained.

'That's rich, coming from you. You never said a word while she was here,' Audrey accused.

The girl flushed. 'There didn't seem much point, after the tea we'd eaten.'

'Well, there's certainly no point now,' Audrey said, savagely.

'If we'd all spoken up, she might have believed us.'

'She knew! Miss Hubbard, I mean. She knew. It's my belief she was prepared for the rep coming,' Barbara said.

'How can she have? She probably just does better food on Sundays, in honour of the Sabbath.'

'No. I reckon she must have heard you talking, and got the wind up, man,' said Eileen. 'I bet that's why the meals improved – she wouldn't know exactly which day the rep would land, so she wasn't taking any chances.'

'Yes, and I'll bet the standard of cooking will drop again, now the danger's past,' Barbara said.

'You can bet your life it will,' said Audrey.

'And none of us will dare complain again.'

'Well, some of us daren't complain this time,' said Muriel. 'But when you all get sick of starving, we will complain again, we just won't be so obvious how we go about it next time. And next time, you'd better all back us up.'

'Come on, it's done now. We don't want to be at each other's throats so let's forget it and get our jobs done, so we can put the gramophone on and have another go at dancing before bedtime,' said Joan.

'Oh, Christ! Don't say the jitterbuggers are going to be pounding the planks again, to those same bloody tunes, over and over again,' Audrey protested, still in a foul temper. 'I'll go mad!'

'Me too,' said Barbara.

The jitterbuggers laughed unfeelingly, and as soon as

their work was done they pounded the planks without mercy until Miss Hubbard came in at nine o'clock, to pack them off to bed before half past. Muriel thought she detected something sinister in the smile the warden gave them, and malevolence in that gleam in her eyes. She got ready for bed with an uneasy feeling that Miss Hubbard knew – everything. Her suspicions were later confirmed.

'Never mind, girls,' Miss Hubbard said, softly, as she put the lights out. 'No hard feelings. I'll give you something nice for your breakfasts.'

With her thick socks on and her back aching just a little less than usual, Muriel lay awake, wondering exactly what the warden had in store for them.

Chapter 6

'Prunes!' Audrey exclaimed. 'You call prunes something nice? I can't stand them. They make me sick!'

Miss Hubbard's eyes narrowed. 'You'll get what you're given, in my hostel. Prunes is all there is, like it or lump it. So get them down you if you know what's good for you, and leave 'em if you don't. My advice is: eat your fill – because you'll get nothing else. If you choose to go hungry, it's your lookout. Run off and phone the War Ag, if you want,' she added, with a disdainful sniff. 'See where it gets you.'

Prunes was all there was, so the girls forced down what they were given in sullen silence, and they did not like it. The warden stood with a grim little smirk on her face and a triumphant glint in her eye, evidently enjoying her revenge as she watched them spit prune stones into their bowls. As deep as the ocean, that one, Muriel decided.

Audrey looked ready to explode. In any clash with this woman, Audrey would certainly come off worst, Muriel thought.

'Come on,' she said, looking directly at the warden.

'Leave this old prune to stew in her own rancid juice. She's not worth it.'

The smirk was gone. The old prune gaped at her, and stood like a stranded fish with her mouth opening and closing, lost for a reply. Muriel rammed her hat down on her head, grabbed her coat and taking Audrey by the elbow she stalked out to the lorry, steering her friend firmly out of harm's way.

Audrey looked back at the warden and grinned. Some of the other girls started to snigger and most were chuckling by the time they got in the lorry.

Eileen was in stitches. 'It was so funny! She looked as if she was chewing a mouthful of wasps, trying to think of a come-back!' she gasped. 'I wonder if she'll manage to dream one up before teatime?'

'A bit late in the day, if she does.'

Somebody struck up a song – 'In ee-leven more months and ten more days I'll be out of the calaboose!' and the rest took up the refrain: 'In eleven more months and ten more days they're gonna turn me loose . . .'

Except for Muriel, the rest joined in, and they were still singing when the driver let down the lorry's tailboard and half a dozen of them jumped onto the road, beside fields that were covered with January morning frost and so foggy that they could barely see two yards in front of them. He refastened the tailboard, then bade them a cheery farewell and jumped back into his cab.

'Good luck, lasses,' he called. 'Rather you than me!'

'Just make sure you're back before we're all frozen solid,'

Muriel shouted as he revved up the engine and pulled slowly away. With his eyes on the road he gave them a backwards wave. There was nothing for the girls then but to take their implements and stumble along the uneven ground to start wresting wurzels from the frozen earth.

'All right for some,' Eileen moaned as they took their places along the rows. 'I wish I had nothing else to do but ride about in a cab all day.'

'A couple of months ago I could never have imagined myself out at this time of day and in such weather, to do a job like this,' Barbara said.

After half a morning's hard labour, their noses were red with the cold. Muriel's hands were so near to frostbitten she had lost all sensation in them, and she had a terrible stomach-ache. She straightened up, to ease her back.

Eileen did likewise. 'I cannot wait to get back to the hostel for a decent meal, and a chair beside the fire, man,' she said. 'It's the only thing that's keeping me going.'

'I've got to go to the toilet,' Muriel said. 'It must be those bloody prunes. They're never long acting on me.'

'Why, there's no toilet here, man. There's no toilet for a mile, and you know what that one's like.'

'I'll never get that far, and I can't hang on any longer.'

'When you've gotta go, you've gotta go,' Audrey laughed.

The very thought of pulling her breeches down in the open air gave Muriel the horrors. It was something she would never get used to if she lived to be a hundred, but there was no finesse in the fields and the only way to get any privacy here was to hide behind a hedge or a tree. A couple of the others had already squatted behind a nearby hedge, but Muriel was determined to get as far away from the rest of the party as possible. In acute distress she stumbled frantically along the frost-hardened furrows in the direction of a clump of trees barely visible about a furlong distant, falling once in her hurry, and wrenching her ankle.

She reached the trees and struggled desperately with frozen fingers to unfasten the buttons at the side of her breeches. She finally succeeded, but when the time came for the more intricate job of fastening them again she could feel neither fastenings nor hands, nor get her frost-deadened fingers to work properly. After what seemed an age of trying she heard a voice calling her name, and the ghostly shape of a man loomed through the fog. As he drew nearer she recognised the uniform of a prisoner of war.

He nodded towards the direction from which they had come and spoke in broken English. 'All right?'

A German! And she was alone. She felt the hairs rise on the back of her neck.

'All right?'

She looked down at the side opening of her breeches and made another brave attempt to get her fingers to work. She failed, and might have staggered back to the girls just holding them up if she could have been sure of both her grasp and her ankle. She looked up, and met his eyes. 'My buttons,' she said.

With a polite little bow and the ghost of a smile he stepped up to her and took hold of her waistband. She

studied his face while his eyes were lowered to the fastenings, and the light touch of his hands made her heart race.
How handsome this fair-haired Nazi was, how regular
and masculine his features – and what nice manners he
had. German fingers were evidently much better disci-
plined than English ones, for her buttons were soon
fastened. He moved two or three steps away and looking
directly into her eyes, held out a hand.

'*Komm.*'

Two minutes ago she could not have imagined being
asked to take the hand of a German. Two minutes ago she
would have felt it a betrayal of her own country to do so.
The mere idea would have repelled her. But an aeon had
elapsed in those two minutes and erased all barriers
between them. She looked into his blue German eyes and
her heart turned somersaults.

'*Komm mit,*' he urged, and with a broader smile and a
tilt of his chin he beckoned her with the fingers of his
outstretched hand.

She hesitated, then took his hand and holding it as
tightly as her frozen fingers allowed, she tried to walk,
keeping her weight as far as possible off a left ankle that
was so painful she thought she might have broken it.

The German put an arm tightly round her waist to
support her. After a few steps he gave up, and lifting her
into his arms he carried her across the furrows and through
the morning mist, safely back to her own party. The girls
were crowding round a small fire lit by his fellow
prisoners.

'You took your time – skiving off and leaving us to do all the work!' Audrey exclaimed, 'so when the prisoners came across, we sent one of them to find you. We thought you'd fallen down a rabbit hole.'

More like a button hole, Muriel thought. 'I've wrenched my bloody ankle in a rabbit hole, anyway, and it hurts like hell,' she said, stealing a furtive glance at her rescuer.

The girl nearest to the fire looked up with a mock frown: 'I suppose you all know that fraternising with the prisoners is against the law.'

'Shove over, then, and don't warm your hands at the prisoners' fire, if you're so bothered about the law,' Audrey said. 'Let Muriel get near it, instead.'

'Bugger the law! All I care about is getting my hands warm,' the girl said, but she moved over just the same.

The German pointed to Muriel's ankle, and then to the farmhouse.

She shook her head. 'I don't think I'll get much help there.'

He said something, then knelt and took off her boot. She winced as he examined her ankle, and then said something to another prisoner, who translated for him. 'Not broken. We go, now.'

Muriel gave her rescuer a tentative little wave as they went, her heart thudding.

'How does he know whether your ankle's broken, or not?' Barbara demanded. 'Has he got X-ray eyes? We ought to get you to a doctor.'

'Where's the nearest telephone box?'

'Miles away. We've no bikes, and it'll take hours to walk it.'

That put paid to the idea of a doctor. The girls turned again towards the fire and warmed their hands, and then got back to work until the farmer came at 'lounces' with a bucket of tea. They ate their sandwiches and then got back to work. The Germans returned as evening drew on, and helped them to finish their rows.

'Why, fancy them coming back to help us, man,' Eileen said, when they were back in the lorry.

'Yes, who'd have thought it?' Barbara commented. 'I can't say I welcome it, either, them smarming round us while our own men are God knows where.'

Muriel opened her mouth to say a word in the prisoners' defence, then looked into Barbara's wounded eyes, and held her tongue.

'That lad that came to find you was the same one that was looking at you in the Land Rover,' Audrey told Muriel when they were out of the lorry and the other girls were going in to the hostel.

'Rubbish.'

'No, God's honest truth. His name's Ernst Müller, with two dots over the "u". One of them was telling us they're all Kriegsmarine. They were rescued after their U-boat got depth charged in the Atlantic.'

'Oh, bloody hell, don't tell me! Kriegsmarine!' Muriel repeated, and wondered why she was so horrified. It would have been just as bad if Audrey had said Luftwaffe.

Still, the U-boat arm of the Kriegsmarine was responsible for depriving Hull of untold numbers of its husbands, fathers, brothers and sons – and she, a daughter of Hull, had taken the hand of a Kriegsmarine submariner, and looked into his deep blue eyes, and been sunk.

'Woolton Pie – again!' Eileen groaned. 'Soggy carrots and turnips in HER rock-hard pastry, after a freezing cold day in the fields. We'll be lucky not to break our teeth on it. If I weren't bloody starving, I'd throw it at her!'

'It is possible to make it almost edible,' Barbara said, 'if you do it in a slow oven, well seasoned with a bit of thickening and very little water, and put sliced potatoes on top dotted with a bit of marg, instead of pastry.'

'Why don't you tell her? Give her a lesson in cookery. Take it over completely, and send her out to the fields, that would be even better,' said Audrey. 'I bet she's made a boatload. We'll get the rest of it tomorrow, you watch.'

'Well, I'm sorry to say it, but I don't think there's much point in complaining again,' said Joan. 'Do you, Muriel?'

Muriel said nothing. She was as unconcerned about her Woolton Pie as about the pins and needles in her fingers or her aching back. Her head and heart were full of Ernst Müller. And how could she, after everything they'd done to Hull? After everything the other girls had told her about Newcastle, and London, Coventry, Liverpool, Plymouth, and everywhere else the Nazis had devastated? When she could hear poor Barbara in the next bunk, crying herself to sleep every night over her lost husband? It was sheer treachery.

'Muriel?'

Muriel started. 'What?'

'You looked as though you were in a trance. I said: do you think there's any point complaining again?'

Muriel looked down at her Woolton Pie. 'Not really,' she said. 'The Prune says there are no choices in her hostel, and the rep says she's got no fault to find with her meals. She told us to like it or lump it this morning, so it looks as if we'll be lumping it.'

'You've changed your tune. It's a bit much, though . . .'

Muriel drifted off again. It was treacherous, but it made no difference. She couldn't help it. And after all, governments gave their orders, and everyone had to do as they were told, or else. None of the war was Ernst's fault any more than it had been hers. Like her, he was too young . . .

After tea she went to the bathroom and examined her face in the mirror. The few spots she'd had were almost gone, and all the hard work was trimming that little roll of fat from her midriff. Her hands were a mess, sore and chapped and with broken nails, but that couldn't be helped. On the whole she looked very well indeed, and from what Audrey had said, maybe he thought so too.

The following day a suppressed excitement fizzed and effervesced inside her as she climbed into the lorry. She might see Ernst again. They might even come and light another fire. But there was no sign of Ernst or any of the other German prisoners all day. The weather was an overcoat warmer, as her father would have expressed it, and a wind had blown the fog away.

But cold and fog with Ernst would have been better than these warm south-westerlies and this glorious sunshine without him, and her disappointment was keen. Maybe later, or tomorrow . . .

'Ooh, this is a nice surprise,' she said, at supper that evening. 'Surprise hotpot.'

'It is, an' all! There's a bit of scraggy mutton floating in the veg,' Eileen said.

'Aye, that's what I mean,' Muriel said, 'finding a shred or two of meat is the surprise. It's my birthday on Sunday. I wonder if she'll bake me a cake?'

'A prune cake, maybe,' Eileen grinned.

Audrey laughed outright. 'That might give us all a laugh; watching her fall over herself to get to the closet as soon as she's swallowed it!'

Some of the other girls chuckled, obviously in the mood for a bit of fun. Muriel took the joke in good part, laughing as much as the rest. 'Why don't we all go down to the village, see what the pubs are like, maybe have a glass of something?' she suggested.

'The village pubs on a Tuesday will be as dead as I feel,' said Audrey. 'I'm game at the weekend, though. We'll go on Saturday, then we can all have a lie-in on your birthday.'

'What about a walk, then?'

'It'll soon be dark.'

But Muriel was bursting with energy and exuberance, and couldn't keep still. 'Anybody for the jitterbug?'

'Too bloody tired,' the others chorused.

So she went out for a brisk walk alone. When she returned, Joan had recovered enough to jitterbug with her for half an hour before they collapsed into bed.

Chapter 7

The German prisoners seemed to have disappeared off the face of the earth. The wurzels were almost all up by Friday night, so two of the girls were sent to help with the threshing at a farm about four miles away from the hostel. They were all sick of the very sight of wurzels, and Muriel and Audrey were not sorry to be the ones chosen. A half-moon still hanging in the dark cloudless sky gave just enough light to see by when they set out on heavy, khaki-coloured, standard-issue War Ag bikes, with beetroot sandwiches in the carrier – along with oilskins, although they'd had no rain for days. With luck it would be fine and warm again, with balmy south-westerly breezes blowing.

'I'm always glad when it gets near to my birthday,' Muriel said as they pedalled along with their hats jammed firmly down on their heads. 'Even if it's still cold, it still means the light nights are coming and the snowdrops are out in the Park. I've never known it as nice as this, though. It's like spring.'

Audrey gave a wry smile. 'We won't forget your birthday, Muriel, honest,' she said. 'You've reminded us too many times. We'll take you down to the pub on Saturday night, and you can buy us all a drink.'

'No fear. It's up to you to buy me one; it's my birthday.'

'Nah. The birthday girl's the one who has to stand a round.'

'Rubbish!'

They could hear an engine rattling away as they approached the farmhouse.

'They've been 'ere sin' five o'clock, so as Old Mr Whittaker could get his fire lit and get some steam up to power t' thresher. Mother's given 'em their breakfast, so we're all ready for work. It's a good job for us we've had so many windy, sunny days to dry corn, after all rain we had in January. If that 'ud carried on, all hard work would have gone for nothing,' the farmer's daughter told them, as she took them to a field where they saw the source of the noise – an old steam engine which had a leather belt running to power the massive contraption beside it.

'Ever seen a threshing machine before?' the man in charge of it asked, removing his flat cap to scratch his balding head.

'No.'

The lads with him looked very happy to hear it.

'Right, a couple of lads will be working on corn stack, pitching sheaves to two lads standing on t' thresher. They'll be feeding the corn into drum. That beats grain out of ear, then it goes over sieves to clean it, and it comes out into sack. They weigh two and a quarter hundredweight when they're full, so the lads'll carry 'em to cart. Straw comes out from other end of t' thresher. That gets collected into sheaves and tied with hay bonds. Then sheaves get pitched to straw stack and built up wi' corners square – that's how to make a straw stack. That's skilled work, that is – and carrying grain sacks to cart is heavy work; it 'ud be too much for you. You'll be carrying chaff sheets; that's a job we usually give Land Girls – it don't take a lot of skill – not too complicated for a pair of townies,' he said, handing them a couple of large hessian sheets. 'Spread 'em out down there. You rake all chaff and rubbish out from underneath t' thresher, and pile it onto them sheets, and when you've got a good pile you get all four corners together and carry it into fold yard. It does for litter.'

'What, for the animals?' Muriel asked, stupidly.

'Well not for you, unless you're desperate,' he grinned.

'Be handy when you've had any prunes,' was Audrey's dry comment.

The lads started laughing, and the foreman allowed himself a chuckle, tickled pink at his own wit. 'Mr Whittaker's lad will be running up and down to pump to fetch buckets of water so's he can keep plenty of steam up and we can keep it moving,' he said, still grinning. 'Don't trip over him when you're chaff carrying. Right, let's get cracking.'

That was the instructions over, so they spread their chaff sheets out and watched the lads on the stack pitchfork the sheaves to the others, who by now were perching on top of the thresher, to feed them into the roller drum which Muriel guessed would bash the grain out of the ears. It did, and the grain ran out of one part of the machine to be bagged, the straw from another to be baled. They waited for the chaff to collect under the machine, and started raking.

Those balmy south-westerly breezes were not quite so welcome now. As the job progressed, chaff and dust found its way into their mouths, noses, eyes, ears, hair and even into their clothing, and it irritated like hell.

Audrey spat the dust out of her mouth. 'This must be the worst bloody job going,' she frowned.

'Pitching the sheaves off the corn stack can't be that hard, either,' Muriel said. 'I can't see any skill in that. We'll plump for that job, next time.'

'I think I'd rather heave sacks of grain, given the choice. Let some other idiot rake chaff.'

When the sheets were full, they gathered the corners together and held them tight to heave the bundles onto their backs. Muriel staggered under the load and followed Audrey to the fold yard with the enormous weight of it swinging behind her, pounding her backside with every step. Audrey had started walking back to the threshing machine and Muriel was just shaking the last of the chaff off her sheet when her heart gave a joyful little throb and her eyes lit up at the sight of Ernst Müller walking out of the cowshed.

That answering light in his eyes and that tiny twitch of his eyebrows as he smiled at her put a smile on her face she couldn't wipe off. He gave her a broader smile, and a little wave. She returned a wave. They stood, gazing and smiling at each other – until both remembered what they were supposed to be doing and with a few backward glances got back to work.

Audrey was already at the raking. 'This is worse than wurzels,' she said.

Muriel pulled some of the chaff out of her hair, wishing she had a mirror. 'We haven't been at it half an hour, and you look filthy already, so I must look as bad.'

It was annoying, but it couldn't be helped. She carried chaff to the fold yard with her stomach fluttering, staggering hopefully under the loads, but without catching another glimpse of Ernst.

A couple of hours later, the farmer's wife and daughter came from the farmhouse carrying a bucket of tea, a bag full of scones and some enamel mugs. The threshers stopped for a welcome drink and a bite, and very glad the chaff-carriers were to slake the dust from their throats.

'It's Muriel's birthday tomorrow,' Audrey solemnly announced, as she took a scone from the bag that the farmer's daughter was offering.

'Shut up,' Muriel laughed, also taking a proffered scone.

The gaffer raised his scone in salute. 'Happy birthday, Muriel,' he said.

'Aye, happy birthday,' some of the lads echoed.

'I'll kill you, Audrey,' Muriel promised.

'Seeing as it's Muriel's birthday, I think it's time,' Audrey said, when they'd finished, 'that someone else took a turn at chaff carrying, and we got a chance to feed the sheaves into the drum, or something.'

'All right,' the gaffer nodded, 'you can do the pitching up, and she can feed the machine.'

Four of the lads looked apprehensive.

'I'm all right with chaff carrying,' Muriel said.

Audrey whipped round and stared at her in astonishment. Muriel avoided her eye. Ordinarily she would have leaped at the chance of something more interesting and less dusty and back-breaking, but it was only the chaff carrying that got her into the fold yard, so chaff carrying it had to be.

'All right, then. She can keep on chaff carrying, and you can have a turn at pitching up. Then you can have a turn at feeding the machine. Let's keep everyone happy,' the gaffer said.

The lads, with their chaff-carrying time halved, immediately looked only half as unhappy. Audrey took her coat off, swapped her rake and hessian sheet for a pitchfork, and the job was underway again. Half an hour later a shriek arose above the rattle of the steam engine. Everybody stopped, to see what the matter was.

Audrey had tossed her pitchfork aside, and her hand was thrust deep into her shirt. 'Something's dropped down my neck,' she shouted, and pulled out – a mouse.

She jumped and threw it aside, to insensitive guffaws of laughter from the lads. 'Ugh! Ugh! Ugh!' she shuddered.

Remembering Audrey's barb about the prunes, Muriel laughed as heartily as the lads. Her chaff carrying had not been rewarded with another sighting of Ernst, but at least she'd had no mice down her front.

★　★　★

'Chuck your sandwiches to the pigs and have some dinner with us,' the farmer's wife said, when the threshing was finished, and the hundredweight bags of grain had been stacked on a cart. 'We've got some German prisoners working for us today, but they can eat when you've finished. You'll not want to fraternise.'

'I don't mind, if it saves you the trouble of having two sittings,' Muriel offered, in the true spirit of wartime self-sacrifice.

One of the lads gave her a suspicious look. 'Fraternisin's agen the law, in't it?' he demanded.

'It wouldn't really be fraternising, though, would it? I bet they can't speak a word of English, and we don't speak German. How can you fraternise with someone if you can't understand a word they say? And it'll be a lot better for Mrs . . .'

'Winter,' the farmer's wife prompted.

Muriel flashed her a smile. 'Mrs Winter, if she can get the dinner all over and done with at once.'

They could hardly object to making things better for Mrs Winter, so – more or less willingly – threshers and Land Girls seated themselves on benches at one end of the huge old oak table in a kitchen which ran the full length of the farmhouse. The farmer came in and sat at the other end, with the prisoners on his right and left. They nodded polite acknowledgements to the people at the table, and received stony stares from the gaffer and his lads in return.

With her cheeks flaming from the heat of the massive iron range at the end of the room, the farmer's wife brought a tray with two enormous, steaming shepherd's pies and set them on the table, then went back to the range for two more. The farmer's daughter brought a pile of hot plates wrapped in a tea-towel, and the sons brought dishes piled high with carrots and Brussels sprouts. The daughter and two sons placed themselves tactfully between prisoners and threshing party. Mrs Winter went and slid two deep apple pies with well-sugared tops into the oven, slammed the door and then came to the table and dispensed generous helpings of steaming shepherd's pie onto the plates before sitting beside her daughter.

'Tuck in, then,' she said.

Muriel hesitated for a minute or two, then put a forkful to her lips, almost burning them. She lowered the fork and watched a couple of the threshing lads for a moment. They were both looking at the Germans as if they'd escaped from a freak show – much the same way, Muriel realised, as she herself must have looked at the man who'd been showing them his photos in the Land Rover. The gaffer was taking no notice of them at all, and Audrey was asking Ernst for the salt and pepper, and generally behaving as if the prisoners were just the same as everyone else. Muriel cast a sly glance in Ernst's direction, and their eyes met. She looked quickly away and with a secret little smile distractedly swallowed a mouthful of scalding shepherd's pie.

'This is the first really good meal I've had since I left home,' she coughed, with tears in her eyes.

'Me too,' Audrey agreed, and started a discussion about terrible hostel food, their very peculiar warden, rationing, the wonderful weather, farming, and everything but the war. The prisoners contributed nothing to the conversation, other than an occasional murmur of appreciation to Mrs Winter. Muriel did her best not to make her absorption with Ernst obvious to everyone else in the room, but her heart raced every time he stole a glance at her.

One dishful of deep apple pie and custard and several mugs full of tea later, the threshers thanked the farmer's wife kindly and went to get their machines on the road. Muriel and Audrey helped her to clear the table, and offered to help with the washing up.

'No, she don't like strangers in her kitchen,' the farmer warned them, sinking into a large Windsor chair by the range. 'Come and sit beside the fire for five minutes afore you go.'

Audrey and Muriel took their chairs and placed them by the fire.

'Come on,' the farmer beckoned the hesitant Germans. 'Come and get a warm beside the fire.'

They were all more than warm enough after the hot meal they'd eaten, but the prisoners brought their chairs and sat down, Ernst directly opposite Muriel.

'It's Muriel's birthday tomorrow,' Audrey said.

'Is it? How old are you, then?'

Muriel laughed self-consciously. 'Eighteen.'

Audrey said something in German, and pointed to Muriel. The Germans smiled and nodded, and the farmer sat up and took notice. 'You talk German, then,' he observed.

'What did you say?' Muriel asked.

'I told them tomorrow's your birthday.'

'I didn't know you spoke German.'

'I'm not likely to forget the words for tomorrow and birthday. I had a German grandfather that never forgot mine. He was a pork butcher in Leeds.'

'Aahhh,' Muriel said. Audrey's strange attitude to the enemy began to make sense, now.

The farmer's eyes narrowed. 'You're not a German spy, are you?'

'Aye, I'm going to invite Adolf to your place for his dinner if he ever gets round to invading.'

Muriel's eyes widened in alarm. 'Careful, Audrey, he might think you mean it!' she said, not at all in jest. 'And there's probably a law . . .'

'There probably is,' the farmer said, 'but don't look so worried, lass. I was joking as well as her.' He reached into his pocket and began to fill his pipe from a tobacco pouch, then offered tobacco to the two prisoners. Neither of them smoked.

'I brought 'em from camp to fill some of them bomb craters in, that their airmen made in my fields,' the farmer said, nodding towards the prisoners. 'I reckoned the Jerries made 'em, so the Jerries can fill 'em in again. That seems fair. But that young 'un, Ernst, he knows something about cattle – brought up on a farm in Germany, as far as I can make out. Just helped me deliver a young heifer of a calf – he's patient, and clever. Saved me having to send for the vet, I reckon. The older one, Willem, he's been doing all real hard work. Wrong way round, but there you are – young un knows something about cattle and older one don't. Good workers, though. Both on 'em.'

Both prisoners alerted at the sound of their names and the farmer nodded to them, but made no attempt to make them understand him. He fixed his eyes on the girls.

'How long have you young women been Land Girls, then? I ent seen either o' you afore.'

They told him their stories, and gauged his interest from his drooping eyelids and his loosening grip on the pipe he held. Ernst caught it just as it dropped and put it in the hearth, preventing the burning contents of the bowl from spilling onto the hearthrug. Then prisoners and Land Girls sat for a while smiling at each other, until Wilhelm thought of something to say.

'Happy birthday, Muriel.'

'It's not today, it's tomorrow. Valentine's day,' she smiled.

'Valentine's day,' Ernst repeated, and putting his two forefingers together he slowly separated them to inscribe a heart in the air, then placing his upturned palms beneath the imaginary heart he pushed it towards her, his eyes never leaving her face.

They watched his little mime and burst into laughter. 'Ah, that's sweet,' Audrey teased. 'Best Valentine you'll ever get, Muriel!'

Muriel blushed and smiled, and looked deep into Ernst's blue eyes for a moment before looking away. To gaze for longer must have counted as fraternising, although the feelings he stirred in her were far from fraternal.

'*Ein schönes Gesicht,*' he smiled.

At the sound of their laughter the farmer stirred, stretched himself and yawned. 'I must have dozed off for a minute. Where's my pipe?'

'In the hearth. You nearly dropped it,' Muriel said.

He picked it up. 'Gone out, only half smoked, as well,' he grimaced, knocking the ash out before putting it back in his pocket and getting to his feet. 'Ah, well, back to work then, lads.'

'Not for us; it's our half day,' Muriel said, trying not to let her glance linger too obviously on Ernst as they went to get their bikes.

'Shall we save them for later?' Audrey asked, tilting her chin towards the beetroot sandwiches, still in the carriers.

'What do you think?'

They made a detour to the pens, and took great satisfaction in taking Mrs Winter's advice and chucking them to the pigs, before cycling back to the hostel in companionable silence, helped along by the wind at their backs. At last the hostel came into view, bathed in the light of the bright winter sun, and Audrey stopped.

'I'll tell you what, Muriel,' she said, thoughtfully, 'if you don't tell anybody my granddad was a German pork butcher, I won't tell them you got a Valentine from a German prisoner.'

'What Valentine?' Muriel asked, pretending ignorance.

'Only the best bloody Valentine I've ever seen in my life, if you include the look in his eyes when he gave it to you.'

The colour rose to Muriel's cheeks. 'You're on, then,' she nodded.

When she looked in her pigeonhole for her post, she found letters from her mother and Doreen, and an expensive Valentine card that could only have been from Bill – posted in Liverpool and inscribed inside: *to my dearest Podge, from guess who?* Well, he'd obviously spent a bit of money on the card, so he hadn't wanted her to be in any doubt about the sender. Podge, indeed! That cheeky little devil would never change, but she couldn't help smiling at him, sometimes.

She went to give herself a thorough wash, and when she saw her reflection in the bathroom mirror thought what rotten luck it was that Ernst had had to see her looking such a mess. She looked as if she'd been down a coal mine. What a mucky little street-urchin of a lass, to be given such a beautiful, make-believe Valentine!

Downstairs in the common room, Barbara was reading the *Daily Mail*.

'What's happening in the world, then?' Muriel greeted her.

'It looks as if the Red Army's chasing the Germans out of Kharkov, and the Yanks are getting Rommel out of Southern Tunisia - if you can believe what you read in the papers,' she said.

'That's good news. Maybe the war will soon be over,' Muriel said. It was on the tip of her tongue to ask Barbara if she'd heard anything about her husband, but she had second thoughts. If Barbara had heard anything, she would have told them.

Chapter 8

Except for those who'd gone home for the weekend,
the girls descended on the village en masse that evening,
all out to enjoy themselves. Few of them had had either
the money or coupons for clothes that looked any
better than the Land Army uniform, so most of them
wore that. Still walking on air after her encounter with
Ernst, Muriel led the way into the Dog and Duck. The
inside was gloomy, lit only by candles burning in
sconces, and the place stank of beer and cigarettes. There
was some sort of meeting going on, and men too old
and lads too young for the forces were paying contribu-
tions to an old fellow who was marking them down in
a ledger.

Muriel sat down at one of the battered old tables.

'That's Bill's chair,' one of the old men glowered.

She gave him a smile. 'I'll just keep it warm for him.'

The only youngish farmer in the place gave an exag-
gerated wince, sucked in his breath through pursed lips,
and winked at her.

'Oh, we're not staying here, are we?' Eileen muttered.

'Let Bill have his bloody chair, man. It's a mucky old place full of miserable old codgers.'

A woman who looked like a cross between old Queen Victoria and Mrs Musgrave sailed towards Muriel like a battleship, raising her arm in the direction of the door.

'Oop, thoo, an' oot!'

'We don't hev ladies in here,' the landlord called from the bar.

Audrey ignored the woman and looked him in the eye. 'Why not?' she demanded. 'Our money's as good as anybody else's.'

The Dog and Duck's version of Mrs Musgrave put her hands on her hips, threw her chin in the air and with her mouth turned down at the corners looked down her nose at them. 'You're makin' a mistake,' she sneered. 'These aren't ladies. No lady sets foot a public 'ouse.'

Muriel was in the wrong position to look down her own nose, so she lifted her chin and stated the obvious: 'You're in one.'

Now the woman moved more like a bull advancing to a red rag, and shook her arm more vigorously towards the door. 'Oot, thoo! Oot! All ov yuh – oot.'

'You're about fifty years out of date,' Audrey said, again ignoring the woman and speaking directly to the landlord.

'Well, I have no wish to stay here. This place would be none the worse for a good scrub. It can't have been cleaned for fifty years,' Barbara said, with a disdainful glance around walls and ceiling the colour of tobacco.

Audrey looked more searchingly, and poured scorn on that idea. 'Clean this ruin, and it'll fall down. It's only the muck that's holding it together.'

'Noo, away wi yuh, or Ah'll bussel ya off i' quick sticks! Ah've a good mind ti report ya to Committee!'

Report her! To the Agricultural Committee! She was so very like Mrs Musgrave that Muriel couldn't help a disrespectful peal of laughter.

Half a second later the chair was yanked from under her, and having just managed to keep her balance she was herded outside with the rest.

'Coome 'ere ageean, an' Ah'll ding yer lugs fo' yuh!' Dire warnings against darkening the door of the Dog and Duck again were directed at Muriel most especially. The effect was to double her up with mirth.

'Did you see the way she looked at us? As if we'd crawled out from under a stone!' Barbara exclaimed when their adversary was back inside her citadel. 'Outrageous!'

'Let's go,' Muriel laughed, 'before we get busselled off i' quick sticks!'

Barbara still failed to see the funny side. 'I'll go in my own good time,' she insisted. 'I don't like being ordered about, and I don't like people looking down their noses at me.'

'Yeah,' Joan agreed, 'she did, didn't she? She looked as if there was a nasty smell somewhere!'

'Take no notice, man. Her nose is too near her fat old backside,' said Eileen. 'That's what she can smell.'

Muriel laughed herself to tears at that, then gasped: 'It's

all right for you lot, but I'll get my lugs dinged if I'm here much longer, so I'm busselling off!'

She started off down the street followed by more than a dozen other girls, feeling as if she'd already had a whole evening's worth of entertainment. Her mirth had subsided to sporadic chuckles by the time they got half a mile from the Dog and Duck – and saw the Half Moon Inn, its timbered gables just visible, aptly enough, under a bright half moon. The sound of men's voices raised in song drifted towards them, to the accompaniment of jolly tunes bashed out on a piano with more enthusiasm than skill.

They opened the door and got through the blackout screens to find themselves in a cosy room with a large coal fire at one end, and lamps that gleamed their light into copper and brass. A group of servicemen gathered around a battered upright piano in the corner.

The landlord welcomed them with open arms.

'This is more like it,' Eileen breathed, smiling from ear to ear.

'What do you want, lasses?'

'Half a glass of cider,' Eileen ordered, importantly.

'It's Muriel's birthday tomorrow,' Audrey announced, as the landlord pulled the cider.

He looked up with a smile that showed a sizeable gap between his two front teeth. 'Oh aye? Which one's Muriel?'

Audrey grasped her wrist, and raised it into the air.

'What a coincidence. It's my birthday today. Do you want to stand me a drink, Muriel?'

'I'd love to, but I'm skint. So no, thanks.'

'Shall I get you one, then?'

She looked him in the eye and gave him a fetching smile. 'If you like.'

He laughed, and so did a few onlookers. 'If I give you a drink, Muriel, will you be my Valentine?'

'As long as you keep it a secret,' she said, gazing solemnly into his face. 'I've already got two others, and I don't want to upset them.'

'Hey, Muriel, if I get you a drink, can I be your Valentine, as well?' a man called from the other end of the bar – a very presentable man of around thirty-five with fair hair, hazel eyes and a hail-fellow-well-met air. The smart checked tweed jacket he wore gave him the look of a prosperous farmer.

'Didn't I just see you in the Dog and Duck?' she asked.

'That you did, and I'll never forget seeing you in the Dog and Duck to my dying day,' he grinned.

'How did you get here so fast?'

'By car. I passed you on the road. Will you be my Valentine?'

'Tell me your name and I'll put you on the list for next year,' she promised. 'I've got too many for this year, now.'

'He's a Goodyear, one of the biggest names in these parts. You'll find that out if you're here any length of time,' the landlord chipped in with a wink and a knowing nod. He beckoned her towards him, and lowered his voice. 'Play your cards right, and you'll do all right there,' he advised, in an aside intended to be heard by everyone.

Muriel looked towards 'a Goodyear' and appraised him carefully before turning back to the landlord to answer him in a similar stage whisper. 'Only one of the biggest? Who's the biggest, then? I ought to be talking to him.'

One or two of the locals exchanged sly grins. Goodyear looked a little put out, but he laughed, and looked even more interested.

'I'll tell you what, Muriel,' the landlord said, with a twinkle in his eyes, 'I've got a barrel of pear cider that wants using up. We'll have a party – me and you – and invite all your friends.'

The pear cider flowed into glasses, and since it was on the house most of the girls were soon sipping it – despite the taste. Muriel, who had never tasted anything alcoholic in her life before, thought it was horrible but declared it 'not bad', and drank the whole glass to prove it. Audrey urged the few girls who pulled faces at the taste not to be so fussy; they shouldn't look a gift horse in the mouth. The landlord refilled Muriel's glass and the locals watched them all with interest.

The man on the piano struck up with 'Happy birthday to you'. The servicemen sang lusty good wishes for Muriel, and everyone in the place raised a glass to her. Then they played the whole tune again and toasted the landlord.

'Come and sing us a song, then, Muriel,' the pianist demanded, when the toasts were over.

'Yeah! Give us a song, Muriel!' they all demanded.

'I can't sing.'

'Course you can. Everybody can sing.'

'I can't. They won't even let me sing in the lorry going to the farms.'

'Just join in with us, then.'

The pianist struck up a comic song. The oldest-looking paratrooper assumed a doleful expression and began: 'I've been married to the wrong woman for a dozen years . . .'

'and it's more than a man can stand . . .' the rest chorused, soon supported by locals and Land Girls, until the whole pub reverberated with the tune. Muriel laughed, and sang loudly and off-key – and nobody cared! What good company they all were, and how happy she was. This was better than coupon counting; this was what she'd joined the Land Army for. Freedom, and fun. Oh, and serving her country, she remembered. There was that, as well.

The others suddenly stopped singing, and with everyone's eyes fixed on her she sang half a line on her own before realising it. When the laugh was over, one of the men put two cigarettes to his lips, and lit them both.

'We thought you were kidding when you said you couldn't sing. Now we know,' he said, with a broad grin. 'You sound like a strangled alley cat.'

'Told you,' she said, pursing her lips round his proffered cigarette.

Other paratroopers were lighting cigarettes for other girls. Audrey was already smoking.

'Don't inhale,' Eileen warned, taking a cigarette herself. 'If you do, you'll be sick.'

'It's not proper smoking if you don't inhale,' Muriel protested. 'In for a penny, in for a pound! That's my motto.'

'That's a good motto, Muriel!' the paratrooper agreed. 'It would be a waste of a good fag.'

One-of-the-biggest-names-round-here backed Eileen's advice. 'You will. You'll be ill. Don't inhale, Muriel.'

Muriel ignored him. There would be no wishy-washy pretence at smoking for her, she decided. If she was going to smoke at all, she would make a proper job of it. She inhaled deeply, and determinedly suppressing a coughing fit squinted down her nose to watch the smoke stream out of her nostrils. It was pretty impressive. Eileen watched with a disapproving shake of her head. The paratrooper nodded encouragingly. When the performance was over Muriel wiped her streaming eyes and laughed to see Audrey imitate her. It was hilarious. It was the best night of her life. Everything was hilarious.

'Well, might as well fill your glasses, lasses, while our host's giving the stuff away,' Goodyear said, and took their empty glasses to the bar.

'Glasses, lasses,' Muriel repeated. 'He's a poet.'

'I call it cheeky,' Eileen said. 'He thinks because he's one of the biggest names round here he's got a right to be familiar – cheeky bugger. We're ladies. Tell him, man, Muriel.'

But Muriel was distracted by a couple of the paras who had begun to blow smoke rings. She watched, mesmerised, and then tried to copy them, determined to master this new and impressive social accomplishment. She was conscious of Goodyear's eyes on her as he returned with brimming glasses of pear cider, and threw him a smile. What would he say – what would he think – what would he do – if he knew that a Kriegsmarine submariner had carried her the length of a field, and given her his heart? And taken hers, in exchange? What would he say if he knew that? What would any of these paratroopers say, preparing to risk life and limb to defend their country from Hitler and his Nazis? They wouldn't be joking with her then. They'd be tarring and feathering her instead.

Her heart almost stopped at the thought and she gave a little shiver. That was not so funny. It was so far from being funny that it almost sobered her up.

The paratrooper gave her a queer look. 'Somebody walk over your grave?'

'It felt like it,' she shuddered, and shook the feeling off.

Never mind, none of them were going to say anything, because they weren't going to find out. She threw herself again into talking, smoking, drinking and laughter.

'What's your second name, Muriel?' Goodyear asked.

'What's your first, come to that?' she demanded.

'It's John.'

'Hello, John,' she said, and after pausing for thought, added: 'Anyway, I don't know why I'm talking to you, if you're only one of the biggest names round here. Mine's the biggest name where I come from. I don't think someone who's got the biggest name in a place ought to be talking to someone who's only got one of the biggest names.'

'You're a cheeky little missus! Well, where do you come from?'

She doffed the ash from the end of her cigarette in a swaggering sort of movement, and removed a sliver of tobacco from the corner of her mouth in a gesture she'd seen in the films, and thought rather smart. 'Morley Villas!' she announced, at last.

'So what's the biggest name in Morley Villas?'

Muriel laughed. She was not to be trapped so easily. 'You're going round in circles, John. I'll tell you when you're the biggest name round here.'

'All right, then. Give us a kiss, Muriel.'

'Get out of it,' the paratrooper said. 'I saw her first.'

'No you didn't; I saw her in the Dog and Duck, before she ever got here. Give us a kiss, Muriel.'

'No fear. I'm quite fussy who I give my kisses to. Where's the biggest name round here? I might give him a kiss, if I fancy him.'

John Goodyear looked wounded. 'Come on, Muriel! Where's Morley Villas?'

Before she could answer, someone announced that the fish and chip shop was open, and there was a rush for the door, with the Women's Land Army at the head of the stampede. They had all been paid their fourteen shillings in wages that day, and the landlord's party humour had left them enough money to squander on a decent supper.

Muriel got to her feet. 'Pardon me! I don't want to be at the back of the queue.'

'I doubt if you'll ever be at the back of the queue for anything,' John Goodyear said, standing aside to let her pass.

She stumbled over a chair and disdaining his proffered arm, made her unsteady way outside. He followed her, along with a few of the locals. The night air hit her like a sledgehammer. Her legs wobbled and she suddenly found herself sitting in the road. John Goodyear helped her back onto her feet.

The locals, now standing round the door of the inn, burst into guffaws of laughter.

'We wondered when it was going to hit you!' one of them called.

'That stuff's been in the cellar for years – since before the old landlord went.'

'Aye, and this one's tried to unload it on every stranger who walked in the pub. He's finally succeeded.'

'And then only by giving it away. It must be lethal by now.'

'You'll have some stinking headaches in the morning, lasses,' one of them jibed, as the girls streamed across the street to the chip shop.

Eileen turned to face them. 'You rotten old . . .' she slurred, 'why didn't you tell us?'

Muriel looked dizzily up at John Goodyear. 'Hey, Big Name! Why didn't you warn us?'

'What, and spoil their fun?' he asked, nodding towards the locals. 'And Big Name yourself, if you're the biggest name in Morley Villas. Tell you what, though. I'll treat you to fish and chips to make up for it.'

'I hardly drank any of that stuff,' Joan said. 'It was horrible.' She glanced at her watch, and looked dismayed. 'Do you realise it's ten o'clock? That clock in the pub must be wrong. There'll be a hell of a row when we get back. We'd better do without the fish and chips.'

Barbara drew herself up into five foot six inches of mildly inebriated dignity and resolution. 'I shall be having my fish and chips, and the warden may do as she pleases about it. I'm tired of being treated like a schoolgirl,' she said.

Muriel regarded her with admiration. Barbara wasn't going to be pushed around by the warden, so why should any of them? 'Good for you,' she slurred. 'Let's get in the queue.'

'Aye, better soak some of that booze up,' John Goodyear advised. 'And better drink a couple of glasses of water apiece before you go to bed tonight.'

Since John Goodyear's offer only applied to her and none of the other girls, Muriel insisted on paying for her own fish and chips – not wanting to be the only one of the girls beholden to someone who was only *one* of the 'biggest names round here'.

In view of the disgraceful, drunken condition of the majority of the girls, a couple of the army lads offered them a lift back in the lorry, judging it unsafe for them to cycle. Their bikes were left in the barn behind the pub. Muriel refused the offer of a lift from John Goodyear, and went with the rest. The hostel was in complete darkness when they got back, except for a light shining in a tiny attic window that she had never noticed before.

The driver's mate let the tailboard down and the girls jumped out, so used to the action that only the hopelessly intoxicated stumbled.

Barbara pointed to the light. 'Look at that! Who'd have thought our stickler of a warden would be so careless?'

'Don't worry. There are no ARP wardens round here,' the driver called.

'Lucky for her. They'd have her in court.'

The door was locked. Audrey banged on it. No response. She rattled the letterbox. Still no response.

'We'll leave you to it, then, lasses,' the driver called. His mate was back in the cab, and they drove off.

Muriel stooped to the letterbox and called through it, sing-song style: 'Hey, Miss Hub-bard! You're showing a li-ight! You'll have the Air Raid Warden after you.'

They heard movement from deep within. The warden eventually unlocked the door and appeared before them wearing a murderous scowl, along with a dressing gown, thick bed-socks, and hairnet. Muriel just managed to stifle the laughter rising within her.

'You're late! And you're drunk! I'll have words with the War Ag people about this.'

'And I'll have words with the magistrate,' Barbara countered. 'You're showing a light.'

'You're drunk. I can smell it on your breath.'

'There's a light in the attic,' Joan insisted, looking her

straight in the eye. 'It's against the law! We're all witnesses, and we're not all drunk. Most of us are stone cold sober.'

The warden's eyes flitted warily round the group, then a thought seemed to occur to her, and she clutched her chest. 'Oh, dear! Oh dear me! If there is a light in the attic it means Elinor must be walking again.'

'Who?'

'The ghost.'

'What ghost?' Audrey's voice was loaded with contempt.

'Elinor, I said. The ghost of Elm Hall. The daughter of the family – she was carrying on with one of the grooms, donkey's years ago; it caused a terrible scandal. They locked her up in the attic. She used to signal to him with a candle from that window.'

'Ghost of my arse!' Audrey exclaimed. 'You've been up there yourself, or someone has.'

Muriel walked unsteadily to the stairs. 'Only one way to find out,' she said, full of bravado and pear cider. The other girls followed her up to the first landing.

'Come on, then,' she urged, at the door to the attic stairs.

Eileen shrank back. 'No thanks,' she said, and she was not alone. Most of the other girls were reluctant to go any further as well.

'You're not scared, are you?' Muriel jeered.

They answered by melting away into bathrooms and dormitories, leaving only Barbara and Audrey standing with her at the bottom of the attic stairs.

Muriel lifted the latch and opened the attic door to look up into darkness. An icy and ill-omened draught swept downwards, causing the hairs to rise on the back of her neck. Tales of ghosts did not seem quite so ridiculous now.

She shivered. 'It's cold.'

'We ought to go up. Somebody's got to put that light out,' Barbara said.

Duty-bound, Muriel started up the narrow, winding staircase closely followed by the other two. She hesitated at the top, her nerve failing.

'Go on!' Barbara urged her.

The moon was visible through the tiny window, and a lighted candle on the sill cast flickering shadows on the wall. A cloud drifted across the moon, obscuring its light. They heard an eerie scraping sound. The candle spluttered and died.

'Aagh!' Panicked, Muriel turned and almost slipped off the narrow end of one of the twisting treads as she scrambled down the staircase, driving the other two before her. 'She's there! Elinor! Aaagh! The ghost!' she gasped. 'Go on, down!'

Audrey and Barbara nearly fell over each other in their eagerness to get back to safety, with Muriel close on their heels clutching, like the warden, at her heart. She spilled out her tale of seeing the ghost of Elm Hall to the other girls who, half undressed, half washed, one or two with toothbrushes still in their mouths, crowded round her, listening.

Later on, safe in her bunk she thought of the horror on Audrey and Barbara's faces, and then the wide eyes and dropped jaws of the other girls as she'd babbled her nonsense about seeing the ghost, and couldn't hold her laughter in. It was so funny! How could they have believed it? How could she have believed she'd seen anything herself, even for a moment?

'What's so funny?' Barbara demanded.

'She's hysterical, man. It's delayed reaction,' said Eileen.

'You're all barmy. There are no such things as ghosts,' said Joan.

'You wouldn't be so sure if you'd seen the look on Muriel's face when she saw it,' Barbara asserted.

Audrey groaned. 'Are we at sea? My bunk won't stay still. I feel as if I'm being tossed in a gale.'

'So's mine,' Muriel said, her laughter subsiding.

'Why, mine's just spinning,' said Eileen. 'Round and round. I wish I could be sick, man. I'd feel better if I could be sick.'

'I bet that old farmer was right. We'll all have stinking headaches tomorrow,' said Barbara.

'I just hope that ghost stays in the attic, where she belongs,' Muriel joked. 'What will we do if she comes downstairs, and gets into bed with one of us?'

Eileen took her seriously. 'We'll know if it feels colder. It always feels colder, when ghosts are walking,' she said.

'Aye. Nearly as cold as the cold room at the Maypole grocery.'

'How many ghosts have you seen, then, Eileen?' Joan challenged her.

The warden snapped the lights off. 'Shut up, you lot, and get to sleep!'

'How can we sleep, when one of us has seen a ghost?' Eileen demanded.

'You've seen her?'

'Muriel has.'

'Well then, you'll keep away from the attic, and not meddle with the spirit world, if you know what's good for you. Just get to sleep.'

'Bugger her!' Eileen said, after she'd gone. 'It's Sunday tomorrow, and when I finally do get to sleep, I'm going to sleep all day.'

Audrey agreed. 'Not half. Thank God we won't have to work.'

'Mm,' Muriel mumbled. But no work meant no hope of seeing Ernst Müller, which meant a day wasted. And on her birthday, as well.

Chapter 9

Someone was playing a jazz record downstairs, rending the peace of a bright Sunday morning. A clarinet solo screeched its way through Muriel's aching head like an express train. Her mouth tasted like a compost heap. Eileen had been right. If only they could have been sick, and got rid of all that head-aching, stomach-churning pear-poison.

She lifted her head carefully from the pillow and looked round, bleary-eyed. Except for Barbara, the rest were up and gone, leaving their beds neatly made.

Barbara looked at her and smiled. 'How's your head?'

'Terrible. How's yours?'

'Not as bad as yours, by the look of you.'

'That bloody racket downstairs. What do they have to make such a bloody noise for?'

'Joan and the other teetotallers? Audrey asked them to be quiet and they said they weren't going to have their only day off buggered by people who don't know when to stop guzzling rotten booze. Happy birthday, Muriel.'

'What!' Muriel groaned. 'I'm dying. I'm dying, on my

eighteenth birthday. I was born at three o'clock in the afternoon, and I'll never see three o'clock again.'

Barbara's laughter jarred painfully. 'Yes, you will, but you've missed breakfast. And the Prune wouldn't let us save any for you.'

Muriel threw back her covers and rolled cautiously and slowly out of her bunk to step ever so gently towards the bathroom. The hot water was all gone. She washed in cold, carefully cleaned her teeth and then dressed and went downstairs, where she breakfasted on the couple of glasses of water which she vaguely remembered John Goodyear telling her to drink before she went to bed.

She peeped into the common room and saw Joan, enthusiastically jitterbugging with a few other girls, all with shoes off and in their socks, the better to leap, slip, slide and generally fling themselves about. Now Muriel saw Audrey's point about being driven mad by people pounding the planks to the same bloody tunes. Now she was totally in sympathy, though annoyingly unjustified in expressing her objections with similar force.

'Would you mind just turning it down a bit?' she called, above the racket.

They laughed at her. 'What's up? Too much of that lovely pear cider?'

'Go and get a couple of aspirins from the warden. They'll soon put you right.'

'She looks a bit pale round the gills, though,' one of them said, evidently gifted with at least a grain of human sympathy.

'Yeah, but I don't think it's through seeing any ghosts,' Joan grinned. 'Get out for a walk in the fresh air, Muriel, where you can't hear us. Blow the cobwebs away – or the alcohol fumes!'

She went and put the needle down on another record, and they all danced on, as noisily as before.

Muriel's eyes narrowed. She pursed her lips. Just you wait, Joan; I'll get you back for that, she thought, and closed the common-room door.

Snowdrops were blooming in the unkempt garden of Elm Hall, and even with her splitting headache, Muriel's heart lifted at the sight. She had always loved her birthday – before this one. Even now she felt that hers was the best date possible for a birthday, because it meant the year was on the turn, the dark evenings were over at last, and the world was being reborn. This was the sunniest, most glorious February she'd ever known and to be out of the warren of streets off Holderness Road and in the country in such weather was a delight. A blow in the garden might not be a bad idea. She got her coat and walked to a rustic bower in a distant corner and sat down, inhaling deeply. The smell of spring was in the air, summer was coming and there would be no more living like moles. Let there be light – light and warmth. They were already coming home from the fields in daylight, and soon the mornings would be light, as well.

Coming home. She smiled. She'd actually begun to think of the hostel as home, but it was better than home.

Here she had a ready-made circle of friends she could never have had at home. Here there were girls from all over the country and from all walks of life – girls she'd never have had the chance to meet if she'd stayed in Hull working at the Maypole, and despite – or because of – the banter, they were like one big, happy family. Here there was no mother constantly shoving her oar in, dishing her orders out and laying down the law! Granted, there was the warden, but they'd got her under control last night without much trouble. They were all taking charge of their own lives now and having a bit of freedom.

The thought struck her that had it not been for the war, they could never have had such freedom. Without the war she would never have met a certain German submariner. Her heart lifted further at the mere thought of him, and the rush of memories stirred by that thought – of the deep blue of his eyes, his tiny, bewitching smile as he'd fastened her buttons, of the strength of his arms as he'd carried her, of that beautiful Valentine that had no existence outside their minds and hearts. A pleasant little tingle shot down her spine, and she shivered. What was Ernst Müller with two dots over the 'u' doing at that exact moment, she wondered? He couldn't be working, on a Sunday. He would be in the prison camp, but where, precisely was the prison camp? She would have to find that out. They never let the prisoners out, except to work – except, maybe, to go to church on Sundays. It was around eleven o'clock. He might be in church at this very moment. She might start going herself, in the hope of seeing him. Many of the girls already did go.

She breathed deeply, got to her feet, and set out for a long walk. It would be an effort, but the scenery would be her reward, and the fresh air might blow her headache away.

'I'm absolutely starving. I hope today's dinner's as good as last week's,' she told Audrey at one o'clock, as they filed into the dining room and took their seats.

'I've got something to show you, if we can get a minute on our own,' Audrey said.

'What is it?'

'Shh. Show you later.'

'Fancy going up to the attic for a ghost hunt when it gets dark?' Joan laughed, pulling out her chair and sitting opposite to them.

'Maybe another day. They only come out when we're full of cider.'

'How are your headaches?' Joan asked. 'They make a good case against your idea of not looking a gift horse in the mouth, I reckon, Audrey. Most gift horses are only fit for the knacker's yard.'

'Did you have a good time at the Half Moon, Joan?' Audrey asked.

'Yeah, I did.'

'Well, that was because most of us let our hair down. And we wouldn't have let it down so much if it hadn't been for the cider, would we?'

Joan opened her mouth to argue, then saw the dangerous glint in Audrey's eyes, and let the matter drop – but
she was at least half right, Muriel thought. The party at
the Half Moon Inn had been a lot of fun, but she would
be a bit more moderate with the booze herself next time.
Her headache was going, but to waste even half of a beautiful Sunday through self-inflicted illness was a crime.
There would definitely be no more morning-after headaches for Muriel.

The warden took her place at the head of the table, and
the girls on kitchen duties came in relays, bearing dishes
of vegetables, gravy boats, and arms full of plates with the
meat already on them. The girls stared at the meagre helping placed before them, and then all looked towards
Audrey and Muriel.

'We are definitely not getting our meat rations,' Muriel
protested, feeling herself elected to speak. 'We're supposed
to get double rations, working on the land.'

'You get everything you're due to,' the warden
snapped. 'Everything!'

'I know what a ration of meat or cheese looks like. I
could cut it to within a sixteenth of an ounce when I was
at the Maypole,' Muriel insisted.

'Be thankful for small mercies,' Barbara said. 'At least
there's no beetroot.'

She spoke too soon. A couple of the other girls were
just setting dishes of it on the table, whole, boiled, and
unappetising.

They helped themselves sullenly to vegetables, and

apart from asking each other to pass this condiment or that dish of vegetables they ate in silence – except for Audrey, who muttered, more than once: 'I'm sick of this.'

They went inside the library and after checking that the coast was clear, Audrey closed the door and then dragged the library steps to the wall of books behind it.

'The shelves are wide, and the smaller books are arranged in double rows, so you can't see the row behind. So I was looking behind some of the smaller ones to see if I could find a good detective novel, and instead I found . . .' she went up the steps and pulled some books off a high shelf in the corner and handing Muriel a book bound in red Morocco announced: 'this!'

An English–German dictionary. Muriel's heart leaped. She had burned with curiosity about Ernst Müller – what part of Germany he came from, what his home was like, whether he had any brothers and sisters and how old they were, and how old he was, exactly? And most important of all, whether he had a sweetheart in Germany? At her next meeting with him, she would know the words for sister, brother, sweetheart, and how old. At last she had a chance of understanding him, and making him understand her.

'You're a godsend, Audrey,' she said, and then her brow creased in perplexity. With German and English engaged in a fight to the death she would be letting herself in for a lot of hostility and suspicion if she let anybody see her trying to learn the enemy's language – and where could she hide, with nineteen other girls constantly milling around and Audrey her sole ally among them? Only the lavatory, and even there she wouldn't be left in peace for long.

The door opened, and Joan walked in. Muriel hurriedly handed the dictionary back up to Audrey with the words: 'No, I don't fancy that one, either.'

'What are you looking for?' Joan demanded.

'A bit of light reading. A murder mystery, for preference, but we can't find any.'

'I'm not surprised. There's probably only a lot of highbrow stuff in this place, Shakespeare, and Latin stuff and that. What do you want to waste your time with a lot of dusty old books for, anyway? Come and have a dance with us.'

'All right. You coming, Audrey?'

'Nah. I'll stay here, and waste my time. I might even find something good, if I look hard enough.'

After five minutes' dancing Muriel's headache took a diplomatic turn for the worse, and she made her excuses. She was quickly back where she really wanted to be, in the library with Audrey, poring over an English–German dictionary and looking up the words '*Komm*', and '*mit*'. They meant exactly what she'd thought they meant, which was very much like English.

'I was looking for a ghost, and guess what I found?' Muriel said softly later that afternoon, on meeting the warden in the hallway, just as she returned from a visit to her sister's.

Miss Hubbard looked at her, apparently uncomprehending.

'Go up to the attic, and Audrey will show you,' Muriel insisted.

'I don't know what you're talking about.'

'I think you do. None of the other girls know yet, so either you go up there now, or I'll have the rep here faster than you can say "War Agricultural Executive Committee", and then everyone will know. You've got two seconds to decide which it's going to be.'

Two seconds was more than enough. Miss Hubbard went. Muriel waited for a few minutes and then followed, taking care not to be seen by any of the other girls.

Miss Hubbard was wringing her hands as she knelt by the door to a cupboard that opened at floor level into that part of the roof space where it was too narrow for anybody to stand upright. Inside the cupboard were bags of sugar, blocks of butter and cheese, a flitch of bacon, and boxes of tinned food. Audrey stood over her, her jaw tight and brows drawn together in a frown.

'What's the penalty for stealing other people's rations again, Audrey?' Muriel asked.

'That they be taken to a place of execution and hanged by the neck until dead, if I've got anything to do with it,' Audrey said. 'I'd put the rope round her neck myself.'

Muriel looked at the cringing creature kneeling at their feet and felt embarrassed for her. 'Well, I don't think it's as bad as that, but it's bad, all the same. Cheating people out of their rations when they're working for the government must be worth six months with hard labour at least, I should think.'

The warden looked up and gave a little gasp of fear.

'So why'd you do it?' Audrey demanded. 'There's more than you could eat yourself if you lived to be ninety. You must have been planning to sell it.'

The warden shook her head. 'No.'

'Where's it been going, then?'

'My sister's. A bit to friends, sometimes. Just saving some.'

'Friends who live in the country, surrounded by farms? What do they need our rations for?'

There was no answer.

'Well, your sister and your friends will have to manage on their own rations from now on, because they're not getting ours, and we've done with starving, while you hoard,' Audrey threatened. 'Have you got that?'

'Yes,' Miss Hubbard whispered.

'What beats me,' Muriel said, 'is how you managed to have a meal ready good enough to impress the rep. How you knew. And you did know, didn't you?'

Miss Hubbard nodded.

'How?'

'My sister heard you. She's the telephonist,' Miss Hubbard said, and cringed, as if expecting a blow.

'Another one, then, that deserves six months with hard labour,' Audrey exclaimed.

'Oh, don't!' Miss Hubbard almost sobbed. 'She's got three bairns!'

'You should have thought about that before you

robbed us all. I'm going to report you, and I've got no sympathy for either of you. You deserve everything you get,' Audrey said, staring at the warden with a look so implacable it made Muriel sorry for her.

'We can't do that, Audrey,' she said. 'Think about her poor bairns, losing their mother.'

'Think about us,' Audrey said, 'out slaving like navvies all day, and coming back to less than half rations of the stuff that's been provided for us. No wonder I've lost piles of weight.'

'But do we really want to be so vindictive we get anybody locked up?' Muriel demurred.

'Well, my friend doesn't want to be vindictive,' Audrey said, 'but we're owed arrears of rations, and I want it all. So if you don't want to get what you deserve, you'll start by making sure you put plenty of that Spam out at teatime. And make sure we get the rest of the stuff as well, other-wise you'll know about it, and so will your sister – bairns or no bairns. Got it?'

The warden had certainly got it. 'Yes,' she said, 'but you'll have to bring the Spam down. I shan't be able to fetch it, without being seen.'

'We'll bring enough down for teatime, and you can leave the rest of the stuff up here. I'll do a stocktaking, just like we used to do at the Maypole,' Muriel said, 'and make sure we account for everything.'

'All right,' the warden mumbled, reluctantly.

Audrey jerked her head towards the stairs. 'Buzz off, then. And you can leave the key with us.'

Trembling, the warden obediently crept back down the attic stairs.

After a moment's silence the two girls looked at each other and smiled. 'Well, that was a turn up, wasn't it?' Muriel said. 'If I hadn't come up here to read my dictionary in peace . . . I nearly had a fit when I heard you coming up the stairs.'

'Aye, if you hadn't been so desperate to hide it, we'd never have found her stash.'

'Perfect place to hide it, though, eh?' Muriel said, looking round the room, festooned with cobwebs and overlaid with dust, and still gloomy in broad daylight. 'Nobody in their right mind would want to spend much time in here, unless they had a good reason.'

'Yep, the perfect place, the thieving . . . I can't understand why you were so soft on her,' Audrey said.

'Not because I've got much sympathy for her, if that's what you think – but would you really want to get anybody locked up, especially if they had bairns depending on them?'

Audrey gave a sardonic laugh. 'I bet that's a barefaced lie as well.'

'Well, there is another thing. We want our full rations in future, and we're going to get them. But like you said, we're owed the arrears – and they've got to be paid to us and not to anybody else. Seeing as we didn't get this stuff when we should have had it and there's quite a little stockpile, the odds are that the War Ag will reckon it's more than we need, and take most of it away,' Muriel said. 'They might even call it evidence, and take it all away.'

Audrey's grim little smile slowly broadened into a wide grin. 'You're a crafty little so and so, aren't you?' she said. 'Aye, there must be a hundredweight of sugar, at least.'

'Aye,' Muriel nodded. 'I don't think she's given much to any bairns, has she?'

'She must have had a hell of a lot through her hands, if she has. What are we going to do with it, then?'

'Lock the cupboard and let the ghost of tragic Elinor stand guard over it — and that'll be all the better for me. I quite fancy the idea of getting the place cleaned up and coming up here on my own sometimes for a little read, when the weather gets warmer. If we play our cards right the warden will help us to put the others off coming up here at all.'

'How's she going to do that?'

'You'll see — if it works,' Muriel said. 'I'm looking forward to teatime, though. Aren't you?'

'Not half,' Audrey laughed.

Chapter 10

'All right, lasses?' the landlord greeted them when they got to the Half Moon Inn, to collect the bikes.

'As well as can be expected, after you tried to poison us all off with your bloody pear cider,' Eileen said.

'Why, you can't complain; you got your money's worth. And it wasn't that bad, just well matured, that's all.'

'Lethal, you mean. We've had headaches all day, me and Muriel, and Audrey as well. And Barbara and . . .'

'Why, that just goes to show what a good night out you had. I'll tell you what, though. If you don't want to come in the pub for a glass of my best cider, I'll let you into the barn at the back of the pub, to see the film. I get one every Sunday night for the younger end in the village. It'll cost you ninepence each, though. I charge them, so it wouldn't be fair not to charge you.'

'What's the film?'

'Horror. You've just got time to go in and get a seat. We start at half past seven.'

Audrey and Muriel smiled at each other. That might

just fit the bill. 'What do you think, lasses?' they turned and asked the other girls. 'He's got a horror film. Cost you ninepence.'

'Is it a talkie?'

The landlord looked offended. 'Of course. We might be a bit behind the times in Griswold, but we're not out of the Ark altogether.'

'Well, we're here,' Barbara said, 'so we might as well see the film before we ride back again.'

The other girls were all quite keen, so the ones who had money lent ninepences to the ones who'd brought none, and they took their seats on straw bales and benches.

The programme started with a cheery newsreel showing the heroic efforts of the Women's Land Army, which was greeted with a chorus of jeers and catcalls from the villagers, and opposing cheers from all the representatives of the Women's Land Army present in the audience. A revue picture followed, and then came the main production. Villagers and Land Girls settled down to watch a spooky story set in a hellish castle with black bats flying out of soaring turrets and rats scurrying around dank dungeons where the corpses of forgotten prisoners hung in chains. Rattling coaches raced at breakneck speed through nights of drifting fog or horrible thunderstorms towards creaking drawbridges which they reached the instant before they were drawn up. Young virgins disappeared by the score, never to be seen again – all accompanied by spine-chilling discords belted out by an insane organist in the castle hall.

Land Girls and villagers sat on the edges of their seats and craned their necks to see when the vampire Count bared his enormous fangs and sneaked up on his latest defenceless young victim. The young heroine saw his shadow on the wall and turned to face him with eyes wider and bigger than his teeth, shrinking back in terror until he had her trapped against the wall, next to the mantelpiece . . .

This was too much for the young lad next to Muriel, who sprang to his feet and yelled to the celluloid heroine at the top of his lungs:

'Hit 'im wi' candlestick, lass!'

The suspense was ruined as the audience burst into laughter. The heroine made no attempt to grab the handy candlestick, preferring to let the Count sink his teeth into her neck. This was too much for the agitated youth next to Muriel, who could endure no more and left the barn.

'He'll probably have bad dreams for a month!' Muriel grinned, to another roar of laughter. The rest of them watched until dawn began to break on the screen and the Count was safely back in his coffin with his teeth dripping blood and a sharpened stake held firmly against his chest. A carpenter's mallet was poised to drive it in, gripped in the manly hand of the hero.

Before the mallet had struck even once, the villagers rose as one body and raced for the door, scrambling over benches and bales to get out first and almost trampling both Land Army and each other in the rush. Muriel looked around, expecting to see a fire somewhere, but there was none. The girls looked at each other, shrugged, and turned back to the screen to see the vampire properly disposed of.

'Vermin control,' one of the girls remarked. 'Be funny to see a lot of 'em threaded on a line – like we string rats up, wouldn't it? But why did the natives scoot so fast, do you think?'

'I reckon they were all desperate to get out before the National Anthem,' Eileen guessed, but there was no National Anthem. Presumably the village had no record-ing of it.

The landlord enlightened them when he came to run the film back to the beginning and take the reel off the projector. 'Pea and pie supper at the Methodists',' he said. 'That's what they were in so much of a hurry for.'

'That sounds all right. Why didn't they invite us?' Muriel demanded.

'What, after seeing you rolling out of my pub, three sheets to the wind?' he laughed. 'Not really the Methodist way, is it? Come in now, and have a glass of something. You've got plenty of time.'

'Yeah, going by your clock, we'll have plenty of time,' Joan said, looking at her wristwatch. 'Going by mine we've got exactly half an hour.'

The landlord looked towards Muriel and displayed the gap between his front teeth in a coaxing smile. 'Come on, you've got time for one, to celebrate your birthday.'

Audrey spoke for her. 'Nah. We've got to work tomorrow.'

'Aye, better get back, I think. We were late yesterday. We'd better not do it too often,' Eileen said.

'Come next week, then. Give the lads a treat,' he said, with another broad and gappy smile. 'You'll have to buy your own drinks, though – unless you can get them to pay! One of my customers is killing a pig, and he's bringing some sausages. I'll do 'em in the oven – save you having to queue at the chip shop.'

They would definitely come next week, they told him, making a promise they had every intention of keeping.

'Why, that was one of the best meals I've had in a long time, man. I haven't seen butter spread that thick since before the war,' Eileen said, as they lay in bed that night, with their War Ag bikes safely stored at the back of the hostel.

'And a decent helping of Spam, instead of a couple of slices you can see the plate through,' another girl said.

'Yeah, I don't know what's got into our warden. She spoke to us as if we were human when we got back from the village.'

'Do you think she's had a religious conversion?' Laura asked.

'Doubt it. But she gave us decent meals last Sunday as well, if you remember.'

'Are you calling that muck she gave us this dinnertime *decent*?'

'What's that noise?'

'What noise?' Muriel asked, innocently.

'That noise – it's coming from the attic. It sounds like someone walking about.'

'I can't hear anything,' Audrey said.

'Well I can,' Barbara said. 'She's right. It sounds as if someone's tramping about in the attic.'

'You're imagining things. That vampire film must be preying on your minds,' Audrey said.

'Wasn't it a scream when that young lad next to me got up and shouted?' Muriel chuckled.

'And then the vampire bit her! Not much of a heroine, was she? She should have listened to him.'

'Give it a rest, girls. We'll be up at the crack of dawn tomorrow and out, muck-spreading all day, or some other stinking, back-breaking job.'

Joan lifted her head off the pillow and propped herself up on her elbow. 'They're not imagining anything. I can hear it as well. You must be deaf, you two.'

'You don't think it's the va-ampi-ire, do you?' Audrey said, in sepulchral tones.

'No, I don't,' said Joan.

'Maybe it's Elinor, walking. Signalling to the ghostly groom.'

'Funny if she signals from the front of the house,' Joan sneered. 'The stables are round the back.'

'Shh!' Eileen said, and sat up in bed, listening intently. She shuddered. 'There is. There is someone up there – or something.'

'Nip up to the attic, and see if anybody's up there, Joan,' Audrey said.

'Why me?' Joan protested.

'Because you don't believe in ghosts. You could go and have a look round, and put everyone's mind at rest without being scared out of your wits.'

'Not without getting frozen to the bone, though. And what if it's an escaped prisoner, or a man with a gun, or something?'

'Or a vampire, maybe? Well, I'm not risking seeing Elinor again,' Muriel said. 'She made my hair stand on end yesterday, and I was drunk. If I saw her sober, I'd have heart failure.'

'I'm not going either, and that's flat,' Joan said.

The pacing in the attic went on, until the fear in the dormitory was almost palpable. And then it stopped.

Carrying a couple of spades over one shoulder, the farmer strode swiftly forward along a narrow lane bordered on either side by leafless hedges and trees, through whose stark branches the bright winter sun glinted. He was tall and thin, and the thick thatch of corn-coloured hair under his flat countryman's cap gave him something of the look of a scarecrow. Muriel would have put him in his sixties, but he was no less energetic for that. They trotted along after him with their baskets, struggling to keep up. He suddenly veered off the road and into a field and along the hedgerow to the highest ground, where a long straw-covered mound of earth ran north to south.

'This is a tatie clamp,' he announced, driving the spade into the northernmost end of it. He dug away through a thick layer of earth to reveal the heap of potatoes sandwiched between equally thick layers of straw underneath.

'It's like a burial mound for spuds,' Audrey said.

'It's not like anything. It's a tatie clamp, and I've opened it,' the farmer said. 'What I want you to do is get this job done while weather's fine. I want you to dig all taties out o' this clamp then I want you to pick 'em over and chuck rotten 'uns out so they don't turn others bad. Fill baskets with good 'uns then tak 'em and chuck 'em in riddler. If there's any shoots on 'em, I want you to rub 'em off by hand afore you chuck 'em in baskets. Then one of you will have to slide riddle back'ards and for'ards, like this' – he jerked the riddle backwards and forwards, suiting the action to the words – 'until all little 'uns have fallen through bars onto this wire netting underneath. You can tak turns doing this – it's hard work. We can't sell little 'uns for ware, so I want you to put 'em to one side, and bag bigger ones up. We keep little 'uns for stock feed. All right?'

'Come again?' Muriel said, with a straight face. 'I didn't quite catch what you want us to do.'

He stared at her for a moment, apparently lost for words, exasperated at the unbelievable stupidity of the typical townie Land Army recruit.

She gave him an apologetic smile. 'Sorry.'

'Weren't you listening?'

'I was, but you were going too fast. What do you want us to do, again?'

'Right. Listen, this time. I want you to . . .'

A snort of laughter exploded around the vicinity of Eileen.

The farmer stopped, and began again. 'I want you to . . .'

'Are they prisoners you've got working at the other end of that field?' Muriel asked.

He turned a sour look on her. 'They're Ities. They like singing and making up to women, and they're not particularly fond o' work.'

'So we've heard.'

'Well, you've heard right, then. So you've no need to bother about them. What I want you to do is dig taties out o' this clamp . . .'

'What's ware?' Eileen asked.

'Stuff we can sell for people to eat.'

'Do you want us to dig the taties all out at once?'

He looked at them dubiously, and changed his mind. 'No, maybe not all at once. Dig enough to sort good from bad, and riddle little 'uns out and fill some of sacks, then you can dig some more, and get 'em riddled and in sacks. I don't want you to go right through clamp and open 'em all to light, if you're not going to be able to finish bagging 'em up afore you go. Look,' he said, evidently on the edge of desperation, 'I'll *show* you.'

He gave them ample demonstration and they set about doing what he wanted them to do. Muriel's dedication to the task was unhindered since Italian prisoners provided no distraction for her. At midday 'lounces' the farmer's wife brought them tea with sugar, but no milk. She apologised, telling them that in winter every drop they produced had to go to the Milk Marketing Board.

'What, all of it?'

'Every drop,' she said. The cows gave less milk in winter, so there was none to spare. They had a quota and they had to fill it, even if that meant going without themselves. They needed the money.

The 'Itie' prisoners saw the tea and walked the length of the field to join them. The farmer's wife gave them beetroot sandwiches. They had no food of their own, since they'd already eaten their ration of one thick slice of bread lathered with marg, which was all they were given to last the whole day. They drank tea, told the girls how '*bella*' they were and sang them some operatic love songs. With the devil in her, Muriel loudly sang them something in return – that might have approximated to '*O Sole Mio*' had it been sung by someone else. The agonised prisoners finished what tea they had left, trying to cover their ears at the same time, and then retreated to their own field with much haste and little decorum.

At mid-afternoon lounces the farmer's wife gave them all apple pie with their tea. The Italians joined them to eat, drink, laugh and chat, and apply their wandering hands here and there, but they seemed to have lost their enthusiasm for singing.

After they'd gone, the girls worked with a will, and to the farmer's amazement they managed to get all the potatoes up, riddled, and in the sacks. They left him unexpectedly happy with their day's work.

Muriel was not happy. She went back to the hostel disappointed, with all the questions she'd had for Ernst still unasked. Why could those bloody prisoners not have been German? It had been a waste of a day – the only consolation being that after all the hard work, they might just get something fit to eat.

'What's wrong with the warden?'

'Has she run out of beetroot and prunes?'

'Rissoles! I didn't think she had enough meat left for rissoles.'

'And two each! Bloody hell, things are looking up.'

With generous helpings of buttered and seasoned vegetables, Muriel noted. The pudding was apple pie and custard, which might have been very good, had the warden been a passable pastry-cook. Maybe they could arrange some instruction for her – from Barbara, preferably. Still, they'd had a rattling good meal, all told.

As the girls left the dining room replete with food and favourable opinions about it, Muriel and Audrey glanced towards each other. Their eyes locked. Barbara was one of the last to leave, and she saw it.

'You two know something,' she said.

'We do; we know Miss Hubbard needs someone to teach her how to make decent pastry. What about it, Barbara?' Audrey said.

'You read my mind,' Muriel smiled.

Barbara dismissed the idea. 'Miss Hubbard's not likely

to want any lessons from me,' she said. 'I can't quite put my finger on it, but there's something going on, and you two are up to the neck in it.'

They turned faces of injured innocence on her. 'What, then?'

Barbara was not deceived. Her eyes narrowed and she gave a sardonic little smile, nodding slowly. 'I don't know, but there's something,' she said.

Chapter 11

'She doesn't miss much, Barbara. We'll have to be careful,' said Muriel.

She was hoping for another lift with the German POWs as she and Audrey turned for the hostel after a short walk, although common sense told her that they would have returned to the camp at least an hour ago. Instead, they were hailed by John Goodyear, who stopped his car to offer them a lift, and a job. How would they fancy being milkmaids on his farm?

'No, thanks,' Muriel said. 'We've never milked cows before.'

'You'd soon learn. You could live in one of the cottages. Have it to yourselves, just the two of you. Have your meals with us, if you don't want to make your own. Our housekeeper's a damned good cook.'

'No thanks,' said Muriel. Being stuck on the same farm all the time wouldn't improve her chances of seeing Ernst again.

'It's a nice cottage; it's got roses round the door in summer. Come and have a look.'

The girls looked at each other. Muriel was quite curious to see Goodyear's farm and his cottage, and Audrey didn't seem averse to the idea either.

'All right, we'll have a look, but we're not promising,' she said, 'and you'll have to take us back to the hostel afterwards.'

'I know that.'

They got in the car, and a twenty-minute journey along deserted by-roads took them to Thornhill Farm, an isolated farmhouse with its many and varied farm buildings surrounded by acres of fields.

'It's all Goodyear land, as far as the eye can see,' he boasted. A couple of farm workers were leading six shire horses back to the stables. Half a dozen cows stood in the yard close to the cowshed, with many more in the fields.

John Goodyear stopped the car beside a short terrace of six cottages, some distance from the farmhouse.

'The cowman and his wife live in that one,' he said. 'You'd be next door, in this one.'

It was a pretty, well-maintained little cottage, with a green door, green painted sash windows and a slate roof, identical to the cottages adjoining, and even smaller than her home in Morley Villas. Muriel pictured herself as Mrs Müller, the cowman's wife, living somewhere similar. Would it be in England, or in Germany? It would have to be England. Inside, the cottage floor was flagged. There was no tap.

'Where do you get the water, then?' Audrey asked.

'There's a pump, outside.'

He waited at the foot of the stairs while they went up to see the bedroom, which contained a washstand with basin and ewer.

'We'd have every drop of water to carry,' Muriel said.

He heard her. 'Only up, not down,' he called. 'You can chuck the water you've used out of the window.'

'What about the stuff in the chamber-pot?' Audrey muttered, eyebrows raised. 'Do we chuck that out of the window, as well?'

He failed to hear that. 'Give it a week, see if you like it,' he called, encouragingly.

They went downstairs. 'We'll think about it,' Muriel promised.

'You'd like it,' he urged. 'Having your own cottage would be handy; you'd have nobody ordering you in for a certain time, no warden waiting at the door with the rolling pin. You could have visitors, as well.'

'Have you got a wurzel to spare?' Muriel asked.

He looked taken aback. 'What do you want it for?'

'A doorstop.'

'Funny thing to use for a doorstop, but I've got thousands,' he said. 'You can take your pick.'

She took her pick from a pile in the barn. They started the journey back, with the conversation ranging from the landlady at the Dog and Duck, the landlord of the Half Moon and his pear cider, the trials of the farmer's life, the advantages of cottages over hostels and back again.

'What about it, then?' John Goodyear asked, bringing the car to a halt near the hostel.

'Just give us a few days to talk it over. We'll let you know,' Muriel said, as they got out and slammed the car door after them.

He wound his window down, and poked his head out of it. 'All right. Decide before the weekend. See you in the Half Moon on Saturday, then.'

They stood together and watched him roar away down the road in his car.

'One oil lamp downstairs, one candle upstairs, no bath, no running water, no electricity, no drains, an earth closet and a piss-pot under the bed,' Audrey said.

'You've forgotten the roses round the door!' Muriel protested.

Audrey cared nothing for the roses. 'Bugger that!' she said. 'We can have as many visitors as we want, and do as we like – as long as we're up every day at four o'clock in the morning to milk his hundreds of bloody cows! We'd want to be in bed before nine o'clock if we had to get up at that time.'

'Yep! Come and go as we like,' Muriel nodded. 'It's all right for him, coming and going on his four wheels, but we wouldn't be doing much coming and going, living at the arse-end of nowhere with only bikes for transport – and the War Ag probably wouldn't let us take the bikes, if we were at the same farm all the time. And how many visitors do you reckon we'd get?'

'Not a lot. Stay where we are, then?'

'Not 'alf,' Muriel grinned. 'And now we've got the warden tamed, we might get a few dances organised.'

'Will Elinor be walking again tonight, do you reckon?'

'No, let's give her a rest; I think we went overboard with it yesterday,' Muriel grimaced. 'I didn't mind getting Joan rattled, but I ended up feeling quite bad for the rest of them, especially Eileen.'

'We'll have to watch out for Barbara, though; she doesn't miss a trick, that one. I hope she doesn't go ferreting about in the attic.'

'She won't find anything. The door to Mother Hubbard's cupboard's locked again; I went up and checked,' Muriel said. 'Not that I'm worried about the rations, but of all the girls in the hostel, Barbara's the least likely to have much sympathy for people who fraternise with the enemy.'

'We can't blame her, can we?'

'I'm not blaming her. I'm just saying it might be a bit awkward if she caught me reading an English–German dictionary, that's all. So I'd rather put her off coming up to the attic at all, if I can.'

'All right. We'll trot Elinor out again on Saturday night, shall we?'

'Good idea. Then the girls can catch up on their sleep on Sunday, poor things. I'm not sure whether the walking will be enough to put them off, though. Maybe we ought to have a manifestation.'

'Get Miss Hubbard to dress up in a sheet and run round the dormitory howling and dragging a bicycle chain, maybe?'

The thought was irresistible. Muriel's dark eyes danced. 'That might be a laugh, mightn't it?' she chuckled. 'Aye, let's do it.'

'There's never been any such thing as "rained off" at any of the other farms we've been to,' Muriel remarked to the farmer's wife the following day. 'This is the first time we've ever been brought inside when it's rained.'

She and Audrey were three miles away from the hostel, at a thirty-acre farm run by Jack and Cissie, a couple in their fifties. They had been planting broad beans when the rain had started, and since it showed no sign of a let-up the farmer had brought them inside to sit by the fire and mend sacks – what he called a 'wet-weather job'. It was a very pleasant change to sit by the kitchen range and hear the gentle hissing of the fire, and the sound of the pelting rain on the window pane, and the howling wind dashing a rose-branch against it to make a persistent scratching noise on the glass. What a treat it was to be warm and dry inside, rather than wet and cold in windswept fields that were turning to mud.

Cissie, the fair, rosy-cheeked, bustling farmer's wife sat between them in her flowery printed wrap-around apron, showing them how to do blanket stitches round the holes using a sack-needle and string, and then stitch through the stitches until the hole was closed up.

'Well, we've gotten most of t' outside work done this month, it's been that fine and sunny – up to now, that is. It's a dowly lookout today, though. Mice have been at this pile of sacks, most of 'em; so we'll get 'em mended. It'll mek a change for you.'

'Dowly? What's that?' Audrey queried.

Cissie glanced at the window. 'Dowly – you know – wet, miserable, bad.'

'We saw a couple of men repairing the hedges,' Muriel probed. 'Are they your farmworkers?'

'No. They're Germans. We've 'ad 'em afore. They're good workers – ones who are willing to work at all, that is. One o' guards from prisoner o' war camp was telling us that some of 'em refuse.'

'You wouldn't think they'd have the option,' Audrey said, 'but I suppose it's like taking a horse to water – you can't make it drink, if it's not having it.'

'No, and trying to force them 'ud be more trouble than it was worth. But ones we get are good workers, and quite a few of them are used to farm work. My husban' would sooner have Germans. That young 'un we've got just now is as brant as a hoose side. He fair reminds me of my eldest. My husban' reckons they're a lot more like us than Italians are.'

'What's "brant"?'

'Straight. Holds himself tall and straight, proud, like – some people might call it conceited, but I don't. I like a man with a bit of pride in himself.'

'They might have all your hedges done before the guard comes to fetch them, then,' said Audrey.

'Not today they won't, not by looks of it, anyway,' Cissie said, casting a glance towards the window, where the rain drummed louder and the rose-branch scraped more insistently against the glass. 'My husban's gone to fetch them inside as well. He'll set 'em on cleaning cowshed.'

'That's nice; I wouldn't like to think of 'em drenched and shivering,' Muriel said, and to show her patriotism added: 'although I suppose it's no better than they deserve.'

'Well, we don't go by what they deserve,' said Cissie. 'We know nothing about 'em, really, and anyway, it's not up to us to decide what they deserve. We go by Golden Rule.'

'What's that, then?' Muriel asked.

Cissie looked dumbfounded for the moment. 'Well! Do unto others as you would have them do unto you, o' course. Didn't anybody ever teach you that?'

'Oh,' Muriel said. 'Well, I know that. I just didn't know anybody called it the Golden Rule. We never went in for religion much in our family.'

Cissie looked as if she could well believe it, and directed Muriel's attention back to stitching sacks.

Muriel stifled a sigh. If only there were jobs like sack mending for men, they might have sat cosily working together. The prisoners had been too far away for her to see their faces properly, but she knew in her bones that one of those prisoners was Ernst just from the way he stood and moved. She would have recognised his bearing anywhere – straight and confident, capable, commanding even, just as a man ought to be. It was no surprise to

Muriel that they were working on the same farm again. Fate had decreed it. It must be Ernst Müller, but he was outside in the cowshed and she was inside in the kitchen, and rack her brains as she might, she could think of no way to cross the divide.

Eventually Cissie got up to put the kettle on and began to fry the remains of her Sunday dinner in dripping. Left-over beef, mash, cabbage, roast potatoes, gravy, all went in the pan, and then she put out two plates and went to the door and called her husband.

Audrey and Muriel looked at each other. They might have been invited in, but it was plain that there would be no farmhouse dinner today. Not so lucky now as when they were with the threshing team.

'You can eat your sandwiches in here, if you like,' Cissie said.

Muriel put aside the sack she'd just finished and got to her feet. 'We've left them in the carriers. I'll just go and bring them in.'

Cissie nodded. 'I'll make us all a nice cup of tea. Give Jack another shout, will you?'

'All right,' Muriel said, and shouted to Jack as soon as she got outside, but not too loudly, since she'd had the happy thought that he must be in the cowshed, supervising the prisoners. Obviously, the best thing to do would be to go over there and have a look. The bikes were leaning against the farmhouse wall so she took her oilskin from her carrier and holding it over her head quickly tucked her sandwiches and dictionary under Audrey's oilskin, and went out. She walked across the yard with a secret little smile, but halfway across had a sudden attack of doubt that Ernst could really be there – followed by acute misgivings about his Valentine. She'd probably read too much into it, or she'd let Audrey convince her there was more to that light-hearted little mime than there really was. It had probably been no more than pleasantry, mere chaff, like the stuff she'd been carrying – and she'd built it up into a grand passion by her own wishful thinking. Her steps slowed, and when she reached the entrance to the cowshed, she felt almost afraid to go in.

'Hello! Hello!' she called from the entrance. 'Are you there, Jack?'

'Aye, lass, come in.'

She went in, and saw Jack attempting to converse with Wilhelm. 'Your dinner's ready,' she said, smiling from ear to ear.

'What's tickling you, then?'

'Nothing in particular. Maybe the thought of a nice cup of tea,' she said, searching the cowshed for Ernst, finally casting her eyes upwards. There he was, standing on a plank above the cows – with a bucket of whitewash and a brush. Muriel gave him a smile and a wave, attempting to convey her sheer delight to him, and casual politeness to the farmer. 'Are they your prisoners?' she asked.

'British Army's prisoners, more like – I've just got 'em on loan. They're a better bargain than you Land Girls, though,' he teased. 'Get through work in half time you tak.'

'Ha! We know when we're not appreciated,' she exclaimed, with eyebrows raised and the corners of her mouth dropping, managing to feign offence while electrified with excitement and pleasure both at Ernst's presence and the farmer's satisfaction with him.

'Course you're appreciated – when there's no skilled men.'

She let that pass, preferring to concentrate on the prisoners. 'It's a lot easier to talk to us than them though, isn't it?' she said, smiling at Wilhelm as they turned to leave, but prudently not waving to Ernst again.

'It is if we get lasses who understand way we talk. It's no better, if they don't.'

The rain was slackening off a bit, but Muriel held her oilskin over her head again as they walked back across the yard. 'We've seen those two before, at another farm, when we were threshing,' she said. 'The young one's called Ernst. He helped the farmer with a heifer when she was having her first calf.'

Jack nodded sagely. 'If she was a heifer, I reckon it would be her first,' he ragged her.

Muriel retrieved her sandwiches and followed him into the kitchen, hanging her oilskin on one of the pegs behind the door.

Jack and his wife sat to the table with their mouth-watering left-overs, and the girls joined them with their sardine sandwiches which, though vastly inferior to hot farm dinners were certainly preferable to the beetroot they were so very familiar with – a familiarity that had succeeded in breeding contempt to the point of revulsion.

'Either of you two lasses play whist?' Jack asked.

Audrey brightened, and sat up straight. 'Aye, I like a game of whist,' she said. 'We used to play a bit at home before my dad got called up.'

'There's a whist drive at the village hall on Friday night, in aid of comforts for soldiers. If you want to come, we can call for you on way. You'd get to know a few of the Griswold folk there.'

'Aye, I'd love to play,' Audrey said. 'What about you, Muriel?'

'I wouldn't mind if I could play, but I can't.'

'You've got time to learn rudiments, between now and then,' Jack said.

'Are the rudiments enough, though?' Muriel demanded. 'I once read about a man being killed for leading the wrong card.'

'That wasn't whist, it was bridge, and it was in America,' Cissie laughed. 'A woman shot her husband. We don't take cards that seriously here – ours is only a friendly game, for comfort fund. And quite a lot of us are Methodists, so we're not big card players. Nobody minds losing.'

'Well, thank goodness for that. All right, then, if Audrey can teach me enough before Friday night, and you all promise not to kill me if I get it wrong, I'll come,' Muriel said.

'We'll call for you about seven, then,' Jack said.

'Do you know where we are?'

'I should think so. I've lived round here all my life. I remember Elm Hall when old squire lived there.'

'Did you ever hear anything about a ghost there?' Audrey asked.

'A woman did away with herself there once, one of old squire's great aunts, I think,' Jack said, 'but that was long before my time. Long before my father's time as well, I shouldn't wonder. Supposed to have been a big scandal, though.'

'What happened?'

'She'd been carrying on wi' stable lad, as far as I know. I never took much interest in it.'

Cissie enlarged on the tale. 'She'd been carrying on wi' a stable lad, so family got shut of him and set about marrying her off to someone she didn't want to marry. So she did away wi' herself − or they did away wi' her. One o' two.'

'Goodness! Do you reckon the family might have done her in, then?' Muriel exclaimed, recognising in a flash how useful it would be to instil that sinister and romantic tale into the heads of all the other girls in the hostel. And it might even be true! 'The warden told us something about a ghost, but I thought it was a cock and bull story,' she said, probing for more information.

'Well, it hardly matters now, any road up. They've all been dead for donkey's years,' Jack said, putting an end to the discussion.

The kettle boiled, and Cissie got up to make tea and fill

four cups and two enamel mugs – and put milk in them all. 'Take these two to prisoners, will you?' she asked Audrey.

'I'll go,' Muriel volunteered, putting aside a half-eaten sandwich and taking the two mugs.

'Don't be long coming back, or yours'll be cold,' Jack said.

Luckily the rain had stopped, and the oilskin was not needed. Muriel walked the distance between the farmhouse door and the cowshed with one hand holding the two mugs, and the other firmly pressed against the dictionary under her jumper.

Ernst and Wilhelm came and took their tea, with no '*bella bella*'s or '*O sole mio*'s – just a quiet courtesy. They each had one thick slice of bread spread thickly with margarine, which she knew from the Italians was a fifth of a loaf, not much to fuel a grown man for a day's hard labour. Ernst smiled, and the light in his eyes showed such pleasure that Muriel glowed with relief and delight, thinking it wonderful how much can be said with a look, without even uttering a word. Her last, lingering doubt that she had read too much into that Valentine disappeared. Both men watched her with a puzzled interest as she thrust her hand down the front of her green V-necked jumper and withdrew the dictionary and then sat on a straw bale and opened it at the English word 'brother', putting her finger under the German translation. Ernst stooped to look over her shoulder at the word. She turned to him with a querying expression, her face so close to his that she could see the folds in his cobalt blue irises. She flushed, slightly.

He shook his head. '*Nein*.'

He didn't understand. With her right index finger still under the word, she raised one, two, three and then four fingers on her left hand, still looking at him in that same questioning manner and feeling as if she were playing charades. He laughed, shook his head again, and then raised his right hand with the thumb and index finger forming an 'O'. He had no brothers. She turned the pages to find the word 'sister' and put her finger under the German equivalent of that. This time he raised three fingers, smiling and nodding at the same time.

Wilhelm looked on, sipping his tea.

They hardly noticed him. 'You've got three sisters, then,' Muriel said, gazing into his blue eyes.

'Three sisters,' he repeated, with a wide smile.

He took the dictionary from her, and with a question-ing look at her, held his finger under 'sister'.

'One,' she told him, holding up one finger. 'And one brother.'

'*Ein Bruder*.'

'Yes. He's twelve.'

She hadn't enough fingers to express that, so it was back to the dictionary.

A few minutes later Audrey appeared at the entrance. 'Far be it from me to interrupt your billing and cooing, Muriel, but your tea's gone cold and you haven't finished your sandwich, and if you don't come quick, you won't have time. He wants us planting beans again in five minutes, now the rain's gone.'

Muriel thrust the dictionary back into her jumper, collected the cups and with smiles and a regretful '*Auf Wiedersehen*' she left Ernst and Wilhelm and followed Audrey out of the cowshed. She was totally unconcerned about either the sandwich or the tea, especially now that the new arrangement with the warden almost guaranteed a substantial evening meal – but it would be better to avoid arousing suspicion of fraternising. The girls walked together towards the farmhouse, striding over puddles made bright by the sun. At the farmhouse door Muriel glanced back to the cowshed, and saw both Ernst and Wilhelm standing outside, looking towards her. A quick wave, and she went inside to gulp her cold tea and finish her sandwich under Cissie's curious gaze.

The arc of a rainbow stretched wide over the blue sky when they set out through fields bathed in sunshine. Raindrops on trees and hedges sparkled like diamonds. From the topmost twig of an ash tree a blackbird was singing his heart out, his silences filled by the shriller tones of a thrush. Sparrows chirruped in the hedges and high above them all the silvery notes of a skylark rippled through the cold, clean air.

Muriel stood entranced, listening and watching with her boots in the mud and her mind and heart in paradise. Beside her, Audrey was already stooping to plant beans in the sodden earth.

Chapter 12

Audrey's limited skills as interpreter were called upon every day at Iounces, and the dictionary was thumbed through without let up in the days that followed. Before Thursday came, Muriel knew that Ernst's father was dead, that his mother was called Ursula, and that she was struggling to work in some munitions factory in Germany while keeping a home for his three sisters. Seventeen-year-old Eva worked in a hospital. Rosa, aged fourteen, and Gretchen, eleven, were at school. Ernst loved his mother and sisters and since his father had died he considered it his responsibility to look after them. He worried about Rosa the most. Out of the three she was the one who was the soonest crushed, who took everything to heart. Muriel admired his loyalty, and thought it wonderful for them to have a nice big brother feeling responsible for them – not that he would be doing much to look after anybody in Germany from a prison camp in East Yorkshire. Still, she concluded, it's the thought that counts. Catch Arni feeling as if he ought to be looking after her!

Like many of the poorer farmers in East Yorkshire,

Ernst's grandparents were struggling to keep a small farm going in a place near Hamburg. Before the war, Ernst had been able to help them. Now they had to manage alone – or maybe not, Audrey suggested. Maybe they had British prisoners of war working for them, same as Ernst was working for the farmers in East Yorkshire. It was a bad job all round, but one piece of the Ernst Müller jigsaw filled Muriel with joy – he had no girl in Germany.

At midday lounces on Friday she and Audrey sat in the barn with him and Wilhelm, drinking tea from enamel mugs. Muriel had a sudden impulse to tell him she'd been offered a job as a milkmaid, and turned it down because she'd never milked a cow. With the help of Audrey, the dictionary, and a merry game of charades, she managed to get most of the message across. Ernst took her by the hand, and led her into the dairy, where he scrubbed and dried his hands, and by smiling, nodding and pointing got her to do the same. Then with milking-caps on they proceeded to the newly whitewashed cowshed, where he sat her on the milking stool beside the best milker. He patted the cow's neck and gave her a lot of soothing words, then crouched close to Muriel, and tried to show her how to grasp the teats, one in each hand, and squeeze – crouched so close that her heart raced, and she felt as faint as a heroine in a Victorian romance – in sore need of the smelling salts.

Milking was harder work than she could have imagined. She pulled and heaved, and got no more than a few unwilling drips out of those stubborn teats. Ernst laughed, and showed her again. It seemed so easy when he did it – the milk flowed out in a swift and constant stream, directly into the bucket. Muriel tugged with renewed vigour. The cow bellowed and moved out of the way, kicking over the milking pail. Before Muriel could stoop to retrieve it, the infuriated cow swished her tail vigorously round, lashing her in the face and knocking her backwards into Ernst.

Smelling salts were no longer needed. The force of the blow had dispelled any tendency to the vapours. 'Ouch!' Muriel's hand flew to her stinging cheek as she sprawled on the floor, half lying on Ernst. She felt him shake with laughter.

'She don't like you milk,' he managed to say.

'And I don't like her smacking my chops, either!' Muriel exclaimed, turning to face him. He wrapped his arms round her, drawing her to him until their noses almost touched.

'Not much of a milkmaid, am I?' she joked, making no attempt to free herself. Ernst had stopped laughing, and she was transfixed by the intensity in the blue eyes that were searching hers.

His arms tightened their hold.. Her heart raced, and she lowered her eyelids, expecting to feel his lips against hers . . .

Instead, Audrey's voice boomed: 'Hey, you two!'

A beautiful moment was ruined. Muriel looked up and saw her and Wilhelm walking rapidly towards them. Ernst stood up and helped her to her feet.

'Sorry to spoil your fun and games, but it's time we got back to work!' Audrey said.

'You're a real pal, Audrey!' Muriel grimaced. 'Thanks a lot.'

In Griswold's village hall a dozen green baize-covered card-tables were ready and waiting, each with a pack of cards and a little enamel device to show which suit was trumps. Their little party was among the first to arrive, and Muriel and Audrey sat at table one, East–West opposite Jack and Cissie's North–South, indulging in a little idle chit-chat as they waited for the games to begin.

'Are you sure everyone's just playing for fun?' Muriel asked, with some trepidation.

'Aye, it's just a fund-raiser, so's lasses' knitting circle can mak some woollies for lads in army,' Cissie said.

'You'll be all right, Muriel,' Audrey encouraged her. 'We've made a fair bit of progress, playing in the hostel.'

Playing at the hostel with girls she'd known for weeks was a bit different to playing with the cream of Griswold at a proper whist drive, she thought, as she watched all the local worthies stream into the hall until every table was filled bar one.

A disgruntled-looking old chap looked pointedly at the large pendulum clock hanging on the wall. 'We'd better mek a start, then. None on us wants to be up all neet.'

'We can't very well start wi'oot 'em,' the Master of Ceremonies protested.

'Are we ganna sit here all neet, waitin' for 'em then? Wor if they don't come at all?'

'We'll just gi' 'em five minutes,' the MC insisted.

The old chap heaved an impatient sigh, threw himself back in his chair and stared pointedly at the clock.

'Owd Sammy Mawson,' Cissie whispered. 'Nothing ivver suits 'im.'

After a long two minutes of its relentless tick, tick, ticking John Goodyear came in with three others.

'"King" waits for nobody, I suppose,' Owd Sammy Mawson scoffed, 'ivery bugger else waits for him.'

'Theere's a sample o' kettle callin' pot grimy arse, if yer like,' Jack snorted. Owd Sammy Mawson affected not to have heard.

John nodded to Jack, and was taken aback to see Muriel there. 'Well, if it's not the lass with the biggest name in Morley Villas! Fancy seeing you here,' he greeted her as they passed. 'I wouldn't have had you down as a card player!'

'We'll soon see whether I'm a card player or not,' she laughed. 'I know this much though, John – I'll never make a milkmaid.'

The older men with him looked on with interest as John made a comic little grimace of disappointment, but a roomful of people waiting to start the game left no time for either introductions or argument so they walked on to the empty table at the bottom of the room.

The late arrivals settled themselves, the man in charge gave the word, the players cut for trumps, and battle commenced. Audrey and Muriel did fairly well, holding their own with all the games against Cissie and Jack before they had to move to the next table. They did not disgrace themselves there, either. Muriel began to think she was playing damned well for a beginner and the gleam of approval in Audrey's eyes convinced her that it was so. She was gaining such confidence in her skill as a whist player that she had time to eavesdrop on snatches of Jack and Cissie's conversation with their new opponents. 'Beans planted, Brussels sprouts gathered, kale cut, and carrots dug,' she heard Jack boasting. His hedges had wanted re-laying for years, they'd been full of gaps at the bottom, now they were all cut back and re-laid, by a couple of German prisoners. They were good workers, them lads – they'd even whitewashed the cowshed, so that now they were up to scratch with everything on the farm, in spite of their lads joining the forces . . .

By the time they were half-way through the hands at table number three, Muriel considered herself a born whist player.

Then she saw Jack looking directly at her, and heard him say to the new couple at their table: 'She's as blithe as a linnet, when she sees one of our . . .'

One of their what? One of their prisoners! What else could it be? A frisson of terror ran through her. Surely he couldn't have twigged about her and Ernst – she'd been so discreet! She was craning her neck to hear more, when she was startled by a sharp order from Sammy Mawson.

'Wake up lass! It's your turn! Follow suit, will yer?'

More concerned about what Jack might be telling people, Muriel snatched a card from her hand, spanked it down and found she'd won the trick. The play passed on, but she was too busy wondering what Jack had been saying to take much notice of it. The thought of everyone within a hundred miles of Griswold knowing she was worse than fraternising with one of the cogs in Hitler's war machine was disturbing. She seriously doubted it would make her very popular anywhere, and it would make her most especially unpopular with Barbara and the crowd of RAF men and paratroopers who frequented the Half Moon Inn.

Sammy Mawson suddenly leaned forward with eyes like a hawk, and pointed his gnarled old finger at her. 'You're cheatin', miss!'

Muriel jerked back from the stabbing finger and stared at him, astounded. 'Hey? What?'

Audrey stared at Sammy, her pale blue eyes bulging. 'Just a minute, we don't cheat. You'd better be sure of your facts before you start accusing people,' she said.

Sammy replied by standing up and calling for the director. The flow of pleasant chatter stopped, and Muriel felt everyone's eyes on her while an inquisition commenced into who played what, card by card and trick by trick.

The director finally found against Muriel. 'Look there – you played a heart, when you should have followed with your diamond, and you took the trick because hearts were trumps,' he told her. 'Two rounds later, you played the diamond.'

Muriel's face glowed like a beacon. 'I just didn't see it,' she said.

Sammy glared at her. 'Cheatin',' he repeated.

She stiffened. The thought of having to kowtow to this horrible old man sickened her but some sort of apology seemed to be due. 'I'm very sorry,' she said, distantly, while looking straight through him. 'I didn't see it.'

The director was very sympathetic. 'Don't worry, we've all revoked at one time or another. You're not the first to make that sort of mistake, and you won't be the last. Even Mr Mawson's not above making a mistake now and then.'

The proper penalty was awarded against Muriel and Audrey, and play continued without further mishap until they'd played the sixth table, when a serving hatch at the end of the room was opened by one of the ladies. Two others stood in the narrow kitchen beyond, one of whom was filling an enormous teapot with water from a Burco boiler while another was busy spreading pork dripping onto bread cakes. The lady at the hatch began setting out milk, sugar, cups and saucers on the counter and people who'd already finished their games went to line up for refreshments.

Jack stood behind Muriel and Audrey at the serving hatch. 'You had a bit of bad luck theer,' he grimaced. 'Most other folks 'ud a let it pass, and said nothing, but o' course, Sammy had to mak a song and dance aboot it.'

'I got a bit distracted by what you were saying.' She turned towards him and smiled, her eyes searching his face for any reaction.

He looked blank. 'I wouldn't have thought anything I had to say 'ud distract anybody. What I was sayin'?'

John Goodyear's party had finished their game. He was making his way towards her, and she had no intention of going into it with him listening. She would save it until Jack was giving them a lift back to the hostel.

'I forget, now,' she said. 'It just struck me at the time.'

'Well, the cup that cheers but don't inebriate,' John Goodyear greeted her. 'You weren't at the cider before you played that hand, were you?'

'I was not.'

He nodded towards the hatch, where one of the women was pouring tea into a line of cups, and laughed. 'You won't get the same buzz off that that you got off the Half Moon's rank cider!'

'Or the headache, either.'

Still smiling, he asked: 'Was it bad?'

'It's put me off pear cider for life. Probably all cider. Probably all alcohol.'

'Shame,' he commiserated, 'but don't give up on it yet. And what makes you think you'll never make a milkmaid?'

'Cows,' she said.

'And anyway, we'd rather live in the hostel, where we've got plenty of other lasses for company,' Audrey chipped in. 'There'll be a good few in the Half Moon tomorrow night, looking for the blokes they've got friendly with. See if any of them are interested in being milkmaids.'

'I will, if you're not interested,' he said, and joined his own party at the back of the queue.

Muriel and Audrey tossed their pennies into the dish for cups of tea and bread cakes and returned to their table with their mouths watering, thinking they had the best of the bargain.

Audrey sank her teeth into her bread cake, smeared with salted pork fat. She gave a rapturous sigh. 'Oooh! Mucky dripping!'

'Don't talk with your mouth full,' Muriel said, and bit into hers. The bread was new and soft, and the dripping was succulent. Conversation stopped for a few minutes, while they savoured every mouthful.

John Goodyear now had his tea. He turned towards them and raised his cup in salute, looking as if he'd be over to join them, given the slightest encouragement. Muriel flashed him the briefest of smiles and then turned to Audrey, as though deep in conversation. John drifted off, to find company elsewhere. She was relieved that they never had to play against John Goodyear, since he and his partner were also East–West and moved from table to table well ahead of them.

They clip-clopped home in the trap at about half past ten, under a clear sky and a bright full moon, with the whole party laughing – about Muriel's having been awarded a box of chocolates as a booby prize after the scores had been announced, to the applause of the whole hall.

'You could tell he felt sorry for you,' Cissie said,

referring to the director. 'I was sickened when Sammy Mawson got first prize though!'

'I might have been sickened if it hadn't been a diary – when we're half-way through February,' Muriel said. 'Mine was a better prize than his. I bet the director swapped them.'

'I'd rather have had yon bottle-opener that Goodyear got, than any diary,' Jack said.

'I think he's sweet on you,' Cissie said.

'Who?' Jack asked

'Muriel. I saw him give her quite a few sly glances.'

'How old is he?' Muriel asked.

'Thirty-five.'

'He's an old man, then,' she said, dismissively.

'At thirty-five?' Cissie protested. 'I wish I was thirty-five again.'

Muriel pulled a face. Thirty-five. That was getting on for forty – unthinkably old for a girl of eighteen. Ernst, on the other hand, was twenty – the ideal age-gap, to her mind.

'Why isn't he married, then?' Audrey demanded.

'He went to university, and after that he knocked about with a few of the young women he'd met there, but none of them came to anything.'

'There must be something wrong with him,' Audrey said.

'There's nothing wrong with him. He's just a bit fussy, that's all.'

'Or none of his young women wanted to go and live at the back of beyond,' Muriel said.

'If I had a dowter, I'd marry her off to him i' quick sticks, if I could,' Jack said. 'He's his father's only lad – he gets everything when owd man's happed up, and he's got nigh on 1,000 acres. They had twenty-four horses till not long sin', but they've swapped half of 'em for three tractors. Twelve horses and three tractors now – think on that! He's got fields stretching for miles.'

Jack evidently expected her to be impressed, but John Goodyear's acres left Muriel cold. She was inclined to think as Audrey did. Thirty-five and not married? There must be something wrong with him. But she wasn't concerned about John Goodyear, one way or the other. Half-way back to the hostel she could bear the suspense no longer. For better or worse, she had to know what Jack had been telling those people at his table. With her pulse racing and her heart in her mouth she exclaimed, as if suddenly calling something to mind: 'Oh! I've just remembered what it was that put me off my game, Jack! You were saying: "She's as blithe as a linnet, when she sees one of our . . ." and I wondered what could make anybody as blithe as a linnet, but I didn't catch the rest.'

Jack took off his cap and scratched his head. 'Why, I can't say as I remember saying it,' he said, and replaced the cap.

'You did,' Cissie said, after a pause. 'You were talking about our lads. You said: "She's as blithe as a linnet when she sees a letter from one of our lads."'

'Oh, aye, so I did,' Jack said. 'She must have ears like a bat.'

'Aye. No secrets where she is,' Cissie said.

Muriel laughed. There certainly was a secret where she was, had they but known. She herself was the secret – a secret made flesh. 'Well, you were looking straight at me, Jack, so I obviously thought it was me you were talking about,' she said.

'Nay, you're blithe all the time, not up and down, like our Cissie.'

'He's right. I am,' Cissie said. 'Down, when I haven't heard from the lads for a bit, happy when they write, and twice as blithe as any linnet when they're coming home on leave.'

The conversation turned to the couple's two sons. The danger was past and all Muriel's tension ebbed away. She could rest easy, and laugh now at the terror Jack's innocent little comment had caused in her guilty mind.

'Are you coming next Friday, then? Shall we give you a lift?' Cissie asked, when he drew the horse to a halt outside the hostel.

'What's it in aid of, again?' Audrey asked.

'Nothing for the Land Army, you can bet your life on that,' Muriel said.

She was right. It was for cigarettes for the soldiers. The girls decided they would go, as much for the supper as the whist.

'All these "do's" to get money for the soldiers!' Audrey exclaimed, when they stood together waving Jack and Cissie off. 'What about us? What about raising some money for comforts for the Land Army?'

'Aye, what about it? A few bottles of shampoo and bars of nice, scented soap wouldn't come amiss,' Muriel said.

'I wondered what was wrong with you, just before you played that heart,' Audrey said. You looked as if you were going to fall off your chair.'

'I nearly did. I thought he was telling all Griswold I was fraternising with the enemy.'

'Well, you are.'

'I know I am, and so are you. But I didn't think it would do me much good if everyone else knew it.'

'Maybe you should pack it in, then.'

'I'm not packing it in,' Muriel said. 'But I wouldn't blame you, if you did.'

'Nah. It's all the government's fault, anyway. They can't have us working alongside the so-called "enemy" and expect us not to talk to 'em. They should keep them locked inside their prison camps and do without their labour, if they want to stop people fraternising. So that's my attitude from now on, and if anybody opens their mouth about it to me, that's what they'll get.'

Audrey's stolid common sense put some heart into Muriel. If she intended carrying on with Ernst – and she did intend to – it would have to be her attitude as well. She would have to be less faint-hearted about things, and not jump at every shadow, or fall to pieces at every whisper.

She gave an emphatic nod. 'Aye, that's the style. And we'll go to the whist drive next week and win first prize, just to rub Sammy bloody Mawson's nose in it.'

Chapter 13

Ernst and Wilhelm were already hard at work when Muriel and Audrey arrived at Jack and Cissie's farm early the following Monday morning. They were digging manure from a pile in a field next to the fold yard and loading it onto the cart. The girls laughed and held their noses as they rode by on their way up to the farmhouse, where they leaned their bikes against the wall and went to get their orders for the day. They found Cissie kneeling on the pegged rug beside the range, kneading dough.

'I can't do with you in the kitchen today, lasses, it's my day for baking. I'll leave you a couple of bottles of tea outside the door when it's time for your lounces. You can take the Germans theirs, as well.'

Jack gave them the task of mucking out the fold yard, which was deep in weeks' worth of dung compressed with the straw that had been spread regularly on top of it to soak up the liquid. Provided with shovels and wheel-barrows the girls started digging, much to the amusement of the Germans, who laughed and held their noses before turning for the ploughed fields with their cartload. The girls dug and wheeled load after load to the adjoining field to dump it beside the old manure heap, where Jack intended to leave it to rot down for another year. When the job was done, he sent them off with a couple of bottles of tea for their lounces, a four-pronged, round-tined fork each, and wheelbarrows laden with manure – to help the Germans with muck-spreading.

Rosy and invigorated after pushing their barrows full of well-rotted manure, they paused for a moment on a slight rise in the lane to watch two tiny figures of men at the far end of a ploughed field, still quite a distance away. They were moving slowly forward with the horse and cart under a wide blue sky, working rhythmically as they went, with the birds wheeling above them. For how many years, for how many long centuries must that same scene have been re-enacted in these same fields, Muriel wondered, and with the thought came a profound sense of connectedness to the land and its past. She filled her lungs with cold, crystal-clear air, and smiled at her poetic fancies. Life in Holderness Road had certainly never inspired any such romantic notions. Living in the country was having a strangely spellbinding effect on her – but why, she could hardly imagine. The air might be crystal-clear, but just at that moment it had more than the whiff of manure. And there had been very little glamour in her day so far – up before the crack of a cock's fart and out in the dark and the freezing cold to spend half a day shovelling cow muck into a heap, and then bring more muck to spread on ploughed fields – what was poetic about that? To put the matter at its plainest, it was shit that Ernst and Wilhelm were spreading, not fairy dust, she thought, and she came out of her trance, laughing.

Audrey looked at her and grinned. 'What's up with you?'

'Us,' she said. 'What we've got ourselves into – spreading piles of muck onto ploughed fields.'

'We could be doing many a worse thing,' Audrey said. 'We could be cooped up in a munitions factory, with a foreman who thinks he's Hitler.'

'There are some farmers who are no better, going by some of the tales Laura tells.'

'Aye, well, we don't have to put up with them for long if they're that bad; the War Ag rep's told at least one of them he'll never get any more Land Girls.'

'She has. I suppose she's pretty fair, all told,' Muriel agreed.

They pushed on to the field and set their wheelbarrows some distance apart, facing the men and working towards them.

Muriel lifted a fork full of manure and threw it feebly onto the field, where instead of scattering it landed in one solid lump. She saw Ernst laughing at her, and taking a forkful himself he scattered it in a wide arc, and then dug and scattered another in the same manner.

'Show off,' she shouted, but he was probably too far away to hear, and wouldn't have understood anyway.

Both men strode quickly towards them, to give them a

demonstration at closer quarters. Ernst stood behind Muriel and with his hands clasped over hers on the dung fork, tried to toss the dung as before, with little effect but a lot of laughter. He kissed her cheek and whispered in her ear '*mein Liebchen*' and other sweet German nothings she could only guess the meaning of. They made her blush, all the same.

Audrey, much taller, soon got the hang of it through simple demonstration. Muriel was also managing better when the time came for midday lounces.

They left the horse and cart in the field and walked along a narrow footpath towards a clump of trees on slightly higher ground, carrying their lounces of cold tea and sandwiches wrapped in newspaper. Ernst took off his coat and spread it on a fallen log, with a smile and a sweep of his arm inviting Muriel to sit on it.

She laughed at him, and picked it up. 'Put it on, you idiot,' she said, handing it back to him. 'It's cold!'

'It's cold,' he repeated with a mock shiver, and wrapped his coat around her, more as an excuse to give her a squeeze than to keep her warm, she suspected.

'What's the German for "idiot"?' she asked, handing him his coat for the second time and seating herself on the log. He put it back on and sat beside her, and they laughed as they each took a swig from a bottle of tea, surveying the clear blue sky beyond the fields and big white clouds which seemed to be sitting on the horizon. A fresh south-westerly breeze kept the scent of manure in their nostrils, but it truly was not all that cold. The wind seemed to have blown away the most biting chill.

Ernst and Wilhelm had already eaten their slabs of bread and margarine, but the girls had thoughtfully brought double their usual quantity of sandwiches, made and packed right under the nose of the unprotesting warden.

Muriel offered a cheese and beetroot sandwich to Ernst, and got a polite but reluctant refusal. To save further argument she took the sandwich and slapped it in his hand.

He laughed. '*Dankeschön.*'

'You're welcome.'

Audrey gave a sandwich to Wilhelm. 'You'd think we'd all have bad stomachs, touching food after doing a job like that,' she commented, watching them eat.

Muriel observed their chapped and filthy hands with none of the horror she would have felt during those distant days at the food shop. 'We should, by rights, shouldn't we? Miss Chapman would never have stood for this, in the Maypole.'

They all ate hungrily, caring nothing about grubby hands and the stench of manure in their nostrils – or what Miss Chapman's opinion on it might have been. When the food was eaten they drank cold tea out of the bottles and managed to make a little headway with conversation.

Ernst turned to Muriel. 'Nice,' he said, looking at the sky. '*Sonnenschein.*'

'*Sonnenschein,*' she said. 'Do you reckon that's sunshine, Audrey?'

'Yep.'

'It amazes me,' Muriel said, 'how many of our words are similar: milk − *Milch*; cow − *Kuh*; sunshine − *Sonnenschein*; brother − *Bruder*; my − *mein*. And when it comes to words like water − *Wasser* and *Butter* − we say "butter" exactly the same way in Yorkshire. That can't be a coincidence, to my mind.'

'It's not,' Audrey said. 'Remember the Danelaw?'

Muriel took a bite of her sandwich. 'Never heard of it,' she said, through a mouthful of bread and beetroot.

'What'd they teach you, at that school of yours? Didn't you ever learn any history?'

'If I did, I can't remember it.'

'Well, after the Romans had gone, this part of the country was invaded by Vikings and Danes. It was the Danelaw when King Alfred was burning the cakes, and for a long time after, if I remember rightly.'

'Danes and Vikings aren't Germans, in case you haven't noticed.'

'They're not far off, though, are they? Denmark's not that far from Germany, is it?'

Ernst stood up, took a penknife out of his pocket and began to cut into the bark of a tree.

'What are you doing?'

'*Ernst und Muriel*,' he said.

Muriel laughed. 'So they do that in Germany, as well, do they? Our lads usually do a heart with an arrow through it, as well,' she said, then thought that that mouthful of English had been too much and too fast for him.

But he nodded, still chipping bark away from the tree. *'Ernst und Muriel – immer,'* he said, eventually.

'What's "*immer*"?'

'Always,' Wilhelm said.

'Always,' Ernst repeated, looking directly into Muriel's eyes. They leaned towards each other until their lips met in a kiss, and she felt she could have followed him to the ends of the earth.

'Oh for pity's sake! Just look at that, Wilhelm. Isn't it enough to make you throw up?' Audrey mocked, and putting her fingers to her mouth made a couple of retching movements.

Wilhelm smiled indulgently. *'Ja.* Very nice,' he said.

Without a word to anybody, the two conspirators escaped from the Half Moon Inn two full hours before closing time that evening and pedalled away on their War Ag bikes as furiously as a full moon and shielded bike lamps would allow, leaving all the other girls enjoying a rousing sing-song round the piano with some very attentive servicemen.

Back at the hostel they knocked and entered the warden's private quarters, intent on constructing a convincing ghostly Elinor from a dressmaker's form, an old long white nightgown, a wurzel, a couple of hanks of brown wool and a long, lace net curtain – everything except the wurzel supplied by Miss Hubbard.

They stepped back when they'd finished, the better to admire their handiwork, and it was very good. 'Well, if that doesn't convince them, nothing will,' Audrey said.

When they had rehearsed the warden in her own part in the drama, they went upstairs with a dud light bulb and a small set of stepladders, to make sure none of the girls would be able to throw too much light on their carefully created phantom.

Audrey set up the stepladders under the landing light and using a towel to protect her fingers she took the bulb out of the socket and handed it down. Muriel took it and cut the power off at the switch. 'Better not electrocute yourself,' she said, handing Audrey the dud bulb. 'One spook will be enough. We don't want two of you wandering about.'

Mission accomplished, they went back downstairs to return the stepladder and give the good bulb to the warden, and then back upstairs to enjoy long soaks in hot baths while awaiting the arrival of their victims. By the time the others got back they were sitting together by the common-room fire dressed in their pyjamas, innocently sipping cocoa.

Audrey looked at the returning revellers from under sleepy eyelids, and put a hand over her mouth to cover a huge, faked yawn. 'Time I went to bed, I think. We've worked like navvies today, me and Muriel.'

'Why, you've missed the best part of the night, you two,' Eileen said. 'We've had a marvellous time. I laughed until I ached.'

'But not as much as my head ached, last Sunday morning,' Muriel said. 'I vowed I wouldn't get in that state again, so we came away and had a nice bath, with nobody else hammering to get in the bathroom.'

'Aye, we needed it, after shit-shovelling all day,' Audrey said.

'And tomorrow morning we'll be up jitterbugging, with all you lot begging for mercy.'

'Speak for yourself. I won't be doing any jitterbug-ging,' Audrey said.

Barbara contemplated her for a moment, and then looked at Muriel, equally thoughtfully.

Muriel got to her feet, feeling uncomfortable under Barbara's scrutiny. 'Well, I'm off, lasses. See you in the morning,' she said, and retreated, thinking it prudent to avoid any awkward questions she might come out with.

Audrey picked up the empty beakers. 'I'll just give these a rinse, and then I'll be joining you – and I won't need any rocking tonight,' she said.

Tragic Elinor walked on cue, about ten minutes after lights out, just as everyone was falling asleep and before they were dead to the world.

Eileen started up. 'Listen! What's that?'

'What's what?'

'That noise again – footsteps! It's her – she's walking again.'

'Go to sleep,' Audrey groaned. 'You're imagining it.'

Muriel's suppressed laughter came out as a snort. 'You've had one too many, Eileen. Is your bed spinning?'

Eileen's voice sounded taut and shaky. 'I've hardly had anything, man. One gill of cider, and that's all!' she protested. 'I can hear it, I'm telling you!'

Her almost palpable fear had its effect on the others. What a wonderful effect their tales of the blighted bride were having, Muriel thought. A few hints and scraps of information, and the girls' imaginations did the rest – or most of them did.

Laura sat up, to listen more intently. 'I can hear it as well,' she shivered. 'It's true, she is walking.'

'Something is, I'll grant you that,' Joan said, 'but I reckon it's on this side of the grave.'

'Somebody?' Barbara suggested, in a way that sounded warning sirens in Muriel's head.

'Somebody? Who, then? It's nobody from our dorm,' Laura said. 'We're all here.'

'Put the light on, Joan, and make sure,' Muriel commanded.

'Put the light on yourself,' Joan said.

'Listen!' Eileen said. 'It sounds as if she's going downstairs . . .'

'Oh, oh!' Laura whimpered.

The girls were worked up into a satisfactory state of near hysteria – except for sceptical Joan – and the warden's footsteps had receded. The time for the climax of their carefully prepared drama was at hand. Muriel screwed her courage to the sticking place and pushed her doubts about Barbara to the back of her mind.

'I'm willing to go and have a look, if one of you lot will come with me,' she said, fears about the success of her scheme putting a convincing apprehension into her own voice.

'Go on, Joan. Go with her. You're the only one who's not scared of ghosts,' Eileen urged.

'I didn't say I wasn't scared of ghosts!' Joan exploded, springing out of bed. 'I said there were no such things. I said they didn't bloody exist!' She groped for her dressing gown, and struggling into it bounded across the room to snap the lights on and reveal five startled girls blinking in the light, all present and correct, and not an empty bunk.

Joan turned and wrenched the door open. Expecting as much, Muriel had dropped out of her bunk to stand behind her, and Audrey was at the door almost as quickly. There on the landing by the casement window, as if looking out of it, stood the eerie figure of poor, star-crossed Elinor, dressed in her fatal wedding gown and with her face covered by a long bridal veil. She looked so truly spirit-like that Muriel almost believed the sham herself, though she knew it for nothing but a dress form in a long nightgown, topped by a wurzel with a couple of hanks of brown wool for hair and a large net curtain over the whole.

Joan shrank back for a moment, then groped for the landing light-switch. She found it, and flipped it down – with no result. The apparition stood undisturbed in the gloom by the casement window, illuminated only by the light from the dormitory, and looking so real that even at that critical moment Muriel couldn't help feeling a stab of fear, along with enormous pride in their creation. She would have liked Joan to be afraid as well, and to run back into the dormitory and hide under her bedcovers quaking with fear, but Joan was made of sterner stuff. She bounded forward, grabbed the spook by the shoulder, and cried: 'Gotcha!'

The phantom's all too solid head fell off its shoulders and landed with a thump on the floor – and then to Muriel's horror and amazement Joan collapsed beside it.

With commendable presence of mind, Audrey shut the dormitory door, blocking everyone else's view and leaving Muriel and Joan alone on the landing. As quick as lightning, Muriel sent the wurzel and its bridal trappings over the banister rail and down into the darkened hallway below. The dress form followed. Muriel then dropped to her knees beside the prostrate Joan, and gently slapped her cheeks, but Joan was in a dead faint.

'Help! Help!' Muriel shouted, in a panic that she might actually have killed her.

Then Audrey rushed out of the dormitory, closely followed by Barbara and the rest of the girls, and one or two girls came out of dormitories further down the corridor to see what the rumpus was.

Joan slowly opened her eyes and gazed at them all, struggling to speak. 'Her head dropped off,' she said, at last. 'Was she beheaded? Her head dropped off . . .'

But Barbara was not with the rest of them, surrounding Joan. Instead, she had her hand on the banister rail and Muriel's heart sank when she saw her walking slowly and deliberately down the darkened stairway. Two minutes later she returned, bearing the wurzel complete with headdress.

'Her head dropped off, you said, Joan,' she said,

holding the object aloft for everyone to see. 'Well, here's her head, but now she appears to have lost her body. Rather careless of her, isn't it?'

Joan sat up and stared at the thing, completely befuddled.

Muriel looked at the wurzel and then at Barbara, devoutly wishing she could do a ghostly disappearance herself – float through the casement window, or fade through the landing, perhaps. The girls stared for a moment or two in stunned silence, then cries of indignation came thick and fast.

'Shame!'

'What a terrible thing to do!'

'Who? Who did it?'

'I was terrified.'

'I was scared out of my bloody wits, man!'

'What a stinking, rotten trick!'

'It's a wurzel!' Audrey said, in tones of innocent surprise. Muriel's eyes popped, and she gave her friend a disbelieving smile, suspecting her of a treacherous attempt to disassociate herself from the hoax.

'That's right, Audrey, it's a wurzel,' Barbara said, pleasantly. 'You're not going to tell us you've never seen it before, are you?'

Audrey was silent. Joan got to her feet, helped by Muriel. 'I could kill you, Audrey,' she said, her cheeks burning with fury. She shook off Muriel's hand, and rounded on her. 'And you, as well. You're as thick as thieves, you two.'

Muriel said nothing. She and Audrey certainly were as thick as thieves, they'd been caught red-handed, they had no defence, and it was vain to hope for a pardon. The rest of them, especially Joan, had every right to tear a strip off the culprits. She'd been so cocksure that there were no such things as ghosts – until confronted by their 'Elinor'. Then her staunchly held convictions had collapsed like a pricked balloon, and her image of herself as the only rational person in the place was demolished. Now she was sure it was only Joan's pride that had suffered, Muriel's smile became a little conceited. She'd taken her down a peg, and had a highly satisfactory revenge for the pear-cider torture of last Sunday morning. They'd exposed Joan as being no more rational than the rest of them, and as susceptible to fear of 'ghosts' as everyone else. Now the score was even.

The ominous silence was broken by a snort from Eileen, and then a stifled snigger. The snigger swelled to laughter, and then loud and helpless laughter, joined by Laura and then Barbara. Barbara, who hadn't been heard to laugh all the time they'd known her, Muriel thought, her own smile broadening. Tension evaporated as one by one they were all infected. Girls poured out of the other dormitories to see what the joke was, and then stayed to join in the merriment, until resentment and irritation were blown away in gales of laughter. Then Barbara cruelly ordered Muriel downstairs to retrieve the dress form, and made her and Audrey set 'Elinor' up again so that the girls could admire the artistry that had taken Joan in so completely.

'You believed in ghosts as much as me, in the end,' Eileen ragged her. 'At least I never fainted.'

'You didn't see it, did you? If it had been you, you wouldn't just have fainted – you'd have died!' Joan said, and disappeared into the dormitory. She returned to deal Muriel a hefty and unexpected blow on the side of her head with a pillow. 'And I wouldn't have fainted either, if it hadn't been for these two!' she said. 'They deserve a good hiding for that.'

That was the cue for the rest of the girls, who all ran for their pillows amid shrieks of laughter, to give the ghost-raisers the punishment due to them.

Chapter 14

They were up and out early the following morning, to escape the other girls and cycle to the Methodist chapel in Griswold wearing their full Land Army uniforms, so that if Ernst came he would spot them straightaway.

The chapel was a welcoming little place, heated by an iron stove and with oak furniture that looked the colour of honey and smelled of beeswax. The pews at the back had reserved notices on them, Muriel noted. They spotted Cissie and Jack in one of the pews further down and went to join them. Shortly after they were all settled they heard the escort filing the German prisoners into the pews at the back. She turned, and seeing Ernst managed to exchange a smile and a lingering look with him and that was all. Not so much if looks could kill – rather, if looks could make love! That thought and his closeness had her tingling with excitement for the whole of the service. When the war was over she would be Mrs Müller, no matter what the obstacles, and then how they would make love. She was acutely aware of Ernst even with her back turned – knowing that he would still be looking at her even if discretion forbade her to look any longer at him.

At the end of the service the prisoners were marched out by their escorts, leaving the congregation to sing the last hymn without them, cutting off all opportunity for any contact between them. It seemed pointless, considering that so many of these folk had daily contact with the prisoners on their farms. Muriel looked at Cissie and Jack, and felt an immense gratitude to them for their refusal to judge, and their going by the 'Golden Rule'. And what was Christianity supposed to be about anyway, if not loving your enemies?

When the strains of the last hymn died away she filed out with the rest, looking for the most strategic seat for the following week – the one that would give the greatest opportunity for seeing Ernst, and letting him see her. With no opportunity for closeness or conversation, their eyes had to do the talking – and they had shown that they could do it very well, given the chance. Next week she would sit at the end of the pew nearest to the ones the prisoners occupied. If Ernst saw her there every week, he would do his best to be on the one directly behind. Then they might be able to exchange a word, or pass a note.

The Germans were gone when they got outside. Muriel and Audrey stood with Jack and Cissie making trite but friendly conversation about chapel business with other comfortable, pleasant men and women like them. They had an interesting few moments when Cissie introduced them to a woman in her late forties who bore a strong resemblance to Miss Hubbard:

'This is Mrs Beckett; she's your warden's sister. You can probably see a likeness.'

'We can!' Audrey exclaimed, almost triumphantly. 'And are you the sister that operates the telephones, Mrs Beckett?'

'She is!' Cissie beamed. 'You want to talk to anybody, you get Sarah, and she puts you through to 'em straightaway!'

Mrs Beckett nodded and smiled slightly.

'You haven't got your children with you. I suppose they must be too young to sit through the service,' Muriel said, scrutinising Mrs Beckett's iron grey hair, the sagging cheeks and the wrinkles round her mouth and eyes.

'Oh, excuse me; I've just seen someone I've got to talk to . . .' Mrs Beckett said, and chased off towards a woman further along the road.

'Too young to come to service?' Cissie echoed, watching her go. 'Whatever gave you that idea? Her lads aren't too young to be in army, and dowter's married wi' a bairn of her own.'

'Your ears might be good, but you want your eyes testin', lass,' Jack laughed as he and Cissie climbed into the trap.

'I just thought I'd heard someone say her bairns were young. See you tomorrow, then,' Muriel smiled.

'That you won't,' Jack said. 'We're up to scratch, for now. You've worked yourselves out of a job, lasses.'

Muriel's face fell.

'I might have work in a week or two when we start wi' lambing, and drilling sugar beet.'

'You've been good lasses. He'll ask for you by name,' Cissie promised them. 'Won't you, Jack?'

'Aye. All right, then,' he promised.

'Worked ourselves out of a job, if you like! I damned near asked him if he was keeping the prisoners on,' Audrey said, watching them go.

'I bet he is, with a couple of cows ready to drop. I bet he keeps Ernst at least, to help with the calving,' Muriel said, 'in which case I won't be seeing him anywhere else. And what do you make of the "three bairns", then?'

'I never believed it in the first place. "Bairns" twenty years ago, maybe. But she played the sympathy card, and got herself out of trouble.'

'She had me fooled.'

'I know that. Things aren't going too well, lately, are they?' Audrey said, with a wry smile.

Muriel knew she was referring to their antics of the previous night. 'No, they're not. I'll have to find somewhere else to read my dictionary, and we'd better make sure Miss Hubbard's cupboard's never left unlocked. You'd think she'd have had the sense to hide the evidence as soon as she heard it come flying over the banister rail, though, wouldn't you?'

'She's got as many brains as a frog's got feathers,' Audrey fumed.

'She can't have been downstairs more than two minutes before it came crashing over,' Muriel said. 'She can hardly have had time to get back to her office.'

'It makes you wonder how she got away with pinching the rations for so long.'

'You don't need brains for that. Just a safe hiding place and a nasty enough manner that nobody wants to get on the wrong side of you.'

'I thought she'd have come to stop the riot, but she was nowhere to be seen. Funny, that, wasn't it?'

'Maybe she was hoping they'd kill us,' Muriel grinned, with a mischievous twinkle in her dark eyes, and then added, quite seriously: 'but I begin to suspect Miss Hubbard's only stupid when she wants to be.'

'Maybe. There's one thing certain, though,' Audrey said. 'We'll never live that prank down, as long as there's a Women's Land Army.'

Chapter 15

Jack and Cissie were not the only ones who were up to scratch with the work. Few other farmers had any use for the Land Girls during the following week or two, so some of them volunteered to go home for a spot of unpaid leave. With little chance of seeing Ernst that week, Muriel was among those who opted to take unpaid leave and go home for a few days. Even with the full ration and a bit on top, hostel cooking couldn't compete with her mother's. Besides, she wanted to see Doreen and Arni. She was dying to catch up on all their news and to tell them about Ernst, desperate to get her feelings for him out in the open – at home if not in the hostel. All she had to do was think of the right way to go about it. She'd been quite encouraged by the attitude of some of the farmers to the Germans. Cissie and Jack, and Mr and Mrs Winter at the threshing, had all treated the German prisoners well, and seemed to like them. But then, none of them had had their houses bombed, or lost friends or relatives – and they were getting a lot of hard work out of the Germans for very little in return, so they had every reason to like them.

Even so, Muriel had every hope that she could soften up her family. They were pretty fair-minded, and when she explained that the bombing in Germany was as bad if not worse than it was in England, and that the ordinary people in Germany were no more responsible for the war than they were themselves, they would give Ernst a chance. She would just say that they'd been working near some Germans, and they really weren't evil monsters, and lead up to it gradually.

Then she remembered what her own feelings about the Germans had been, and knew that if anyone had tried to tell her while she crouched under various staircases in Morley Villas that she would ever love a German or give a tinker's cuss how many bombs the RAF dropped on Germany, she would have called them a liar – and why would anybody in Hull be any different now?

The train was crowded, mainly with forces people and Land Girls. Audrey had decided to go home as well, and the girls were lucky enough to get seats in one of the compartments. One of the Tommies facing them, probably in his mid-twenties, sat brazenly ogling Muriel. She ignored him, although it did give her a bit of a boost to be the object of such open admiration from a very good-looking man. But the admiration was overdone, and she instinctively knew him for the sort who only wants a woman to enhance his love affair with himself.

He leaned forward, refusing to be ignored. 'All right,

sweetheart?' he said, unctuously. His companions watched him with a lively interest.

'As well as can be expected,' she sighed, with her eyes downcast, fiddling demurely with the buttons on her good coat.

'I've been waiting for a girl like you all my life,' he vowed. 'Got a young man, have you? You're too good for him, if you have.'

Muriel eyed him, and gave a little smile. They could have a bit of fun with this one. 'Oh no, it's not that!' she said, straightening up and leaning eagerly towards him, before sagging again and sighing, 'but I've got three bairns.' She crossed her right hand over the left, as if to conceal the lack of a wedding ring, and added, 'Twins, and then the youngest.'

'Aye, and a right set of little demons they are!' Audrey burst out, quick to see the game. 'I don't know how you keep your hands off 'em! I'd skelp 'em, if they were mine.'

The 'young mother' looked at her with round, reproachful eyes, and defended her brood. 'Oh no, I couldn't do that! They might be a bit high-spirited, but they're not bad lads, really, just a bit too much for me, on my own with 'em.'

'Too right, too much,' Audrey said. 'Too much for anybody. They've wrecked your mam's house, just about. I don't think she's got a stick of furniture they haven't scratched, or broken, or gouged lumps out of. She's hardly got a window pane they haven't cracked. And what about that time she had to get a man to dig the drains up because your youngest kept shoving stuff down the lavvy – just to watch it disappear? You let 'em get away with murder.'

Muriel gave her a half-witted smile and turned a pair of wide and hopeful eyes on her admirer. 'Take no notice, they're good lads, really, only what they need,' she said, lowering her voice, 'is a good man, to play football with 'em, boys' games, and that. And maybe be a bit firm with 'em, now and again. That's all they need really, but I can't do it; I'm too soft. When I get married, though, we'll be able to leave my mam's, and get some-where as a proper family.' She gave her quarry a caress-ing smile, leaned eagerly towards him, and ignoring the stifled laughter of his friends simpered, 'So – you've got no lady-friend, then?'

His eyes widened, and the colour drained from his face. 'I have – I have!' he said, jumping to his feet. 'I'm engaged. We're getting married. Next week.'

Muriel's idiot smile was gone. She frowned and her eyes flashed fire. 'What! You're engaged? Getting married *next week*! When you've just told me you've been waiting for a girl like me all your life?'

He did not think fit to argue, but grabbed his kitbag and stumbled out of the compartment with the look of a hunted animal. She sprang to the door and called after his retreating figure, fast disappearing down the corridor, 'You're just like all the rest of 'em!'

She watched him stumble over someone's luggage and fall headlong into the ticket-collector, then took her seat again and glared at his friends with pursed lips, flushed cheeks and folded hands. Hardly able to contain their mirth they got up, collected their baggage and followed him.

'Cheerio, idiots,' Audrey laughed as the last one escaped, and sinking back in her seat she triumphantly put her feet up on one of the vacant seats opposite.

Not for long, though. Passengers standing in the corridor soon saw their opportunity, and Audrey had to give way.

They parted company in Hull Railway Station, when Audrey boarded the train for Leeds. 'See you Sunday, then,' was the joint farewell.

Muriel took the bus to Holderness Road, viewing the devastated city all the way. She'd barely been away three weeks, and in so short a time had almost forgotten how bad it really was. There was nothing here that would encourage anybody to admit to any sort of sympathy for the Germans.

She cheered a bit when she turned onto Sherburn Street, and then up the footpath dividing tiny Morley Villas, with its six houses mercifully intact. She looked towards Bill's house before going into her own, hoping he'd be on leave to see her clear complexion and her brilliant wasp waist from all that bending and lifting and straightening up she'd been doing for the past month. Let him try calling her 'Podge' now! She'd make him eat 'podge'. He'd be begging to take her out again, and she'd refuse – make him choke on his 'She's Too Fat for Me.' Shame about her hands, though, she thought, looking regretfully at the chapped backs and split finger-ends, calloused palms and dirty-looking, broken nails.

Arni was at home.

'And why aren't you at school, then?' she demanded.

'Why aren't you off digging carrots, or milking cows somewhere?' he countered.

'We've been sent home. Not enough work for all of us. So what mischief are you up to, now?'

'Eggs! Got to know about some condemned ones on the docks, dumped off a Polish ship that caught fire!'

'So he went down to liberate 'em,' their mother said, with a smile and the light of maternal pride in her eyes.

'There's trays and trays – full of 'em.'

'They've probably gone off.'

'They haven't gone off. They smell of smoke a bit, and some of 'em are cracked, but they're all right. We've had some, fried,' their mother said.

'Have a look,' Arni said.

Muriel followed him into the yard, noting the new electric cooker as they passed through the kitchen – and saw Arni's go-cart stacked with them – trays and trays, just as he'd said. She took a couple of cracked ones, and broke them one by one into a cup, sniffing suspiciously.

'Give up!' her mother jeered. 'You know when an egg's off, you don't have to get your nose in it. They stink to high heaven.'

Muriel delved under the sink for a couple of spuds. 'Right. I'll have chips and two eggs, then. Better use 'em as fast as we can, before they do go off.'

Her mother put the chip-pan on the new cooker. 'What do you think to this, then?' she demanded. 'Your dad bought it for us when he came home on leave, just after you hopped it to the Land Army. He was none too pleased about that, either, I can tell you.'

Muriel concentrated on the cooker, choosing to let the comment about her dad's disapproval slide into oblivion. 'He must be doing all right, then,' she said, focusing on the cooker. 'It's a bobby-dazzler.'

'It's bang up to the minute! No soot on the bottom of your pans, like with cooking on the fire. It's smashing,' her mother beamed, and they traded gossip about the new cooker and other tales of Morley Villas for tales of life in the Land Army and embellished versions of hostel pranks while Arni went to dispense a few of his condemned eggs to the neighbours.

'I wish I knew how to make advocaat,' Muriel said. 'That would be a good way of keeping some of them. I could take some back to the hostel if we made enough.'

'Not much chance of that; you need loads of sugar, and brandy. I don't know how we'd get that. I don't think even our Arni could manage to find any brandy. Anyway, you never know. Go down to the library, and see if you can find a book on how to make it.'

She'd said no more about Muriel's defection from the Maypole all the time they'd been talking. That little blow for independence seemed to have been forgiven if not forgotten. Muriel slid the peeled and chipped potatoes into the sizzling fat, and judged it to be just the right moment to open with: 'We've been working near some German prisoners of war . . .'

Almost before the words were out of her mouth Arni came bounding in, and stood in the kitchen doorway, bursting with the news. 'Bill's dead! Bill Peterson's ship got torpedoed – all hands lost. His mother just got the telegram.'

After a moment's stunned silence, Muriel's mother pushed past Arni and ran through the house and out of the front door, still in her apron. Arni followed close on her heels, across the footpath and into the Petersons' house. Muriel followed them as far as the front door then stopped, unsure whether to go or stay, considering she'd given Bill his marching orders barely four weeks previously. She went inside again and stood at the bay window in the living room in an agony of indecision, looking over to Bill's house directly opposite. As she looked, she saw Mrs Peterson draw the curtains, plunging the house into mourning. For Bill! For the lad who'd been her constant companion from the time they could toddle across to each other's houses until he'd joined the Merchant Navy. A lifetime of laughter and joking, and fallings-in and fallings-out gone – wiped away because of a U-boat torpedo. Muriel sank down onto the sofa with her head in her hands – until she smelled burning.

The flames from the chip-pan were roaring half-way to the ceiling and little blobs of grease were blazing merrily all over the beautiful new stove when she reached the kitchen. She stood and watched it for a moment, as one hypnotised. Then the problem of how to put the fires out without burning her hands off or setting the whole kitchen alight brought her back to the present, and even took her mind off Bill for the moment. She grabbed a towel, and stood at the kitchen sink wringing it out in cold water with the flames nearly setting fire to her clothes . . .

'Why didn't you think to put the bloody switch up, before you walked away and left it?' her mother demanded, when she beheld the ruin of her kitchen. Her once-beautiful cooker was a sorry-looking object, its dazzling days well and truly over.

'Same reason you didn't,' she said. 'Bill.'

'I wasn't the last out of the kitchen, you were,' her mother protested, and then her anger evaporated. 'Well, it's nobody's life,' she said. 'At least the house didn't go up in flames, and you're all right. It could have been a lot worse.'

'How's Auntie Ivy?'

'How do you think? How would you be, if you'd just got to know your bairn had drowned? You'd be better answered if you went over there to see for yourself. She wants to see you, anyway,' her mother said.

'I can't go.'

'What do you mean, you can't go? What's stopping you?' She looked again at her cooker, and heaved a sigh. 'Bloody Germans! They're evil. If it hadn't been for them, none of this would have happened. Bill would be alive, and I'd still have my nice shiny cooker. And you haven't had anything to eat yet.'

'I couldn't. I couldn't eat a thing, now. And I'd have come across with you, if I hadn't fallen out with Bill.'

'Go now, then. Go, and tell Ivy you're sorry.'

'I can't face it.'

'What are you going to do, then? You've known him all your life; you can't act as if nothing's happened. You'd better go and give your condolences, and get it over with. Then you can go down and get the rations, before the shop shuts. I've got enough flour and lard to make a bit of pastry for an onion flan, then we'll have run out of nearly everything – except eggs.'

Chapter 16

The bell above the Maypole's door gave its familiar tinkle as she went in. Amid the wreckage in the streets outside, the shop looked like an oasis of cleanliness. Inside it was as cold as ever, but the welcome was warm.

Miss Chapman's eyes lit up at the sight of her and she smiled. 'I'll serve this customer, Ada. You go and wash a few of the jam-jars, will you?'

Ada disappeared into the back of the shop, Muriel gave her order, and Miss Chapman packed her shopping bag, cut the coupons and took the money. Then with Ada out of sight, Muriel discreetly gave Miss Chapman the half a dozen eggs she'd removed from the bag before handing it over.

'Our Arni again,' she said, keeping her voice low. 'He got them from the docks, trays of them. Supposed to have been condemned, but they're all right.'

'Arni again! But fancy you bringing them for me! What a treat; I'll give a couple to Ada and share the rest with my mother. That was kind, especially after I beat you to the parachute silk,' Miss Chapman smiled, and there was a mischievous twinkle in her eye. Then she stopped smiling and gave Muriel a very penetrating look. 'Come up to the staff room; we'll have a cup of tea, and you can tell me all about the Land Army.' She called Ada back: 'You can manage on your own for five minutes, can't you Ada?'

There was nobody in the shop. Ada could certainly manage on her own for five minutes.

Miss Chapman put the kettle on. Muriel had talked for a minute or two about Griswold and life in the Land Army when Miss Chapman interrupted her.

'Muriel, something's wrong.'

Had she not heard the sympathy in Miss Chapman's voice nor seen it flowing from the kindly blue eyes behind those owl spectacles, Muriel would have kept her composure. As it was, she burst into tears. 'Oh, Miss Chapman, we've just had some terrible news!' she choked. 'You remember Bill Peterson that I was going out with a few weeks back? Well, they got a telegram today; his ship was hit by a torpedo, and he's been drowned. He's dead, Miss Chapman! I went to see his mother, and I felt so aw–awful . . .'

Miss Chapman put a protective arm around her. 'My poor girl, my poor girl! Come and sit down.'

'It's ter-terrible. I didn't know what to say . . .'

'There's not much you can say, Muriel,' she said, softly. 'That's War. The men get killed or maimed, and the women weep. They had submarines in the last war. And it's not only the soldiers who get killed now, with these air raids. They're wicked, wicked people, the Germans.'

She pulled Muriel closer, and Muriel wept

uncomforted, nestled against that soft and ample bosom that had never nursed a child, nor ever would. Motherly Miss Chapman would never be a mother, and that reflection only added to Muriel's mountain of grief. She cried it out and Miss Chapman tried to console her until she gave a shuddering final sob, the tears stopped flowing, and Miss Chapman left her for a moment, to make the tea.

As they drank it, Miss Chapman did her best to bolster her up, pouring praise on her bravery for giving her job up so resolutely in the teeth of all opposition, to help her country. Muriel listened and sipped the tea, unable to speak for the lump in her throat and tears threatening to burst forth again.

Miss Chapman saw it. 'Time's a great healer, you know,' she said, softly. 'You're a brave little lass, Muriel, and in time, you might meet someone else you like.'

Muriel gulped the tea and sniffed back the tears. Miss Chapman had no idea. She already had met someone else she liked; she had met someone she loved, and she daren't as much as speak his name. It wasn't losing Bill that she was crying over so much as the sheer impossibility of having Ernst. She'd gone against her mother and father to join the Land Army and make friends while helping her country, but this was something else; she couldn't go against them in this. This was too enormous. She couldn't shame them in front of all the people whose sons had been killed, homes demolished, lives destroyed by tying herself to someone who had lain in wait at the bottom of the ocean to kill those poor lads who were just trying to feed them all. It would single her out as a traitor, and set her apart from everyone else she cared about. If only Miss Chapman knew what was really grieving her! She wouldn't have much sympathy then.

'Really, you will,' Miss Chapman urged.

'You didn't.'

'No, but that's different. My young man was still alive – just – not well, for a long time. Perhaps you'll meet a nice young farmer in a year or two, and marry him. Just make sure he's got a widowed father for me,' Miss Chapman said, attempting a joke. 'I'd leave my job like a shot then, and let him keep me in comfort for the rest of my life. I'm not too old for that.'

Muriel gave her a watery smile. 'From what I've seen of farming, there's more hard work than comfort, but I'll do my best.'

'I wouldn't mind milking a few cows now and then,' Miss Chapman urged, with a resurgence of the twinkle in her eyes.

You just want to show off your parachute silk knickers, Muriel thought, and that sudden and wicked idea brought a genuine smile to her face. 'All right. We'll be mother-in-law and daughter-in-law, then,' she said. 'You'd be a nice mother-in-law, and you'd love the countryside, Miss Chapman. Anybody would.'

'That's what we'll do, then. I'm going to the spiritualist church tomorrow. I'll get the spirits to help us,' Miss Chapman said, and jumped up. 'My goodness! I must have been here half an hour. That poor girl downstairs . . .'

She fled and was already taking a customer's order when Muriel got down the stairs, but looked up to give her a reassuring smile and a nod, and wave a kindly good-bye. Muriel collected her shopping bag and left the shop, envying the new assistant, Ada. If only she could go back to the Maypole, so that she wouldn't have to see Ernst and tell him there could be no 'Ernst und Muriel' – ever.

She cycled back home thinking of Ernst all the way – until she dismounted at the narrow footpath that separated the houses on either side of Morley Villas to walk the few steps home and looked towards Bill's house, its curtains closed, concealing the devastated people within.

'How am I going to tell our Betty?' Bill's mother had asked her an hour or so ago. 'She idolised him.'

Betty would be home by now, knowing the worst. Muriel suddenly had an uncanny feeling that Bill was behind her – such a strong sense that she turned around, but there was nobody there. The times he'd followed her up that footpath, times without number, ever since they'd both been infants in the same class at Buckingham Street Mixed Infants. Now she would never hear his tread again. Never again would he sneak up on her unawares to grab that inch of fat around her waist and bait her with his laughing: 'Hiya, Podge! Give us a squeeze, then!'

She shivered. The fat was gone and so was Bill. Morley Villas was plunged into mourning because of a U-boat in the Atlantic – one of those Wolf packs that were hated and feared by everyone. An image of Bill flashed into her mind, not laughing now but gasping, struggling for dear life as ship and crew sank to the bottom of the sea. It was unbearable, too terrible to think about, and her tears began to gush again as she drowned in sympathy. And what mercy could a captured German submariner expect from anyone in Morley Villas, or anywhere in Hull, or anywhere like Hull, come to that?

Inside, Arni and Doreen were both very quiet. Muriel examined her face in the mirror over the mantelpiece – swollen and blotchy, but not a spot to be seen.

Arni threw his comic aside and looked up at her. 'Bill thought the world of you. I don't know what you chucked him for,' he said.

'We fell out, that's all.'

'People do, you know. And they might have fallen in again, given half a chance,' their mother said. 'Ivy thought so, anyway.'

'She did. She told me we'd have got back together in the end. Poor Auntie Ivy, she was talking about when . . . when we were both little, what good pals we were,' Muriel said. 'We were a pair of imps, nothing to choose between us for mischief, she said.'

Her mother smiled. 'When you first started school the teacher had to sit you at opposite ends of the class, because of the devilment you got up to if she let you sit together. She reckoned you two were more trouble than the rest of the class put together. When you weren't falling out, you were hatching mischief together: a right pair of scamps. We used to take you up to East Park sometimes, hoping to wear you out before bedtime, but it never worked. You wore us out.' She shook her head. 'We had some happy times when you were little, me and Ivy. Well, that's all over, now, thanks to Hitler and his Nazis, set of murdering swine they are. It would be a good job if *they* were all at the bottom of the sea.'

'Aunt Ivy asked if I'd got my Valentine. He sent me a lovely Valentine,' Muriel said, instinctively changing the subject, as if to deflect such ill will from one German, at least.

Tears sprang to Doreen's tender young eyes. 'Poor Bill.'

'No chance of you getting back together now,' Arni said.

'I pity Harry, when he finds out his lad's dead,' their mother said, speaking of Bill's father. 'That'll be a nice letter for Ivy to have to write.' Fuelled with anger she jumped up and went into the kitchen, to snatch the onion and egg flan out of the oven and slam the oven door. They heard her slap it onto the table and crash plates and crockery down after it.

'Come on, then. Your tea's ready,' she called.

They trooped through to the kitchen, to see a mouth-wateringly browned flan set before them. 'You don't see many fresh eggs these days, and there's six in that,' their mother said.

'I wouldn't care if I never saw an egg again, if we could have Bill back,' Doreen said.

'I gave Auntie Ivy a load of 'em for nothing,' Bill said,

as they sat down. 'At least they'll be able to have an egg for their tea.'

'I shouldn't think they'll have any appetite,' Muriel said. 'I know I haven't. I couldn't swallow a thing.'

She excused herself and went upstairs to the bedroom she shared with Doreen and sat looking over to Bill's house. As children they would stand and wave to each other from those bedroom windows when they were supposed to be asleep, she and Bill, but now the curtains were closed and the house looked dead. She stared at it for a while, then found pen and paper to write a note, not to Bill's mother or anyone else, but to herself – a strict instruction:

Forget Ernst Müller, with two dots over the u.

'What was that you were saying about Germans?' her mother asked. 'Just before our Arni came in, you were on about working near some Germans. The news about Bill put it out of my mind, till now.'

'I said we've been working near some of them.'

'There must be more to it than that.'

'Well, there isn't. We've been working near them, and they seemed all right. That's all there is to it.'

'Aye, they'll be all right as long as they can't be anything else,' her mother said, 'but just let them get the whip hand again, and you'll see a different side to 'em, like Ivy's poor lad. You keep well away from 'em.'

Muriel packed her bags and went to catch her train with Arni's magnanimous gift of a bag of eggs, boiled hard to stop them from smashing and making a mess of the rest of her things – as well as to keep them from going off. Arni seemed to be improving a bit, what with his sympathy for Auntie Ivy and his generosity with the eggs, and it had been nice to see Doreen and her mother, but deep down Muriel was glad to be leaving home and all the talk of what might have been. Thoughts of home would be forever tinged with grief in Muriel's mind and she was glad to escape it. She had cried out all her grief for Bill, and for his mother and Betty, and felt lighter for it.

Chapter 17

Audrey was waiting for her on the platform of Hull Railway Station. 'Did you have a nice time with your twins and the baby, then?' she joked.

Muriel shook her head. 'I'm glad to get away.'

They boarded the train with three minutes to spare and took their seats, then Muriel poured out her tale of woe.

'Well, I'm sorry about Bill and I'm sorry for his mother. And it doesn't help you, does it?' Audrey said, after hearing her out. 'You'll get some stick, if it's Ernst you want, and so will he. There'll be plenty of hard feelings, for years and years after the war's over. Not from me, but from the vast majority. I know my grandparents had a rough time of it, long after the Great War ended. Really rough. And this war's raked all that nastiness up again. As they do.'

Muriel eased herself back into her seat, and stared out of the window, glad to be out of the cramped, dirty, blasted city, all grief and tribulation, and speeding back into the countryside with its space and never-ending skyline, its earthy freshness, and its *peace*. She hated unhappiness, and was looking forward to seeing the girls again, to give them their nice surprise of eggs for tea, and above all to catch up on their news and hear conversation that was bright and cheerful, and not full of grief and gloom and hatred of all things German.

The further they got from Hull the more optimistic she began to feel about a future with Ernst Müller. It might be possible, after all. 'It's different in the country, though, isn't it?' she said. 'People like Cissie and Jack never say anything wrong about Germans – just the opposite. There's hardly any bad feeling about them at all among the farmers.'

'The farmers have got no reason for grudges, have they?' Audrey reasoned. 'They don't get their houses bombed night after night. They don't get torpedoed. They get a lot of cheap labour instead of all that. They get all the good, and the folk in places like Hull and Coventry get all the fire and blast. Their grudges will last into the next generation; you can bank on that. My mother and her brother took some stick at school just for being half-German, all sorts of spiteful tricks.'

'Like what?'

'The worst was when a couple of the kids shouted to my brother – "Oh, come and have a look at what we've got, in this tin," and he went, thankful they were being nice to him for a change,' Audrey frowned, 'but what they had in that tin was meths, and when he bent his face over to see, one of them chucked a lighted match in it, and singed his eyebrows and eyelashes off. He's lucky he wasn't blinded.'

'That's terrible,' Muriel said, and she could believe it;

she'd heard enough anti-German talk in Hull. Well then, the only thing to do would be to leave Hull forever and settle in the country, near people like Jack and Cissie, and that would be no hardship. It was what she wanted to do, anyway. Why should she break it off with Ernst? If she could have done anything to bring Bill back she would have done it, but it was beyond her power. She pitied his family from the bottom of her heart, but Bill was lost, and she couldn't mend it, whatever sacrifice she made. And none of it was Ernst's fault, anyway. He hadn't started the war. He didn't give the orders.

She abandoned her resolution to abandon Ernst. She could hardly wait to see him again.

The hostel was unnaturally quiet when they got back, no gramophone playing, no dancing, no girls tearing around the place, no groups of chattering, laughing girls to be seen anywhere, just a few subdued readers and letter-writers sitting round the fire in the common room with the radio playing softly in the background.

'What's up?' Audrey demanded. 'What's wrong with the jitterbugging? It's like a bloody morgue in here.'

There was a deathly silence. Barbara looked up from her chair next to Laura's, her face pale, and Muriel's heart contracted. Her missing husband must have been reported dead.

Laura got up and left the room.

'Oh-oh!' Audrey said, sinking onto a chair, 'I seem to have put my foot in it.'

Muriel took the seat next to Barbara. 'What's happened?'

'Well, we set out to the Half Moon last night, all in good spirits, and intending to enjoy ourselves, until we found out that the chap Laura was hoping to meet had been shot down over Germany with a couple of others a couple of nights ago. The rest of the men didn't give much for their chances. It put rather a damper on our evening.' She got to her feet. 'She probably won't want company, but I'll just go and see how she is.'

'It's bloody awful, man,' Eileen said, when Barbara had gone. 'She'd hardly known him two minutes, but she'd marked him out for her husband, and he was dead keen on her, an' all.'

'You don't have to know a man long to know he's the one you want,' Muriel said. 'It can happen the first time you look into their eyes.'

'Aye, and that's the way it happened with Laura, and now . . . It's knocked her sideways.'

'Yep. And it's opened Barbara's wounds up again,' Joan said, in her broad Norfolk accent. 'She's had no news about her husband, and it's been months since he went missing. They've got a lot in common now, her and Laura.'

'They're the only two in the hostel who know what it feels like to have someone missing, and not know whether they're dead or alive. The rest of us can only guess,' Eileen said. 'It's no wonder they've got a bond.'

The warden had gone to see her sister, leaving the girls to make their own tea. Muriel put the boiled eggs out with a heavy heart, with only the briefest mention of Arni's resourcefulness instead of the entertaining anecdotes she might have told under more cheerful circumstances.

'Well, thank you, Arni,' a girl called Vera from one of the other dorms remarked. 'At least we'll have an egg. The food's gone off again, since you went on your holidays.'

'Did you have a nice time at home?' Eileen asked. 'We never thought to ask you.'

Audrey said yes, and Muriel told the girls all about Bill Peterson. 'We went out together for a while, but we'd had a falling-out. It was Bill that sent me the Valentine.'

Laura came up to her and put her arms around her, her eyes full of tears. 'Oh, Muriel! Oh, Muriel, that makes it so much worse,' she choked, and drew Muriel's head tenderly onto her shoulder.

There was silence for a moment and then, 'You'd probably have got back together if it hadn't been for them, and been happy for the rest of your lives,' Joan said, her cheeks flushed with anger.

Barbara exploded. 'Bloody Germans! I hate them all! I detest them! I wish them all in hell.'

That chorus was immediately taken up by the other girls, with the sole exception of Audrey. Muriel listened to the stream of vitriol poured out on Germany and all things German and wondered how she could face admitting her love for the man she'd marked out as *her* husband, in the teeth of all this hatred?

★ ★ ★

'Opening a potato clamp and riddling spuds today, lasses,' the farmer told the four of them when they arrived. 'Have you done it afore?'

They assured him they had done it before and needed no further instruction, so he gave them spades and directions. They were making their way to the field when along came a party of German prisoners and a lone little Tommy with a gun walking behind them. Muriel smiled at them as they passed, whereupon the biggest man among them started towards her with a mouthful of German swear words, and then spat at her.

Muriel jumped back, and before she knew what was happening Barbara flew at the man with her spade, beside herself with rage. He jumped out of the way just in time to avoid it crashing down on his neck.

The little Tommy instantly raised his rifle and pointed it at Barbara. 'Stop! Or I'll shoot!'

Eileen screamed. Audrey leaped forward and threw her arms round Barbara's waist, to drag her away.

'Go on! Get on! Get a move on! *Schnell! Schnell!*' the Tommy ordered, herding them on at the point of the rifle.

'God, man, Barbara, you nearly got shot!' Eileen exclaimed, watching them go.

'It would have been worth it, if I could have broken his neck,' Barbara said, and unleashed a tirade of the foulest abuse at the prisoners' backs – abuse that they could still well hear.

The reaction of that prisoner to an innocent smile had been shocking enough, but to Muriel, Barbara's raw and unrestrained hatred was the most shattering thing. Barbara, who she'd imagined the most self-controlled of them all. She turned distractedly to Audrey. 'What did he say?' she demanded. 'What did he say to me?'

Audrey's face closed like a clam. 'How do I know?' she shrugged. 'Don't ask me.'

Muriel looked at her open-mouthed for a moment and then realised her mistake. She'd made it obvious to anybody who cared to look that Audrey could speak some German, at least. Luckily her gaffe seemed to pass unnoticed.

'I'll bet that bugger never spits at another Land Girl as long as he lives,' Eileen said.

'I don't know why they let him out of the camp. I can't see him volunteering to help feed the English,' Audrey said.

'They ought to lock him in the bloody prison camp and throw the key away for what he just did. Leave him to starve,' Barbara said, 'instead of keeping him in comfort and feeding him on stuff we've worked to produce. It makes me sick!'

After a long, hard day, the four of them were back at the hostel, exchanging gossip with the other girls while waiting to get washed, but none of them had a story to match Eileen's tale of Barbara, the Nazi, and the pint-sized Tommy with his gun. As other girls arrived, she told the story again, with embellishments, until almost every girl in the hostel knew about the German who'd spat at Muriel, and nearly had his head taken off by Barbara for his trouble. And who would have thought that quiet, dignified Barbara even knew the meaning of some of the swear words she shouted after that German? She might have got shot, if it hadn't been for Audrey. With her eyes flashing again with indignation, Barbara added a detail here and there, to round-eyed stares and approving nods from the girls. Audrey and Muriel kept fairly quiet.

The food dished up that evening was awful – a return to the dreaded, soggy Woolton Pie, as bad as it had ever been, if not worse. There were exclamations of disgust and disappointment from the girls, which all ran off the warden like water off a duck's back. It was wartime. She did the best she could with what she had. Muriel and Audrey both looked silently towards her, their faces impassive but conveying the message: we'll have words about this later. It did not have the desired effect. The warden seemed unperturbed.

They ate without relish while, by popular demand, Eileen repeated the story of the spitting German and the spade-wielding Land Girl, for the benefit of the few who hadn't yet heard it and the many who wanted to hear it again. She had rehearsed it so often and was so much in the acting role by this telling that she added more detail, including: '. . . and Muriel was standing there like a head-less chicken, squawking: "What did he say to me? What did he *say*?"'

There was a burst of laughter at that piece of mimicry.

'– to Audrey,' Eileen continued, as soon as the laugh had died down, 'as if Audrey was supposed to know!'

Audrey smiled, and said nothing. The brick Muriel dropped had been picked up, and put on display for all to see and wonder at. Muriel held her breath, expecting the worst, until she realised that they weren't wondering. Not one of the girls seemed to have twigged to it.

She blushed, and gave a nervous laugh. 'I don't know how I expected anybody to know,' she said, 'but it gave me such a shock, to be spat on and sworn at, I hardly knew what I was saying.'

The girls regarded her with the utmost sympathy. Amid their chorus of comforting words and soothing noises Muriel was neither comforted nor soothed. She was too aware of the warden, who was looking at her with eyes like a rattlesnake. If the significance of that unguarded question was lost on her, it would be a minor miracle.

'She's under a lot of strain,' Laura said, dolefully. 'It's hard to keep your mind on things, when you're like that.'

Strain or not, there was business in hand, and when the meal was over and the clearing up done, Muriel and Audrey went to knock on the warden's door.

'You're at it again, then,' Audrey accused her, grim-faced.

'At what?' Miss Hubbard scowled.

'Stealing our rations.'

'What rations?'

'The rations in the cupboard in the attic, as well as the rest of it.'

'What cupboard in the attic?'

'Old Mother Hubbard's cupboard full of other people's rations, in the attic!' Audrey exclaimed, producing the key.

'I don't know as there's ever been a cupboard in the attic. If there is, I never noticed.'

'We'll go up there, then, and see.'

The warden's frown was ominous. 'Don't you dare to dish your orders out to me. I'm not going anywhere.'

So the girls took the key and a couple of bicycle lamps upstairs to the attic. Mother Hubbard's cupboard was bare. There was nothing inside it now but empty roof-space.

Audrey held up the key, which they'd taken on holiday with them. 'Some bloody use that is, now. We thought ourselves as cunning as a pair of vixens, but we've been out-foxed.'

'What idiots we are!' Muriel exclaimed. 'It can't have been hard to get the door off, when you come to think about it; she only had to unscrew the hinges to lever it off. Look, you can see where the paint's broken over the hinges and the screws.'

'I wonder how long it took her to think of doing that?'

'Not as long as it took us, evidently.'

'What are we going to do, then? Go to the War Ag again?'

Muriel grimaced. 'Well, we could, but they might start asking awkward questions, like why didn't we go to them in the first place,' she said. 'We should have split on her straightaway. I wish we had, now. I wish we'd split on her as soon as we found the stuff, and let them deal with her. We were too soft for our own good, there.'

'We? You were, you mean. I'd have happily thrown her to the wolves.'

'You would,' Muriel conceded, 'and now it's our word against hers, and it's obvious she'll lie her head off. I'm just glad I put that dictionary back on the library shelf. It would have been bad if she'd found that, because I think she latched on when Eileen was telling everyone I asked you what that German had said. Oh, I could kick myself! Sorry, Audrey.'

'Well, it's done now. No good crying over spilt milk.'

'I'm not crying over spilt milk. I'm crying over all that Spam. And all that corned beef and powdered egg, and sugar! I wonder where she's stashed it?'

'At her sister's, probably. Flaming hell! We can't let her get away with it. Can we?'

'We'll tackle her again. See if we can put the wind up her.'

They went to the office again and made a brave attempt.

'Where's all that corned beef and Spam? And what about the dried eggs, and sugar?' they demanded.

But the warden stuck to her denials. She fixed her serpent's eyes on them and with nostrils dilated and mouth tight and hard she demanded to know what Spam? What corned beef and sugar? There had never been any. She'd never seen any cupboard in the attic, but then she didn't go poking about in places that didn't concern her. They were a pair of liars, nothing but mischief-makers, the dregs of the cities trying to get more than their fair share by trying to intimidate an honest woman who was doing her best. They'd lied to the other girls about ghosts, and they'd gone into her private quarters without invitation and stolen her dress form and her net curtain just for the pleasure of terrifying them – and then they'd damaged her property by throwing it down the stairs. She'd heard the other girls accuse them of being as thick as thieves with her own ears. They were a pair of thieves and hooligans. They ought to be locked up. It was only out of the kindness of her heart that she hadn't reported them to the police.

At the end of the interview the girls' fury was tempered by their absolute conviction that, if put to the test, there was no false accusation that Miss Hubbard would not make, nor any lie that she would shrink from telling, and telling so well that she would be believed, since her lies would be mixed with half-truths. She was certifiably dangerous.

'Well,' Muriel said, when they were alone, 'last time we crossed her, she fed us on prunes. This time, it might be strychnine. Maybe we ought to warn the rat-catchers among us to be careful to keep their stuff under lock and key – and find out what the antidote is.'

Audrey's face was white. 'Remember what Laura said? "I'm not reporting her, she'll bear a grudge forever and she'll make sure she gets her own back."'

'"And you won't get anywhere when you've done!" Hmm! She knew what she was talking about, didn't she?' Muriel said.

'No ill-feeling,' Audrey said, 'but I wish to God we'd gone to the War Ag as soon as we found the stuff. We would have got somewhere, if we'd done that.'

'I know,' Muriel said. 'It serves me right, for trying to be clever. I could be sick. On top of everything else, to be beaten down by someone like her – it's more than flesh and blood can stand. It just puts the tin lid on every rotten thing that's happened since we went home.'

'Never say die, though, eh?' Audrey encouraged.

'No! Never say die!' Muriel declared. 'Round two to the Prune, that's all.'

Chapter 18

As Laura had said, Muriel was under a lot of strain, enough strain to keep her awake for hours that night. She'd gone to the hostel because she wanted friends, and now she was one of the most popular girls in the place, with lots of friends – wonderful friends. Her company was sought out by everyone, but if they found out about Ernst, she would be shunned. And at some point they would find out, because although she was certainly capable of a little fib here and there, Muriel was quickly discovering that her talents for serious, sustained concealment and deception were far from exceptional. She was too impulsive to carry it off. At some point she would open her mouth and put both feet in it, and then except for Audrey every girl in the hostel would turn against her.

The incident with that horrible man who spat at her had shown her all too clearly how quick they had been to forget the help and kindness they'd had from many of the other German prisoners. Scratch the surface, and how deep the feeling ran against the Germans! And they'd never accept Ernst at home – her own family, Bill's family, even Miss Chapman, they'd all cast her out, and now it was just the same here in the hostel. If she were set on having Ernst, she wouldn't have one friend in the whole world – apart from Audrey. It would be just the same for him, among his own people . . .

And what was it, Muriel wondered, that had prompted that prisoner to spit and snarl at her in return for a smile? Was it pure Nazi evil – or something more personal? Perhaps someone he loved had been killed, maybe in one of the RAF raids over Germany – because those heavy, four-engined Lancaster bombers were certainly not flying over there to drop messages of love.

It made no odds. He was German and therefore he hated the English, and most of the English that Muriel knew hated the Germans just as passionately. There was too much sheer, virulent hatred on both sides for any marriage between them to stand a cat in hell's chance. It took more courage to love one German than to fight the whole German nation these days, and Muriel did not delude herself – it was the sort of courage she lacked. She couldn't face everything it would mean. She liked having friends, lots of them, and she could not stand alone.

She remembered that look she'd had from the warden, and shivers ran down her spine. Miss Hubbard missed nothing; she might well have pounced on the real significance of that question which seemed to have passed the others by, and she was the sort who would enjoy wielding power over anybody, and over Muriel Dearlove above all. If she got wind of anything, Muriel knew she could expect no mercy. She'd be had up for fraternising, if not for being a fifth columnist. It was all right for Audrey to talk about telling people it was the government's fault for putting prisoners and Land Girls together, but that would never wash with the authorities. She couldn't risk courts, fines, or maybe even prison. The very thought of it almost made her heart stop.

It was impossible to carry on with Ernst. Some people might be able to carry it off, but she was not cut out for a life in the shadows, of not daring to open her mouth for fear of giving herself away. Words sometimes had a habit of jumping out of her mouth before she realised it was happening. And even if she had been capable of guarding her tongue, everything was against them. There was no future for Ernst and Muriel, and she had to face it.

She had to face it, and she deeply did not want to face it. Ending it with Ernst was the last thing on earth that she would have done, had it been possible to avoid it. She saw no sign of him all week, and every night she returned to the hostel in turmoil, disappointed at not having seen him, and yet relieved at the reprieve for 'Ernst und Muriel'.

The girls evidently thought jolly dance music an affront to their bereaved friends, so the hostel was shrouded in a pall of gloomy silence. The food was filthy, and that was borne, if not without complaint, at least without urging responsibility for reporting it onto either Muriel or Laura. Muriel and Audrey occupied themselves for an hour or so each evening in playing whist with any of the other girls who would give them a game. The standard of play was not high, and the practice they got gave them no great hopes of beating Sammy Mawson that Friday night.

Jack and Cissie were already in their places, sitting North–South when Muriel and Audrey arrived at the Methodist Hall with Barbara and Vera.

'We called for you last Friday, but Miss Hubbard said you'd gone home,' Cissie told them.

Muriel rolled her eyes. 'We went home for a few days, seeing as nobody had any work for us, and we didn't want to starve,' she said, in such a way that Jack laughed. After a bit of banter with him, and a promise of work as soon as they had any from Cissie, the girls took their places at a table further down the room, Muriel and Audrey sitting East–West, to ensure an opportunity of more conversation with them. John Goodyear and his party arrived last again, to jibes from Sammy Mawson, which they ignored. John Goodyear gave Muriel a smile and a wink as he passed, and sat North. Play started as soon as his party was seated.

Muriel was determined to be cheerful and keep her mind on the cards. There would be no mistakes about following suit this time. In spite of her resolution, she and Audrey lost as many games as they won, which did not make Audrey happy. *It's not whether you win or lose, but how you play the game* was not a philosophy that she subscribed to. They arrived at John Goodyear's table just before the break for supper.

'All right, Big Name?' Muriel greeted him.

He looked up and laughed. His partner, an older man

of remarkably similar features, smiled, but looked puzzled.

'Ha ha, a bit of a joke between us,' John informed him. 'This lass says she's got the biggest name in Morley Villas, whereas we've only got *one* of the biggest names round here.'

'Hello, Mr Goodyear,' Muriel smiled, correctly assuming the older man to be John's father.

'Where's Morley Villas?' he asked.

'Best part of Kingston upon Hull,' she answered, certain that they would never go and look. 'Not been bombed, yet.'

Though not usually desperately competitive, Muriel sat up and took even more notice than she had when playing against the other pairs. Against this table, she was whole-heartedly with Audrey; winning mattered. She gave the game her whole attention and made little conversation.

'You're not on form tonight, Muriel,' John Goodyear said, after the first couple of games. 'I put it down to a deficiency of pear cider.'

Muriel glanced furtively round the Methodist Hall, her eyes wide in mock alarm. 'Shush,' she said. 'Remember where we are!'

'Come to the Half Moon tomorrow, and I'll buy you a decent drink,' John offered, not to be put off.

'What do you think, Audrey? Shall we go?'

Audrey's mouth turned down at the corners, and she gave a non-committal shrug. 'Maybe. See how we feel tomorrow.'

John raised his offer. 'Come, and I'll buy you both a drink.'

'We might,' Audrey promised. 'Did you go last Saturday?'

'Yes, you weren't there.'

'Did you hear anything about the raid?'

'Not a lot. They don't talk shop much, in the pub. A rear gunner and a couple of other lads killed, as far as I can make out.'

'Aye. Engaged to one of our Land Girls, that rear gunner,' Audrey said.

'We never asked you whether you got any milkmaids,' Muriel said.

'We did – if you want to call Itie prisoners milkmaids. They come up from their camp every morning, in time for mucking out. Not quite the same as a pair of lovely Land Girls in the cottage, though, is it?'

'Aren't they a bit rough on the cows' teats, the Ities?'

'They're not rough on 'em at all. We've got the latest machines!' John boasted. 'We don't milk by hand!'

'Until it breaks down,' his father said, dryly. 'Then we milk by hand. We're back to old ways, then.'

'The old ways are the best, you know,' John said, with a wink at Muriel. 'Just like the old jokes.'

The older man said nothing but Muriel could see he felt the jibe. She liked John less for humiliating his father, and less still for involving her. The girls won three games to two, and although they would have preferred to annihilate John, they had to be content.

At break-time Muriel sat with Audrey, Barbara and Vera. One of the farmers had killed a pig, and baked sausages were on offer with the bread cakes and dripping.

'It would have been worth coming, just for the supper,' Vera said, 'after the swill we've had to eat at the hostel.'

'Well, we did our best,' Audrey said. 'It's a shame more of you didn't back us up.'

'Funny thing is, it picked up for a bit, and now it's worse than ever,' Barbara said. 'Odd, that, isn't it?'

'It seems to be the pattern, according to some of the other girls,' Vera said. 'It improves for a bit, and after a week or two it's just as bad again.'

'Far be it from me to accuse her, but it's not unknown for people to hoard stuff,' Muriel said. 'But it's no good going to the War Ag again until we can prove everything we say. All we can do is bide our time, and keep a lookout.'

Chapter 19

Muriel sat opposite Audrey at Cissie and Jack's table and managed to restrain herself from asking about the prisoners, although she would have dearly loved to know whether Ernst was still working for them.

Before they'd finished the first hand, Audrey casually asked, 'Have you still got the prisoners – Ernst and Wilhelm? Or have they worked themselves out of a job as well?' and Muriel's heart leaped at the mere mention of Ernst's name.

'Aye, we've still got 'em, and they can still get through twice as much work as any lass, Land Girl or no,' Jack teased.

'Go on, then, prove it. Tell us what they've done that we couldn't,' Muriel scoffed, and then listened closely to every detail of the week's doings on the farm with a secret glow of pure pleasure to hear Ernst so well spoken of. It almost renewed her hopes.

Her head was still in the clouds when they sat with their next opponents, a married couple in their thirties. She came back down to earth when the conversation turned to the bombing in Hull, and they told her they'd recently had to tell their evacuees – from Hull – that their parents had been killed and their home destroyed by a German bomb.

The last hand they played was against Sammy Mawson and partner. Muriel managed to avoid revoking, but they lost four hands out of five, to Sammy's unseemly delight and open contempt for his opponents. They watched him step up to the MC to be awarded first prize when the winners were announced.

'"Cock of the midden, crowing on a dung heap," that's what my mother would say about him,' Muriel breathed in Audrey's ear.

The applause was polite, but unenthusiastic. None of the Land Girls got a mention – even the booby prize was awarded elsewhere. They cycled back to the hostel soundly defeated.

'That Sammy Mawson! He's unbearable,' Muriel said.

'Ooh, we've got to bring him down a peg,' Audrey exclaimed, 'absolutely got to. We've got to get some practice in, lasses, or stop going altogether. I can't stand that old so and so rubbing my nose in it every week.'

'Is that the bloke who won first prize? I thought he looked dead arrogant. We never played against him,' said Vera.

'You wouldn't, sitting North–South. Lucky you, is all I can say.'

'Well, at least our fighting men will have a few extra ciggies. That's one consolation,' Barbara said.

'Not the only one, either. It was worth coming just for the supper,' said Audrey.

'I enjoyed myself, getting to know a few of the Griswold people,' Vera said. 'They're not a bad lot, are they? Apart from Sammy Mawson.'

'Plenty worse,' said Audrey.

'Don't sit here on your own. Come to the Half Moon, Laura,' Muriel pleaded. 'I'm going. It'll do you good to get out.'

Laura shook her head. 'No. I don't want to. It's not the same for you, Muriel, your Bill was never in the Half Moon, but it's where I met Guy, and it's the last place on earth I'd want to be now he's not there. It would break my heart.'

Audrey sat down beside her. 'We'll stay here with you, then.'

'No,' said Laura. 'It wouldn't help me. Nothing helps, because nothing can bring him back. You go. I don't want to be rude, but I'd rather be left alone.'

They had to leave it at that. So, apart from Barbara and one or two more who decided to stay behind as well, the girls got on their bikes and cycled to the Half Moon, leaving Laura sitting in the common room, staring into the fire.

Sammy Mawson was just going into the Dog and Duck as they passed, with a carrier-bag. 'Going to visit your lady friend, Sammy?' Muriel laughed. 'Give her a kiss from us!'

Sammy scowled like a gargoyle, but wasn't quick enough to reply. The girls rode off, their bikes wobbling as they shook with laughter.

'Just the sort of pub for him, miserable old bugger,' Audrey said.

They were greeted with glad smiles and words of welcome when they walked into the Half Moon Inn, with airmen and ground-crew offering to buy drinks for their favourite girls. There was no mention of the men who'd been lost – within Muriel's hearing, at least. A brown-haired chap with a flying brevet on his uniform smiled at Muriel and offered her a cigarette. She took two.

'I'll just take one for my friend, as well, shall I?'

'Be my guest. You're the girl who sat down in the road,' he said.

'Will I ever live it down?'

'Probably not. Where's Laura?'

'Didn't want to come,' Muriel shrugged.

'I've got something for her.'

'From Guy?'

He nodded.

'What happened?' Muriel asked, looking into his brown eyes. 'Is there any chance at all he might have survived?'

He shook his head. 'No. He got the chop,' he said, and abruptly turned his face away. A moment later and without a word to them he walked to the piano and began to rattle out a tune.

The next minute John Goodyear was beside them, with one arm round her waist and the other round Audrey's, hugging them both into him. 'What'll you have, girls?'

'What's on offer?' Audrey asked.

'Cider. There's never much else.'

So cider it was. The girls stood with him at the bar, sipping it and quizzing the landlord about the raid.

'You don't get to know a lot from the RAF,' he said, without his usual smile. 'All I know is Laura's bloke was a rear gunner; and they haven't a great survival rate. Three other lads bought it as well, but they don't talk shop to outsiders; they tend to keep it in the family.'

'Careless talk costs lives . . .' Muriel said, and put her cigarette to her mouth.

'Keep mum,' John added, placing a finger on his lips.

'You can see it takes its toll on 'em, though, without asking.' The landlord paused and with a glance towards the piano player shook his head, looking deadly serious. 'I've seen 'em before, jollying themselves along, trying to shrug it all off. They look as if they're hardly out nappies, some of 'em. Queer thing is they're all volunteers, on these night raids, or so I'm told, although you'd wonder how they managed to get anybody to volunteer for it.'

'Defending their country and the people they love, I imagine,' Muriel said. 'Give us a light. He gave me a fag, and forgot to light it.'

John produced a handsome cigarette lighter and lit her cigarette and Audrey's.

'They've got more guts than me,' the landlord said. 'I admit it.'

'So do I,' John Goodyear said, and raised his glass. 'Here's to the boys in blue!'

'Well, they come out to get away from it all. They don't like misery, so slap your happy faces on,' the land-lord said, raising his glass. 'The boys in blue!'

Others were coming to be served, so they drank the toast, and moved away from the bar.

They smoked and drank, sitting with John most of the time. The missing men weren't spoken of, and it seemed tasteless to ask any of the RAF men about them. To Muriel it seemed even more depressing than Bill's death. At least they'd talked about him, cried over him, and railed at the people responsible, rather than behave as if nothing had happened.

A few men and girls gathered round the piano for a sing-song – less boisterous than the first time they'd been at the inn. Muriel left Audrey with John and stood with them, but refrained from singing.

'You said you had something for Laura,' she said, to the pianist, at the first pause in the flow of playing, while others were going to the bar.

'Yes.' He put his hand inside his jacket and pulled out an envelope. 'Give her this, will you? And tell her Howard said it was quick; he didn't suffer.'

'I will, but I don't know whether it'll be a comfort, or break her heart. She's really upset.'

He shrugged. 'I dare say she will be, for a little while.'

'A very long while, I think.'

His bright brown eyes gave her a searching look. 'You want to know how much any of us are missed?' he asked, now quite composed. 'Stick your finger in that glass of cider, and when you take it out again, try to find the hole you made. It's like that with us. When we're gone, someone else fills the space, and the show goes on as if we'd never existed.'

'Not with everyone, it doesn't.'

'With most people, I'm afraid it does,' he said, and turning back to the piano he struck up with a lively rendition of 'Roll out the Barrel'.

Muriel tucked the letter safely into her handbag, and went back to sit with Audrey and John Goodyear.

She took a gulp of cider. 'I need a ciggie. There's too much misery in the world. Give us a ciggie, John.'

'I don't approve of women smoking. It's not good for their delicate constitutions.'

'You didn't mind before, when you gave me a light.'

'Only because the landlord would have given you one if I hadn't.'

One of the paras tossed a full packet of Woodbines in her direction. She caught them, and gave one to Audrey before putting another to her own lips.

'Thanks,' she said, throwing him back his packet. He was beside them in an instant, with a light.

'Keep it. I've got enough,' he said, thrusting the packet on her.

'What about me?' John demanded, watching them inhale.

'What about you, what?' Muriel asked, with feigned surprise.

'What about offering me one?'

'I don't approve of men smoking,' she said. 'Not the ones who won't give me a cig, anyway.'

'He'd flown,' Laura said, 'as rear gunner on twelve bombing runs, and it had taken its toll. His last was the thirteenth, and he had a really bad feeling about it. He seemed to sense his luck wouldn't hold out. And he was right, wasn't he? So that was the end of another tail-end Charlie. My poor Guy.'

'He must have been very brave, to feel like that, and still go,' Audrey said.

Laura made a cynical little 'Hmm-hmm', and shook her head. 'He might have been brave to start with, but bombing run after bombing run – it can wear the strongest nerves to shreds, and they're supposed to do *thirty*. "When you get on that bus to ride to the plane, you can actually smell the fear on people," he told me. He had the most awful jitters. He said he was physically sick before getting in the plane the last couple of times – just vomited – on the tarmac.'

'Couldn't he have got out of it? Asked for another job for a while, or something?' Muriel asked.

That drew a short, sardonic laugh from Laura. 'Not a chance! If he'd done that, it would have got him tarred with the LMF brush. For airmen that's a fate worse than death. That's what forces most of them into going on to breaking point – and beyond.'

'What's LMF?'

'Lack of moral fibre. That's the label the top brass stick on them, and it's a total and deliberate degradation. They don't go on the bombing runs they're scheduled for, or they turn back to base for some reason, and they're disgraced for life. They're stripped of everything – rank, buttons, flying brevet, and shunted off to be treated as a lower form of life in some menial job somewhere. They'd rather die than suffer the shame of it. And Guy did.'

Muriel took hold of her hand, and gave it a squeeze of sympathy. 'Howard said to tell you it was quick. He didn't suffer.'

'He'd tell me that no matter what; even if he'd seen him shot down in flames, so it's not much comfort. They should never have put him "on" that night; he was a bag of nerves. I wish he'd never gone, but they dread refusing even more than going. Oh, yes, the whole show's set up to make sure none of them try to get out of it. They know what's in store for them if they do.'

'I am sorry, Laura,' Muriel said.

Laura stared at the envelope Howard had sent. 'I hardly dare open it.'

'Shall we leave you alone?' Audrey asked.

Laura shook her head. 'I'll read it later. I can't even cry about it. I feel frozen inside – such an awful emptiness.' Looking directly at Muriel, she said: 'Well, you've got your own troubles. They killed your young man at sea, and they killed mine in the air – he took his flight from the world on that run. Jerries! We should never have had an Armistice. We should have done for them all the first time round. We should never have given them the chance to start another bloody war.'

Muriel looked into Laura's bleak eyes, and saw the terrible frozen void that came with the death of all hope. And Laura's 'we should have done for them all' chilled her even further.

'What terrible times we live in,' she said.

Chapter 20

At chapel the following morning Muriel was keyed up with nerves, waiting for the German prisoners to be filed into their pews, forbidding herself to turn or look at Ernst. But at the sound of their boots in the hall quite a few people turned to look, including Audrey, Eileen and Laura, and Muriel couldn't help herself. Ernst beamed a bright and rapturous smile at her. She gave him a sad and surreptitious one in return. The service passed her by, her head was too full of what lay in front of her to heed it – but the hymns were uplifting, and sung in German as well as English. The concluding hymn was 'Glorious Things of Thee are Spoken' and the power and resonance of the prisoners' voices made her tingle. She knew that Ernst would be looking towards her, and she dare not as much as steal a glance at him, for fear of giving herself away by bursting into tears.

The last strains of the hymn died away. The congregation stayed in their places until the prisoners were safely in their transport and on their way back to the prison camp, and then they shuffled out. He was gone, and Muriel felt as if her heart would break. Outside the chapel people lingered, standing in little groups, gossiping with their friends. Cissie and Jack came over to speak to them but the warden's sister kept well clear.

'We forgot to mention on Friday – we've got some work, if you want it,' Cissie announced. 'Sowing Brussels for the main crop, and keeping an eye on the ones we sowed last month.'

'Will you still have the prisoners?' Muriel asked.

'No. We got them to do all hard work, tilling soil and preparing seed bed,' Jack grinned. 'Then we sacked 'em so we could let you put a few plants in.'

'Like the few broad beans we planted?' Audrey said.

'Aye,' he laughed. 'But this time bed's so soft plants'll jump in on their own.'

'Is that all right, Laura?' Muriel asked. 'Are they allowed to bespeak their own workers?'

'Just this once, then. Although we try to keep to a rota – give everyone a fair turn at the good farms so nobody's lumbered with the bad ones all the time.'

'Which sort is ours, then?' Jack laughed. 'Good, or bad?'

'They volunteered for it, whichever it is,' Laura shrugged.

'That system works as well for the farmers, I reckon,' Jack teased, 'nobody's lumbered with worst Land Girls all the time.'

'The Land Girls are all good,' Muriel declared.

'We'll be there on Monday,' said Audrey.

So, the prisoners were at Jack and Cissie's no longer, Muriel thought. Her ordeal had been postponed.

Sunday dinner consisted of a couple of ounces of fatty shoulder of something that had been advertised as lamb but would have been more accurately described as the lamb's great grandmother, dished up with lumpy gravy. The vegetables, as usual, had been boiled to extinction, but there were more of them than the girls could stomach. Dinner was followed by sour apple pie and watery custard. Miss Hubbard did not dine with them.

'I notice she didn't let herself in for any of that!' Vera observed, as they cleared the tables.

'Can you blame her? She cooked it herself.'

'Why should she eat the muck she dishes up to us, when she can go round to her sister's and get a decent Sunday dinner?' Audrey demanded. 'Would you? I suspect the meat's a bit more plentiful there, and the apple pies are sweet, with sugared tops.'

'Yes, made with our sugar ration,' Vera said.

Some of the girls laughed.

'I hope her sister's as good at cooking as she is, and she's crippled with indigestion,' Joan said, 'not that I'd ever wish her any harm.'

There was more grumbling over the washing up.

'A thousand and one pots, pans, dishes and cooking utensils, used to produce a meal like the one we've just been forced to eat! It seems a bit excessive, wouldn't you say?' Barbara commented.

'And every single one of them left for us to wash up. No clearing up as you go for her. I've had enough of it. I'm going to make a formal complaint to the War Ag,' Laura said.

After a chorus of approval and support from Barbara, Eileen and Vera, they all buckled down to the task of washing and drying dishes and scouring pans. After a few minutes, Muriel said tentatively: 'But you said it was pointless when we did it – and you were right, as it turned out.'

'The food improved amazingly, though. And it was passable for quite a while afterwards,' Barbara said, encouragingly.

'But remember your spiteful cow of a games mistress. You were scared of her, and I reckon the warden's even worse,' Audrey cautioned.

'Well, things sometimes happen that put other things into perspective, and if some people can risk their lives against German gunners and fighter planes, I should be ashamed to be frightened of a nasty old cat like Miss Hubbard, shouldn't I? What do I care, anyway? Well, I don't, not now. All the Miss Hubbards in the world count for nothing now, as far as I'm concerned.'

'She's an old cat with long, sharp claws though, Laura, man,' Eileen warned. 'That's how she gets away with murder.'

'She does, and it's time we put a stop to it. I'm going to put my complaint in writing.'

'Well, if you're going to do it at all, that'll be the best way. I certainly wouldn't recommend telephoning, with her sister earwigging on your conversation,' Audrey snorted. 'That's what happened to us. Let's just hope she hasn't got another one in the post office, censoring our letters.'

'If you do complain, every girl here will back you up – I'm sure of it,' Barbara said.

Audrey and Muriel looked at each other, imagining the torrent of lies the warden might unleash against them as soon as she was cornered. It would be far better for them to have nothing to do with the scheme and avoid any trouble, but there was no way they could decently get out of it.

After a slight hesitation Audrey nodded. 'Aye, all right, then. We'll overlook the fact that damned few of you backed us up when we tried it.'

Muriel put the last dried plate back in its place. 'I'll go along with it,' she said. 'You make the complaint, and we'll back you up.' She hung her tea-towel on the oven door and turned to the others. 'Come on, let's get the bikes and go for a blow round a few country lanes. It's a shame to waste a nice day chewing the fat about *her*.'

Four of them went: Muriel, Audrey, Eileen and Laura, out for a long cycle ride in the East Yorkshire country-side. The rest chose to stay in the hostel, reading and writing letters. Spring was in the air, the weather was mild, and the air fresh and invigorating. They cycled at a steady pace through Griswold and out the other side, along familiar lanes, and then the less familiar, and finally along byways altogether unknown to them, along lanes and bridle paths overhung with trees just coming into leaf, or lined with primrose-studded hedgerows. They came to rest on a rise to gaze at fields and hedgerows of every shade of green and brown spread out like a patchwork before them.

'Look over there!' Audrey nudged Muriel and pointed to a barbed wire fence, surrounding a few huts with corrugated iron roofs.

Muriel shivered.

'Are you all right?'

'I suddenly thought of that man who spat at me,' she said. 'Are they German prisoners, or Italian, do you think?'

They mounted their bikes and cycled right up to the fence, to find out. A sentry in a greatcoat with a rifle slung over his shoulder came to warn them off.

'Are they Jerries, or Ities?' Laura demanded.

'Jerries.'

'How many are there?'

'What you see. Enough to fill half a dozen huts.'

'I wonder how many of our lads are in prison camps in Germany?' Eileen mused. 'I wonder if Barbara's husband is in one just like this?'

'It must be awful to be a prisoner. How long will it have to go on?' Muriel said, turning her bike. 'The war, I mean.'

'I don't know, man, but I hope someone can remember which way we came,' Eileen said. 'It'll be getting dark before long, and I don't fancy going round in circles all night.'

'Where's your sense of direction?' Audrey asked.

'I don't know, Audrey, man. I must have dropped it somewhere, and I've never been able to find my way back to it.'

Audrey gave a mock sigh, and shook her head. 'Follow me, then.'

Muriel was the last to follow. She took particular notice of the way, although she knew it was to no purpose.

Chapter 21

After a couple of peaceful days with Cissie and Jack, they were sent with a few other girls to sow early potatoes at the farm where they'd learned the art of riddling. A group of German prisoners were working nearby, with Ernst among them. Muriel firmly suppressed an impulse to wave to him and tried to keep her mind on the job, with Audrey working on one side of her, and Barbara at the other.

'I've never seen you look so fed up,' Barbara told her. 'You were always the one that cheered us all up and now you look as if you've got the weight of the whole world on your shoulders.'

Muriel gave her a half-hearted smile. 'I never really had much to be fed up about, until now. I must have led a charmed life. Pity I never appreciated it.'

'We all have a habit of taking things for granted, until,' Barbara threw her hands in the air '– hey presto – they've gone.'

'Aye. Because some big fat obstacle – like a war – gets waved over us like a black magician's wand,' Muriel said, bitterly, 'so that the thing we want more than anything else in the world, is the very thing we can't have.'

'Or the very man,' Barbara said.

Muriel nodded.

'We're in the same boat now, sort of,' Barbara said. 'But I'm sorry it's happened to you, Muriel.'

'We're not in the same boat at all. I hope your husband will come back to you, and you'll live happily ever after.'

'It's looking less and less likely,' Barbara said, and they both returned to the tedious, back-breaking job of setting potatoes by hand.

As always, the Germans finished their quota before everyone else and, as always, they came across to help the girls finish theirs. Muriel found herself working an arm's length from Ernst, but an open field, surrounded by other prisoners and Land Girls, was not the place for a private conversation. Still, there was no alternative, and the agony of not having matters settled between them was something she could no longer endure. She walked off and went behind a tree in the hedge. After a while, he was there beside her.

When she was sure they were both out of sight, she burst out with it. 'It can't be Ernst and Muriel any more, Ernst! We're at war. It was a dream.'

His blue eyes searched her face. '*Nein*. War ends. Peace. No enemies.'

'Too many people killed. A boy at home, killed!'

'I did not kill him.'

'I know, but people blame all the Germans, and hate all Germans,' she said. Her heart throbbed painfully, and her throat felt tight. If only she could have made him understand that they would hate his children as well, that they would all be hated and hounded – but words failed her. Again she shook her head, this time with tears in her eyes. 'No *Ernst und Muriel! Nein!* Two wars!'

He shook his head. 'I not start the war, Muriel! The war not my . . . *meine Idee war das nicht. Denkst du, ich sass am Tisch bei irgendeinem Politiker, um diesen Krieg zu planen? Denkst du, ich bin ein Admiral, der entscheidet, wohin das Wolfsrudel fahren soll.*'

'But you all followed Hitler . . .'

'You know how bad things in Germany, before Hitler came? *Zwanzig Jahre lang haben wir gehungert. Wegen des Versailler Vertrags, wegen der Reparationen. Leute sind vor Hunger gestorben. Dann kam Hitler. Er hat den Versailler Vertrag gebrochen und die Reparationen gestoppt!*' He paused, struggling for the right words. 'Hitler gave men work. He put food on German tables and made . . . *er machte uns wieder stolz, Deutsche zu sein. Hitler ist gekommen und Deutschland erblüht.*' His voice was becoming louder.

'Sh! Sh!' She put a hand over his mouth to quieten him. 'You sound as if you love him! I bet you were in the Hitler Youth,' she accused.

'*Warum nicht der Hitlerjugend angehören?* Everybody was in the Hitler Youth! *Wir wollten Deutschland von Ketten befreien; wir wollten unsere Länder zurückgewinnen. Nochmals Krieg mit England wollten wir nicht!*'

She stared at him, feeling his passion but hardly understanding a word he'd said, which seemed to her to under-
line the difference between them.

Seeing that she hadn't understood, he stopped, and
mimicked eating, carrying his hand to his mouth. 'And
this,' he said, pulling at his clothes, 'we want food, homes,
clothing, like any people. *Nur Verrückte wollen Krieg.*'

'You're German, and I'm English, and we're at war!'
she said. 'There can be no *Ernst und Muriel.*'

He shook his head vehemently, pointing rapidly to her,
then himself, then her. 'We are not at war!' he said, his
voice rising again. '*Unsere beiden Länder sind im Krieg gege-
neinander, aber,'* . . . he struggled for the English, '. . . I am
not at war with you, Muriel.'

She saw the pain on his face through a haze of tears,
and backed away.

He attempted to hold her. 'Muriel! *Die Britische RAF
hat ihren Teil beigetragen zum mutwilligen Töten. Unschuldige
Frauen und Kinder waren auch Todesopfer, aber dir gebe ich
nicht die Schuld dafür.*'

The tears brimmed over her lower lids and spilled
onto her cheeks. She shook her head. 'It doesn't matter,
Ernst. It's what people believe, and there's so much
hatred stirred up it's frightening. They'll never accept
us, never! You marry a nice German girl, and I'll marry
an Englishman. Better for us both. Better for our
children.'

'What Englishman?' he cried.

'Any Englishman!' she choked, and fled.

Both Barbara and Laura gave her curious looks when she had pulled herself together enough to return to work.

'What was that all about?' Laura asked. 'What was he saying to you?'

'How do I know?' Muriel said. 'I don't speak German. We were having a bit of a dispute about Hitler, I think.'

'You look pretty upset about it.'

'I'm not upset at all,' Muriel contradicted, and the rebuff was so pointed that Laura shrugged her shoulders and moved away.

After a day of back-breaking work, everyone but Muriel fell to and devoured everything on their plates that evening, while she listlessly pushed hers round on her plate.

'You haven't touched a thing, Muriel,' Barbara remarked, when most of them had finished eating.

'No appetite.'

'I wish I had no appetite,' Joan said, 'so I wouldn't have to swallow this muck.'

Muriel gave her a feeble smile. 'If you want to lose your appetite, lose the man you love. Better still, throw him away. That'll make you lose your appetite for everything. For living!' She got up and left the room, and ran upstairs to throw herself on her bunk, where she re-lived the end of Ernst and Muriel, sick at heart.

Her world turned grey. For her, all the colour leached out of the bright spring-time. Dreary day followed dreary day, sowing beets, sowing early potatoes, muck spreading, drilling seeds and all the jobs that come with spring-time. She ate enough of the hostel food to stay alive, and joined in the jitterbugging, but the bright face she tried to put on with the other girls slipped, now and then. Her misery at her loss gave her an intense sympathy for others who had suffered loss. On Saturday afternoon she wrote a long letter to Bill's mother full of incidents from their childhoods and expressions of sympathy and friendship.

She excused herself from chapel the following Sunday morning. 'I'm quite tired. I wish I'd slept better, and I've got a bit of a pain in my chest; probably sickening for something. I think I'll give it a miss. You go without me.'

They went, and Muriel wrote separate letters to her mother and Arni and Doreen, then paced restlessly around the garden waiting for Audrey to get back with news of Ernst.

'Did you see him?' she demanded, when the other girls had gone in and she and Audrey were alone in the garden.

'I did.'

'What did he look like?'

'He looked miserable. What do you expect? He had it bad for you. I hope you're satisfied.'

'Don't be like that! I'm not satisfied at all,' Muriel protested, but that was not quite the truth. The grief she felt at having made Ernst unhappy was mingled with a bitter kind of gladness – at this reassurance that his feeling for her had been as genuine as hers for him.

She saw nothing of him for days, and the days length-
ened into weeks, but he was her first thought on waking,
and when she closed her eyes his face was there. Day and
night she was either thinking about Ernst, or trying to
devise ways of stopping herself from thinking about him.
The preoccupations 'Ernst' and 'not-Ernst' fought a
constant duel in her head, but it came to the same thing
in the end. It was always Ernst.

She dreaded seeing him again – but looked for him,
everywhere.

'I think what shocked me the most, was walking into the
Half Moon, and being told he'd died, while other people
were drinking and joking and enjoying themselves as if
nothing had happened. "Sorry to have to tell you this,
Laura, but Guy's had it," they said, and there's that
bloody piano rattling away in the background, and
people *laughing*! I went cold, and I just ran, it jarred on
me so much,' Laura told them, one Saturday afternoon
in the middle of April. And it really must have made an
impression on her, Muriel thought, because she'd told
them the same thing at least a dozen times before. Laura
leaned back in her garden chair, and put her nose in the
steam from the tea they'd just brought out, testing the
rim of the cup with her lip – to hide her watering eyes,
Muriel suspected. Laura didn't take a sip. The tea was
milkless, and still scalding.

'It's bloody bad luck, when people die, but it's war,'
Audrey said, brutally tactless as usual, and as usual telling

the truth, from her seat beside Muriel on the broad trunk of the fallen elm. 'So what can you expect? People are dying every day. If the whole RAF plunged themselves into deep mourning for every one of their chaps they lost, they'd never be out of it. It would depress the hell out of them. There'd be no morale at all. My guess is the lads who escape want to celebrate living for another day, and make the best of it while they can.'

'Yes. I think it's the only way they can survive – to leave the mourning to the nearest and dearest, for now anyway. It might seem heartless, but it's the only way,' Barbara agreed. 'People couldn't carry on, otherwise.'

'They must feel it, though, deep down. They go to bed, and a bunk that used to have a warm body in it is suddenly empty, or they sit down to a meal, and there's a chair, without the lad that used to sit in it – you can't *not* notice things like that. And they're supposed to carry on as normal,' Muriel said.

'I bet they try bloody hard not to notice, because they can't afford to dwell on it,' Audrey said. 'It would paralyse them.'

'It's over a month ago,' Laura said, when the threat of tears had passed. 'I can hardly believe it. You can hardly believe these horrible things are happening at all, sitting in this tangle of a garden, so peaceful, and with the birds singing and everything bursting into life again. It's lovely, but horrible that some of the chaps aren't here to see it.'

'So, let's be like them, and not talk about horrible things – carry on as if it's not happening. And you cheer up, Muriel,' Vera said, sternly, 'and start eating your lovely dinners.'

'Lovely dinners!' Audrey exclaimed. 'I don't think any of us will ever eat a lovely dinner here. Have you heard any more from the War Ag, Laura?'

'No. I told you, I eventually got a curt little reply promising a visit that never materialised.'

'Never will,' Audrey said. 'I think we buggered complaining to the War Ag for good, me and Muriel.'

'I was just being sarcastic when I said lovely dinner. Anyway,' Vera said, turning back to Muriel, 'you've been miserable too long. If you get much thinner, you'll fall down a grating. And you'd probably never have got back together with Bill, anyway, so stop eating your heart out.'

'Well, he did send me a Valentine, if you remember,' Muriel said, 'and that was long after we fell out.'

Joan nodded her agreement. 'That's true, but it's no good thinking about it, so you cheer up. Let's see a bit of the old Muriel, who used to plague our lives out. I know it's terrible when people you love die, but we can't think about it too much while there's still a war to fight. There'll be plenty of time for grieving when it ends.'

'Lads are forever disappearing,' Eileen said. 'Not dying, but being moved about all over the place. You never get to know what happened to them, most of the time.'

'I've been in love with more boys than I can count. They're here today and gone tomorrow, getting moved here, there and everywhere. They're here, and I'm in love with them, and then they're gone, or I'm gone, like when I came up here from Norfolk – and it's not long before I'm in love with someone else,' Joan laughed.

'I'll never be in love with anybody else!' Laura vowed.

'I've been in love thousands of times,' Vera boasted. 'It's different for Barbara, she's married, but you two will be in love with someone else before you can say Jack Robinson. There's more fish in the sea than ever came out of it, that's what my mother says.'

'I got sent up to Griswold as a punishment for being a bad girl, and I wasn't very happy about it, either,' Joan confided. 'I never told you that, did I?'

'Bad girl? In what way? Or shouldn't I ask?' Muriel asked, and leaned towards Joan, all ears for the rest.

'For being too fond of the Yanks,' Joan grinned. 'They put six of us together in a hostel in North Norfolk, and it just happened to be opposite a big house where a lot of GI signallers were billeted. My goodness, we used to have some fun with them. They're lovely. There were about three of them for every one of us and we were in the Black Swan with them every night unless there was danc- ing at their base, and they didn't half have some money to splash about! We had some high old times, until a lot of the posh end of the village complained to the War Ag – miserable old buggers.'

'Why, some people cannot stand to see anybody having a good time, Joan, man,' said Eileen.

'No, they can't! So they shifted us girls all out and split us up. Those toffee-nosed War Ag women made us feel

like a lot of tarts, just for being friendly with the Yanks.
Well, they're supposed to be our allies, aren't they? So we
ought to be friendly, but the War Ag didn't seem to think
so. They didn't keep two of us together. We got scattered
all over the country, and I was sick about it, not only
because of missing the Yanks, but because I can't get
home to see my mum so often now.'

The others sat gaping at her throughout this revelation.
Eileen laughed incredulously. 'But you hardly take a
drink, Joan, man – when we go out, you're more sober
than the rest of us!'

'I'd never have believed you were the type to scandal-
ise a village, Joan,' Barbara said, in mock reproach.

'Anybody would be the type, next to those Americans,'
Joan assured her, with a wide grin on her face. 'They're
good fun – really friendly, and free and easy with their
money – and their fags and Hershey bars – everything.
They're a smashing lot of boys, and don't you believe
anybody that tells you any different.'

'That's how you got so good at jitterbugging, then,'
Muriel said.

'Why, good for you, Joan, man. I've never been near
any Americans, but I've been in and out o' love wi' plenty
of English lads. And you'll be the same before long,
Muriel.'

Muriel nodded, willing to be convinced. She was looking forward to being the same. She would be glad to fall
in love with someone else.

Then for some unaccountable reason Doris Chapman

appeared in her mind's eye, clear in every detail from her blonde hair and her tired blue eyes behind their owlish glasses, to her ample figure and swollen ankles – a woman who had not been in and out of love a thousand times, but had been faithful all her life to one blighted man. Loving, patient, faithful, wasted Doris.

Chapter 22

'What do you think they were trying to tell us yesterday afternoon, then? When we were sitting in the garden?' Laura demanded, fresh out of the bath and still barefoot and wrapped in towels.

Muriel was lying on her bunk, flicking through a magazine. 'I don't know. Is there a bathroom free?'

'There was nobody on the landing waiting to dash in when I came out. Well – what do you think they *meant*?'

Muriel sat up. 'I don't know. Just trying to jolly us along, I suppose. Cheer us up a bit.'

'Or shut us up, more like. Barbara's been good, but most people soon run out of sympathy.'

Muriel's eyebrows rose at that. She had been assiduously comforted by all the girls, not in any overt way, but by a hundred small kindnesses – a gentle word here, a quick hug there, an offer to take a letter to the post, or fetch her a cup of tea.

'I don't think they have. I think they just don't like to see us miserable.'

"'Laugh and the world laughs with you. Cry, and you cry alone.'"

'Well, that's true enough. There aren't many people who enjoy crying. But I wouldn't say they're unsympathetic, Laura.'

'I'd say a lot of them are.'

Muriel sprang down from her bunk and got her sponge-bag and towel out of her locker and pausing by Laura's bunk put a hand on her shoulder, to give her a comforting squeeze. 'Not deliberately, I'm sure. It's just that people don't know what to say, a lot of the time, Laura. And maybe they're frightened of making you cry again, so they just don't talk about it. Look, come out with us tonight, instead of staying in, fretting about things you can't change. Think about it,' Muriel said, and then hared off towards the bathrooms, before anybody else beat her to it.

Strange, she thought, that Laura felt the lack of sympathy, when she herself could have done with a lot less. She'd washed away the worst of her grief for Bill in that first cleansing deluge of tears, but her hopes for the future hadn't rested in Bill. Her real grief was for the death of her hopes for '*Ernst und Muriel*', and for better or worse she had strangled them at birth, rather than face what '*Ernst und Muriel*' would be up against. She'd been getting sympathy under false pretences, but the girls all meant well, and she either had to pull herself together or be comforted beyond endurance.

She chose to pull herself together. Life had been too

dreary for too long. Something had to happen to cheer it up, and she was the only one that could make it happen. Grow up, she told herself, and stop acting like a child, crying for someone you'll be a lot better off without. Crying didn't suit her. She didn't want to cry at all, and she certainly didn't want to cry alone. Laura was probably right. The other girls were fed up of seeing them with faces as long as fiddles. She would have her five inches of water for a bath and get her war paint on, then sally forth with the rest of them, to whoop it up in the Half Moon Inn.

Muriel sat with Audrey, watching John Goodyear queuing at the bar to get drinks for them. His dad was a widower, and a nice old man, judging by what she'd seen of him at the whist drive. If she ended up married to John maybe she could get Miss Chapman fixed up with his dad, and keep that promise she made. She could invite Miss Chapman round to stay, and play Cupid.

'Daft thoughts we have, sometimes, don't we?' she commented to Audrey.

'Such as what?'

'Such as marrying a bloke we don't fancy, just so we can get his old dad for someone else.'

'Aye. That really is daft. I suppose you're talking about John Goodyear.'

'I am.'

'Has he asked you to marry him?'

'No, but I get that feeling off him. He definitely fancies me.'

Audrey's face was a study. She gave a low chuckle, and cast her eyes heavenward. 'You're not big-headed or anything, are you? Anyway, fancying you and marrying you are two different things, lass. Have you come into a fortune? Because I doubt he'll be marrying anybody without a ha'penny to scratch her arse with. He don't strike me as that type at all.'

'Well, I've got to admit, I still have to scratch mine with my fingernails,' Muriel grinned. 'So what type does he strike you as?'

'A charmer, when it serves his purpose – and the type that never gets the worst end of a bargain. I wonder what he thinks Morley Villas is?'

'A row of swanky mansions in The Avenues, or somewhere, I reckon. Not a tiny little terrace at the peasants' end of Holderness Road. Huh!' Muriel exclaimed, bridling at the mere possibility of John's looking down on them, 'who does he think he is, anyway? I'm not sorry we didn't go to his place as milkmaids, even if he has got a flaming machine.'

'Neither am I. I'm sorry you jacked it in with Ernst, though,' Audrey said, softly.

Muriel was suddenly looking at her friend through a blur of tears, and the lump forming in her throat kept her from answering for a minute. When she spoke her voice was low. 'So am I. But I can't go against everyone else – absolutely everyone else I know, Audrey, apart from you – I just can't. Or go through what your grandparents went through, either. I'd love to marry Ernst, but we'd be tormented to death for it, for the rest of our lives, probably, and maybe have our bairns coming home from school without their eyebrows, or something worse.' She shook her head. 'I can't live like that. You can put up with bairns coming home without their gym kit now and again, but coming home without their eyelashes is beyond the limit. Like you said, your uncle's lucky he wasn't blinded.'

'He got over it,' Audrey said. 'They all did. You'd be all right if you settled somewhere in the country.'

'I thought so to begin with, but it's even seeping into the villages now, the hatred. Remember the last time we were at the whist drive when that couple were saying they'd just had to tell their evacuees that their house was bombed flat, and their mam and dad were dead? Imagine having to tell a bairn that! They hadn't got much good to say about the Germans, either,' Muriel said, with her eyes on John Goodyear, just pocketing his change. 'Anyway, let's change the subject. He's coming back – but if you ever get the chance to talk to Ernst again, try to make him understand why I broke it off, will you, Audrey? Before it went too far?'

'It had already gone too far when he carved your initials into that tree, as far as he was concerned, anyway. Probably before that, even,' Audrey said. 'He's gone on you, Muriel. Some blokes are like that.'

'Like Vera said, there are plenty more fish in the sea – for Ernst as well as for me,' Muriel said, and with a sigh, she looked away. Vera was sitting with Laura in the far corner of the lounge and caught her eye. She gave Muriel a wave, with a significant little jerk of her head towards Laura, who was too engrossed in conversation with an aircraftman to notice. There was a light in Laura's eyes and an animation in her face that told the whole story. She was very much attracted to him. And how long had it been since the death of her tail-end Charlie, the sworn love of her life, Muriel wondered? Six weeks, maybe? Laura had evidently taken the girls' advice to heart – she was cheering up with a vengeance. Poor Guy, Muriel thought, not that it could hurt him now, but she was glad that Howard wasn't in to see it.

She nudged Audrey, and gave a sardonic little snort. 'Just look over there; Laura looks as if she's reeling another one in.'

John was back from the bar with three glasses of cider. He put the drinks down on the table and sat beside her.

Muriel took a deep breath and pulled herself together. 'Thanks, John. Give us a ciggie, will you?' she smiled, her voice loud enough to be heard by the servicemen standing nearby.

He drew his eyebrows together in a look of comic despair, took a gold-plated cigarette case out of the inside pocket of his jacket and snapped it open. They had barely put the cigarettes to their lips when he was there with a light. Muriel smiled and inhaled, and then sat back to perfect the art of blowing smoke rings, while John watched her with resigned disapproval and talked about farming. But blowing smoke rings was a knack that had lost the fascination it had held for her before, and she soon got tired of it. She sat up and put the ciga-rette out.

Audrey spotted the para she had been talking to on their first visit to the inn. She excused herself, and went over to have a word with him.

'What's up, Muriel?' John asked, after she'd gone. 'You've lost your sparkle. You're not your usual bubbly self tonight.'

She gave him a bright smile. 'Nothing. I'm all right. What's that you were saying about silage?'

He burst out laughing. 'I see. That's what it is – my conversation.'

'No,' she assured him, 'that's not it, honest.'

'Well, if you're really interested, I'll repeat it.'

'Oh, I am. I'm a Land Girl now. I ought to know everything there is to know about silage.'

He gave another chuckle. 'Well, then, it will interest you to know that I'll be moving all my stock out of the silage fields before long, and spreading some fertiliser to give the grass a good six weeks' growth before I cut it . . .'

Muriel listened, while gazing round the room at the people there – all enjoying themselves, or pretending to – but try as she might to buck herself up and join in the fun, for her everything seemed to have lost its colour and its savour. The place was full of charming, good-looking young men, and not one of them interested her. John Goodyear was right – all genuine lightness of heart was gone. She slowly dipped her finger into her cider, and took it out again, looking in vain for the hole.

★ ★ ★

After Muriel had refused the usual offer of a lift from John Goodyear, she cycled back to the hostel with the others.

'I'm glad I let you persuade me to come out, Muriel,' Laura said, as they rode along. 'I didn't really want to come, but I feel as if it's done me good. And I had to face it sometime, didn't I?'

'Either that, or stay in for the rest of your life,' Muriel agreed.

'Well, Guy wouldn't expect me to do that. It's very hard, but life does go on. All the airmen say that. Guy told me in his letter that he wouldn't want me to be in mourning for the rest of my life, so I'm glad you made me come out. It's bucked me up quite a bit.'

It was plain to see that Laura wasn't going to be in mourning for the rest of her life whether Guy would want it or not, Muriel thought, judging by the looks that had passed between her and that aircraftman. 'Go for one of the ground crew, next time round,' she said. 'It might be less of a heartbreak.'

'Why, you seemed to be getting on all right with old Big Name, Muriel, man,' Eileen said. 'No chance of him copping it, is there?'

'No, he's doing such a vital job, you know. The whole war hangs on making proper silage.'

'That chap you were talking to was ground crew, wasn't he, Laura?' Audrey said.

'Yes, but I'm not thinking about anybody else at the moment.' Laura said, hastily. 'I expect it'll take me a long time to get over losing Guy.'

'Well, he certainly looked as if he was thinking about you,' said Vera.

'Did he?' Laura said, with a little smile. 'I can't say I noticed.'

But that glad little smile told Muriel that for Laura, consolation was close at hand. Guy would be occupying her thoughts less and less, and the gap he'd left would be filled as easily as Howard had predicted.

How perverse it was that the girl who'd been so steeped in her grief that she'd almost had to be dragged out of the hostel against her will should be going back so uplifted and with her sights so obviously on the future, whereas the one who'd gone out determined to cast off all her cares and woes and enjoy herself should return with her spirits dampened and incapable of lifting herself out of the doldrums. But '. . . my young man was still alive . . .' Muriel seemed to remember Miss Chapman saying. So how could she have taken up with another?

'I'm not going to the Half Moon next Saturday,' she suddenly announced. 'I'd rather go to a dance. Anybody fancy going to the hop in the village hall?'

A few of the girls had already tried the village hop.

'What – and stomp round the room to Victor Sylvester records with lads in their farm boots, while the village girls sit there looking daggers at you?' one of them laughed.

'Making you feel about as welcome as the bubonic plague,' another chipped in. 'I've tried it, so no, thanks.'

'Don't expect them to do the jitterbug, either. It's like the land that time forgot. They're all about a hundred years behind the times, still pulling their forelocks to their betters. I'd rather be at the Half Moon with people who are living in the twentieth century.'

'Besides that, most of the lads are too young – about fourteen, a lot of them. The older ones are in the forces – the ones who've got anything about them, that is. Couldn't wait to get away and see a bit of life, I should think.'

'Let's hope they don't regret it,' Barbara said.

Chapter 23

The following week, Muriel was sent with Audrey and a few of the other girls to work for a Farmer Hogg, to clear out the ditches so that the field drains could empty into them. The farm had been neglected for years, and the new owner was on top of them the whole time, riding up and down on his horse shouting curt orders. All the regular farm workers seemed terrified of him. The girls had stood it for a whole morning and were ready for lounces when they looked up at the sound of his guttural accents berating one of the youngsters: 'Keep your mind on your work, you stupid . . .' He let his riding crop do the rest of the talking. A lad not much older than Arni cowered away as he raised it, but not quick enough or far enough to prevent the full force of the blow landing on his shoulders.

Muriel's blood boiled. 'Leave him alone!' she yelled. The farmer turned his horse and rode it so far up to her she thought she was going to be trampled. Then he towered over her, spilling out a lot of invective in an accent that was completely unfamiliar, smacking the crop against his boot all the while.

Work stopped, as all the girls stood up to watch. Muriel put her hands on her hips, looked him in the eye and surprised both herself and him. 'You hit me with that thing, and I'll have the law on you,' she warned.

'Aye, and she's got plenty of witnesses,' Audrey said, looking first at him and then pointedly at all the other girls.

The smacking stopped. He pointed the crop at them, with a sharp order to them all to get back to their work and quick about it.

At lounces one of the farm workers came across to talk to them, his weathered, wrinkled face wearing an almost toothless smile, especially for Muriel and Audrey. The old farmer had been a good old lad, he said, but he'd let the farm go. Now this new boss had come, and he meant to get it up to scratch. He'd run a farm in Africa before that. He was used to treating his workers like slaves, and had brought his African ways back to England with him.

'You should all get together, and stick up for your-selves,' Audrey told him.

The old man shook his head. 'Nay, first one as did it he'd turn out; make an example. They'd lose job, and cottage. He'd only have to do it once, then rest 'ud fall into line.'

It was plain that everyone hated the man, but none of the workers wanted to be the first to stand up to him. Getting on the wrong side of him meant losing not only their wages, but their homes as well, and since most of them were too old to be taken on by anybody else, they had to put up with it. Muriel hadn't seen anyone pull a forelock to the 'new boss' yet, but the idea of anybody like that farmer having so much power over her that he could lash her with a riding crop and get away with it made her think that there might be some pretty big drawbacks to life in the country – for people who didn't own the farm.

The boss came to drive them back to work before they'd had time to swallow their sandwiches, and kept them slaving a full half-hour after their time, with the lorry waiting to take them back to the hostel. The driver gave them a ticking off, and at the hostel they were greeted by the warden's sour face and her complaints about their lateness. She'd failed to see why everyone else should be kept waiting for them, so all the rest had eaten and cleared up. Their tea was in the kitchen, and if it was stone cold it wasn't her fault. They tried to explain that the farmer wouldn't let them leave on time. Her response to that was to tell them they'd better clear up after themselves, and make sure they got back on time tomorrow.

The food was stone cold, since the warden had made not the slightest attempt to keep it hot, and it was twice as unappetising as a result. They ate it, and then went to find Laura to complain yet again.

The following day was just as bad: 'convict labour', Barbara called it. They slaved all day under the farmer's watchful eye, and when the lorry came and they attempted to leave, he sat in front of them, determined to squeeze more work out of them than he was due to.

'You can go when you've finished the work I set you,' he snarled.

Muriel, Audrey and Barbara were equally determined to leave, and tried to walk past him. He attempted to drive them back, and only succeeded in knocking Barbara down with the horse.

'What are you trying to do – kill her?' Muriel shrieked. Audrey got past him and ran like a hare towards the lorry. He turned the horse and shouted her back, and for a couple of seconds Muriel thought he was going to ride her down, until he turned again.

Muriel dropped to her knees beside Barbara, until Audrey came back with the driver. Barbara winced. 'It scraped its hoof right down my leg,' she gasped.

'Pure accident,' the farmer rasped to the driver. 'It would never have happened if she'd been watching what she was doing. You all saw what happened, didn't you?' he shouted to his own workforce. He got no answer; they continued to watch in silence. 'She walked into the horse,' he repeated, his eyes fixed like gimlets on the driver.

Barbara's leg was pouring blood. They didn't stop to bandy words with him, but pulled her boot and sock out of the mud. With one hand on Audrey's shoulder and the other on the driver's, Barbara hobbled to the lorry, bleeding profusely. The others followed, unimpeded by the farmer, who was riding towards his own workers, waving his riding crop at them and urging them back to work.

War Ag sent an ambulance to take Barbara to the

nearest field hospital, where the doctor found a two-inch strip of flesh scraped off her calf, and a broken ankle.

The rep who came to Elm Hall from the War Ag later that evening to see them about the incident was not the same one they'd had before but a Miss Fawcett, a much younger woman. The lady who had just escaped being crushed to death by the falling elm had been obliged to leave to take care of her ageing father.

The warden stayed with them the whole time Miss Fawcett was listening to their sorry tale and was called on to verify how late they'd been getting back the previous day. The girls took the opportunity of making a point about the cold food. Miss Hubbard responded that if she'd known what the trouble was, she would have kept the food hot, but − and here she looked directly at Audrey and Muriel − *some* of the girls in that party were quite difficult and unreliable. She had just assumed they were up to some prank, somewhere. And knowing what *some* of the girls were like, she would be quite interested to hear the farmer's side of the story. They had quite a habit of reporting people for no good reason except to cause trouble, some of them.

The rep nodded. She would hear the farmer's side of the story the following day.

'I don't care what he says; I'm never going back there again,' Audrey said.

The warden looked at the rep, and with a pursing of the lips and a sideways glance at Audrey told her as clearly as words could have done that there sat one of the *some* who took the prize for being difficult and unreliable, et cetera.

'I'd like you all to go tomorrow, except Barbara, and I'll be going with you,' the rep said, pleasantly, her expression very sweet, and her eyes very determined.

Young Miss Fawcett was at the hostel the following morning before the lorry left for the farms, not in her usual clothes, as they'd expected, but in the Land Army rig-out. She would be working with them, she said – the only way to find out what was really going on. On the way to the farm the girls asked her if she'd seen Laura's letter, and tried to tell her about the terrible food. She had not seen the letter and although she listened to their complaints she appeared not to give them much credence – probably warned against them by the previous rep, Muriel thought.

The farmer was at the farm gate waiting for them when the lorry drew up, sitting astride his horse, crop in hand. When he'd counted them all in he ordered the rep to hold the gate open for him, and then asked where Barbara was.

'Not coming,' the rep said, briefly. 'I'm here as a replacement.'

'It might please you to know that you've broken her ankle,' Audrey informed him.

He turned his gimlet eyes towards her and pointed his riding crop at her. 'You,' he snarled, 'get off my land. I don't need your services, and I won't be paying for them.'

Audrey looked towards the rep, expecting instructions as to what to do. None came, so flushed and furious, she yanked the gate open again and stormed off his land and back into the lorry. After witnessing what had happened the previous day the driver had mercifully waited a moment or two, to see how things went.

Farmer Hogg's temper had not been improved by Audrey's open challenge. He gave full rein to his domineering, slave-driving instincts and Miss Fawcett had ample opportunity to see his cowed workers and his behaviour towards the girls for herself. When five o'clock came she had seen more than enough, and told them that their day's work was over and they would be returning to the hostel. The farmer rode up to stop them leaving exactly as he had the day before, whereupon Miss Fawcett introduced herself as the representative of the War Agriculture Executive Committee, showed him her credentials, and told him very clearly that they would not be sending any more Land Girls to his farm.

Muriel turned to the other girls, and yelled: 'Hip, hip?' She was answered by a chorus of glad hoorays. They gave three rousing cheers and got off his land. Despite their exhaustion after nine hours of almost unrelenting hard labour, they walked towards the lorry with a spring in their steps, laughing all the way.

Back at the hostel, Miss Fawcett very politely asked the warden if she would mind her joining the girls for tea, since she'd done a day's hard work with them. Miss

Hubbard replied, just as politely, that she wouldn't mind at all. It would be her pleasure.

'What happened to you after you got chucked off the African penal colony?' Muriel asked Audrey, while they were queuing to get washed.

'I ended up working on another farm,' she said, and then murmured, 'Met a couple of nice lads there.'

Muriel looked at her sharply, and could barely bite back the question: Ernst?

They went downstairs to a very tasty Lancashire hotpot, followed by adequately sweetened apple turnovers. They all enjoyed it, although Muriel would have been much happier to see a more representative sample of Elm Hall's bill of fare put before the War Ag's rep – but Miss Hubbard was far too crafty for that, she thought. That woman certainly knew how to watch out for herself, no doubt about it.

After they'd eaten, the rep thanked the warden, complimenting her on her cooking. She took Barbara aside and had a few private words with her, then said a cordial goodbye to them all and left. It was a fine late April evening, so without inviting any of the others, the two who were most notoriously difficult, unreliable, and as thick as thieves, went out for a walk together.

'Did you see Ernst?' Muriel asked, her heart jumping in anticipation of news of him.

'Both of them. Ernst and Wilhelm.'

'Did you explain – why I had to break it off?'

'I did my best.'

'How did he take it?'

'All right.'

'How is he, then?'

'Seems to be getting over it all right,' Audrey said, impassively.

'Oh,' Muriel said, and her stomach suddenly felt like lead. Her shoulders slumped, and the world looked bleak. She knew that the breach between them had been her own doing; she knew that she should have been glad that Ernst's unhappiness had been short-lived, but she was not glad, because it took him further away from her. She recovered herself enough to say: 'Oh, that's good, then. It's the best way all round, for everyone,' while deep in her heart she screamed: *NO-OOO!*

Easter fell late, at the end of the warmest April since records had begun, and some of the girls were taking advantage of the Bank Holiday to go home for an extended leave. Joan decided against going, because it was a long journey to Norwich, the trains would be packed, and she had an idea that there might not be much going on at the American bases because of the Easter weekend. Some of the GIs were quite religious, she said. Muriel and Audrey volunteered to stay and let those girls go who were keenest to get home. Barbara didn't want to struggle on the trains with her leg in plaster to go home to an empty flat. Laura and Vera stayed for reasons connected with their fellow visitors to the Half Moon, and Eileen stayed because the rest of them were staying.

The whist was off that week, on account of Good Friday, so Muriel and Audrey played whist in the hostel all evening, with any of the depleted little band of Land Girls who would play with them. A couple of the girls from another dormitory turned out to be real card sharps who played a mean game. Muriel was glad of any occupation that would drive Ernst out of her mind for a while, and after a few hands and a little tuition began to hope that she might improve enough to beat Sammy Mawson. Laura and Vera went to the Half Moon with a few of the others.

Chapter 24

On Saturday night, Laura was ready and raring to go out with the rest of the girls. Muriel half-heartedly got ready and cried off at the last minute, reluctant to face another night of talking about farming to John Goodyear while watching Laura with Guy's replacement. Neither did she want to see Howard's reaction, if he happened to be in. She let them go without her.

Barbara was writing letters by the stove in the common room, sitting on one chair with her plaster-of-Paris-encased leg resting on another. After exchanging a few words with her, and getting the feeling that her conversation was not welcome just at that moment, Muriel got up and drifted into the library. The unseasonably warm weather made it comfortable to sit in, so she sat there alone, poring through the only book in the room that could be of no earthly use to her now, with a few more scattered around her in case anybody came in.

An hour and a half later she was startled by sounds outside the door and hurriedly concealed her book, snatching up another in its place. The door handle turned and the hinges creaked like the door of Dracula's castle.

'I thought I might find you here.'

'You're back early!'

'Aye. I talked to John Goodyear for a bit. I told him you weren't coming. He bought me a drink, I'll give him that, but then he spent the rest of the time we were talking looking over my shoulder, ogling every other woman in the room. Probably looking for your replacement.'

'A fair wind to his arse,' Muriel laughed. 'I hope he finds one.'

'It's clear I'm not in the running, anyway,' Audrey grinned. 'I'm not his type.'

'Whose type are you then?' asked Muriel, intrigued. 'That paratrooper you were talking to?'

'Maybe. He's all right. We had a drink together, and a chat, and then I suddenly felt shattered. I came away to have an early night.'

'You're dead keen on him, then,' Muriel grimaced.

'Must be, mustn't I?' Audrey grinned. She held up a packet of cigarettes, and rattled the few left inside. 'He gave me a few fags, anyway. Come on, let's go and see if the old Prune's left any tea leaves in the pot that we can soak again, so we can have a cup of tea and a fag.'

'All right. You go and put the kettle on, and I'll be with you as soon as I've put these back.'

Audrey looked curiously at the books, but said nothing. After she'd gone, Muriel put them back in a flash and went to join her. They had a smoke while the kettle boiled, then poured out a beverage that Audrey described as 'witch piss', and took their cups into the common room, with one for Barbara. There were a few other girls in there, including Eileen, all just back from the Half Moon and laughing and chattering about their evening.

'That letter seems to be taking some writing, Barbara,' Muriel commented, knowing that it couldn't be to Barbara's husband, since she had no idea where he was.

'Yes, it is,' Barbara said, pleasantly. 'I'm writing a letter to Farmer Hogg, telling him how he injured me, and how much compensation he owes me for the injury and the loss of earnings. Then I'm taking out a summons against him. You threatened to have the law on him, Muriel, and I'm going to do it. I'm calling what he did to me assault and battery. It's a criminal offence, as well as a civil one. I ought to know; I used to work in a solicitor's office.'

Muriel and Audrey watched each other's eyebrows rise, and their eyes widened.

'Well, I only threatened. I don't think I'd have carried it out even if he'd hit me; I wouldn't have known how. And he probably *is* a magistrate, Barbara. Have you thought of that?' Muriel said.

'He might very well be, but there are rules, and if the magistrates trying the case don't follow the rules, I shall appeal to a higher authority.'

'The War Ag won't be pleased,' Audrey said.

'I don't care whether the War Ag's pleased or not. The War Ag didn't get inches of flesh torn off its leg, or get its ankle broken, and it can hardly be seen to obstruct justice, can it? And you'll be my witnesses, I hope.'

Audrey grinned. 'Course we will,' she said, with obvious relish. 'Nothing I'd like better than to see him come to grief.'

Barbara gave her a dubious look. 'Just tell the truth in such a way that it's not too obvious you've got an axe to grind yourself.'

'But I have got an axe to grind,' Audrey said, 'so would it be truthful if I didn't make it obvious?'

The warden put an end to the legal quibble by poking her head round the door, and announcing that it was half past ten and high time they were all in bed.

'It's Sunday tomorrow,' Audrey said. 'There's no reason for us to go to bed.'

The warden scowled, and insisted that there was. That was the rule, in her hostel. It kept them in the proper routine for getting up for work.

Audrey, who had come back from the Half Moon early for the express purpose of having an early night, now wouldn't have gone to bed to save her soul from damnation. Barbara openly stated that she was not a child who needed her routine ordered by anybody else, and she was heartily sick of being treated like one. Muriel stood by her friends.

The warden's face turned from red to puce, and the veins bulged on her forehead and her neck. Everybody else in the room took one look at her and obediently filed upstairs.

Then Miss Hubbard strutted up to Barbara and started wagging a finger in her face. 'I thought you were better than the common herd of townies but no; you've turned out to be no better than this pair of shit-stirrers! No wonder that farmer got fed up with you – he did right to knock you down – I wish he'd knocked you into the middle of next week! All of you! You'd try the patience of a saint!'

Barbara's face was soon a match for the warden's. She was beside herself. Muriel collapsed into nervous giggles at the sight of them, eyeball to eyeball, like two Furies. Then the warden turned and strode from the room, pushing her roughly aside as she made for the door. They heard her storm upstairs and start the banging of doors.

She soon swept downstairs again, and back into the common room. 'There's two of 'em still out, and it's quarter to eleven!' she shouted. 'It's like Liberty bloody Hall here. It's time there was some discipline.'

'She thinks she's governing Holloway!' Audrey exclaimed.

'But I'm not, and more's the pity, because that's where you lot belong. You'd know about it then! I'd have you all on bread and water – making mischief for honest people! I'd have you breaking rocks! That farmer ought to have given you a horsewhipping, disgusting crew you are. Never mind reporting *me* – *I'm* going to report *you*.'

'And I'm going to report you,' Barbara said, eyes blazing.

'And I'm going to report *you*. And I'm going to report

these two – and I know plenty about them, don't think I don't.'

'And I'm . . .'

The warden abandoned this pantomime-like exchange and went into her own quarters, locking the door behind her. She came out again half an hour later, and left the hostel, locking the front door after her.

The three of them stayed up for a while to demonstrate their independence in case she came back, and then got tired of sitting it out and went to get ready for bed. Laura and Vera were still out. Muriel went downstairs to unlock the door for them, but the spare key was gone from its hook in the hallway. She went to the back door. That key was also gone from its usual place next to the radiator key and the shed key. The key to the kitchen door was gone as well. They were locked in like prisoners, as if they actually were in Holloway. She was just on her way back up to the dormitory to tell the others when she heard someone at the front door.

She called through the letterbox, 'Who is it?'

The reply was accompanied by snorts and giggles. 'Who do you think? It's us – Laura and Vera.'

'She's locked us all in, and taken all the keys. Go round the side and I'll let you in through the library window.'

With more snorts and giggles the latecomers clambered unsteadily through the long library window, and got around the blackout blinds in that hilariously light-hearted mood usually brought on by the refreshments served in the Half Moon Inn. When the inn had closed they'd decided to go for an illicit spin with their aircraftman friends in one of the government's vehicles – and had enjoyed themselves no end.

'I'm surprised at you, Laura,' Muriel began, and then shut up. She sounded too much like the warden.

While the latecomers got washed and ready for bed, Muriel went into the dorm and joined the others, who had just exhausted their discussion about the warden. The verdict was that she ought to be in Broadmoor, not Holloway. The news that they were locked in as if they actually were in Holloway drew outraged demands to know what they were supposed to do if a fire broke out. Laura and Vera came in and put the lights out before getting into bed, apparently unconcerned about the warden's antics, or the danger of being burned alive in their beds.

'What a shame it's too late to ring the War Ag,' Eileen said.

'Never mind,' said Joan, 'she'll get it all when we ring her tomorrow.'

'Whoever rings her tomorrow will have a long ride,' Muriel commented. 'She's locked the office door, as well; we can't get to the telephone.'

They were just settling down to sleep when the lights were snapped on again. The warden entered the dormitory like a cat stalking a mouse and stood facing Laura with eyes narrowed and nostrils dilated. There was a suppressed violence in her manner, like some predatory animal preparing to spring. It was all wasted on Laura, who was still too much under the influence of her intoxicating evening to be affected by it.

'How did you get in?' Miss Hubbard demanded, softly.

Laura dragged herself up, to face her inquisitor. 'I walked through the wall – like Elinor,' she said, and burst into a fit of the giggles.

The warden gave her a twisted smile. The light in her eyes was not pleasant to behold, and she suddenly slapped Laura's face with a crack that sounded like a rifle shot. The giggling stopped.

'Right,' she said. 'You've had me up all night, so you can get your own breakfast tomorrow, and your own dinner, as well. See how funny that is.' With that she turned and left the dormitory, snapping the light off on her way out. Laura's laughter burst out anew and with redoubled force, soon joined by Vera's and the rest of the girls'. The warden's progress down the stair was accompanied by howls of laughter.

Chapter 25

The worst three troublemakers were the first in their dorm to get out of bed the following day. The few girls remaining in the other dormitories were already downstairs. They had heard the row, and wisely stayed out of it. The warden was nowhere to be found, and was not answering to the knock on the door of her private living quarters. They found the kitchen cupboards padlocked and not a scrap of food left out for them, not a spoonful of tea, not even a match to light the gas, or the stove in the common room. The doors were locked, as before.

Muriel climbed out of the library window and cycled into Griswold to telephone the War Ag, but there was no answer – not surprisingly, on Easter Sunday morning. She got back to the hostel at around ten o'clock, to find all the girls up, dressed, and mutinous. There were fine lines of bruising on Laura's face, corresponding to the outline of the warden's fingers, but most of the girls were more concerned with their own empty stomachs and the lack of food than the state of Laura's face.

'From bad food, to no food,' Barbara said. 'I wonder if she means to starve us all day?'

'Does anybody know where her sister lives?' Joan demanded. 'We should go round there and drag her back, or at least get the keys off her.'

The sister lived in Griswold, but nobody knew quite where.

'She goes to the Methodist chapel,' Audrey announced. 'I'll collar her there.'

While Laura and Vera were still in bed, the regular and the occasional chapel-goers sallied forth to the service on their War Ag bikes, along with others who had never been to chapel in their lives, but were determined to secure their food supply, and see the fun.

Muriel went with them for the first time in weeks. Inside the chapel Audrey sat where she could be best seen by the prisoners, and Muriel sat beside her. When the prisoners filed in, Muriel looked for Ernst with her heart in her mouth, and didn't know whether to be glad or sorry not to see him among them – but when Audrey turned round after smiling at Wilhelm there was such a glow on her face that she looked as if a lamp had been switched on inside her head.

She loves him! Muriel thought, and the thought quite stunned her. It preoccupied her throughout the whole of the service, even more than her hunger or the scheme to corner the warden's sister.

Back outside, they were hailed by Jack and Cissie, who were coming to talk to them. Out of the corner of her eye, Muriel saw the warden's sister scuttling off as fast as her legs would carry her. Audrey chased after her, and the rest of the Land Army chased after Audrey. Muriel watched, until she saw the warden's sister like a fox at bay, surrounded by a pack of hungry girls.

Cissie and Jack stared in pure astonishment, and they were not alone. A good many of the congregation also had curious eyes on the warden's sister and her entourage, and the heated discussion going on between them.

'What's that all about?' Cissie asked.

'It's about breakfast, dinner, and tea,' Muriel said. 'We're starving, and Miss Hubbard's seen fit to take herself off somewhere and leave us without a bite to eat. She's gone, and everything's locked up. We've had nothing this morning and we'll have nothing for the rest of the day, unless we can find her. We tried ringing the War Ag, but there was no answer.'

'Ring army base,' Jack said. 'Ring RAF base, see if either of them'll feed you, being as we're all supposed to be in it together, now there's a war on. If not, you two can come to us, but we can't feed everyone.'

'Well, it's an idea, anyway,' Muriel said. 'Thanks, Jack.'

The other girls came back, and the warden's shaken sister went on her way.

'She denies all knowledge,' Audrey said. 'Her sister's not at her house, and nothing her sister does is anything to do with her, she says. She wouldn't give us her address, though, so we could go and see for ourselves.'

'I'll give you her address,' Jack said. 'There's a fork in

road after you get past Dog and Duck. You always take main road on your right, back to Elm Hall, but if you bear left instead and go up Pinfold Lane – she's at number six.'

'If Sarah says she's not there, she's not there,' Cissie insisted, with a reproachful glance at Jack. 'An' Sarah was walking in opposite direction, so there'll be nobody there.'

'Be a waste of time, then,' Audrey said.

They all went to ring the Army and Air Force camps, as Jack had suggested, and got a reasonably sympathetic hearing. Both promised to 'see what they could do'.

Later, as they were passing the Dog and Duck, they all halted, and looked thoughtfully towards Pinfold Lane.

'It's not much out of our way, is it?' Muriel said.

'Let's go and knock. I'm not convinced our warden's not there – in spite of what Cissie says,' said Audrey.

'Neither am I,' Joan said. 'I think that was just a sample of locals ganging up against outsiders.'

'Away, then, man,' Eileen said. 'She might even come to the door hersel'. We'll have her then.'

With their expedition up Pinfold Lane successfully completed, the chapel-goers all clambered back into the hostel via the library window, to be greeted by Barbara and Laura, both bursting with their news.

'You'll never guess who's been!' Barbara said. 'Miss Fawcett! She rolled up in her Morris Minor just before you got back; said she'd hoped to be invited to dinner. We asked her in, but she wouldn't climb through the window – said she didn't want to risk snagging her Sunday-best nylons. She's gone back to the War Ag to see if she can find any keys and something to feed us all with.'

Muriel burst into a peal of laughter. 'Oh, hell! We've rung the Army and Air Force bases as well, to ask them to send us their left-over dinner instead of chucking it in the swill bin,' she said, her eyes dancing. 'How's that for cheek?'

'Huh!' Audrey snorted. 'I always knew we'd be eating pigswill before we'd finished, and we'll be having it for Easter Sunday dinner.'

'That's if we're lucky and they bring it,' Eileen said. 'If Miss Fawcett turns up with bread and cheese as well, we'll have more than we can eat, man.'

'There's no such thing as more food than I can eat,' Joan said. 'I'm absolutely bloody starving. And if none of 'em bring any food, we'll starve to death.'

'You won't be starving much longer,' Muriel said. 'Somebody will have to do something. Be a laugh if they all turn up at once.'

'If only the warden could see what's been going on here, she'd cack hersel',' said Eileen. 'She thinks she's got us right under her thumb, sitting here starving, waiting on her rolling in at teatime – but she's one off!'

'The warden?' Barbara exclaimed, eyebrows raised. 'Did you track her down?'

'We did. We thought we might find her at her sister's, but there was nobody in,' Joan said.

'But the lass next door was out in her garden, and she told us we'd find our Miss Hubbard three doors further up,' said Eileen. 'And we did!'

'And whose house do you think that was?' Muriel asked, hugging herself with delight.

Her face pink, and smiling in anticipation, Barbara shook her head. 'For heaven's sake, tell me!' she pleaded.

'Sammy bloody Mawson's!' Audrey and Muriel chorused.

'Aye! And they looked so cosy together when we looked in you'd have taken them for an old married couple, man,' Eileen chuckled. 'I wouldn't be surprised if the old hen gets her feathers ruffled there, now and again.'

'Ugh! What a thought! But no couple were ever better matched, I'll give you that,' Vera said.

Miss Fawcett was the first to arrive, with a key for the front door and another for the office. None for the locked kitchen cupboards, unfortunately, but a car full of loaves, blocks of cheese, pots of chutney, tea and milk compensated for that. Some of the girls had just gone out to carry it all inside when a Land Rover drew up, and out jumped four army volunteers for the mercy mission, all friendly with the girls from their evenings at the Half Moon Inn. With much joking, mostly on the lines of England's answer to Hitler running Elm Hall, they carried in containers of sliced beef in gravy, mashed potato, roast parsnips, mushy peas and spotted dick and custard for 'afters', in quantities beyond the girls' most hopeful imagining. Next came the RAF in the shape of Laura's aircraftman and his pal, with their offering of roast pork with crackling, stuffing balls, roast potatoes, cabbage and – spotted dick and custard.

The bread and cheese was brushed aside, and the containers of still warm food laid out in the kitchen. Plates, knives and forks were soon produced and one War Ag rep and ten famished girls began to help themselves and carried their loaded plates into the dining room. Barbara had put the boiler on in anticipation of Miss Fawcett's return, and Laura let her food get cold while she made tea for the servicemen.

'There are some beautiful parquet floors in this place. It would be ideal for a dance,' Laura's new admirer commented, taking a cup of tea from her.

'Not much chance of that with our warden,' Joan said.

'No. She calls it Liberty Hall, but I assure you it's not,' Barbara said.

'Since she isn't here to defend herself I suggest we stay off the topic of Miss Hubbard,' Miss Fawcett said.

That put a damper on the conversation for quite a while, since the girls' heads were so full of Miss Hubbard that nobody seemed able to think of anything else to talk about. The meal was soon finished, many hands made light of the washing up, and the clean containers were carried back to the vehicles they came in. Laura had thoughtfully put more water to boil after making tea for the servicemen, and an order for 'cups of tea all round' was soon fulfilled. Girls and servicemen strolled round the hostel, into the library, the common room, and then most drifted into the garden with their tea.

Joan put a record on, and she and Muriel tried to teach a couple of the lads to do the jitterbug. Both seemed to have two left feet and no sense of timing. The girls abandoned the effort and turned the gramophone off.

'Hopeless,' Joan commented, out of their hearing. 'Not a patch on the Yanks.' They joined the others in the garden and were there when the warden returned.

'Who invited them here?' she demanded, glaring at the soldiers and RAF men.

'I did,' Audrey said.

The warden shook her head, breathing heavily. 'I ought to have known. I'll have something to say to you later. Get off this property, you lot! You're trespassing,' she said, rounding on the servicemen. 'You've no business here, and it's time you went.'

They all looked towards Miss Fawcett, who the warden had not noticed.

'Let them stay a little longer,' Miss Fawcett said. 'After all, the girls would have had nothing to eat today, had it not been for them.' The servicemen seemed happy to stay, and the girls seemed happy to detain them a little longer.

Miss Fawcett led the warden into the house. They heard her say: 'If you knew even half of what I've had to put up with, you wouldn't blame me . . .'

The two of them went into the office and firmly closed the door. The girls could only imagine the rest – but it was evident that the warden had no intention of going down without a fight. After about half an hour Miss Fawcett called Barbara into the office. Five minutes later she emerged, red in the face and with her eyes blazing – not a good omen, Muriel thought. Then it was Laura and Vera's turn. They came out pale, and with heads bowed.

Then Muriel was called in, together with Audrey.

'Miss Hubbard has made some very serious accusations against you,' she said. 'Among other things, she accuses you of going into her living quarters without her permission, to take items of her property.'

'We had her permission!' Audrey exclaimed. 'She knew all about it. She helped us.'

'Hmm,' the rep said, eyebrows raised in frank disbelief. 'Miss Hubbard also says that you damaged her dress form by deliberately throwing it down the stairs.'

The friends' response to this accusation was silence. Muriel could hardly pretend that tossing the dress form over the banister rail had been anything but deliberate.

'Defiant! She's a defiant little madam, that!' the warden exploded. 'I've done my absolute best with both of them, but they're a pair of liars and troublemakers and they'll never be any different. And that one,' she said, tilting her head in Audrey's direction, 'that one speaks German. They think people are stupid, but they give themselves away. She's probably a fifth columnist. And the other one,' indicating Muriel, 'is as thick as thieves with her. They go drinking in public houses to meet servicemen every Saturday, to pump them for information.'

'These girls have names, Miss Hubbard,' Miss Fawcett said. Receiving no reply she asked: 'Why didn't you report your suspicions to the police?'

'I did. They took no notice. Said I had no evidence.'

Throughout much of the interview Muriel had been looking over the warden's head towards the office cupboard, an antiquated, oaken piece as big as a wardrobe. 'Open that cupboard,' she suddenly said.

'See what I mean?' the warden said. 'No manners at all. I don't take orders from you, miss.'

Muriel scrutinised the warden's face and saw that she was shaken.

Miss Fawcett scrutinised Muriel just as intently. 'Open the cupboard, please, Miss Hubbard,' she said.

'I'm sorry,' the warden said, 'but I haven't been able to find the key for a day or two. One of the girls has probably taken it.'

Acting on an impulse, Muriel went to the cupboard and pulled at the doors. It was locked. She turned and opened the top drawer of the warden's desk. The warden grasped her wrist, and shut the drawer. Miss Fawcett ordered the warden to open the drawer. The warden refused, whereupon Miss Fawcett said that she intended to see what was in that cupboard, even if she had to break the lock to do it. She calmly ordered Muriel to fetch a couple of the servicemen to assist them. The warden gave in then, and let her open the drawer and take the keys. Miss Fawcett chose the likeliest-looking one and opened the cupboard, to reveal a sizeable hoard of sugar, tea, powdered milk, powdered egg, and every other variety of non-perishable rationed food that could be imagined.

Miss Fawcett turned to the warden. 'I think you'd better explain yourself.'

Miss Hubbard had nothing to say.

'That's not all of it,' Audrey said.

Miss Fawcett turned a look of astonishment on her. 'What do you mean, not all of it?'

'It's not as much as she had before, is what I mean,' Audrey said, 'and we haven't had any of it.'

'Now it's your turn to explain yourself,' Miss Fawcett said.

So Audrey made it very clear that the hoard they'd seen in the attic had been twice the size of the one that was now in the cupboard. The rest must have been hidden elsewhere, or disposed of.

Miss Fawcett demanded to know why they had not reported the matter immediately to the War Agricultural Executive Committee. The culprits answered by grossly overstating their sympathy for Miss Hubbard and their wish to avoid getting her into trouble, and by understating their own determination to keep all the hoarded rations for themselves and their friends. They entirely forgot to mention their use of threats of exposure as a means of forcing Miss Hubbard to bend to their will.

Miss Fawcett believed their explanations and saw straight through their attempts to whitewash their own base motives. She gave them both a severe reprimand for not reporting the matter, and for using their discovery to blackmail Miss Hubbard. Miss Hubbard was also given a severe reprimand, and a choice – she could either pack and leave without making any difficulties, or she could face criminal prosecution. Miss Hubbard chose to leave, and on the instant. Let the War Ag find someone else to look after this pack of ungrateful townie brats; she was sick of them all.

They left her to her packing then, with a warning to be sure to leave all the keys and any more hoarded rations behind her.

Miss Fawcett thanked the servicemen for their trouble, more or less dismissing them. The girls waved them off, then followed Miss Fawcett into the kitchen to make a meal of bread, cheese and chutney.

'What made you come on Easter Sunday, of all days?' Vera asked her as they ate.

'What better day to come for a sample of what you eat?'

'Why, we didn't think you believed us, when we were telling you about the food. We thought you'd been got at by the other rep,' Eileen said.

'She did have an influence, I admit,' Miss Fawcett smiled, 'but I thought you all looked rather gaunt. Not at all what people who are getting double rations ought to look like. So in spite of the wonderful meal Miss Hubbard gave us, I wasn't entirely convinced.'

'You're dead crafty,' Eileen said.

Miss Fawcett laughed. 'Not really. I just like to see things for myself. The problem now is getting someone to hold the fort, while we appoint another warden.'

'I vote for Barbara!' Audrey said, almost before Miss Fawcett had finished her sentence.

Muriel, Laura, Vera, Joan and everyone else also voted for Barbara.

Barbara blushed a bit, smiled, and said she'd rather act as warden than do anything else, while her leg was sore and her ankle encased in plaster. So Barbara was duly elected hostel warden, pro tem.

Miss Fawcett stayed to see Miss Hubbard off the premises and collected the keys from her. Then she got into her Morris Minor, declaring that she had had a most interesting afternoon. It had been quite exhilarating, in its way.

'Wait till tomorrow, when the others get back and we tell them what's been going on,' Muriel said. 'They'll get the shock of their lives.'

Chapter 26

They saw nothing of Ernst or Wilhelm during the whole of the following week. Muriel would have loved to hear more about Audrey's last encounter with Ernst, but now that she'd been assured he was 'getting over it all right', she felt she'd forfeited any right to mention him, in Audrey's eyes, at least. She would also have liked to broach the subject of Audrey and Wilhelm, but couldn't think of a way to do it without seeming too inquisitive. Audrey was saying nothing about either man and Muriel felt she couldn't say anything about them either. Talking about the men in the forefront of both their minds had suddenly become taboo.

It was busy on the farms the following week, but good to work in the sunshine and fresh air, knowing that when they got back to the hostel tired and hungry one of Barbara's hot meals would be ready for them. They got the whole of their meat ration now, nicely cooked in hotpots and stews, which made them wonder where half of it had gone before – to Sammy Mawson's, Muriel guessed. But even vegetable pie was palatable the way

Barbara did it – not soggy and tasteless like Miss Hubbard's, but well seasoned and not overcooked. There were always puddings or well-sweetened apple pies to follow the main dish, and later a supper of cocoa with fruit cake or scones, an unheard-of indulgence when the Prune was in charge. Barbara was making lavish use of the warden's hoard while it was still theirs, before the War Ag came to claim it. Miss Fawcett had wrought quite a change in all their lives, and as Barbara said, no new broom ever swept cleaner than she had.

Despite the better food and the changed regime, Audrey decided to go home the following Saturday, which fell on May Day. Muriel imagined her, talking openly about Wilhelm with her mother and her uncle. She would surely have no blanket condemnation of Germans dinned into *her* ears, in either of their households. How Muriel envied her. She had a letter from her mother later in the week saying, among other things, that the U-boats were fighting a losing battle according to the papers. Pity they hadn't lost it altogether before poor Ivy's Bill went down, but at least the other poor lads might be a bit safer. They were getting some stick from the RAF as well. They were getting a dose of their own, now.

Muriel wrote back with the news that she would be dancing at an American Army base the following week-end, and she'd known that the Germans were getting a dose of their own ever since she'd arrived at Griswold. They could hear the bomber squadrons flying over to Germany almost every other night, and they sometimes met some of the air and ground crew in the local pub. One girl's bloke had been killed during a raid, she said, but the lads didn't say much about any of it. Careless talk costs lives.

'This is where I was before I got sent to Griswold,' Joan said, with her head sticking out of the carriage window when they were in the last stages of their journey to her mother's in Norwich. 'I stopped at one of the farms round here for a bit before I went to the hostel, and I had to go round with a horse and cart selling milk round the village we're just coming up to – measure it out of a churn into the customers' jugs. The housewives used to give me cake, or biscuits. I hardly needed any dinner, when I'd finished. It was better in the hostel than living on the farm, though. Company your own age. More fun.'

'Everybody says that,' Muriel agreed. Since Audrey was going home for the weekend, Joan set herself the task of jolting Muriel out of the doldrums by taking her to Norwich, to stay with her mother and sister. They would go to a GI dance, and spend some time with boys who really knew how to enjoy themselves. If that didn't cheer her up, nothing would, Joan said. Muriel gratefully accepted the invitation.

'When I think how soft I used to have it here, it crazes me,' Joan moaned as she took in the view. 'And I bet the next lot of girls didn't turn out any better than us.'

'I bet they didn't.'

'Some Yanks were stationed near the farm, and I used to see them whizzing round the lanes in their jeeps, and sometimes they'd go hedge-hopping in their monoplanes. They didn't half used to scare the cattle and horses. There, over there,' Joan said, pointing to a distant farmhouse, 'that's where I was. The Yanks used to come to the farm door and buy eggs and butter. Oh, they were lovely. Always so clean and smart, and polite.'

'I wonder what they think to us,' Muriel said.

'They think we're all right. After three dates, they wanted to marry you, some of them, but I used to back off when it got to that stage. I could never leave my mum, not for anybody.'

'Three dates?' Muriel repeated, imagining that the dates from date palms must be associated with some strange American courtship ritual.

'Dates you've arranged to meet on. You know – calendar dates. After you've been out together about three times. That's what they call going out with someone – dating. I thought everyone knew that, from the films.'

'Oh, aye,' Muriel said, as the light dawned. 'I just never thought of anybody saying it in real life.'

It was a very dubious expression on the face that stared back at Muriel from the long mirror in Joan's mother's bedroom. Joan was already dressed and ready, and was sitting at the kitchen table downstairs, telling her mother all about Griswold. They had eaten very little after arriving, in anticipation of stuffing themselves to bursting point at the GI base.

'Are you sure this frock's really good enough, Joyce?' she asked Joan's sister. 'It's a bit plain for a posh dance.'

'It's not a posh dance,' Joyce reassured her. 'It's nothing out of the ordinary, for them. Anyway, most GIs hardly notice frocks. They're more interested in your face and figure, and whether you can dance.'

'Hmm!' Muriel grimaced at herself, not entirely convinced about the frock. The rest of her looked all right though – dark hair curled with Joyce's tongs, eyebrows plucked and pencilled into a fashionable arch, and lips painted a vivid red.

'Come on then, get your coat and let's be off. Best foot forward.'

They collected Joan, and went out through the front door of the family's terraced house in Magpie Road to walk through the street in their Land Army coats and dancing shoes until they reached the spot where an American Army truck was supposed to be picking them up. Other girls began to gather, and talk about the GIs, the music, and above all, the food, until Muriel's mouth began to water. At the appointed time the truck appeared. Muriel, Joan, her sister and their friends were hauled in and whisked away in a hair-raisingly fast, madly exciting and bumpy ride north-west along the Fakenham Road. They soon reached the American airbase, and stopped beside a hangar. The band music they could hear was as good as anything Glenn Miller played, and when they got inside they found couples already dancing.

'I love to be on the dance floor,' Joan's sister said, as the three of them stood on the edge of it, waiting for partners.

'Are you as good at dancing as Joan?' Muriel asked, as a GI approached them.

He asked Joyce for a dance. She put her hand in his. 'Better!' she threw over her shoulder as she took the floor with him.

Joan and Muriel were soon whisked onto the dance floor as well, and Muriel found that everything Joan had said about the GIs was true. At last the band stopped for a break, and food was served by the canteen system. Muriel grabbed a plate and followed a queue of people passing along a long table, filling their plates with whatever took their fancy. Chicken drumsticks, slices of ham, cheese, and pastries of different sorts. At three points along the table stood huge iced cakes, with inscriptions on them – WLA, WAAF and ATS, and vats of butter, jam, and something called peanut butter, which Muriel had never seen before. She watched, horrified, as the GI in front of her spread half a week's ration of butter on one slice of bread, and then topped it with peanut butter and a week's ration of jam. Joan and Joyce didn't bat an eyelid, evidently not quite so fixed with the idea that eating more than two ounces of butter in a week was verging on criminal, and quite used to seeing two weeks' rations consumed in one sitting. They were passing down the table ahead of her, happily employed in piling their plates and surreptitiously stuffing chunks of this and slices of that into their handbags.

'Weigh in, honey,' the GI in behind her said. So Muriel weighed in until her plate was loaded, regretting the fact that she lacked a brazen enough face to follow her friends' example, and fill her handbag into the bargain.

'It's like another world!' she murmured to Joan when they sat down to eat. 'How is it that the Americans can manage to get so much food into the country, when we can barely get enough to feed ourselves?'

'I dunno. Perhaps the Germans don't torpedo their ships,' Joan shrugged. 'They get it, anyhow.'

A young woman with a West Midlands accent further along was holding forth about the Germans. 'My father used to go to Germany on business, even during the phoney war. He used to take us sometimes, until things got too hot,' she said. 'He liked a lot of them, but after Hitler took charge some of them began to think they were world-beaters. He used to say: "I could do with the Germans, but they really have got the idea that they're the Master Race."'

'It's instilled in them. They're surly as well, even to their own, a lot of the time,' another girl said. 'There's a German prisoner of war camp near where I live, and some of them would have been willing to work for their keep, if they hadn't been bullied out of it by the rest.'

Muriel's thoughts flew to the bullying Nazi, who'd spat at her. She could quite see how a few of that sort could intimidate the rest.

'They're brought up to think they're better than everyone else – anything you can do, we can do better, sort of
style.'

'It must be a national characteristic. Scratch the surface,
and they're all the same underneath. Arrogant.'

And Ernst, Muriel thought, while the conversation
flowed on in the same vein – was he the same underneath? He was certainly bossy – their national characteristic, maybe. '*Komm mit! Komm!*' he'd ordered, and with
such an air of authority that she had *komm*ed! Trotted to
him as docile as a lamb! Well, perhaps not trotted, but
staggered and stumbled, at any rate. She wondered why
she had, and then threw in her two penn'orth about bossy,
arrogant Germans.

'They are bossy,' she said. 'They'll have us all goose-
stepping like them if we ever let them take England over.'

The words were no sooner out of her mouth than she
shrivelled inside.

'You've got Uncle Sam's Army here now, honey.
We're here to stop them in their tracks,' an American
airman grinned.

But now she felt like a traitor, and it was a conversation
she wanted no further part in. She gave the airman a
pained smile and walked away, over to a table full of
glasses of orange juice. And really, when she thought
about it, no German could possibly be any worse than
that bloody English farmer who'd knocked Barbara down
and broken her ankle. But no, she hadn't thought about
it. Instead she'd let herself be carried along by all that

anti–German talk until she'd betrayed the man who'd sworn undying love to her, and betrayed her own feelings into the bargain.

So what? she asked herself aggressively, like someone out of an American gangster film. So what? It could never be any good. He was German, she was English, that was the end of it. She gave a bleak little laugh then, at the thought that it was the end of something that had never really begun. They'd never so much as been to the pictures together. Even the Valentine had been a mirage. They'd exchanged a few kisses, and that was all. She was talking herself out of something that had never existed.

The American airman who was going to save England from the Germans walked across to her.

'You seem pretty upset, sweetheart. Don't be. They're good fighters, but we've just kicked their asses in Medjex. Yesterday's fighting in Tunisia was the bloodiest in the whole African campaign, but we came out on top – and they're taking some punishment at home from our bombers. Don't worry. They can't win. They've got too much against them.'

She was upset, too upset to reply. The band struck up with a lively number.

He offered her his hand. 'Come on, honey, let's dance, and forget the Germans.'

He led her onto the dance floor, for a jive so fast that there was no room in her head for any thought except movement and rhythm and staying on her feet. The music was better than Joe Loss, better than Glenn Miller, or any other dance band she'd ever heard. It was exhilarating. She lost herself in trying to follow his lead and catch his hand after the spins. Then just as a jitterbug contest was being announced from the stage he spun her too fast – she missed her hold and skittered across the dance floor – to land in the lap of another Yank.

'You get women throwing themselves at you in England, Fred,' the man beside him laughed.

Fred's blue eyes were wide and round, and his crew-cut fair hair emphasised his look of surprise. 'Gee, honey, you only had to ask!' he said. 'Sure I'll give you a dance.'

But Muriel's partner came over to apologise, and claim her back.

Fred held on to her. 'Catchers keepers,' he said. 'She's mine, now.'

Muriel laughed, spread her hands and shrugged. A minute later she was on her feet with Fred, and lining up with other couples, waiting for him to have a number pinned onto his back. They were well matched. He was slim and very well proportioned, and only about five inches bigger than her. He lifted her hand, now scrubbed and bleached clean, and commented on the calluses, chapped backs and broken nails.

'Women's Land Army,' she explained.

'Sure, WLA; I know that, but some girls say it stands for We Love Americans,' he grinned.

She grinned back. 'It might as well – round here.'

Joan and Joyce were also in the queue, with other GIs. When the contestants were all numbered, the band struck up again, and Muriel found herself jitterbugging to a tune she'd danced to a thousand times before, in the hostel. Fred danced with less force and fury than her other partner but with better timing and more finesse. They synchronised perfectly.

'Gee, honey, my mom . . .'

But she lost the rest, concentrating on the dancing until, one by one, other couples were asked to leave the floor. She spotted Joan and Joyce occasionally, both dancing like demons, but in the end she and Fred were the only ones still on the dance floor, and couple number nine were acclaimed the winners.

Fred was ecstatic. 'Honey, you're dynamite! Wait till I tell my mom I won a jitterbug contest – with an English lady! She'll never believe it. And I don't even know your name!'

'Muriel,' she grinned. 'Muriel Dearlove.'

'Muriel Dear Love,' he echoed, his blue eyes gazing into hers. 'Well, Muriel Dearlove, here's Fred Sears, at your service. But not the Sears and Roebuck Sears, honey,' he joked. 'Don't get too excited.'

Muriel didn't get excited at all. The joke was lost on her, since she'd never heard of Sears and Roebuck, or their catalogue of mail order goods, which she soon learned was sent to every corner of America.

A man came to take their names and occupations, and their shoe sizes, of all things. When they were called up to the stage, the Master of Ceremonies took Muriel's hand. 'This little lady does a farmhand's work, but she sure doesn't jitterbug like one! Congratulations, honey. You deserve to get a medal at the end of the war, but for now, here's something for your leisure hours.'

He gave her six pairs of size 9 block-heeled nylons. Unheard-of luxury! She was delighted. Fred got three pairs of silk socks.

In the kitchen in Magpie Road, Joan and Joyce opened their handbags and tipped out the loot – another feast for their mum. Chicken drumsticks, cheese, a banana and various other squashed but still quite tasty odds and ends.

Muriel emptied her own bag, which she'd filled when the dance was nearly over and she'd realised that all the rest of that beautiful food was destined for the bin. 'I was wishing I'd had two stomachs,' she said. 'They brought tinned peaches and ice cream out for pudding, but I was too full to eat much more.'

'I only wish they'd have a dance every night,' the girls' mother said. 'We wanted for nothing in this house when they were both going out with the Yanks. Then Joan had to go and get herself moved up to Yorkshire, and spoil it all.'

'Yeah, and then I teach the Yorkshire lasses to dance, and bring one of 'em down here to pinch six pairs of nylons off me. I wish I'd never brought her now!' Joan declared, and only half in jest. 'She only just pipped us to the post. Me and Jim were the last to be ordered off the floor.'

'You lucky so and so!' Joyce exclaimed, with covetous eyes on the nylons. 'They're like gold!'

Muriel pushed two packets each towards them.

The sisters pushed them back. 'They're no good to me, they're too small,' Joyce said.

'We'd push our toes through the end the first time we wore them. You keep them, but remember who it was that helped you to win them,' said Joan.

'Okay, honey,' Muriel grinned, in her best Yankee accent. 'You brought me here to cheer me up, and you've sure succeeded.'

'What did I tell you? The Yanks know how to enjoy themselves, and they treat you like a lady.'

'They do,' Muriel said. 'They can talk a donkey's hind leg off, as well.'

'Yeah, you never have to think of much to say when you're with them,' Joyce said, 'and they're as smart as paint.'

'They're great boys, and honey, can they jitterbug!' Muriel mimicked. 'That was the best dance I've ever had in my life, that contest.'

'Yeah, well, you remember who taught you, and don't you dare scare the life out of me with any more ghosts,' Joan warned.

That piqued Joyce's curiosity. 'What's all this about ghosts?' she demanded, so they sat up till two o'clock in the morning, while Joan told that, and other tales of Griswold.

Chapter 27

The following day, Muriel was in agonies watching Joan shilly-shallying about instead of getting ready, when they had to catch the last train north. When she was finally dressed and her bag was packed, Joan decided that she couldn't go without saying goodbye to the neighbours. Instead of the promised two minutes, she took a quarter of an hour. Even so, with Joyce and her mother helping them to carry the luggage, they finally managed to get to the station and onto the platform with two whole minutes to spare, much to Muriel's relief. To Muriel's surprise, Fred was waiting for them, with a parcel. He thrust it into her hands.

'I won it in a crap game. It's too small for me, but it should fit you okay. And honey – thanks for the best dance I ever had.'

'Oh, I've just got time to go to the toilet,' Joan said. 'I hate going on the train.'

She dumped her luggage and disappeared. Muriel called her back, but her protests fell on deaf ears. The train's engine started, and the porter began to slam carriage doors. Muriel snatched up her suitcase and looked frantically for Joan.

Fred caught up to the station-master. They saw him gesticulating towards the ladies' waiting room. Another minute ticked by, then the station-master shook his head, and gave the signal. The last carriage door was slammed and the train began to move. Muriel was on tenterhooks, torn between making a dash for it and getting on without Joan, or waiting a moment longer. She waited too long, and watched with anger and dismay as the train pulled out of the station without them.

Joan eventually sauntered back to them. 'Oh, dear,' she said, looking at the clouds of smoke and the back of the far-distant last carriage. 'Has it gone?'

Muriel was hopping mad. 'You did that on purpose,' she accused.

'No, I didn't,' Joan said, complacently, 'but the War Ag owes us a day for the Easter bank holiday anyway, so we might as well have it today.'

Fred poured oil on troubled waters. 'Better take your cases back, I guess,' he said. 'Then how about I take you to the movies, Miss Dearlove?'

Miss Dearlove accepted the invitation. They took the luggage back to Magpie Road, and then Joan went to telephone the hostel and explain how unlucky they had been to miss their train, and how terribly sorry they were. Muriel went to the pictures with Fred, and Joan went off with her sister – to meet their favourite GIs.

★ ★ ★

'Why, did you meet anybody nice enough to fall in love with?' Eileen asked, when they were sitting in the common room the following evening.

'I did, and he gave me a silk shirt,' Muriel said, pulling at the collar of the one she was wearing. 'Said he won it in a crap game. It's a bit big, but it feels lovely on, after the bloody War Ag shirts. He gave me chocolate and ciggies, as well.'

'What's a crap game?'

'You're as wise as I am. Something to do with dice, I think,' Muriel said.

Feeling as rich as Croesus she handed her cigarettes round and thought: why bother with Germans? They're the enemy. They're bossy, they don't speak the language, they've got no money, they don't feed you, they don't get you six pairs of nylons or give you silk shirts, or chocolate or chewing gum or cigarettes, and they can't take you dancing, or to the pictures. Why bother? What have the Germans got to offer? Nothing. Not a darned thing, honey – except to bring a heap of trouble down on your head from everyone else. She would be better off with an American.

'What's he like, then?' Vera asked.

'Nice. Nineteen, and not all that much bigger than me. He talks about his mother a lot – "Gee, honey, my mom just couldn't believe I got all the way over to England without getting lost, and losing half of my luggage!" Then when we were walking through Norwich to the pictures, he says: "Gee, honey, if my mom could see me now, finding my way around England, she'd be so surprised!"'

'He sounds like a bit of a mother's boy,' Laura said.

'He's not really. I think he's just a country boy that's never been away from home before, like a lot of the Yanks. Like a lot of ours, come to that.'

'Like us, except most of us come from the towns,' said Vera.

'Doesn't sound as if his mother thinks much to him, anyway,' Audrey said.

Muriel laughed at that. 'She probably does, she probably loves him to bits. I know I would, if I were his "mom". But I saw why she might be worried when we got to the pictures, and he couldn't find his money. He was feeling in all his pockets, and you could see the panic on his face. He'd broken out into a sweat before he finally found it – in the first place he'd looked.'

'He sounds like an idiot,' said Audrey.

'Leave him alone, will you?' Muriel laughed. 'He's just a young lad, having to fend for himself in a strange place. It's quite endearing, really.'

'You had a good time with the Yanks, then,' Audrey said.

'I did. I wish you'd learn to dance, Audrey, you'd enjoy it.'

'Nah,' Audrey said. 'I've got two left feet.'

Muriel smiled and shook her head, knowing it would be pointless to press the argument. She turned to Barbara. 'Have you heard anything from Farmer Hogg, yet, Barbara?'

'No, and I didn't really expect to.'

'Are you still taking him to court?'

Barbara's eyebrows twitched upwards, as if she were surprised by the question. 'Well, he can't be allowed to get away with it, can he?' she said.

Her calm grey eyes and quiet determination made Muriel smile. 'No, he can't,' she agreed.

'I don't know as we want this pair in here, after all the trouble they've brought down on our Sadie,' Sammy Mawson told the director, when Muriel and Audrey walked into the hall for an evening's whist that Friday.

'Our Sadie,' Muriel noted. They were related, then. The girls stopped in their tracks, and the hum of conversation died down, the better for everyone to hear what these mischief-making townies had to say for themselves.

'Go on, get out of it, trouble causers,' Sammy said, waving them away.

'If you're talking about our warden, as was,' Audrey said, 'we didn't bring any trouble down on her, she brought it down on herself, without any help from us.'

'And we're a lot better fed since she's gone,' Muriel said, giving him the sweetest of smiles, 'so we'll just leave it at that, shall we?'

But Sammy was not a man to be gainsaid by a slip of a girl. He had no intention of leaving it at that. He was determined to make a public show of them. 'You've done her out of her job and her home,' he glowered. 'She didn't bring that down on herself. It was your spite brought that down on her.'

Sammy's was just the sort of attitude to bring out the worst in Audrey. Her eyes narrowed and her jaw tightened. 'Seeing as you've started this public debate about who's done who out of what, and seeing as you mean to press on regardless, even though we've asked you to drop the subject, we'll have it out,' she said, not troubling to keep her voice down. 'Your Sadie, as you call her, has been keeping us on starvation rations for months. On Easter Sunday she decided she wasn't going to feed us at all – you'll remember that, because that was the day we found her at *your house*, Sammy! So after I'd telephoned the army and the air force, begging for their left-overs because she'd deliberately locked every crumb of food up and we were all famished, the woman from the War Ag came, and found a cupboard stuffed full of *our rations* in *your Sadie's* office! What do you think about that, Sammy? What do all your friends here tonight think about it? You think we're so spineless we're going to put up with that?'

'Miss Hubbard and Mr Mawson, to you, you . . .'

'And that wasn't the whole amount, either, because we'd found a hoard twice the size, weeks before! So how have you been doing for rations, then, Mr Mawson? Have you been getting a share of ours?' Muriel demanded.

'I have not!' Sammy bellowed at her.

'Well, if it wasn't you, it must have been her sister,' Audrey said. 'That follows, because it was her sister who was earwigging on the telephone line when we tried ringing the War Ag about it months ago – and she tipped your Sadie the wink just in time to stop the War Ag rep from seeing what was really going on.'

'It warn't her sister, neither.'

'Well, if you're saying it wasn't you, and it wasn't her sister, you're admitting that Miss Hubbard did pinch our rations,' Muriel said, 'so it must have been someone else.'

'I'm admitting nothing,' Sammy snarled, and then he did what Muriel had tried to make him do at the outset, before all these damaging revelations had come to light. He shut up.

'Very wise,' Muriel said. 'Seeing as the woman from the War Ag told Miss Hubbard that she wouldn't be prosecuted if she didn't make difficulties. And now you're making difficulties for her, because if you hadn't said anything about it, we wouldn't have said anything about it, Mr Mawson.'

There was a deathly hush. Muriel and Audrey were in instant, unspoken rapport. They did not 'get out of it', as Sammy had ordered them to do, but pulled their shoulders back and lifted their chins, and sat with Jack and Cissie as usual, determined to hold their own among these tight-knit village folk who all seemed to be related to each other, one way or other. As they were learning, an offence against one was usually an offence against all, and all closed ranks against outsiders. They were not going to turn tail and run — if any of the villagers other than Sammy wanted them to leave, they'd have to stand up and say so. Audrey started drumming her fingers on the table.

Sammy didn't leave the hall either, but sat with his arms folded, scowling at the floor. The hum of conversation gradually resumed. The girls felt a few disapproving glances cast in their direction, but nobody said a word, except Cissie.

'It's a pity you couldn't ha' done it without getting her the sack, though,' she murmured.

'We did try,' Muriel said. 'But she wouldn't have it.'

'It was the cupboard full of our hoarded rations got her the sack,' Audrey said, 'and she's lucky it wasn't worse than the sack.'

After a minute or two Sammy glanced up at the clock. 'Is Goodyear coming tonight, or what?' he roared.

John Goodyear and his father walked in a minute later. Play started as soon as they were seated. Thanks to their practice with the card-sharps in the hostel, Muriel and Audrey did better than ever before.

'There's an atmosphere you could cut with a knife in here, tonight,' John commented, when play stopped for tea and bread cakes, 'and you two seem to be getting a few dirty looks.'

'Sticks and stones may break our bones, but dirty looks can't harm us,' Audrey said.

'What have you been up to?'

'Nothing,' Muriel said, as if butter wouldn't have melted in her mouth.

He burst into laughter. 'I bet that's what you used to tell your teachers. Where were you last Saturday, anyway?'

'Winning a jitterbug contest, with a GI.'

'How can that stand comparison with talking about silage in the Half Moon?' he joked.

She laughed. 'It can stand it all right. When did I ever win six pairs of nylons talking about silage?'

He raised his eyebrows, fixed a pair of bright eyes on her and gave her a smile and a nod. 'You might win a lot more than that, if you play your cards right.'

Muriel gave him her sweetest smile. 'We seem to be playing them all right tonight, anyway.'

When they got to Sammy's table, he barely spoke and never met their eyes, but sat sullenly through all the hands. It was no contest. Wherever Sammy's mind was, it was not on the game. They won four out of five hands, and annihilated him.

Chapter 28

'We ought to have a dance in here. We ought to throw a party, to thank all the lads in the army and the RAF for coming to the rescue on Easter Sunday,' Joan said, when they sat down to dinner the following day.

Laura promptly seconded her. 'Yes, we should! What about it, Barbara?'

'There'll be a lot of work involved. Who's going to do all that? My time's fully occupied with cooking and running the hostel.'

'We'll all do it,' Laura promised.

'Yeah, we'll all muck in,' Joan said. 'We'll invite the boys from both camps, and make a real night of it.'

'Not all of them, I hope,' Barbara said. 'There's a limit to how many the place will hold.'

'We'll have it next Saturday. Invite them when we go to the Half Moon tonight,' Joan said.

'Oh, the landlord will love us for that,' Muriel laughed.

'Friday, then.'

'Nearly as bad, for him.'

'We should have it the next time there's a full moon,

then it won't be so bad for them to drive in the blackout,' Barbara said.

Laura looked at the calendar. 'That's a Wednesday – two weeks away!'

'A week and a half, you mean,' Barbara said. 'We'll have it on the Friday. If you know you've got to get up the following day, you'll pack them off at a reasonable time.'

'No, we won't. We'll keep them all night, and go straight to work from the party,' Joan said.

'Twelve o'clock's the deadline, whichever day,' Barbara warned, 'or that will be the last party while I'm in charge.'

'Ooh, you are hard,' Vera protested. 'We thought electing our own warden would give us a bit of leeway.'

'Let you turn the place into Liberty Hall, you mean?' Barbara laughed. 'No fear!'

'Will you be fit to dance, Barbara?'

'No. It will be another two weeks before the pot comes off.'

'How's the battle with Farmer Hogg going?' Muriel asked. 'Did he answer your letter? Has he coughed any damages up?'

'What do you think? But I've written again, to give him another chance. If he doesn't answer I shall take further steps.'

Muriel nodded. 'The ones up to the court.'

'Of course.'

Someone started banging the door knocker. Muriel

and few of the other girls flew to the window, to see who
it was. Sarah Beckett, the warden's sister! Muriel went to
the door.

'I've got something to say – and I want everyone to
hear it, so there's no mistake,' she burst out, flushed and
breathing heavily.

'They're having their dinner. What is it?' Muriel asked,
eyes wide with surprise.

'I'll tell you all together.'

'All right,' Muriel said, and showed her into the dining
room. The chatter died away, and the silence reminded
Muriel of the intimidating silence that had greeted her
and Audrey in the village hall the evening before, but
Sarah Beckett had her speech prepared. She stood her
ground and ploughed on with it.

'I've heard what was said at the whist drive yesterday,'
she began. 'I admit I rang my sister after some of you rang
the Agricultural Committee, but that was just to tell her
that she'd better start giving you the meals you were due
to, before she got herself into a lot of trouble. I wish I'd
never done it now, but that doesn't mean I had anything
to do with the rations – I didn't. We might be sisters but
I certainly had nothing to do with *that*. I did my best to
make her stop. I just want to make it clear to *everyone* that
I never touched any of your rations. I've never as much as
had a grain of sugar belonging to anybody else, and I
wouldn't, either. I've got my job with the post office to
think about, and if they got a hint of any dishonesty, that
would be the end of it. So I want my name cleared. If you

want to know where your rations went, ask Sammy Mawson and the landlady at the Dog and Duck. As far as I know he was taking some of the stuff there, and swapping it for drinks.'

'Thanks,' Audrey said. 'We'll see what the War Ag says about it.'

Sarah Beckett went pale. 'I'm sorry to go against my own family, but I've got my job to think about.'

'What relation is Sammy Mawson to you?' Muriel asked.

'Hardly any, really. Third cousin umpteen times removed. Sadie started getting pally with him after his wife died.'

'Do you believe her?' Joan asked, after Sarah Beckett had gone.

'Aye, I think I do,' Audrey said. 'She's a telephonist – nice steady job, not hard work, decent pay – you can understand her not wanting to lose that. And at least she didn't start calling us liars, like her sister did.'

'What do you think we ought to do, Barbara? Do you think we should go to the War Ag?' Muriel asked.

'Well, the rep seems happy to let it drop,' Barbara said.

'It would certainly stir up a hornets' nest in their family,' Audrey grinned. 'You can just imagine half the village siding with one sister and the other half with the other. It might even start the Griswold Civil War.'

'I'd say the warden's been punished enough; she lost her job and her living quarters, so justice has been done there,' Barbara said, quietly. 'I'm tempted to say let sleeping dogs lie.'

'But we're not going to let that woman at the Dog and

Duck get away with it, are we, after her high and mighty attitude to us?' Eileen demanded.

'No wonder she didn't want Land Girls in her pub,' Joan said.

'Well, there's not much we can do about it without involving the police – which might make us very unpopular in the village,' Barbara said. 'We don't want to be at war with them all. Let's sleep on it for a while.'

There weren't many men in the Half Moon that night, so the girls were issuing invitations to everyone there.

'What are you trying to do, ruin me? And in my own pub!' the landlord protested, when he found out what was happening.

'It's only one night!' Muriel told him. 'And they'll have to bring their own booze if they want any, so you might be able to sell them a drop before they come. Then you can shut the pub, and come to the party.'

He looked thoughtful. 'Hmm. You've got it all worked out, haven't you?'

'There's one thing we haven't worked out. Do you know any musicians?'

'Well, some of the lads play the piano, as you've heard. And a couple play the banjo.'

'Oh!' Muriel groaned. 'Not exactly Glenn Miller, is it?'

'No, but look on the bright side,' he said, a smile suddenly brightening his face and showing the gap in his teeth. 'They won't be charging Glenn Miller's prices – they'll be doing it for nixie. And if you get everyone tanked up on my booze they'll hardly notice, and they won't care one way or the other even if they do.'

Muriel bought cider for herself and Audrey, and went to sit with her outside, at the back of the inn.

'Isn't it beautiful? So peaceful,' Muriel said, watching the ducks gliding on the pond, the ripples in their wake tinged red by the setting sun.

The air began to vibrate with the sound of aircraft, off on one of their many midnight flights to Germany.

'Bombers,' Muriel shivered. 'I hope they're not going anywhere near Ernst's mother and sisters. I don't know what he'd do if anything happened to them.'

'Or Wilhelm's wife and sons, come to that,' said Audrey. 'Same thing applies.'

Muriel looked at her. 'I know you love him, Audrey,' she said.

Audrey's face softened. 'Aye. When I'm near Wilhelm, I feel as if I've come home,' she said. 'I've never felt like that with anybody else. Worse luck for me it's not the same for him, isn't it? He's got another home.' There was such a light in her eyes and such a queer mix of joy and sadness in her expression when she spoke about him that Muriel's heart went out to her.

'The very worst,' she said.

Chapter 29

The mere sight of the rising sun, spreading its golden light over the earth, lifted Muriel's spirits. What in the world could there possibly be to beat the sheer joy of being alive in the English countryside in the merry month of May?

She nudged Audrey, who was sitting beside her in the lorry. 'Look at that! Can you wonder that so many folk songs begin with the words: "As I walked out one May morning"?' she demanded, still looking at the dawn.

Audrey looked at that, and appeared unimpressed. 'No. Can't say I ever did. Maybe none of them walked out until the weather got warmer.'

How was it possible to be alive, and not be in love with the earth and everything in it on a day like this? Muriel wondered. 'Well, it's warm now, and it's going to be a lovely day,' she said.

The driver set them down with Eileen and Joan beside a large, undulating field planted with row upon row of turnips, raised up like ribs from the earth. The farmer handed them a hoe each. Their job was to walk between the rows with the hoe and uproot the weeds, or cut their tops off, he said. Weed killing was a constant battle, and he'd prefer them to do it without killing the turnips, as well. One set of Land Girls had destroyed half his plants. They'd only been there for a morning, and he'd never seen a field with so many bald patches. He didn't want a repetition of *that*, he said, fixing a stern eye on them.

With this encouragement they started hoeing. It was monotonous, rhythmic, pleasant enough work, walking side by side, moving steadily forward with the sun on their backs and no other noise than the scraping of the hoes against the earth, the song of the birds, and the sound of their own voices. Whatever a person's troubles might be, such soothing, mindless, repetitious work in the sun and air, surrounded by all the beauty of the countryside, must make them easier to bear, Muriel thought.

'Pity there won't be anybody there to give us a *real* dance, Muriel,' Joan said, talking about the forthcoming party at the hostel. 'There won't be anybody that can dance like Fred.'

'There won't be a band that can play like their band, either,' Muriel said. 'It'll be a piano and a couple of banjos if we're lucky, and dancing to records if we're not. And Barbara does well, but she can't do a spread like theirs.'

'There won't be a spread at all,' Audrey said. 'I'll chip in for their comfort funds till the cows come home when we go to the whist drives, but I draw the line at giving them my rations. They'd better make sure they've had plenty to eat before they come.'

'Ooh, you are mean!' Joan said.

'And they'd better bring their own booze, an' all,' said Eileen.

'And I hope they don't forget to bring some for us,' Muriel said.

'"Will you come to my party, will you come? Bring your own bread and butter, and a bun,"' Audrey chanted. 'Except it was bring your own cup and plate as well, round our way.'

'All we'll be contributing is our company, by the sound of it,' Muriel said.

'That's enough, isn't it?' Joan laughed.

'It'll have to be. It's all we've got, man,' said Eileen.

'We might manage a few scones or something, for a bit of supper . . .'

The chatter continued. Muriel stood for a moment, to breathe the air, take in the view and listen to the lark singing high overhead. She just caught a glimpse of a rabbit, darting out of the hedge, and the white streak of his tail as he took cover again. She turned and raised a hand to shade her eyes against the sun, curious to see how far they had come. Two prisoners of war were repairing the hedges at the bottom of the field, but the sun and the distance prevented her from seeing them clearly. But the way one of them stood, the way he moved reminded her . . . With a terrific fluttering in her stomach she turned back, lamenting the fact that every scrape of the hoe took her further away from him. If it were really Ernst! Oh, if only they could still be friends.

When the farmer's wife came with the tea, the girls walked over to meet her. She gave them their tea and looked towards the prisoners, who showed no sign of walking the distance to join them.

'What's up wi' them today? They usually come for lounces with everyone else!' she said, and started off towards them with tea and bread and cheese.

'I'll take them,' Audrey volunteered.

The farmer's wife took a bottle of tea and some newspaper-wrapped sandwiches out of the bag and handed them over. 'It's quite a walk,' she said.

'It's not that far, and I could do with a nice, brisk walk.'

The farmer's wife shrugged and left with her empty bag.

'What's she want to go running off to them for?' Joan demanded as Audrey started off down the field. 'Why don't they come to us? They always have before.'

Because it was Ernst, Muriel thought, with her feelings in turmoil. That was why they didn't come. He was here, in the same field, and he wouldn't come to talk to her.

She was back to where she'd started, before all Joan's efforts towards cheering her up, she thought, as the lorry rattled along the lanes on the journey back to the hostel. She was devastated, and she had no business to be so utterly devastated. She was the one who had broken it off with Ernst, and she had made it clear that the end was final through the message she'd sent to him with Audrey. No decent man pushes himself where he's not wanted.

Ernst had behaved well, and she was distraught, because deep down she hadn't meant it. Deep down, she wanted him to take her in his arms and drive away all those fears that separated her from him.

Somebody started singing: 'Pack up your troubles in your old kitbag and smile, smile, smile . . .' and the rest joined in. She looked at Audrey, sitting opposite her, now singing at the top of her lungs. Useless trying to talk to her about it, and there was nobody else. Audrey would never understand, because she would have acted differently. Audrey would have stolidly gone on with it, come hell or high water. But she had no opposition at home, and neither, Muriel suspected, had she much imagination. Although she'd had the example of the way her own family had been treated, it seemed to have left no mark on her. Audrey was not susceptible to imaginary terrors. She seemed incapable of meeting trouble halfway, or anticipating how nasty people could be.

She wouldn't look to her friends for comfort any more. She refused to bore them with her misery any longer. She would put a bright face on things, just as she'd seen Howard do, that night he'd gone to the piano and played a jolly tune rather than give way to grief about Guy. She would jolt herself out of it the same way. She refused to pine. Laugh, and the world laughs with you, Laura had said, and even she was laughing now.

A few girls were gathered round the notice board outside the office when they got back to the hostel. Muriel and Audrey joined them, and read a notice from the War Ag, inviting them to apply for week-long courses, with a choice of pig farming, poultry farming, dairy farming, or general farming.

'That might make a change,' Muriel said. 'I might have another go at milking a cow. What do you think, Audrey?'

'I'd rather learn to drive a tractor,' Audrey said.

'You've got some post, Muriel,' Joan said, carrying her own letters into the common room. 'One of them's from Fred.'

'How do you know that?' Muriel demanded.

'Attlebridge postmark.'

The other letters were from Auntie Ivy and her mother, both giving her the latest from Morley Villas. Ivy's letter was full of her hopes of a medium at the spiritualist church and her mother's was unusually affectionate.

So, Auntie Ivy was going to the spiritualist church. Did she ever meet Doris Chapman there, Muriel wondered?

Chapter 30

Fred was coming up to Griswold on a two-day pass, and Muriel and Joan cycled to meet him on the tiny railway platform known as the Griswold Halt, bowling a spare bike along the road with them.

'Gee, I sure am glad to see you two!' he exclaimed. 'I was kinda worried I might miss a train, or take the wrong connection, or something,' he said. Again, his haircut, his round blue eyes and his open, boyish face emphasised his look of relief and surprise at himself for having made it so far without mishap.

'You did well to get here all right; this place is not exactly on the beaten track,' Muriel said. 'What was the journey like?'

'Packed in like sardines, honey!' he said, cheerfully. 'So tight I was worried about getting to the doors to get my connections. A lot of servicemen and quite a few Land Girls on the train, as well.'

'Well, here you are!' Muriel smiled. 'We've booked you a room in the Half Moon Inn. Nobody in the village can remember anybody ever staying there before, so don't expect luxury. The landlord's a good sort though, so you'll be all right.'

'Just don't let him get you drunk on any of his rubbishy old cider,' Joan warned.

'I've never been drunk in my whole life,' Fred said, and repeated, with a laugh: 'Oh, boy, I sure am glad to see you two!'

'This sure is a lovely old house,' Fred said, after they'd taken his luggage to the Half Moon and cycled back together to Elm Hall. The place smelled of polish, after the girls had spent hours trying to give the floors enough slide for dancing.

'It probably was lovely, before they shifted all the old squire's nice things out and filled it with our junk,' Muriel said.

They led him through to the kitchen, where two large pans of soaked peas stood on the cooker, ready to be boiled. Barbara and some of the other girls were busy weeping over the slicing of a mountain of onions, or scrubbing the dirt off old potatoes, and filling the oven with them and the fat, pricked, pork sausages Barbara had managed to get from the landlord of the Half Moon Inn. He wasn't going to need his usual quota that night, she'd told him, and the weather was getting too warm for them to keep very long. Bargaining with the landlord of the Half Moon Inn was no mean feat, but Barbara had convinced him it would be better all round if he sold them at a slight discount rather than keep them and let them go off – especially considering the goodwill it would get him. They weren't going to starve their guests, after all.

Muriel announced Fred's arrival with a fanfare, as the famous GI jitterbugger who'd helped her win six pairs of nylons and, moreover, it was his champion crap-playing she had to thank for her silk shirt. Barbara and half a dozen other girls turned to grin at him. Fred stood smiling and going pink, telling them how he sure was glad to make their acquaintance, and heaven only knew what his mom would say if she could see him now, with all these English ladies.

The girls couldn't take their eyes off him; Fred was the first GI most of them had ever seen.

'Let's put the gramophone on, and have a dance!' Joan exclaimed.

'Wait a minute, before you do that,' Barbara said. 'Do you think you could manage to drag the piano out of the common room and into the dining room, Fred?'

'I'll sure do my best, ma'am,' Fred said, and with a lot of dragging and heaving, and enthusiastic pushing from the girls, he succeeded. Then they dismantled the trestle tables, and stacked them against the outside of the house and then pushed the benches to the wall to make space for dancing.

Tea was a quick beetroot sandwich and a cup of tea, and then the girls began to go upstairs to get dolled up for the evening. Joan and Muriel went separately, one or the other of them staying downstairs to look after Fred.

★   ★   ★

The other guests arrived at about eight o'clock, over twenty of them, a mix of RAF and army, each with their own booze, and enough to spare. The RAF brought crates of beer and glasses they'd borrowed from the mess. Fred and Muriel were already doing the jitterbug to music on the gramophone and girls were queuing to partner him as soon as the music stopped. The new arrivals set up their barrels and crates in the kitchen and poured some drinks, then came to get the party started. Howard sat at the piano and taking up the last tune on the gramophone, he rattled out a version of 'American Patrol', accompanied by his friends on the banjo – rough and ready music, but music all the same.

Laura and Vera took the floor with their partners for a quickstep, followed by Eileen and her partner. The paratroopers who had befriended Audrey and Muriel claimed them for a dance, Joan partnered Fred and half a dozen other couples joined them. Everyone else sat drinking and chatting in the common room or library, or strolling round the garden.

Dancers and sitters-out turned and turned about, and in between checking on the cooking, Barbara took turns at the piano to free Howard to dance. Despite months without practice, her playing was better than his. Fred had asked Muriel for the next dance when Barbara started to play 'Honeysuckle Rose'.

Howard tapped her on the shoulder. 'We need someone to sing this. What about it, Muriel?'

Fred looked at her expectantly.

'Shut up, or I will,' she laughed.

'No, seriously,' he grinned, 'give us a song. You've never heard her sing, have you, Fred? It's an unforgettable experience.'

Fred was obviously impressed. 'Gee honey, you're a singer as well as a dancer!' he said. 'I can't wait to hear you.'

'Just hope you never do,' she said.

Barbara began to play some of the tunes she'd heard so many times in the hostel, and Fred was whisked away from Muriel and pulled into the hallway to do the jitterbug with Joan, and then one after the other of her pupils, with the non-dancers in the common room coming out to watch.

They stuck to the regular suppertime of half past nine, when the delicious aroma of fried onions began to waft out of the kitchen. Strong men were sent out to bring the tables back in, and food, plates and cutlery laid out in the kitchen for people to help themselves and then go and find a place at one of the tables. Muriel and Fred were among the last to set their plates down on the table. Fred had become a favourite with all the girls, which hadn't endeared him to many of the men, but as the conversation and the booze flowed freely and almost everyone imbibed too much, the conversation turned to the war and the sterling work the army had done, beating the Nazis out of North Africa. Fred claimed a fair share of the credit for that for the Americans, and the Brits conceded. The RAF had managed to destroy two massive dams in

Germany, as well, and now Churchill was talking about the coming fight in Europe. Fred and some of the paratroopers began to look a bit apprehensive at that, and the conversation turned to lighter topics. Most of the men pronounced Fred a good chap, one or two saying how impressed they were with his smartness, his good manners and easy friendliness – and how often he thought about his mother.

'Gee, I'm having a whale of a time,' Fred said. 'I sure knew which weekend to choose, didn't I!'

Watching Barbara and Howard deep in conversation with their baked potato and sausage hardly touched, Muriel thought what a lovely couple they might have made – but as Miss Chapman had once said, her 'young man was still alive', so Barbara and Howard were never likely to become the couple generally known as 'Barbara-and-Howard'. Barbara might be in that no man's land of not knowing whether she was widow or wife for years – perhaps forever.

Deep apple pies, well sweetened and flavoured with cloves, followed the first course, washed down with more cider – then girls impatient for more dancing put a record on and began to take down one of the tables to move it themselves. Fred and a couple of other men rushed to take the job from them, the table was out of the door, and Joan grabbed Fred to dance the jitterbug in the corner that had been cleared, watched and applauded by everyone else. Soon the whole room was cleared and the dancing resumed in earnest. Although everyone else could sit a few dances out whenever they liked, Fred wasn't allowed off his feet for a minute until, in the last stages of exhaustion he asked one of the banjo players if he could take a turn at playing that for a while. He played well, but his dancing talents were more in demand than his musical ones, and he was yanked to his feet as soon as he got his second wind.

As the night wore on, the tempo slowed, waltzes and slow foxtrots replaced quicksteps and jitterbugs, and Fred sat down, brought to a standstill by dancing and cider. 'If my mom could have seen me tonight, getting along with all these English people,' he said, with his speech a little slurred, 'she'd have died of surprise!' Shortly afterwards he disappeared, and Muriel and Audrey danced the last waltz with the paratroopers who'd tried to claim them on their first visit to the Half Moon.

At midnight the music stopped, the tables were carried in and set up for the last time, barrels and crates taken out to the lorries, and hearty thanks and good wishes exchanged, with much laughter. Several of the girls' sweethearts went away with a kiss and a fond farewell, and Barbara and Howard looked into each other's eyes as they said a cordial good night. Muriel, Audrey and Joan started a hunt for Fred, who was nowhere to be seen. The RAF had already gone when they found him curled up on the settee in the common room, fast asleep and reeking of alcohol. Seeing the state of him, Audrey flew out of the door to detain the army lorry; Fred was certainly not fit to cycle to the Half Moon alone. Muriel went to the kitchen for two glasses of water.

'Drink this, Fred,' she urged, determined that he shouldn't wake up with the headache she'd had after the Half Moon's pear cider. He obeyed, very unsteadily. A day of travelling in overcrowded trains, worrying about his connections, cycling, shifting pianos, moving tables, non-stop dancing, joking and drinking both beer and cider had all taken its toll, and Fred had to be helped out to the lorry by two of the paras, with an arm over each of their shoulders. They promised faithfully to knock the landlord up and make sure they undressed Fred and put him to bed properly in the Half Moon.

'And put his clothes straight,' Muriel added, 'or he'll look like a bag of rags tomorrow.'

They roared with laughter and left, singing, 'Kiss me Goodnight, Sergeant Major' at the top of their voices.

Many hands made light work of the mammoth washing up and clearing away the following day, and after the first social evening they'd ever been allowed to have at the hostel, the girls did it cheerfully. Long may Barbara reign as warden, they agreed. They loved the new regime, and were already thinking ahead to the next party.

It was eleven o'clock before Muriel and Joan got down to the Half Moon to see Fred with an invitation to have dinner with them at the hostel, both fully expecting him to have a rip-roaring hangover. They found him in the bar, talking to the landlord, bright, clean, smart, and well-kempt as ever, if a little paler.

'I feel fine. That sure was a fine dance we had, ladies. I can't even remember how I got back to the inn,' he said.

The landlord gave them a wink and a gappy grin, over Fred's head.

'Well, you got back and you're all right; that's the main thing,' said Joan.

Fred accepted the invitation to dinner and went to his room to fetch his camera which, he told them, he would have brought the day before, if he hadn't forgotten it.

After dinner they went out into the garden, where Fred took a group photo, and then got Barbara to take one of him with the girls. After that, the gramophone was on again and they danced his legs off until teatime – and again after tea until it was time to repair to the barn behind the Half Moon Inn and pay their ninepences to the land-lord to see his latest rented film.

As always, the barn was full of Griswold youth of both sexes, with a sprinkling of older folk. The first GI ever seen in the village, Fred attracted round-eyed stares from the boys – not least from the lad who'd bolted from the hall at the sight of the vampire's fangs. The older girls ogled him shamelessly. Fred went back to his room to fetch chocolate for them, and chewing gum – which some of them swallowed until warned not to. Fred talked about his family's farm 'out west', and seemed absolutely at home with them all, not all that different from them in experience, Muriel thought, except for the total lack of any tendency in Fred to forelock pulling.

The film was a Western, and the accents on the screen

were very like Fred's accent, which seemed to add to his glamour in the eyes of the young Griswoldians. Instead of bolting for the exit before the film was over, they stayed until after the last credits had rolled, hanging round Fred, demanding he 'talk like that again', and asking him questions about America, until the landlord came to wind the film back and put it back in its box. He sent them all packing.

'I guess they just like Americans,' Fred grinned.

'They like the only American they've ever seen,' Muriel said. 'It's Land Girls they're not so fond of.'

'These little Methodist buggers,' the landlord said, as the last one disappeared, 'they have them signing the pledge before they're out of nappies. What use is that, to me? It's a crime, bringing a child up like that. Never mind, I'll make boozers out of some of 'em, at least. I'll have 'em in my pub getting legless before they're much older.'

'So you're getting them used to coming into the barn to watch the films, and then it'll be a short enough step into the pub, I suppose,' Audrey said, with a wry smile.

'Ooh, God strike me dead if it ever crossed my mind!' the landlord said, with a broad wink at Fred.

The girls all laughed, and Fred looked horrified.

'Come on in for a drop, girls,' the landlord coaxed, with his most jovial smile.

They went in, to keep Fred company for half an hour and see the boys. Before they left him, Muriel generously lent him her War Ag bike to get himself to Griswold Halt in time for the early train the following day, telling him to leave it there and she'd pick it up after work.

'And don't forget to come again to see these lovely girls, Fred,' the landlord said, 'and bring all your friends. I'll make room for you all. There's the barn, if you bring too many to fit into the inn.'

They waved goodbye, with Muriel riding on the back of Audrey's bike.

'What did you think to him, then?' Muriel asked. 'Is he an idiot?'

Audrey laughed. 'Nah. He's a "real nice guy, honey". He's just got about ten years' growing up to do, that's all.'

'I know. I know how his mother feels, now,' Muriel said. 'I won't rest for worrying about him losing himself or his stuff, or something, until I know he's got back all right.'

'Attlebridge to Griswold and Griswold to Attlebridge all on his own. If he does get back all right, he'll never get over himself,' said Audrey. 'His mother will never hear the last of it.'

Chapter 31

'Hello, strangers!' John Goodyear greeted them, when the lorry stopped outside his farm on Monday morning, with ten Land Girls, to hoe his field of wurzels. Muriel and Audrey were sitting at the back of the lorry, next to the tailboard. 'The Half Moon was as quiet as the tomb on Saturday,' he said while passing a bundle of hoes to them. 'Did you have a nice party?'

'Aye,' Audrey said. 'You should have come. We invited you.'

'I'd have been like a fish out of water.'

'Nobody to talk to about farming,' Muriel grinned.

'Except you,' said John. 'We missed you at the whist drive, as well.'

'I'll bet a lot of them did. We gave them all plenty to talk about the week before,' she laughed, 'but that was before you came in. Last week we had too much on, getting ready for the party.'

'I reckon Sammy Mawson must have got first prize, seeing as we weren't there,' Audrey said.

'No, we did, Dad and I. Sammy and his partner

didn't come; first time I've ever known them to miss.'

'I wonder why?' Muriel grinned.

He grinned back. 'Well, there were quite a few people giving their theories, but I suspect you two might be a lot wiser than any of them, about that. Well, work hard, girls, and if you're very good I'll send you some tea at lounces,' he said, and gave the driver instructions to drop them at a field a mile down the road.

'Aye, and don't send it cold and in a bucket, either,' Audrey called, as they drove away.

'Oh, dear, poor Sammy,' Muriel said. 'I wonder how many other people Sarah Beckett went to visit, after she'd seen us?'

'Probably went to drop a bombshell in the Dog and Duck,' Audrey said. 'I know I would have, in her shoes.'

'Maybe in a few other places, as well.'

That pleasant thought kept them going all morning, hoeing miles of furrows between the wurzels, speculating on the goings on between Sammy, Sarah, and 'our Sadie', with an occasional conjecture as to whether Fred caught his train all right, and where he might be now. A few Italian prisoners kept calling compliments to them from further across the field – or what they supposed were compliments, since the word '*bella*' was the only one they understood. The housekeeper came in a pony and trap at noon, with large Thermos flasks of hot tea, and milk. Lounces was enlivened by the company of the Italian Romeos, a good-natured, exuberant set of very good-looking young men who shared the tea and made eyes at them all, and tried to teach them to sing Italian opera by some very tactile methods. Muriel refrained from joining in the singing, out of consideration for the other girls, but she would have been hard put to evade the practical demonstrations on how to breathe and where to find her diaphragm. At teatime the house-keeper brought jam scones with the tea, and very welcome they were. The girls finished their quota well before time, but didn't go across to help the Italians finish theirs. Instead they lounged around, waiting for the lorry and passing round fags given to them by the personnel of the army and RAF.

The office telephone rang just before they went to bed that night. It was Fred, wanting to speak to Muriel, to thank her and all the other girls for a lovely weekend. He was back in Attlebridge, safe and sound, after being almost crushed to death in the trains. He was just about to write to his mom, to tell her about his wonderful English girl, and he sure wished he'd remembered his camera on Saturday, because she just wouldn't believe . . .

His wonderful English girl? Well, where was the harm, Muriel thought, as she hung up. It wasn't likely they'd see much of each other, and a dancer like Fred would always have girls flocking to him like bees round a jam pot. He'd soon find someone else, and that would be the last she'd ever hear from him. The main thing was, he was back in the GI fold in Attlebridge, and safe.

They were at the Goodyears' farm for the rest of the week. On Wednesday John asked Muriel and Audrey again to come and live in the farm cottage, and work with the cows.

'We're going on a course to learn about cows,' Muriel said, 'so we might have a bash at yours when we come back.'

'You don't need to go on a course,' John said. 'I could teach you everything you need to know at the farm.'

'Aye, but we'd rather go on a course,' Audrey said, 'then we'll have a certificate from the War Ag.'

'Will we get any extra money for having this certificate?' Muriel asked.

'Doubt it,' Audrey said, 'if we're relying on farmers paying us.'

'Get out of it!' John grinned, passing them the hoes.

Sammy was absent from the whist drive for the second time running.

'Has he disappeared off the face of the earth?' Audrey asked Cissie and Jack. 'We haven't even seen him going into the Dog and Duck with his carrier-bags.'

'Maybe he's got nothing to put in them, now,' Muriel said, with an air of innocence. 'Has anybody heard anything about him? We haven't heard anything about our old warden, either.'

'Maybe they've run off to Gretna Green,' Audrey said. 'Maybe they're on their honeymoon.'

Cissie had a twinkle in her eye, but her lips were determinedly clamped shut.

Jack laughed. 'I don't know about that, but I've heard

as Sadie's keeping him company on Friday nights, now,' he said.

They tootled off on the train to the training centre. There they were back to square one, or beyond it as far as food and accommodation went. The hostel was a purpose-built one-storey affair with metal window frames, stark and unadorned and without a garden, or anywhere they could sit out with a cup of tea after a hard day's work – a far cry from the 'lovely old house' that had so impressed Fred Sears. Along with ten other girls, they were given Cornish pasties and chips on their first evening there.

'Who do these remind you of?' Audrey said, attempting to cut through the crust.

'Have you seen Miss Hubbard around the place?' Muriel wondered. 'I think she must have got a transfer.'

But no, the War Ag had managed to find Miss Hubbard's double and put her in charge, so they were in for a week of terrible food to go with the Spartan accommodation.

The next morning, the girls were up at half past four to go out and start the fun and games of getting the cows in from the fields. Most of them were easy, amenable creatures who came when called, but the bovine awkward squad ignored the summons, and went as far down the other end of the pastures as they could get.

'Dumb insolence, I call it,' Audrey said as the cows defiantly watched them walking through the fields towards them.

'Aye, defiant and unreliable,' Muriel grinned. 'The dairy herd's version of Audrey and Muriel.'

'That's what we'll call them, then,' Audrey said. 'They're "Muriel and Audrey", from now on.'

The cows made them walk the whole way and waited until they were nearly on top of them, then evaded them and trotted off up the fields to join the rest of the herd.

Once in the cowshed the girls began the process of chaining them up under the watchful eye of their instructor, a middle-aged man with dark hair and heavy, dark-framed spectacles. He showed them how to assemble the gear for the milking machines and have it all ready before washing and drying the cows' udders, and how to test the first squirts of milk from each teat for impurities, which might mean the cow had mastitis and the milk was unfit for human consumption. Then he turned the machine's vacuum pump on and applied the teat-cups, which came in bunches of four and had to be put on within sixty seconds of washing the teats, he said, and those who could get near enough to see solemnly watched the process.

Muriel was first to be supervised doing the cleaning, squirting, examination of milk, and application of teat-cups.

'Hey, Audrey,' she said. 'I never realised that *all* cows have four teats before!'

'Neither did I,' Audrey said. 'Well, how many cows do we see strolling down Holderness Road, or in the middle of Leeds?'

'Not many, but I've had a bash at milking one before, if you remember!'

'Aye, but that didn't guarantee they all had four!' Audrey said. 'Anyway, at least you knew milk came from cows, so you were one up on me.'

'And me!' a good many of the other apprentice milk-maids laughed.

Their instructor proved himself a humourless chap, not given to lightening the day's labour with banter himself, and not the sort to appreciate it in anybody else. He made no comment but his dour face soon put an end to their levity.

One after the other, the girls were supervised, and all given repeated instructions on cleanliness, mastitis, and making sure the vacuum was turned off before they tried to remove the teat-cups. Some of those cows weren't above giving their attendants a hefty kick if they got annoyed, and their aim was usually spot on, said the instructor.

The machine could milk about thirty cows in an hour, but there were over eighty of the beasts, and since the machines didn't get all the milk, the girls had to go round and get the remaining milk by hand.

'John Goodyear's father wasn't all that impressed with milking machines, was he?' Audrey said. 'He said they were always breaking down.'

'And if you have to go round and milk them by hand after the machine's been on, why bother with them at all?' Muriel wondered. 'I bet they cost a mint as well.'

At half past seven, three solid hours after they'd started work, they got their first cup of tea. Then they worked on until all the cows had been hand milked and taken out into the fields.

At breakfast, they devoured everything on the table in short order, and were out again to clean all the equipment and muck out and wash out all the cowsheds. A sandwich and an hour or so off followed, and then it was time to start the whole rigmarole again, bringing the cows in for milking at four. Cows liked routine, and had to be milked at least twice a day, because regular milking done in the right way stopped them getting mastitis, and the more even the intervals between milking, the better the cows liked it, the man impressed on them. It kept them comfortable and calm, so they gave more milk, of better quality. They also liked having the same person to do the milking, but there wasn't much chance of that, with so many girls to teach, and a different set of girls every week, was there? So it was important to be calm and patient, and not upset them more than necessary.

After the day's work, they strolled out with a couple of the other girls to find the village pub, an unwelcoming hole, more dead than alive.

The first couple of days of hand milking brought a few bruises from the more Bolshie cows, who kicked sideways and usually managed to hit the spot, just as they'd been warned. A fair bit of milk was spilled as the battle of wills raged between girls and beasts, until the girls finally triumphed. After hand milking umpteen cows, Audrey revised her opinion of milking machines, and so did Muriel. The machines got through the work in a third of the time, without any strain on their hands. Even so, they went to bed feeling as if their wrists had been broken, and going by the complaints of many of the others, so did they. The following day Muriel decided that she had as much right to be comfortable and calm as the cows had, and tied their back legs together with a strip of old sacking before starting the hand milking, to save herself a bruising. Since the instructor didn't object, as many girls as could find a length of something to tie with followed suit. After a few more days of it her fingers seized up and turned blue, and she was terrified she'd done herself some permanent damage, but most of the other girls were just the same. Some of the girls' hands swelled up like balloons. Nothing to worry about, the instructor said. As soon as the muscles grew used to the strain of pulling on the teats every day, they'd get stronger, the swelling and stiffness would subside, and the pain would stop. It wouldn't be long. Most of the other girls took him at his word, but Muriel's hands and wrists felt so bad she went to see a doctor – who told her the same thing. She just had to keep on milking, although with the stiffness and the swelling, she could barely grasp the teats.

All in all, they were glad when the course was over, and they could take themselves back to homely Elm Hall with its derelict garden, looking forward to feeding like gluttons on Barbara's cooking – if the hoard of rations hadn't been confiscated.

'My bloody hands are still aching,' Audrey said, as they journeyed back to Griswold.

'I thought it would make a change, to learn something new,' Muriel said. 'Now I wouldn't care if I never saw another cow in my life. The only good thing about cows is the milk they give, but I'd rather let someone else collect it.'

What she didn't say was that within the deepest, most secret recesses of her dishonest little heart she knew that the best thing about cows was that they reminded her of Ernst – and since he had a reputation for being good with them she'd had a vague idea that dairy work might bring her into contact with him again. It would be hard not to talk to someone who was in the same cowshed. Her rational mind knew that talking to him would bring more pain than pleasure in the long run, and that going on the course had probably been a stupid thing to do, all told. He'd had enough sensitivity to keep away from her in the fields, so it was idiotic of her to try to sabotage her own best intentions.

'Sorry I dragged you along, anyway, Audrey,' she added, after a pause.

'You didn't drag me along. I wouldn't have come if I hadn't wanted to and I'm not sorry I did, in spite of the hands. I've been thinking I wouldn't mind sticking to the farming life when the war's over, so the more I learn, the better my chances,' Audrey said. 'I'll be glad to get back to Griswold, though. At least the pub's alive. The landlord might be a rogue, but you can have a bit of fun with him.'

Chapter 32

By the time they got back to the hostel on Saturday evening, Muriel had almost forgotten about Fred Sears, 'not the Sears and Roebuck Sears, honey' – and found, to her surprise, that she had three letters from him, and one from his mother. Fred wanted her to get the War Ag to transfer her to somewhere near his camp, so he could see her every week – every day, if possible. He seemed to be getting pretty serious about her, and she saw what Joan had meant about GIs wanting to marry girls after three 'dates'.

The letters were put aside, while the girls all discussed the astounding news about Barbara. Her husband had escaped from a prisoner-of-war camp in Germany, and had managed to make his way into Holland, and from there to Hull. Barbara had gone to Hull at the crack of dawn to meet him. The other girls had had a little time to get used to the idea, and all rejoiced for her, but had been forced to forage for themselves all day, and all had terrible misgivings about what this wonderfully good news for Barbara might mean for them. When the subject had been thoroughly talked out, and the fact squarely faced that this might mean they would lose Barbara as warden, Muriel left the other girls to their doom-laden predictions about the sort of regime they might be subjected to under the her replacement – and turned to her letters.

She wrote a friendly, newsy letter back to Fred telling him about Barbara's husband and the course in looking after cows, and ended by telling him she couldn't ask for a transfer. She had too many good friends where she was, and Griswold wasn't very far from her mother.

Fred's mother had written to ask if there was anything Fred needed, because he kept telling her that there wasn't. Muriel wrote to her to say that Fred had everything he needed – except that he would have liked to have her there to see how well he was managing, winning dancing competitions, and finding his way around England all by himself. Everybody liked him, and if she'd seen him in the hostel the other week she wouldn't have believed how popular he was and how many new friends he'd made. Your baby's managing to survive without you, she thought – but she was too kind to say that in the letter.

Barbara arrived back at the hostel before suppertime, and not alone. A tall, dark-haired, weary-looking chap was beside her, walking with the aid of crutches.

'Welcome home,' some of the girls said, quite shyly.

He looked round the Hall, and gave them a smile. 'Well, this is my home now, is it? It's certainly a big improvement on some of the places I've slept in.' He looked tired out, and after introducing him as 'my husband, Eric', Barbara took him straight through into her own quarters.

Some of the girls went to the kitchen to make some supper, not sure whether Barbara would come out again. Laura put the oven on and got out the baking stuff to knock up scones for them all. Muriel filled the kettle, and threw tea in the pot. Vera put cups and plates out. Half an hour later, when the second batch of fruit scones was just coming out of the oven, Barbara came in to join them.

'He's done in,' she said. 'He's got a few days' leave, until we find out where we go from here.'

'What's wrong with his leg?'

'Knee injury. He wrenched it scrambling over a high wall, and then landing on uneven ground the other side. If it had happened in Germany he'd have been recaptured, but it was in Holland. A doctor told him he's damaged the ligament, and he'll probably have trouble with it for the rest of his life, which he's not happy about but I think might be a blessing in disguise. I hope it gets him a desk job, or discharged from the army altogether. I couldn't go through this again.'

'Oh, we'll lose you, if he does,' one of the girls lamented.

'Yes, you will, and I'll miss you all like hell. But I wouldn't dream of leaving you to starve,' Barbara said. 'I'll stay until the War Ag can get a permanent replacement. Miss Fawcett gave permission for Eric to stay with me tonight, but she'll have to consult the higher ups about him staying any longer.'

'I can't understand why you never got a letter off him,' Audrey said.

'He wrote while he was in the POW camp, but after he escaped, he couldn't. I gave the post office a forwarding address when I gave the flat up, but something's gone wrong somewhere. Maybe in Germany. He says the bombing's far worse there than what we saw travelling through Hull when we came from the docks.'

'It must be terrible, then!' Muriel said.

Barbara nodded. 'That's what I said.'

Most of the girls seemed disinclined to believe it, despite hearing the bombers flying over to Germany, night after night.

Barbara took a scone and a cup of tea for Eric when she left them, saying he would probably be too tired to eat anything.

Joan gave a sly smile. 'I hope he's not too tired to be a proper husband,' she said, after Barbara had gone. 'He's got a lot of making up to do, the length of time he's been away.'

'Bad job about his knee, then,' Vera murmured.

Since Barbara's quarters were entirely shut off from the rest of the girls, the War Ag made no objection to her husband staying there for the duration of his leave. A couple of evenings later he was sitting with them in the common room after tea with the girls talking about the summons Barbara had taken out, when there came a banging on the front door like the crack of doom. Muriel went to open it, to be confronted with the angry defendant in the case.

'Oh! Speak of the devil!' she said.

'Where's Barbara Barstow? You bring her here, this minute! I've got something to say to her,' he snarled, waving something in a long envelope.

'Oh. Just wait there, then, will you?' Muriel said, as if she were speaking to an errand boy, and without another word she slammed the door in his face.

Barbara was already in the hallway. 'Let him in,' she said, 'and show him through to the common room. I'm sure we'll all be interested in what he's got to say, and with all my witnesses here, I don't think it can do me any harm.'

Muriel opened the door again, and with a curt: 'Come in,' led him through to Barbara, her husband, and all the other girls.

He took one glance around the room, and frowned. 'This is a private matter,' he said, waving his envelope at her. 'I'll see you alone.'

'On the contrary,' Barbara said, 'it's a very public matter. It was a public matter when you injured me in your attempt to prevent me from leaving your farm, and it will be a public matter when it's heard in court.'

He glanced down at her ankle, still encased in plaster of Paris. 'It was an accident.'

'As much of an accident as the lashing we saw you give that boy with your riding crop, I suppose.'

'All right. I've come here to try to resolve this matter

in a reasonable manner, and you've obstructed me. So take it to court, and make a fool of yourself. You'll find I've got friends there. Among the *magistrates*.'

'Oh, dear,' Barbara said, 'and I've only got my witnesses and the law. It remains to be seen which will prevail.'

'My money's on you and the law, Barbara,' her husband said, quietly.

The farmer strode towards him and stood there, rising and falling on the balls of his feet, glaring. 'Who the hell are you, and what do you know about it? You weren't there,' he said, and Muriel was certain that if he'd had his riding crop instead of an envelope, he would have been slapping it against his palm.

Until that moment Barbara's husband had looked much the weaker of the two men, pale, thin, unwell, and insignificant, just the sort of nonentity who could be trampled underfoot. Now he rose to his feet, his lips white with anger and his eyes hawkish. 'No, I wasn't there,' he said, quietly. 'I was in His Majesty's forces, and otherwise engaged – and little did I think that my own countrymen would be making war on my wife while I was away defending them and their farms. You injured my wife, and some redress is due. Now, she's written to you in an attempt to resolve the matter, telling you how you injured her and suggesting a settlement. You have seen fit to ignore her letters. I assume that that envelope you're holding contains your summons to appear in court. We'll see you there. Good evening to you.'

The farmer's jaw tightened. He hesitated, smacked his

summons against the palm of his hand, and shook his
head. 'You'll be sorry for this. I'm not a man to be trifled
with. If you're going on with this you'd better get the
best solicitor you can afford, and prepare for a fight. It's
going to cost a lot.'

'In all modesty,' Barbara's husband said, softly, 'I think
I *am* the best solicitor anyone could afford.'

'I've got a score of witnesses who will say it was an
accident,' the farmer threatened.

Muriel jumped up, and went to hold the door open
for him. 'Well, Barbara's got a few as well, and none of
hers will have to tell a pack of lies to keep their houses
and their jobs.' Her dark eyes locked with his for a
moment as he passed by her, and she gave him an acid,
closed-lipped smile.

'I'll tell every farmer round here what you're doing.
The War Ag won't like that.'

Barbara laughed. 'Tell whoever you like. Give them an
invitation to the court, so that they can hear for themselves what really happened. And it's immaterial to me
what the War Ag thinks, because I'll be leaving soon.'

Muriel's heart sank at that news. She looked at Audrey
and the other girls, and saw that they felt the same.

'That War Agricultural woman will never be able to
persuade the farmers to take Land Girls after this. Never!'
the farmer spat.

'Maybe the farmers need the Land Girls more than the
Land Girls need them,' Audrey said. 'TTFN, then – ta ta
for now. See you soon.'

Muriel chased after him as he strode to the front door, and would have opened it for him but he was too quick for her to make a mockery of him by bowing him out, and left her only the very minor satisfaction of slamming the door after him.

They'd just started work when John Goodyear called to her from the bottom of the field: 'Hey Muriel, I've got a job for you.'

'What is it?'

'Come and find out.'

Muriel looked along the row of girls hoeing between his rows of corn with eyebrows raised and a suspicious smile on her face, and they looked at her in precisely the same manner.

'Scream your head off if he starts any funny business,' Joan said, 'and we'll come running.'

'Aye, we will. Tell him we're already suing one farmer, Muriel, man, and he can be next,' Eileen said.

Muriel grasped her hoe and walked towards him. He took her on the long walk back to the stables.

'These two carthorses need to be shod. Take them to the blacksmith's in the village. You can ride one, and the other will walk beside you. Here, I'll give you a leg up.'

She looked at him, horror-struck. 'I can't ride! I've never been near a horse in my life!'

'You'll be all right. Come on, I'll show you.'

She let him give her a leg up, and looked down at him. 'Bloody hell, it's a long way down,' she said. 'What happens if I fall off and break my neck? Miles from anywhere? And I'm not sure I know the way.'

'You won't fall off, you won't break your neck, and they know the way. They're a couple of docile cart-horses,' he said, handing her a canvas bag. 'Here, the housekeeper's made you some sandwiches and put you some tea in a Thermos.'

'What are their names?'

'You're on Barney; the other one's Jotty.'

He waved her off, and they plodded along so steadily that Muriel wondered how they would get there in a week, let alone a day. Then the horses turned off the road, and plodded through fields, down bridle paths, over streams, and along rights of way, passing tiny hamlets she had never suspected existed. It was a beautiful, warm summer's day and the countryside was clothed in various shades of vibrant green, a sight to lift her spirits. Birds were singing lustily and flying about with morsels for their young, and sometimes she spotted a young rabbit sitting at a safe distance watching her, before turning its white tail and disappearing. Muriel sat on Barney's broad back ambling on, looking for parties of German prisoners at work in the fields throughout the whole of her ride and not really caring how long this pleasant journey might take, as long as they got there in the end.

She saw no prisoners, and it was one o'clock before the horses stopped outside the forge and the blacksmith helped her down and took the reins. 'We'll let them graze for an hour,' he said, 'come on, my beauties!'

Muriel was ready to graze herself, and took herself and her canvas bag to sit in the nicest spot she could find, under a chestnut tree at the back of the forge. The sandwiches were generously buttered and filled with lettuce and boiled egg, and the tea was hot and sweet. Muriel ate and drank, and then with the empty canvas bag for padding she leaned against the trunk of the tree and shut her eyes, lulled by the trilling and chirruping of the birds, and the buzzing of insects.

She sensed a shadow looming over her, shutting out the sun.

'Hello! Hello? Are you asleep, lass?'

With a superhuman effort, Muriel forced her unwilling eyes to open.

'No.'

'Come and help me with the bellows, then.'

Muriel helped him with a will, working the bellows while he fashioned the horseshoes.

'Slower, slower, steady on! Whoa, whoa – that'll do, lass.'

He got her talking while they worked about the goings-on at the hostel, showing a particular interest in the disappearing rations and the impending prosecution of Farmer Hogg. Muriel gave him the court date, in case he wanted to hear the details for himself – but the court was too far away, he said, and it would have meant getting his Sunday suit out of mothballs.

'Besides, I've got too much work to do, but it's time someone took him down a peg or two,' he ended, with a sly smile. 'Aye – speed it up a bit, now, lass, a bit quicker! Whoa! That's it . . .'

'I've heard there's going to be a wedding,' he said, as he gave her a leg up onto Jotty's back when the job was finished.

'Oh, aye? Anybody I know?'

He gave her the empty canvas bag and Thermos, along with the news: 'Sammy Mawson's marryin' Sadie.'

Muriel burst into laughter. 'I hope they'll make each other very happy,' she said.

She chuckled about it all the way back, conjuring images of the girls attending the wedding to show all was forgiven, and then throwing rose-petals at the happy couple as they came out of the church. Then she pictured what the newly-weds' faces might look like if they did. No, maybe not. It wouldn't be fair for such city riff-raff to ruin a bride's wedding day – not even a bride like Sadie Hubbard.

It was late when she got back to Thornhill Farm, and the lorry had already gone with the rest of the girls. Muriel and John Goodyear put the horses to graze, and Muriel felt as if Barney and Jotty were two old friends.

'Did you fall off?' he asked her.

'Not once. I quite enjoyed taking them.'

'It'll be too late for you to get your tea, now. Ours is just on the table. Come and have some with us, and then I'll take you back to the hostel in the car.'

Well, what choice had she, Muriel wondered. Still, the sandwiches hadn't been bad. She might as well give the cooking a chance – if it was horrible she could leave it, and at least with Barbara there was always supper. Surely she'd be back in time for that.

'You'll have to telephone the hostel and tell them where I am,' she said. 'They'll be worried.'

'All right.'

She glanced at the grandfather clock in the hallway as he followed her into the farmhouse. 'And you owe me two hours' overtime.'

'I'll pay you in cider,' he said.

'"Hey Muriel, I've got a job for you!"' Eileen repeated, in the most suggestive tones later that evening, when Muriel finally got back and found the girls in the kitchen, waiting for the kettle to boil. 'By, but that was a bloody crafty piece of work, though, Muriel, man. We wondered what he'd done with you when you weren't there for the lorry picking us up!'

'We thought you'd eloped,' Laura said, looking up from her task of stirring a mass of cocoa and sugar into a paste in the biggest jug the kitchen could boast.

'Or he'd sold you to the white slave trade!' Audrey grimaced. 'It's nearly half past nine!'

'He did ring, and tell Barbara I'd be late.'

'So she said, and he told us that, when the lorry came and we went searching for you! "Don't worry, I'll bring her back," he says, and I saw the look on his face, like the cat that got the cream, and I thought: And what happens between now and then?' Vera said, with a very inquisitive look in her eyes.

'I had a very nice pork chop with apple sauce, cooked by his housekeeper, that's what happened,' Muriel said, when she'd taken as much ragging as she could stand about John Goodyear's evil designs on her – 'and he only wants me for a milkmaid. He was asking me all the way back how we got on on that course, so if you don't all stop being rotten, I shan't tell you my news.'

'What news?'

'Sammy Mawson and our old warden are getting married! The banns are up in the church.'

There was a moment of stunned silence, then Audrey laughed.

'Bloody hell! Well, never were a couple better suited.'

'Shall we send them half our rations, as a wedding present?' Vera suggested.

'No, let's send them all!' Joan grimaced.

'Like hell! Let's get a few of them old horseshoes from the blacksmiths and chuck them, instead of confetti,' Eileen said.

Muriel's mouth turned down. 'I'd have brought a few, if only I'd thought of it,' she said.

Chapter 33

Barbara made her complaint, and Muriel was the first of her witnesses to be questioned. She stepped into the box fully confident of her facts and told the three magistrates on the bench how she'd seen Farmer Hogg hit a young lad with his riding crop, how he'd threatened to hit her, how he'd ridden his horse so near to her she'd been afraid she was going to be trampled and how he'd stopped them with the horse when they'd tried to leave his farm – and then put the finishing touch to it all by knocking Barbara down with the horse. Audrey followed with similar evidence, then Laura, and then the driver and the army doctor who had treated Barbara's injury both gave their testimony.

The girls looked at each other and smiled, breathing sighs of relief. They'd braved the terrors of standing up and giving evidence, and the court had the full facts of the matter. It was all cut and dried. The case was open and shut. It was over. They'd won.

But now it was Farmer Hogg's turn. Muriel's bosom swelled with righteous indignation on hearing him tell the court lie after lie, that the whole thing was an accident, and it had all been their own fault. They were provoking parties in the supposed assault. He was an innocent, put-upon farmer, merely doing his best to maintain discipline on his farm and get lazy, sloppy workers to do the work they were paid for – the work that was necessary if they were to be able to feed the country. He denied any liability. He turned the whole case on its head, so that the victims were now the guilty parties, and he was Snow White. The magistrates were nodding gravely, as if they agreed with everything he said. Muriel looked at Barbara in consternation, sure that the case was lost.

Barbara appeared unruffled. When Farmer Hogg had finished, she calmly stood up.

'Did you have a contract with the War Agricultural Executive Committee for the employment of Land Girls?'

'Yes.'

'And did this contract stipulate that the Land Girls were to finish work at five o'clock?'

'Yes, but . . .'

'Yes. And did you attempt to prevent us from leaving your land *after* five o'clock by obstructing our progress while mounted on a horse? Remember that the driver can testify as to the time of my injury.'

'Yes, but . . .'

'Yes. Contrary to our contract you tried to prevent us from leaving your land at the proper time, and that resulted in your horse scraping its hoof down my leg. Is that correct?'

Farmer Hogg's lowering, sullen expression convinced Muriel that he would dearly have loved to give Barbara a lashing with his riding crop at that very moment. He muttered something under his breath.

'Speak up, please,' Barbara insisted.

'Yes!' he snarled.

'That's all, thank you.'

Farmer Hogg's solicitor then called the boy who'd been struck with his riding crop as a witness, and with a little prompting the terrified lad swore blind under oath that he'd never been hit. After the solicitor had finished his questioning, Barbara got up.

'What happens to workers who fail to do what Farmer Hogg has ordered them to do?

'They get the sack.'

'And when they get the sack, what else happens to them?'

'They get turned out.'

'And if you didn't do what Farmer Hogg ordered you to do, do you think you and your family would be allowed to stay in your cottage?'

'No.'

'And did Farmer Hogg make you come here and say things that aren't true?'

The lad reddened to the whites of his eyes and stood gasping like a fish. After a telling pause Barbara took pity on him, and let him go.

Muriel saw a look pass between Farmer Hogg and the chief magistrate, and then Farmer Hogg's solicitor produced a couple more lying employee-witnesses whom Barbara dealt with in similar fashion.

The three magistrates listened, and took note. The one in the middle glanced in the direction of Farmer Hogg with a slight shake of his head.

To the girls' unmitigated joy, and the farmer's fury, the magistrates found in her favour. Barbara got her damages, plus court costs.

'Serve you right!' Audrey told Farmer Hogg, as they sailed past him on their way out of court.

'A triumph for you, and a warning to him. Well done, girls,' Barbara's husband said, with grim satisfaction.

John Goodyear and his father arrived early at the whist on Friday night, and were seated before Muriel arrived with Audrey, and Margaret and Elizabeth, the two crack whist players who'd given them such a good run for their money in the hostel. Sammy Mawson was also present with his partner, looking as surly as ever and as far from a picture of the happy bridegroom-to-be as could be imagined. Sammy always played North, and for sheer devilment Muriel and Audrey decided to play East–West, so they'd have plenty of opportunity to congratulate him on his forthcoming nuptials.

They reached the Goodyears' table first. John brought up the subject of the course in dairy farming they'd been on.

'I forgot to ask you,' he said, 'did you get your certificate?'

'Course we did,' Audrey said.

'Well, we're always looking for milkmaids. Come and try it.'

'We might. Be warned, though, you'll have to treat us very nicely. We sue at the drop of a hat,' Muriel teased. 'We've just had one farmer in court.'

'What? A *farmer*? In *court*?' John's father nearly dropped his cards.

'It's true. Barbara's just got damages from a farmer who knocked her down with a horse. It scraped two inches of flesh off all the way down her calf, and broke her ankle. So she took him to court.'

'What next?' John's father said. 'I wouldn't have thought a Land Girl would have enough money to go to court.'

'You don't need a lot if you can do it yourself, especially if you win,' Audrey said. 'You've seen Barbara at the Half Moon, John.'

'I know. So she's suing farmers, is she? Which farmer was it?' John asked.

His father looked aghast. 'Sueing farmers! Whatever next?' he repeated.

'A Mr Hogg.'

Mr Goodyear looked slightly mollified. 'That's chap as took old Walter's place, John; came from Africa. Oh, well, I've heard he's a nasty piece of work.'

'He is,' Muriel said, and the reference to nasty pieces of work naturally led her to Sammy. 'Have you been invited to Mr Mawson's wedding?' she asked. 'We've heard the banns are up.'

Mr Goodyear gave a burst of laughter. 'We haven't, and I don't suppose you will be, either.'

When the break for tea came, Muriel had the impudence to sidle up to Sammy and congratulate him on his good fortune, in between bites of a bread cake, succulent with dripping. He turned a jaundiced eye on her and told her he didn't want her congratulations.

'What do you want to hold a grudge for, Mr Mawson?' Muriel coaxed. 'Why not let bygones be bygones?'

'Aye, start your married life off on a new footing, Mr Mawson, friends with everyone,' Audrey urged. 'Tell you what, if you invite us to the wedding we'll club together and buy the bride a cookery book – and maybe get a few boxes of indigestion tablets, for you – just to show there's no ill feeling.'

Sammy failed to see the humour, but a few chuckles and several broad smiles on the faces of the Goodyears and other people around them showed that some of the spectators did, in spite of village loyalty.

Play started again, and the friends were disappointed to be beaten by Sammy and his partner, but at the end of the evening when the scores were counted it was Margaret and Elizabeth who took first prize, which was the next best thing to winning it themselves, or so Audrey said.

'See you at the Half Moon tomorrow,' John said, as they left the hall.

Muriel shook her head. 'I'm going home this weekend. I haven't seen them for two and a half months, so I reckon they're due a visit.'

'I'm going home as well,' Audrey said. 'I go home fairly regular.'

'Shame,' John said.

Chapter 34

Muriel packed her things before she went to bed that night. As soon as she got back to the hostel on Saturday she collected her post and stuffed it into her bag, along with a notepad and pen and the carefully wrapped pound of butter John Goodyear had given her for her mother. Then she grabbed one of the War Ag bikes and cycled to Griswold Halt, leaving the bike there to ride back on Sunday.

She managed to get a seat in a dining carriage, and pulled out letters and notepad before stowing her bag on the rack. One of the letters was from Fred. She settled down to read all six pages of news about life in Norfolk and social events at the American airbase, with Fred telling her throughout how much he missed her, and lamenting the fact that although all the girls were good dancers he'd never found a dancing partner as good as her. He was so open and honest and thoroughly *nice* that she wrote a long and newsy letter back immediately, telling him all about Barbara's court case, and the return of her husband 'in the nick of time'. She ended by telling him she missed him, and hadn't danced a step since the party at the hostel. Fred's mother had written to say how much more comfortable she'd felt about him since she'd had Muriel's letter, and she hoped they could carry on corresponding. Muriel wrote back and said she would very much like to keep in touch, and how interesting it was to get the American point of view on things. She had finished both letters before the train arrived in Hull station, and thought her journey time well spent.

The post office was shut, so she got off the bus near the Maypole, and called in to see Miss Chapman, who usually had a spare couple of stamps in her bag. Muriel went to the counter and asked for them, while her old friend Kathleen Moss was being served.

'Sorry, Muriel, I haven't got one,' Miss Chapman told her. 'I've used them all up, writing to relatives.' Muriel must have looked surprised, because Miss Chapman added, with tears in her eyes: 'I've just buried my mother. She died quite suddenly, and I had write to my uncles and aunts to invite them to the funeral. They live in Barton, you see.'

Ada nodded confirmation, looking very sympathetic.

'Oh, Miss Chapman, I am sorry,' Muriel said.

Kathleen murmured her sympathy as well, and then told Muriel: 'I've got a stamp you can have.'

'Thanks,' Muriel said, searching her bag for her purse.

'The tuppence ha'penny doesn't matter; one good turn deserves another. Thank your Arni. He went into my grandmother's house and rescued her parrot, after the last air raid. She couldn't have got to it herself, the place was such a wreck.'

'Well, he's a bit of a risk-taker, our Arni!' Muriel said. 'Did he charge her anything for it?'

Kathleen laughed. 'Course he didn't.'

'It's a wonder. He must be going soft.'

'You're on leave then?'

'Aye.'

'I've only got another year, and then the government will be after me to do something, I suppose – if I'm not married before then.'

'Are you still going out with your fireman?'

'I am. We're talking about getting engaged. He's working tonight, though, so we could go dancing, if you like.'

'That sounds nice. I'll call for you about half past seven, then, shall I?'

'All right. It'll be just like old times.'

'I'm sorry about your mother, Miss Chapman,' she said, when Kathleen had gone. 'It must have been an awful shock.'

'It was. It'll take a lot of getting used to. The worst thing is going home to an empty house. No fire, no meal ready, and afterwards we used to wash up together and talk over the day's events. You never realise how much you're going to miss someone, until they're gone.'

'If I'm ever living in a farm cottage, Miss Chapman, will you come for a holiday?' Muriel asked, on a sudden impulse.

Miss Chapman looked very taken aback. 'Are you going to live in a farm cottage, then, Muriel?'

'I might. And if I do, will you come?'

'You're a good girl, Muriel,' Miss Chapman smiled. 'Yes, if ever you're living in a farm cottage I'll come to see you – but just for a day.'

'No, for a week,' Muriel insisted, sticking her two 2½ penny stamp on Fred's letter and smacking it down to add emphasis.

She posted it further up the road. She'd have to ask her mother to put the right postage on the one to Fred's mother and drop it in the box for her. The post office in Griswold was always shut by the time she'd finished work.

Doreen was plying her skipping rope with half a dozen other girls when Muriel turned into Sherburn Street. 'It's our Muriel!' she cried, and handing the rope to another girl came to greet her, and skip beside her up Morley Villas footpath.

Her mother came to the door of Auntie Ivy's house. 'We're in here! Come and have a cup of tea with Ivy.'

Muriel opened the door of number five to dump her bag in the passageway. Arni poked his head out of the living room to see who it was.

'You're still alive, then,' he said. 'We began to wonder.'

'Hello, Arni. Heard you've been rescuing parrots in distress. It got me a tuppence ha'penny stamp, anyway so thanks!' she said, and went over to Auntie Ivy's, followed by Arni. Auntie Ivy and Muriel's mother were in the middle of a discussion about spiritualism, and it soon transpired that Auntie Ivy often met Doris Chapman at the spiritualist church.

'Any messages from Bill, yet, Auntie Ivy?' Arni asked, eagerly.

'No,' Auntie Ivy said.

'There's a new medium coming tomorrow, though, isn't there, Mam?' Betty said.

The new medium could all but raise the dead, going by her reputation, and Auntie Ivy was expecting great things from her. The longing on Auntie Ivy's face when she spoke about her hopes of reaching her poor Bill brought a lump to Muriel's throat.

'We sometimes end up working near some German U-boat sailors. They say their survival rate is about one man in four, so there must have been plenty of them "passed over",' she suddenly blurted out.

Instead of the expected diatribe against Germans, Auntie Ivy's response was a sad: 'They're all somebody's bairns,' and Muriel's mother nodded.

After about a quarter of an hour of it Muriel could bear no more, and took Doreen and Betty out to join the skipping.

A quiet meal at home, an evening's dancing at the City Hall with Kathleen, and a stroll round East Park the following day with her mother and Auntie Ivy, reminiscing about her lost childhood with Bill, while the youngsters ran on in front, and it was time to catch the train back to Griswold. Muriel boarded it feeling an awful sadness for those lost times in Holderness Road. Odd that her comment about the U-boat sailors had drawn so little reaction from either Auntie Ivy or her mother, she thought, almost as if Auntie Ivy sympathised with grieving mothers in Germany.

'Want a look at this?' a serviceman asked, handing her yesterday's paper. 'I've done with it.'

Muriel thanked him and took it. 'PANTELLARIA OCCUPIED BY ALLIED TROOPS,' she read, and asked: 'Pantellaria? Where's that?'

'Italy, somewhere. They dropped planeloads of Paras.'

Muriel wondered whether any of their friends from the Half Moon had been dropped, and read on: 'The garrison surrendered after an onslaught by 1,000 bombers and the bomb battered island was being occupied by Allied troops. The ordeal and the resistance of Pantellaria, in the Sicilian channel, ended at 1.40 double British summer time today. The air bombardment was supported by naval bombardment. The all out Allied onslaught on Pantellaria began soon after the overthrow of the Axis in Tunisia nearly a month ago . . .'

Bombs by air and bombs by sea, she thought. If any of their Italian prisoners were Pantellarians, it was lucky for them that they hadn't been at home that day.

Chapter 35

'Muriel, you won't half get in a row!' Joan exclaimed after tea the following evening. 'That's government property you're chopping up!'

The weather was warm and the days long, and Muriel was standing at one of the trestle tables in the dining room busily cutting the legs off her dungarees.

'I'm going to get my legs brown,' she said.

'She's right. You'll get wrong off the War Ag, Muriel, man,' Eileen said, gaping at her audacity.

'Be too late by then, won't it?' Muriel said, coolly laying the scissors down on top of the amputated legs and pushing them to one side. 'I'll have my shorts.' She picked up the cotton and snapped off a length, then moistened the end and squinted while she threaded the needle.

'No good talking to her – she'll do as she likes,' Audrey said.

'If I can make a suggestion,' said Laura, 'you'd make a better job if you pressed the hems up before sewing them.'

'Good idea.' Muriel gathered up the body of the

dungarees and trooped to the kitchen forthwith, followed by some of the girls.

They found Barbara giving cookery lessons to a few of the others, who were filling some deep apple pies they'd made for supper and scattering sugar on top.

'Where's the iron, Barbara?' Muriel asked, with the dismembered dungarees held prominently before her.

Barbara shook her head in mock despair at the sight of them. 'It's in there,' she said, indicating one of the cupboards, and added: 'You get no better for keeping, my girl.'

Muriel retrieved the iron. 'I know,' she agreed, cheerfully, 'and you get no worse. I'm glad Eric got his desk job, but oh, Barbara, I wish you weren't going!'

'So do I, in many ways – but it can't be helped,' Barbara said, putting the ironing board up for her. 'He comes first, and since he's had to go to London, I'll be following him after the new warden arrives. Besides, now I've got the plaster off my ankle the War Ag would have put me back to farm work anyway.'

'Not if we'd kicked up a stink they wouldn't,' Audrey protested.

'Officialdom generally gets its own way in the end, no matter how much of a stink people kick up,' Barbara said.

'Well, no good moaning. She's got to go, and that's the end of it,' Laura said.

'And we've got to hide the rest of those rations, before the new warden comes,' Joan said, with her eyes on the sugared tops of the apple pies.

'What's left of them,' Barbara said. 'I've made a bit of a hole in them, I have to admit.'

'I'm glad you did,' Vera said. 'At least we managed a few weeks of gluttony and luxury. And what's the point of *not* letting the next warden have the rations? We can't eat the stuff raw, so we might as well give her a chance. We can't very well come down here in the middle of the night and cook it ourselves.'

Audrey was watching Muriel turn up a hem and test the iron on the inside of it.

'So what are you going to do when the weather gets colder again?' she asked.

'Sew them back on again and let the hems down at the bottom.'

'They'll look terrible.'

'No more terrible than they always look.'

'They will. The top bit will be faded by the sun, and the legs will still be dark.'

Muriel shrugged. 'When they're caked in muck, like they usually are, it will make no difference.'

When the pressing and stitching was done, Muriel went upstairs to try them on, then went back downstairs to show them off.

'You surely don't intend to go to work in them, do you?' Laura said.

'They won't look so bad when I get my legs tanned.'

'They don't look bad now! You'll have all the farmers' eyes on stalks!' Eileen said.

★ ★ ★

Muriel worked in her shorts the following day, with no objections from the farmer. When they got back to the hostel, Barbara introduced the new warden to them, a middle-aged lady called Mrs Hughes. Barbara relinquished the warden's quarters to her immediately and rejoined the girls in the dormitory. A pall of gloom had descended on them all.

'Just promise me one thing, girls,' she said before they went to sleep, 'you won't terrify her to death with Elinor.'

'Ooh, you're putting ideas in our heads now. I'd never have thought of it, if you hadn't suggested it,' Audrey said, brightening up a little.

Barbara chuckled.

'We'll give her a week's trial,' said Joan, 'and if she doesn't shape up, we will. We'll give her the Elinor treatment. Now, don't you go warning her, Barbara.'

They went into the garden before tea on Friday, and Barbara took a group photograph of them with her box Brownie, with the house in the background, then Vera took one of the rest of them with Barbara, and Audrey another with Vera in the picture. Tea was a tasty but quiet meal, with the girls all too acutely aware of what they were losing. Whist was abandoned that night in favour of a farewell party at the Half Moon Inn. Howard played the piano for most of the evening, with Barbara turning the sheet music for him some of the time, and occasionally standing chatting to him when he wasn't playing. John Goodyear had somehow got wind of the party and bought a round of drinks for them all, telling Muriel and Audrey that he'd put in a request to the War Ag for two suitably qualified dairy workers to live in the cottage.

'I hope you get them,' Muriel smiled, and allowed him to light a cigarette for her and chat on about his plans for the farm.

Before they left the inn, Muriel witnessed a very friendly handshake and a lingering goodbye between Howard and Barbara, and Barbara saw that she had seen it. Later, when the rest of the girls had trooped off upstairs to get ready for bed and the new warden had gone back into her own domain, Barbara turned to Muriel and said, quietly: 'You know, when Eric went missing, I never would have believed I could love any other man. I was devastated. I didn't know where to turn, but I had to face it, and learn to rely on myself. He was gone for months, and it's a terrible thing, Muriel, but as the months roll by, you feel the bonds beginning to loosen . . .'

'It's Mother Nature's way, I suppose,' Muriel said. 'Maybe she's too kind to let us grieve forever.'

Barbara gave her a radiant smile though her eyes were glistening with tears. 'You understand.' She drew a deep breath, and let it out in a long sigh, before adding, 'but I am truly glad to have Eric back.'

Muriel nodded. Eric evidently hadn't come back a minute too soon, and it was just as well for all concerned that he hadn't left it any later, she thought.

'There's something I understand, as well,' Barbara said, even more quietly than before. 'That day in the fields, when that prisoner was trying to talk to you. That wasn't about Hitler, Muriel. That was a lovers' quarrel if ever I heard one.'

Muriel's heart contracted. 'Well, if it was, it's over now,' she said.

'What I said about the Germans – I just want you to know, it was only the war, and losing Eric. His sister studied music for years in Germany, and he used to spend all summer there as a boy. He made a lot of friends and if he hadn't learned to speak the language so fluently he'd never have made it back home. He says most Germans didn't want the war any more than we did.'

The tears now welled in Muriel's eyes. 'Well, anyway, it's over now,' she repeated.

Barbara clasped her hand, and gave it a squeeze. 'I'm sorry,' she said.

They shared a last breakfast with Barbara on Saturday morning, and said a last and fond goodbye. 'Keep in touch!' they told her as she waved them off to work.

'Why, I'm half wishing Eric had stayed in that bloody German prison camp now, man,' Eileen said, when they were in the lorry. 'Why couldn't he have been a model prisoner, and stopped there till the end of the war instead of turning up here to bugger things up for us?'

'I'm just glad for her sake he came back when he did,' Muriel said.

'Me too,' said Audrey. 'And he helped her settle Farmer Hogg, didn't he?'

Going back into the hostel after work felt like entering

a tomb, with Barbara gone. They sat down to Mrs Hughes'
version of Woolton Pie in low spirits.

On Sunday morning Eileen chopped the legs off her own
dungarees – to cheer herself up, she said. Joan and Vera
did the same, soon followed by every girl in the hostel
who had a decent pair of legs to show off. Audrey kept
her dungarees long, on the pretext that she had knock-
knees. They went to chapel together, and Audrey
managed to exchange a few smiles with Wilhelm.
Although she looked hard for Ernst, Muriel couldn't
catch even a glimpse of him, and her heart sank to her
boots. Still, it was for the best. In the long run it was definitely for the best – she lifted her chin and squared her
shoulders at the thought – and it would certainly have
been better for Audrey if she hadn't seen Wilhelm,
because her love affair with him had been doomed from
the start. Muriel felt the wrench of parting from Ernst as
sorely as she had on the first day, and she pitied Audrey
from the bottom of her heart for the inevitable end of her
hopes, if she had ever entertained any. It was hard to
know, with Audrey.

Dinner was dished up nearly cold, and was so unappetising they had to force it down. The girls exchanged
ominous glances.

'Where on earth does the bloody War Ag dig 'em up
from?' Joan demanded, after the warden had disappeared
into her own living quarters and they stood in the kitchen
washing pots.

'I don't know,' Laura said, 'but how long do you think we should put up with it this time before we complain?'

'A week,' Audrey said. 'We'll give her a week, and then we'll write to the War Ag, and we'll all sign the letter.'

'And if it doesn't improve after that, I vote we go on strike,' Muriel said.

'Hear, hear,' said Audrey.

Chapter 36

Miss Fawcett was waiting for Muriel and Audrey when they got back to the hostel after a weary midsummer's day spent treading silage. She called them into the office.

'We've had a request for two permanent milkmaids to live in, preferably qualified,' she told them, 'and you are the most suitable candidates, so we'd like you to go.'

'But we don't want to live in,' Muriel said. 'We like it here, with the other girls.'

'The farm's too far away to allow it, I'm afraid. You couldn't get there in time for the morning milking.'

Muriel said no more, but her dismay evidently showed on her face. Audrey looked about as cheerful.

'Look,' Miss Fawcett said, 'you've just had the benefit of going on a course, you two. You've been given a skill, and you shouldn't mind using it for the benefit of your country. There's nobody else as suitable as you.'

'I suppose we'll have to do our patriotic duty, then,' Audrey said, without enthusiasm.

'You will. Since the War Ag's spent money on training you, we think you should give it a chance. Pack your things tonight. You start tomorrow. We're sending you for a month. After that, we might reconsider, if you really hate it.'

'Fair enough,' Muriel said, brightening a little.

They went upstairs to pack and wash, and later went into the dining room for another abysmal meal, served half an hour after the proper time. Miss Fawcett ate with them, and when the girls on the rota for the job were clearing away and Muriel and Audrey were taking their tea into the common room, they saw her take Mrs Hughes into the office.

'I hope she's giving her a roasting about the food,' Audrey said.

'What's it to us?' Muriel frowned. 'We won't be eating it after tomorrow morning.'

Audrey laughed. 'You might spare a thought for our friends.'

Audrey's laughter was infectious, and Muriel smiled. 'I didn't mean it, really,' she said. 'I'm just so fed up about going. You know where we're going to, don't you?'

Audrey nodded. 'I've got a very good idea.'

'There's one consolation,' Muriel said, 'their house-keeper's a good cook. At least we shan't starve.'

When the office door opened and Miss Fawcett came out, Muriel went in to collect her post – yet another letter from Fred. The envelope felt quite fat, and she went out into the garden and joined the few other girls sitting there, looking forward to reading his news. The bulk of the envelope was owing to the snaps he'd enclosed, taken on that Sunday at the hostel. Muriel looked at his photo and thought she liked him more as time went on and she got to know him better through his letters. Honest, decent and uncomplicated – Fred was totally lacking in worldly wisdom, and none the worse for that. She passed the photos round, prompting another wave of nostalgia for Barbara's reign as warden.

'Well, you've got your own way, then,' Muriel said, as she and Audrey dumped their belongings in the cottage next to the cowman's.

'I usually do,' John grinned. 'There's a pile of logs there, and some at the back of the cottage. You'd better light a fire every day for a bit, and stick some warming pans in the beds. They've been aired, but they haven't been slept in for a while.'

'We expect you to take us into the village for whist every Friday, and to the Half Moon every Saturday,' Audrey said.

'That's no hardship. I go myself.'

'And we'll need to borrow a horse to visit the hostel on Sundays, so we can catch up with all the news from the other girls,' Muriel said.

'Can't promise that.'

'We can doss in the hostel on Saturday nights, then,' Audrey said. 'I'm very religious. I can't miss chapel on Sundays.'

'There's a chapel quite near here, in a little hamlet called Bonnick,' John said. 'Congregation of about three.'

'That's no good. The minister in Griswold's the only

one that inspires me,' Audrey said, 'and we do get Sunday off, I hope.'

'Not all of it. The cows need milking, even on Sundays.'

'We might want to have a friend to stay, now and then,' Muriel said.

'No reason why not. I told you that before.'

Muriel nodded and stepped outside the cottage to look at the landscape. All was green. Green wheat and green barley driven in waves by the breeze, so that it looked like the sea, green meadows, fields of green vegetables, and every hedge and tree in full green leaf. How different the land looked, dressed in its beautiful summer clothes. A symphony in green, she thought – a thousand and one shades and tints but – apart from the farm buildings – no colour other than glorious green, as far as the eye could see – until she looked skyward and saw an azure sky and big white cumulus clouds. The blue heavens above them, and a lush green garden of Eden below. 'Paradise,' she sighed, under her breath.

'Have no fear, John, your cows are safe with us,' she said. 'We've been on a course. We're experts.'

'Good,' he grinned. 'You're just in time to muck them out.'

Dinner did not disappoint. They sat down to rabbit in parsley sauce with buttered new potatoes and spring cabbage, all done to a turn and piping hot. The girls did full justice to it, and then the housekeeper put a large rhubarb pie and a jug of custard on the table.

'Show us who's your favourite, then, Auntie Elsie,' John laughed, when she started to cut the pie. 'Auntie Elsie' said nothing but cut a slice far larger than the rest and lifted it into his dish, laughing too.

John's dad feigned disgust. 'See what I've got to put up with?' he said.

The girls smiled, and attacked their smaller portions of sweetened pie, which they soon found were more than large enough. John quickly ate his, and went out to see to business on the farm.

The housekeeper quickly cleared the mountain of crockery and disappeared into the kitchen with it. Since they had a couple of hours' leisure before afternoon milking, the girls sat at the table with John's dad, drinking hot, milky tea.

'She's a very good cook,' Audrey commented.

'Aye. She's got a hundred ways of cooking rabbits, and every one of 'em tasty.'

'A good way of keeping pests down,' Audrey commented. 'Turn 'em into dinner.'

'Aye, they're better on table than in fields, destroying crops.'

'I suppose she's been with you a long time, your housekeeper?' Muriel said.

'Aye. Nigh on thirty years.'

'John can only have been a little boy, then.'

'He was five.'

'I suppose that's why he calls her "Auntie Elsie",' Muriel said.

John's father sat back in his chair and laughed. 'He calls her "Auntie Elsie" because she's my sister,' he said. 'She came to keep house for us after my wife died. She's lived here ever since, and she's been as good as a mother to him.'

'He never said. He just kept calling her "our housekeeper".'

'It's easier to say "our housekeeper" rather than go through all rigmarole of explaining.'

They unpacked and put their things away, then Muriel mooted having Doris to stay for a few days. Audrey had no objection, so Muriel sat down to write to her, care of the Maypole on Holderness Road. It would reach her there all right, and a few days in the countryside would do her good.

They saw plenty of evidence of Auntie Elsie's mothering in the next couple of days. John was her spoiled, petted child. 'Show us who's your favourite, then, Auntie Elsie!' he would say, and he was given the best joint of rabbit or choicest pieces of meat, always the largest slice of pie or any other good thing she had to distribute. The light of sheer adoration shone in Auntie Elsie's eyes whenever she looked at her nephew, and he glowed under her doting gaze. It provided a source of unfailing amusement to Muriel and Audrey. They mocked him behind his back, and occasionally to his face. Audrey said the display of devotion made her want to puke, but Muriel protested it was play-acting on John's part. Auntie Elsie doted on

him, and he just played up to it. Muriel even began to see
John through Auntie Elsie's eyes – a motherless boy who
deserved endless compensation for the blow life had dealt
him in his tender years. She developed quite kindly feelings towards him.

'If I had a dowter, I'd marry her to him i' quick
sticks . . . he gets everything when owd man's happed
up . . .' – making no bones about the fact that the real
attraction was the possessions and the acres, before any
consideration of the man. Country people were quite
pragmatic, in many ways, Muriel had found, and perhaps
they were right to base their life's choices on such hard-
headed practicalities, rather than risk their futures on what
might turn out to be a passing fancy. When she and
Audrey were bringing the cows in from the pasture, or
letting them out again, Muriel sometimes scanned the
wide Goodyear acres and thought that if she married
John, all this beauty might be hers for the rest of her life.

'Maybe I got it wrong,' Audrey told her, when they'd
been at Thornhill Farm a couple of days. 'He does seem
quite taken with you.'

'I quite like him,' Muriel said – and she did. She had
become quite fond of him in a ragging, bantering sort of
way. He was funny and good humoured, and she liked
him. Audrey tactfully avoided all mention of Ernst, and
his presence in both their minds loomed all the larger for
it. The thought of Ernst never failed to give Muriel a
wrench and the knowledge that she'd lost him darkened
the idyllic picture she was painting for herself with John.

Still, she'd been right when she'd told him they had both
better marry their own kind – and there were far worse
fates than being married to John Goodyear.

The thunder rolled and the heavens opened the following day, just as Muriel got to the far end of the pasture to
bring a wayward cow in for milking. By the time she'd
driven it back to the cow house she was soaked to the
skin, and her dark hair was hanging like rats' tails, with
water streaming off the ends. John was waiting for her in
the cow house.

'Where's Audrey?'

'Sheltering in the cart shed.'

'Where's the cowman?'

'In the bull house. We've got five minutes on our
own.' He pulled her towards him, and holding her tight,
kissed her full on the lips, caressing her bottom, then slid-
ing his fingers round the hem of her shorts.

She wrenched herself away and gave his face a resound-
ing slap, with the full force of her overworked right arm
behind it. 'There!' she said, her eyes blazing.

'Ouch!' He rubbed his cheek.

A second later she was sickened to think that he would
soon have the outline of her fingers on his cheek, just as
the warden's had been impressed on Laura's – and what
would Auntie Elsie think?

'Are you a virgin, Muriel?' he asked.

She blushed to the roots of her hair. 'Mind your own
business,' she said.

He laughed. 'You are, then.'

She turned her back, and started to assemble the equipment for the milking.

'I'll do that,' he said. 'I think I'll stay here until my face cools off. You'd better run back to the cottage and get some dry clothes on. Grab an oilskin and take it to Audrey, while you're at it, and get back here as fast as you can.'

Back at the cottage, Muriel found a letter on the mat from Miss Chapman, thanking her for her invitation. Because of all the upheaval with her mother, she was taking a week off work, and would be delighted to visit Muriel at the cottage. She could come on the Sunday before her holiday, which was the 27th of June, or on the Sunday after. Muriel hurriedly scribbled a note back telling her to come on the first Sunday, and bring enough clothes for a few days; they might not want to let her go too quickly. She pushed it into her pocket, put on her oilskin and grabbed Audrey's, then hurried back.

John was busy machine milking the cows with the cowman, a ruddy-cheeked man with the appearance of the typical farmer who was also soaked to the skin. He looked up and gave them a friendly word of greeting. The girls worked under the direction of the two men until the milking was done, with John telling them all about his ideas for the farm. He wanted to divide it into four self-contained units, and keep a close and constant watch on each separate unit's costs and profits. That way each unit could be expanded or contracted according to whichever paid the best. When the government had repealed the Corn Production Act after the First World War, they'd almost lost Thornhill Farm, he said. The price of corn had halved in two years, and many an arable farmer had gone bust and had to get out of farming altogether. They'd hung on to Thornhill by the skin of their teeth, but the men who'd weathered the storm best were the ones who'd switched to stock breeding. 'You need more than one string to your bow in farming,' John said. 'You can't rely on government. They're always chopping and changing.'

'You've got more than one string to your bow,' Audrey said. 'You've got the corn, the cows, and the veg.'

The cowman appeared to be in some discomfort. 'Are you all right?' Muriel asked. She had to repeat the question before he answered.

'Just a bit of earache,' he said. 'It's not getting any better. I'll have to go and see the quack, before long.'

'You'll be all right. It'll soon wear off. You don't run off to the doctor every time your little finger aches,' John said, and continued with his lecture on farming. 'I've got the cows, the corn and the veg, but they all need to be managed and costed separately, so that you can change what you produce as fast as prices and conditions change, cut back on what's not paying, and put your efforts into what does pay. But getting a new idea into a stubborn old man's head is horse work. Worse than horse work. And they're another relic of the past he won't get rid of. Isn't that right, Robert?'

'Eh?' said Robert.

'Deaf or daft, which is it?' John demanded, abruptly.

Robert looked at him, uncomprehending.

'Well, your father did survive, I suppose, and you won't need so many tractors, if the price of corn's going to drop after the war,' Muriel said, in an oblique defence of Mr Goodyear, and to deflect the attack on Robert.

'We will need the tractors; we'll still have to plough and harrow and drill, and move stock feed and veg.'

'I wouldn't mind learning to drive a tractor,' Audrey said. 'I wouldn't mind working with the horses, either.'

'I'll teach you,' said John, 'but it'll have to be in your spare time – when the milking's done.'

Chapter 37

They went to the whist on Friday, walking into the hall with John and his father after everyone else was seated. Sammy Mawson was not there to comment. When they sat down to play against Jack and Cissie, she gave Muriel a very knowing smile. 'I see he's got you up at Thornhill, then,' she said.

'Well, we had been on a course for dairy farming,' Audrey said, 'so it was the War Ag that decided.'

'War Ag's done you a good turn,' Jack said, with a wink at Muriel. 'You'll be all right, there.'

'I see Sammy's not in tonight,' she replied.

'No. Gettin' ready for his nuptials, I reckon. Maybe even having a bath and a shave,' Jack said.

On Saturday the girls called in at the hostel for their post, and came upon girls talking in hushed voices in the garden. They kept John waiting in the car, while they joined the group and heard about all the new warden's failings.

'We'll have to be off,' Muriel said, after about five minutes. 'We've got someone waiting.'

'Oh, before you go, you might like to know we saw the blushing bride this morning, coming out of the church with her new husband. Only she wasn't blushing,' Lorna said. 'The sun was shining on her, though, so we hope she'll be happy.'

'Oh, the new Mrs Mawson,' Audrey said, '– or might it be the new Mr Hubbard? It's a toss-up as to who'll wear the trousers in their house.'

'He'd better behave himself, or he'll get his face slapped,' Laura said.

'Aye, and she'll want him in bed for half past nine.'

'And not for hanky panky, either, I bet,' Joan grinned.

'What did Sammy look like? Had he had a shave?'

'Why, aye, man! And he'd even combed his hair! He looked as if she'd had the scrubbing brush round him,' Eileen said.

'He'd better mind his p's and q's now. Funny, we didn't see her sister among the happy throng, although we looked as hard as we could,' Vera said. 'The landlord and landlady at the Dog and Duck were there though. That's where they had the reception.'

'Probably on what's left of our rations,' Joan said.

'Why, they'll all have dysentery, man, the muck in that place,' said Eileen.

'Oh, well, good luck to them. Life's too short to bear grudges,' Muriel said. 'We'll have to go. See you down at the Half Moon.'

John wanted to know what had kept them so long, so Muriel gave him the news about Sadie and Sammy coming out of the church, man and wife. After that she read her letters from Fred and his mother, with John very keen to know who they were from, and what was in them. She had no objection to telling him.

The landlord at the Half Moon was in party mood as usual, Audrey had a pleasant evening with her paratrooper, who bought her drinks, Lorna and Vera were happy with their aircraftmen, and the rest of the girls seemed to be enjoying themselves with the paras, airmen, and others. Howard asked them all if they'd heard from Barbara, and how she was. Lorna told him she'd telephoned the hostel to say she was settled in a flat in London, and would write to them later. Muriel sat with John for most of the evening.

On the way back, John himself suggested leaving Audrey at the hostel, so that she could go to her favoured chapel for the Sunday service. Muriel demurred, and Audrey knew why, so said nothing.

'Come on, Muriel! Do your pal a favour!' John wheedled.

'All right. We'll both stay, and we'll both go to chapel,' Muriel said. 'I like that minister, as well.'

'Come on, Muriel. You know I can't spare you both.'

Muriel looked at Audrey, and relented. 'All right, then, but there'd better not be any funny business on the way back.'

'It's a promise,' John said. 'Get the lorry to drop you off on Monday morning, Audrey. The petrol ration won't stretch to another journey.'

'You sure?' The question was directed at Muriel.

She nodded. 'You go, and give me all the news when you get back.'

'You might as well get in the front now, Muriel,' John said.

Muriel spotted Miss Chapman standing outside the cottage door talking to John's dad, on her way back from the cow house on Sunday morning – a Miss Chapman that she hardly recognised, decked in her holiday attire, a beautiful lacy-patterned short-sleeved jumper, a linen skirt, and peep-toed sandals. And she was more than just talking to John's dad – she was playing up to him, with the light in her eyes and the smile of the typical woman who is not yet dead, talking to an attractive man of around her own age. When she drew nearer Muriel saw that she was wearing make-up, and she had a faint but unmistakable whiff of expensive perfume. Muriel was suddenly conscious of her own scent, of the cow dung clinging to her boots.

'Right,' John's father said. 'You two will want to talk, but come to us for dinner. I'll give you a tour round the farm, later, if you like, Miss Chapman.'

'Thank you, Mr Goodyear,' Miss Chapman said, beaming up at him. 'I would. I'd like it very much.'

At dinner Miss Chapman ate well, thanked her host and praised the cook. John regarded her with an amused tolerance. After having their offer of help with the washing up rejected, they left the farmhouse and went to sit outside the cottage in the sun for an hour, feasting their eyes on the scenery.

'It's so lovely here,' Miss Chapman said. 'It was the best thing you could ever have done, joining the Land Army, Muriel, although I did miss you at the shop. Still do.'

'Well, we did work together for nearly three years,' Muriel said, 'so you shouldn't be surprised to know I've often thought about you.'

'Really? Well, Ada's a good girl, but it's not the same. There's not the same spark in her.'

'Stay here for a few days, and have a bit of a rest,' Muriel said. 'Stay tonight, at least, Audrey won't be back until tomorrow morning. You've got nothing to rush back for, have you?'

'Not this week.'

'Well, then.'

When John's father came, Miss Chapman changed her sandals for a pair of boots she just happened to have brought with her, and set off with him very happily. She got back after Muriel had returned from the milking, with butter and bacon from Mr Goodyear, and an invitation to the farmhouse for a game of cards after tea, if they would like to go. They decided they would, so Miss Chapman unpacked, and laid her nightie out on the bed and began to titivate herself. Muriel watched her, in her pink knitted silk jumper powdering her nose, and combing her loose, waved blonde hair, still finding it quite a novelty to see her in anything other than working clothes and thinking that Miss Chapman must have been a smasher, in her youth.

Auntie Elsie was no card player, so John partnered Muriel against his father and Miss Chapman for a few games of whist. For all her gentle exterior, Miss Chapman turned out to be a surprisingly sharp player. John's amused tolerance became a little less amused. He sat up and took notice. Now his father was amused, and Auntie Elsie looked up from her knitting. Miss Chapman and Mr Goodyear won the first five hands.

'Where did you learn to play?' he asked her, when they stopped for a cup of tea and a bite of supper.

'We used to play at home when I was young, and then my fiancé and his friends liked a game, and I still play with friends. We sometimes go to whist drives.'

'You never married, though,' John's father commented.

'No. It was not to be. The Great War saw to that.'

'He was killed, then.'

'No,' Miss Chapman said, 'he wasn't killed; that might have been kinder, to us both. He was driven out of his mind – they called it shell shock. There were times when he couldn't sleep at all, and when he did, he had nightmares. We all hoped he would get better, with time and patience, but he never did. He was never the same after the war, poor lad.'

Auntie Elsie looked down into her teacup. 'I might have been married myself, if it hadn't been for the war,' she said. John and his father looked at her, but said nothing.

Miss Chapman's kindly blue eyes turned towards Auntie Elsie, overflowing with sympathy. 'Yes, it dashed a lot of people's hopes, and this war's just the same,' she said, with a quick glance at Muriel.

'What happened to him in the end, your chap?' Mr Goodyear asked.

Miss Chapman sighed heavily. 'Well, he was a wreck, really – twitching and watchful all the time. He used to jump at nothing, and you couldn't reason him out of it. He was quite violent at times, and it got to the stage that his mother was terrified of him. Her neighbours got the police one night, and it ended with him being committed to De la Pole – the mental asylum, you know.'

'Terrible,' Auntie Elsie said.

'To see him come to that from what he was before – it was terrible. It broke our hearts, but none of us could do anything. His mother was a widow, and she couldn't manage him. I had to work for my living. The staff do their best, but asylums aren't nice places to be in. I visited him every Sunday until the day he died, and he always knew who I was; I think that was what kept me going. We used to walk in the grounds on nice days, but he never came home again, poor lad. That's what war does.'

After a moment's silence broken only by the spluttering of the fire and the ticking of the clock, Auntie Elsie got up and cleared the table, refusing an offer of help from Miss Chapman. She could do it quicker herself.

'Elsie doesn't have to wash them,' John's father said.

'One of the farm hands' wives will be in at seven o'clock tomorrow morning for that.'

Play resumed for another round, and after a while Auntie Elsie came in and took up her knitting again. Miss Chapman seemed to have lost her edge, but although Muriel and John did much better, they were still beaten. John's father walked Miss Chapman and Muriel back to the cottage at about half past nine.

'I was surprised someone as nice as you hadn't been snapped up,' he told Doris. 'Now I know why. It's a sad story.'

Miss Chapman coloured a little. 'Count your blessings, one by one,' she said. 'I've got my health. I'm able to work and support myself, and I've got some very good friends.'

'Count me among 'em,' John's father said, 'and call me Peter. I haven't enjoyed an evening at home so much since before my wife died. It was nice to play cards and be sociable in my own house, for a change. We don't get enough visitors, here.'

'It's not easy to get to, but I wouldn't swap it for the world if I were you, Mr Goodyear – Peter,' Miss Chapman said. 'It's such a lovely, peaceful place. A piece of heaven on earth.'

'In summer, maybe. You might not think so if you were working out in the fields in the middle of winter. I reckon Muriel can vouch for that.'

'I can,' Muriel said, 'and I can vouch for the fact that in the middle of winter it's no better working in the freezing cold Maypole grocer's than it is in the fields — except that you don't get rained on in the Maypole, maybe. Peter, this is Doris, by the way.'

He extended his hand. 'We're friends, then. That all right, Doris?'

She took his hand and shook it. 'It is all right,' she smiled. 'Very much all right.'

Chapter 38

Audrey was back the following day, just in time for breakfast in the farmhouse.

'I'll have dinner with Miss Chapman, today, Auntie
Elsie,' Muriel said. 'We can't expect you to do extra
cooking every day.'

'Bring her here,' Auntie Elsie laughed. 'One extra's
nothing to me. I cook for dozens when it's harvest time.'

'Well, if you're sure . . .'

'Course I'm sure. You bring her.'

Muriel was easily persuaded. Auntie Elsie's cooking
would certainly be better than her own, and it would save
her a lot of extra work, apart from being more sociable.

Audrey worked doubly hard to make up for her three
hours off, and with the cleaning and mucking out done,
they went back to the cottage to get washed for another
good dinner. After that, they sat drinking tea in the sun
outside the cottage with Doris, talking for a while.

'I'll go to the farmhouse and ask them to order a taxi
for me when you girls go to do the milking,' she said.

'No, stay another night,' Muriel said.

'You can stay as long as you like for me, Miss Chapman,' said Audrey. 'A month, if you like. Two.'

With that settled, they sank into a comfortable drowse, lulled by the buzzing of insects and chirruping of birds, and the snoring of one of the farm's oversized tomcats stretched out at their feet, well fattened on plentiful mice.

John's father called at the cottage just before the girls set off to do the afternoon milking, to take Doris off on a jaunt round the countryside in the pony trap. They ragged John about his dad's 'romancing' Miss Chapman on their way to the cow house.

'He must think he's sixteen instead of sixty,' John said. 'I'm glad he didn't take the car, anyway, bumping it along the lanes round here.'

'I thought it was your car,' said Muriel.

'Nothing's mine, yet,' he said.

Doris was back when they returned from the milking, with eggs boiled, bread buttered and salad washed for tea – and another invitation to spend the evening at the farmhouse.

'I forgot to ask you, was that minister's sermon worth staying in Griswold for, Audrey?' John asked, when they arrived.

'It certainly was, John,' she replied.

He gave her a crafty, quizzing look. 'What was it about, then?'

'It was the parable of the inquisitive farmer, who was too much of a heathen to go to chapel himself, and find out,' Audrey said, quite unperturbed.

It raised a smile even on Auntie Elsie's face as she sat busily knitting a sock on five needles. Doris commented on the neatness of the turned heel, and said she wished she'd brought her own knitting. She'd had a jumper on the needles for weeks, but had never knitted socks, having no men or children to knit for. Auntie Elsie looked towards John and his father.

'I've no time for knitting anything else but men's jumpers and socks; they keep me going full time, my two men. I've certainly got no time for knitting fancy jumpers.'

'Who's for a game of whist, then?' John's father asked.

John discovered he still had to go and refill the petrol-driven generator and see to the horses, top up their food, water and bedding and settle them for the night. 'We ought to have been rid of 'em,' he said. 'Horses aren't worth keeping now. Tractors are the thing. They're a lot more efficient.'

Auntie Elsie looked up from her knitting. 'John's always one step in front of rest,' she said, with an approving smile. 'He's got a lot of progressive ideas, but his dad's a stick in the mud.'

'I like horses,' his father said, 'so while I'm here, we'll keep 'em.'

John had the last word before he went out. 'No sentiment in business, Dad!'

'It's not only sentiment,' his father said, after he'd gone. 'Tractors are all right when they don't break down, and you can get fuel for 'em. When you can't, horses come in very handy. Not only that, you get the manure.'

'The government will make sure you can get the fuel, Peter,' Auntie Elsie said.

'Government left us in the lurch after the Great War,' he said, 'and they'll do it again, if it suits 'em. I wouldn't trust government as far as I could spit.'

They settled down to play, with John's father partnered with Doris against Muriel and Audrey. Audrey told Muriel they'd had a letter at the hostel from Barbara, and how much the girls were all missing her cooking – 'nearly as good as yours, Auntie Elsie'. Audrey threw the compliment out as an aside, and then she and Muriel followed it with an account of Miss Hubbard's hoarded rations, and the contrast between her and Barbara as wardens, and then how they came to lose Barbara after her husband's escape from a German prison camp.

Auntie Elsie said nothing, but frowned, seeming to disapprove of the criticism of Miss Hubbard.

'Poor man. They're the most wicked people on the face of the earth, the Germans,' Doris said.

'I don't think Barbara's husband thinks so,' Muriel said. 'He'd had holidays in Germany before the war and made a lot of friends there.'

'Well, I've no complaints about any of German lads who've worked on my farm,' said John's father.

Doris went pale. 'You don't mean they come here!' she said, appalled – but not too appalled to play a trump and take the trick.

John's father watched her take it with a satisfied smile. 'Certainly, they come here. They come to most of farms round about and most of us are glad to have them. I'd rather have them than Italians. They're more like us, for a start, and they're better workers than Ities.'

The conversation drifted to the present warden, who was no improvement on Sadie Hubbard, and then on to Sammy Mawson, then Sammy and Sadie, married the day before yesterday, although they must both be around sixty.

'It's never too late, it seems, Doris,' John's father said, with a wink at her. She beamed at him. Auntie Elsie looked sharply up at his use of Doris's first name, and watched them with jealous eyes, suddenly alert to the danger. John came in later and took no part in the conversation but sat reading the paper by the fire with his boots off until nine, and then he glanced at the clock and offered to walk the visitors back to the cottage. They took that as their cue to go and said their thanks and good nights to Auntie Elsie and their host, but politely refused to give John the trouble of putting his boots on again for the short walk back to the cottage, and went without him.

'You brought a lot of clothes, for someone who was only going to stay one night, Miss Chapman,' Muriel said, as they sat over a cup of tea before going to bed. Getting used to calling her Doris was proving to be quite a hurdle.

'I did, didn't I?' Doris agreed, with a twinkle in her eye. 'Well, I thought it might be best just to stay for one day, and see how we got on. You're never sure how quickly you might wear out your welcome, are you? I meant to go at the first hint, but you haven't given me one, so far.'

'We got a pretty strong one from John Goodyear tonight, though, didn't we?' said Audrey.

'He must be tired, and so must you, getting up at half past four. I didn't realise how early you started, before I came here,' Doris said.

'His father's twice his age, and he wasn't showing any sign of being tired,' said Audrey.

'The young need more sleep.'

'He's not young!' Muriel said. 'He's middle-aged.'

'Bloody rude as well, sometimes,' said Audrey.

'He just wanted a bit of peace in his own home after a long day, I expect,' Doris said. 'I'll go home tomorrow. Tomorrow morning, I'll go to the farmhouse and ask Auntie Elsie to telephone for a taxi for me.'

'No, don't,' Muriel said. 'Why should you? John told us they'd no objection to us having visitors, and you're my visitor. You're nothing to do with them.'

'Mine, too,' Audrey said. 'I reckon we'll keep you on as our housekeeper.'

'Well, the spirits foretold a new direction for me,' Doris laughed, 'but I never imagined I'd be keeping house in a farm cottage.'

Muriel's face lit up. 'The spirits!' she said. 'I'd forgotten the spirits! You were going to get them to help us.'

'I did, so here we are!' Doris smiled.

'The spirits, eh?' Audrey said. 'That's a rum one. They should give Mrs Hughes her marching orders and make you the new warden at the hostel. You could get to grips with Elinor.'

'I bet neither of those women were ever engaged,' John told Muriel while they were bringing the cattle in from the fields the following morning. 'It's all eyewash. I know Auntie Elsie wasn't, and I bet your Miss Chapman wasn't, either. These old maids spin romances to make themselves important, sometimes.'

'These old maids? I'm surprised to hear you talk about Auntie Elsie like that.'

'Well, it's the truth. I'm fond of her, but she spins romances about herself sometimes – in fact she lies her head off, and I bet your Miss Chapman does the same.'

'I worked in a shop with her for three years. I've never known her tell a lie. And she certainly was engaged. My mother grew up with her. She knew them both, her and the chap she was going to marry.'

'All right then, I suppose she must have been, but – when's she going home?'

'On Sunday,' Muriel said, feigning surprise, but suspecting what he was driving at.

'On *Sunday*? Look, Muriel, I might as well come clean. I don't want her here.'

'Your dad doesn't seem to mind.'

'Auntie Elsie and I mind. She's fed up of the extra work with cooking and clearing up. She's got enough to do.'

'All right. Doris is my visitor. We'll stay in the cottage. That solves Auntie Elsie's problem.'

'It doesn't solve mine, though. He might end up marrying her, have you thought of that? I've never seen such a gleam in his eye.'

Muriel laughed. 'Why should it bother you if he does? She's too old to have children. She won't be able to take anything from you.'

'If they get married and he dies first, she might be entitled to the farm!'

'Might be?'

'Yes. I'll have to go and see a solicitor, and find out exactly what she could get – of our children's inheritance, if we get married, remember.'

'Your inheritance.'

'Mine and my children's – our children's – if we have any.'

'I didn't realise we were getting married, but I can tell you it would never enter her mind to do a thing like that.'

'I said *if* we get married, and you'd be surprised what enters people's minds when they smell money.'

'Miss Chapman,' Muriel said, with Barbara-like dignity, 'is fifty years old. She's earned her own living all her life.'

'Perhaps she's fed up with earning her own living then, if she can get a doting old man to provide her with a first-class meal ticket. And he's too naïve to suspect.'

'But you're not,' Muriel said. 'Is that why all your other lady friends got the boot?'

'They were all after everything they could get, whether you believe it or not.'

'What about me, then? Am I after everything I can get?'

'You didn't do the chasing, did you? I've had to do the chasing; that makes you a bit more trustworthy. And if we got married . . .'

'I'd have no fears for our children's inheritance,' Muriel said, '*if* we got married.'

Audrey went to the farmhouse at dinnertime, not willing to sacrifice a good dinner for a sandwich, but Muriel went back to the cottage, to have beef paste sandwiches with Doris, leaving it to John and Auntie Elsie to explain to his father why they weren't there.

'I've seen that bull today,' Doris said, as she buttered the bread. 'I've never seen one so close, and the size of it! And the lady next door, the cowman's wife, says it weighs well over a ton. Imagine that! You wonder how any creature can get so big, just by eating grass. She says they keep it because the cows have to have a calf every year, to keep them producing milk, and then their calves are taken away. It seems very cruel.'

'I suppose it is cruel,' Muriel said, 'I suppose a lot of things about farming are cruel, but what else can the farmers do? It's their living.'

Chapter 39

They were awoken at the crack of dawn by a furious knocking on the cottage door. The cowman's wife stood there, fully dressed and frantic.

'Oh, it's my husban'! There's something not right with him. Will you come?'

She looked so alarmed that they quickly threw some clothes on, and followed her into her cottage and upstairs to where the cowman lay. 'He's been in pain all night,' she said, 'we haven't had a wink of sleep, and now look – behind his ear, how red and swollen it is – it's pushing his ear right out.' She attempted to touch the swelling, to show them, but her husband flinched and shied away.

'It looks like a massive carbuncle,' Audrey said, trying to see it in the grey dawn light.

'He's red hot,' his wife said, 'but he keeps saying he's frozen, and he's that dizzy he can't stand up. Just put your hand on his forehead.'

Doris took one look at him and said: 'It's mastoiditis. I've seen it before, and it's dangerous. Somebody will have to get him to a hospital straightaway.'

'He can't walk, he's that dizzy.'

'I'll run to the farmhouse,' Audrey said. 'I've got longer legs than you two.'

After a few minutes she came back in the car with John's father. He helped Robert into it, and since Doris was convinced he would need an operation, Robert's wife packed a bag for them both, and asked Doris to go with them to explain to the doctors.

John set the farmhands to work, and then had to do all his father's routine work on the farm as well as his own, leaving Muriel and Audrey to manage the milking alone. They worked as fast as they could, but were late for breakfast, and after cleaning and mucking out they were also late for dinner. Auntie Elsie took no trouble to conceal her annoyance with Muriel, but at least John spared them his 'show us who's your favourite' games.

John's father and Doris came back in the car just before afternoon milking, without either Robert or his wife. Doris got out of the car to open the farm gate for him to drive through.

'It takes less than an hour and a half to get to Beverley,' John said. 'Three hours would have given him plenty of time to drop them at the hospital and get back here. Where the hell have they been?'

'I don't know. Why don't you ask them?' Muriel said.

'If your cowman had seen a doctor straightaway, as soon as he had earache, it might never have happened,' Audrey suggested.

John missed the implied criticism. 'That's just what he

should have done, the idiot,' he said, flushed with annoyance, 'but our Robert's too stupid to come in out of the rain.'

'He got a good drenching the same time I did,' Muriel said. 'Maybe that's what caused it.'

He turned towards her. 'Well don't you go getting any bloody mastoiditis. We've got enough mastoiditis to last us a lifetime, here.'

'I'll avoid it if I can,' she promised.

John's father parked the car in its spot at the side of the farmhouse, and he and Doris got out.

'What's the news, then?' John called, as they approached.

'He's got to have an operation. The doctor says he'll be off work for weeks,' his father said.

'I knew it! He was the best at dealing with that bloody bull, as well,' John said. 'Bloody idiot! Why didn't he go to the doctor's as soon as he knew something was wrong?'

Maybe because you kept saying things like: 'You don't go running off to the doctor's every time your little finger aches,' Muriel thought, but she managed not to say it.

'Calm down,' his father said. 'We called in at the War Ag, after we'd seen Robert into hospital, and taken his wife to her relations in Beverley. They can probably send us a couple of prisoners.'

'Probably? And they'll probably be a couple of duds, if they do. Let's hope they know something about cattle, that's all,' John said. 'Come on, you two, let's get on with it.'

The girls ran to catch him up as he stalked off ahead of them. His mood was evident even to the cows, and when they got back to the cow house one of them walked into the wrong stall. John suddenly turned on her in temper, and beat her to her knees. She bellowed pitifully.

Muriel began to hate him. 'That's a good way to improve your milk yield,' she said.

'Let me worry about that, will you?' he snapped. 'You might have been on a bloody course, but you're not an expert yet.'

Doris had tea ready for them when they got back to the cottage. 'I hope you don't mind,' she said, 'but I told Peter we wouldn't go to the farmhouse tonight. I said you'd probably be tired.'

'Very tactful,' Audrey said. 'I'd have told the truth – his sister's fed up of having us there, and so is his son.'

'I suppose he knows the truth,' Doris said, mildly.

Whether Peter knew the truth or not, he called on them after tea, to take them all out for a ride in the pony and trap. Muriel hung back, not wanting to intrude on this budding middle-aged love affair.

'Come on, girls,' Doris implored them. 'You can't stay in, on a beautiful evening like this.'

But the girls both insisted that they really were tired, and Doris and Peter drove off on their own.

Muriel was already in bed when she heard the clip-clop of hooves approaching. The pony cart came to a halt under the open window.

'Audrey!' she called, just loud enough for Audrey to hear. 'They're back!'

Audrey came into the bedroom, smiling. 'I'm going to shout down and ask him what he thinks he's doing, keeping her out till this time,' she said, going straight to the window.

'Shush! I can hear them talking.'

They looked down on Doris and Peter's heads, and heard every word.

'I like having you in my house, Doris,' John's father said. 'I'd like you in it for good, not just as a visitor.'

Muriel felt Audrey's elbow nudge her ribs.

'But we haven't known each other two minutes!' Doris protested. 'And what about your son, and your sister? They wouldn't like it at all.'

'I'd like it, and it's my house. They'd have to get used to it.'

'They wouldn't like it,' Doris repeated. 'There'd be an awful atmosphere.'

'Well, then, he's been chomping at bit for years, wanting farm run his way. Maybe I'll split it, make a small-holding for us, and let him manage rest. I'm not getting any younger – maybe it's time for me to take a back seat. There are ways round things, lass.'

'Peter, I manage a food shop in the middle of a city. This is the first time I've ever been near a farm in my life. I've no more idea about farming than the man in the moon.'

'You'd learn. You're not slow.'

'And Auntie Elsie? Two women in a house never works.'

'She'll have to put up with it. And she will, when she knows she's got no choice.'

'That sounds a bit hard.'

'She can stop with John, then. Let her look after him, till he finds himself a wife. I reckon he's got his eye on young Muriel. If they can't get on, Elsie can live in one of farm cottages, and have it all her own way there.'

'They're young. But it's a big step for people our age, John. I'm quite set in my ways, and you probably are as well. The older you are, the harder it is to adapt.'

'Not too hard. It's all possible, and we could have some good times together.'

'It would need a lot of thinking about.'

'Think about it, then,' he said. 'Sleep on it, and we'll talk about it tomorrow.'

He kissed her, and then she slowly got down, and came into the cottage.

'Well I never! Your plan might come right in the end,' Audrey murmured. 'You for John, and Doris for his dad! Who'd have believed it?'

'It was never a plan,' Muriel said, her voice also low, 'it was just a passing idea, in my head.'

'Well, it seems to be working out. She might be your mother-in-law yet!' Audrey said, and discreetly retired to her own room before Doris came upstairs.

Muriel hopped into bed, and a minute later heard Doris's tread on the stair.

'Are you asleep, Muriel?' she whispered.

Muriel opened her eyes. 'No. Did you have a nice jaunt?'

'It was lovely, but I think I've just had a proposal of marriage. "It's all possible," he said.'

Muriel laughed, and sat up. 'Congratulations!'

But Doris shuddered, looking fearful rather than happy. 'I've lived my maiden life for fifty years, and after my young man died, I prayed for something like this to happen, but it was a dream, just a nice idea inside my head. And now it's real – too real – and too late.'

'What do you mean, too real?'

'I mean – it's real! It could really happen! I couldn't face it, Muriel. I'm too old to change.'

There he was, 'brant as a hoose side', just as Cissie had described him, and already mucking out the cow house when they got back from breakfast the following day. Muriel went weak at the knees. He saw her and hesitated – and gave them his polite little bow, with his blue eyes full on her.

She approached, and stood before him. 'How are you, Ernst?' she asked, very politely.

'I am well,' he said, his eyes searching her face. 'How are you?'

'I am well,' she said. 'All the better for seeing you, Ernst.'

He smiled his little smile, but somewhat uncertainly.

Well, that's a start, she thought, with her pulse racing.

★　★　★

Doris was waiting for her at dinnertime. 'That looked a nice young man you were talking to in the yard,' she said.

'He is nice. He's one of the German prisoners. You can tell by the uniforms. They've got bull's eyes on the back and on the legs.'

Doris looked horrified. 'Do you mean they let you work with Germans – on your own?'

'Sometimes – when it's the only way to get the work done. Usually we work separately.'

'Working on your own, with Germans,' Doris repeated, shaking her head. It took her a minute or two to get over that, then she said: 'I've been to the farmhouse, and asked Auntie Elsie to ring a taxi for me.'

'Why?' Muriel said. 'Why not stay until the end of the week?'

'You're very kind, and it's been lovely, but it's Peter. I told you, I've dreamed about someone like him sweeping me off my feet for years, but in your dreams you don't consider what a change like that really means. If he'd lived in Holderness Road I might have dared do it, in spite of being terrified of – you know.'

'What?' Muriel asked.

Doris took a deep breath. Her cheeks went pink, and her voice sank to a murmur. 'You know – the goings-on in the bedroom.' She fanned herself rapidly with her hand for a moment or two. 'I come out in hot flushes, just thinking about it. It's too much of a change, at my time of life. I've left a letter for him with Auntie Elsie, in case he's not back before the taxi comes – to tell him I don't think I can be more than a friend. But you – you're young. You should marry John, and live in this beautiful place for the rest of your life, Muriel. From what I've seen, he really likes you.'

'I'm sorry you're going, Miss Chapman,' Muriel said. 'I'll miss you.'

The taxi came before the afternoon milking, and Miss Chapman fled, to the safety of her maiden life in Holderness Road.

Chapter 40

John strode towards her when she was driving the cows in for afternoon milking with Ernst and Audrey, looking as pleased as punch.

'She's gone, then,' he said.

'Aye, she's gone,' Muriel said, very short.

'Good. Auntie Elsie told me she'd rung a taxi for her.'

'Did Auntie Elsie give your dad the letter she left for him?'

'What letter?'

'What letter!' Muriel repeated, contemptuously.

'Well. Better get on. Make hay while the sun shines, as we say.' He glanced up at the sky. 'That's what we'll be doing tomorrow, I reckon, seeing as we've got a few dry days forecast. Maybe you'll get your chance to drive a tractor, now the visitors have gone, Audrey. Learn how to build a haystack. Cheerio, girls,' he grinned, and went off, without acknowledging Ernst at all.

'Have you got Doris's address?' John's father came to ask, when they were letting the cows out to pasture again.

'Wasn't it on the letter she left for you?' Muriel asked.

'What letter?'

'She said she'd left a letter for you with Auntie Elsie,' Muriel said.

'Huh!' he snorted. 'She's had a hand in this, then, has she? No, I've seen no letter – yet. You'd better give me her address, and I'll write to her.'

'Write to her at the Maypole on Holderness Road. That's where I wrote to invite her to stay, and it got to her all right,' she assured him.

'Did Doris tell you what I asked her?'

'She mentioned something. She thinks she's too old.'

'She's ten years younger than me, and I'm not too old. But I admit, we're getting on, and it's later than we think – so that's why there's not much time to waste. I'm not beaten yet, though,' he said. 'We've got two prisoners to help now – it would be more use if they could live on the farm to see the morning and the afternoon milking done, but still, they get through a fair bit of work while they are here, and you lasses have managed on your own when you've been pushed. So I might get the train into Hull on Monday and go to see her at work.'

'She doesn't finish till half past five, and then you might miss your train home – but Thursday's half day closing. You'd be better off going then.'

He hesitated for a moment, then nodded. 'That's what I'll do then. It'll be better all round – we'll have the haymaking over by then. I'll write to her at this Maypole she works at and tell her to expect me on Thursday.'

'And take it a bit slower with her,' Muriel said. 'It was the suddenness that panicked her, I think.'

Ernst and Wilhelm had gone, and Muriel and Audrey were just finishing the mucking out when John came storming into the cow house. 'I've just had a bloody roasting off my dad, for not being nice enough to your Miss Chapman. He reckons he's going to be chasing after her in Hull on Thursday. There's no fool like an old fool, is there? But why in God's name did you give him her address?'

'Because he asked me for it,' she said, being deliberately dim-witted.

'My God!' He let out his breath in a heavy sigh. 'And after everything I've told you about what might happen to the farm!' He gave her a look of utter disgust and walked away, shaking his head.

The cowman's wife returned just as they were going to the farmhouse for dinner. 'Robert's as well as can be expected,' she told them all. 'He'll be kept in about a fortnight. I didn't pack enough stuff to stay any longer, so I got the train to Griswold, and got a lift part of the way from there. Is your friend still here?'

'She went yesterday.'

'I wanted to thank her; she saved Robert's life. If it hadn't been for her, he wouldn't have been seen so quick, and the surgeon said if it had gone on much longer he might have ended up with meningitis, or an infection in his brain. It was a near thing, the surgeon said. If it had been left any longer he might have died. And he'll have to have a couple of weeks convalescing when he gets out.'

'I wouldn't take too much notice of that,' John said. 'These doctors always make things out to be worse than they are.'

'To make themselves important, I suppose,' Muriel said.

John rounded on her. 'What's wrong with you, lately?' he demanded. 'You've got some sarky little comment to make every time I open my mouth.'

'Well, I'll get back home,' Robert's wife said, hastily. 'See you two girls later, maybe.'

She was tidying her back garden when the girls went back to the cottage for an hour after dinner. 'I'd have liked to thank your friend,' she repeated. 'She was a nice woman.'

'She's so nice that the boss proposed to her, more or less,' Audrey grinned.

'Marry her, you mean?'

'Seems like it, but we don't think it'll come off. She says she's too old.'

'Well, he's a decent old stick. He'd treat her all right. She'd be all right for the rest of her life.'

Muriel left them chatting together, and took her tea to sit in the sun at the front of the cottage, and look at the scenery while getting her legs brown. She was just shutting her eyes for forty winks when Audrey brought a chair out and plonked herself down on it.

'Well, what a good old gossip I've just had with Robert's wife, Edie,' she said. 'It seems your John's had plenty of young women, but none of them good enough for him. He got two different lasses in the family way in his younger days and he's still paying to their bairns – his dad laid the law down for him and made him pay for their upkeep out of his own pocket.'

'Good for him,' Muriel said, fully awake now.

'And then he made him get an apprenticeship for the eldest, and pay for it – he's with the Walkers in Griswold training to be a carpenter and joiner. They've got that wood-yard opposite the Dog and Duck – we pass it every time we go into the village.'

The face of a young Griswoldian jumped into Muriel's mind. 'Candlestick!' she exclaimed. 'Did you get a good look at that lad? I've seen him sometimes as we've passed and thought he looked familiar, but I've only just twigged who he's like. John!'

Audrey nodded slowly. 'Aye, that's the budding carpenter, then, and he'll have to fork out for an apprenticeship for the youngest when he gets to fourteen, as well.'

'Serve him right, then!'

Audrey laughed. 'So after the second bout he learned his lesson, and picked a married woman in Driffield to carry on with for years. Edie says she thinks one or two of her bairns must be his, but he doesn't go so much now, what with the petrol rationing, and everything.'

'I wonder why she told you?'

'I don't know. Maybe she thinks one good turn deserves another, after us coming to the rescue with Robert. "Look out for your friend," she said. "Not that it'll make all that much difference to her – *if he marries her*. He takes no interest in any of 'em."'

'Huh!' Muriel exclaimed. 'And if he doesn't marry me, I might be looking for upkeep and apprenticeships from him if I'm not careful, I suppose she means. What did he say? "No sentiment in business!" No sentiment at all might be nearer the mark.'

'It goes without saying,' Audrey said, 'it would be a bad job for her and Robert if anybody found out she'd told us.'

'You've said it, anyway,' Muriel said, 'and nobody will find out.'

Chapter 41

John had one of the tractors ready with the mower the following day. 'We can't cut the hay till the dew's off it,' he said, 'so I'll set the German lads to mucking the cows out, and then we'll go and have some breakfast. You girls can both have a tractor lesson, today.'

'Aye, well, now we've got no Robert, I'd better go and see to the bull. You give 'em their orders, John,' his father said.

They saw the Land Rover rumbling down the lane as he spoke. It stopped outside the farm gate. Ernst and Wilhelm had just jumped out when they were all startled by a violent banging and crashing coming from the bull house, and yelling from John's father.

'Your dad!' Muriel shouted.

John stood as if rooted to the spot. Ernst leaped over the farm gate and raced to the bull house, stopping to grab a pitchfork leaning against the wall before going in, and closely followed by Wilhelm. A minute later, Wilhelm emerged, dragging John's father by the ankles. Ernst followed very smartly, and barred the door. Muriel's relief at seeing them both safe and in one piece was swiftly followed by shock at the sight of John's father. For a moment she thought he was dead. His lips were white, and his normally ruddy face ashen. There was blood all over his shirt and on his trousers.

'Dad!' John came to life, and ran to kneel beside him. 'Dad!'

His father opened his eyes and struggled to smile at him.

'What the hell are we going to do?' John said. 'We're nearly out of petrol, and there's no doctor for miles.'

Muriel looked down at him, remembering his words: 'You'd be surprised what enters people's minds when they smell money!' So what had entered John's mind, when he heard his dad being gored, and made no move to help him? How nice it would be to get rid of the horses, and split the farm into four, and have it all safely under his own total control, before Doris had the chance to spoil it all for him?

She dismissed the thought as too hideous to contemplate. 'Ring the army!' she said. 'There'll be no shortage of petrol there. See if you can get them to come and take him to hospital. If they won't, try the air force.'

Audrey was already half-way to the farmhouse.

The ambulance seemed to take an age. Ernst and John did their best to stem the bleeding, but daren't move John's father any further because of it, and the risk of doing him any further harm. When help arrived, an army doctor diagnosed several broken ribs, ruptured lungs, a ruptured spleen and possible damage to other internal organs. He gave John's father morphine and set up a drip, and told John his father would be lucky to survive. John got Auntie Elsie to accompany his dad to the hospital, pleading the good weather and need to get on with the haymaking as the reasons why he couldn't go himself. Before they left, the doctor told John that he should have the bull put down.

After breakfast John went into action to organise the work on the farm. He promoted Robert's wife Edie to Auntie Elsie's place. She would do the cooking for them all, with help from one of the labourers' wives. By that time the sun was high in the sky, and the hay nicely dried. John went to cut it with Wilhelm and his farm hands, leaving Ernst to help the girls with the work in the cow house and then feed and water the bull – after it had calmed down. When they'd done that, they could come and help with the haymaking, and have a lesson in tractor driving.

'That bloody beast ought to be shot, never mind telling someone to feed and water it!' Audrey said, when he was out of earshot.

'What? A ton of valuable property? No sentiment in business, you know,' Muriel said. 'He stands there while his father's being gored to death, and then he tells the man who risks his life to rescue him to risk his life again – to feed and water the bloody thing! That takes the biscuit, doesn't it? Don't feed his bull, Ernst! It won't calm down. If he wants it fed and watered, let him feed it and water it himself.'

Ernst laughed at her, his blue eyes dancing. 'No, I don't feed his bull, Muriel!'

'Whatever else we might say about your John,' Audrey said, 'he's no slouch when it comes to organising the work, is he? It comes before everything.'

'He's not my John,' Muriel said.

After mucking out, they went to help with the haymaking, spreading the cut hay out to dry in the field, and at last Audrey got her tractor-driving lesson on the farm's newest Fordson. Muriel was starving by the time a hot and bothered-looking Edie and her helpers brought the dinner out to them in billycans, and ate with them before taking everything back again. The meal was not much better than hostel food, and Muriel found herself wishing Auntie Elsie back home, though not for the pleasure of her company. The girls went to get the cows in for afternoon milking after Edie and one of her assistants brought lounces out at four o'clock. After mucking out, they went back to the meadow, and helped with the hay harvest until dusk, long after the prisoners had gone.

'That was a good day's work,' John said, looking well satisfied. 'That's more use than sitting on your backsides, playing whist. We might get another cut before winter. The corn harvest looks like being good this year, as well. Did that German lad feed the bull, like I told him to?'

'No, he didn't,' Muriel said. 'It hadn't calmed down, and we told him it was too dangerous. It would be murder to send anyone in there, when we've seen what it did to your dad.'

'It hasn't been fed and watered yet, then?'

'No.'

'Just remember this, Muriel,' John said. 'I give the orders on this farm. Not you.'

'I'm fed up with him,' Audrey said on the way back to the cottage. 'I'd like to give him a piece of my mind.'

'Better not give him too much, though,' Muriel said. 'We want to carry on working here as long as he's got Ernst and Wilhelm.'

They looked at each other, and grinned.

Audrey stopped smiling. 'I wonder how his dad's doing, though, poor old bugger?'

'I wonder? I can't say I hold much hope out for him.'

'Can't say I do, either.'

Chapter 42

'He's got fifteen broken ribs, a ruptured spleen, and a puncture wound to his stomach, and they say he's lucky to be alive; it would have killed many a man half his age. They'd given him four pints of blood before I left. But it was pointless me staying in Beverley when there's so much to do here,' Auntie Elsie told all the haymakers when she brought them their afternoon tea and lounces. 'He's too poorly to talk to anybody, and he'll be like that for days, they said. Maybe weeks.'

There were looks of sympathy and murmurs of 'Shame!' and 'Poor chap!' from her audience.

'They think he'll get better, then?' Muriel said, hopefully.

Auntie Elsie shook her head. 'They can't say, but we're not thinking of any other possibility – are we, John?'

'We're not!' John said, vehemently dashing the dregs of his tea onto the stubble.

'A newspaperman came to see me while I was at the hospital, to get the full story, so it might come out in the *Beverley Advertiser*, or the farming paper,' Auntie Elsie said, before departing with Edie and the tea things.

Muriel and Audrey went with Ernst to get the cows in for afternoon milking. John ran to catch them up.

'When you've finished mucking out, Ernst, go in and feed that bull,' he said. 'I went in this morning, and he's quite tame now.'

'He is not tame,' Ernst said.

'Just feed him,' John said, abruptly, and walked back to the tractor.

'Don't feed him, Ernst,' Muriel said, not caring whether John or anybody else heard her or not.

He heard, and turned back. 'You seem quite fond of this chap, Muriel. Are you?'

'I should have thought you'd be fond of him yourself, after he pulled your dad out of the way of a raging bull,' she retorted.

'He didn't. That was Wilhelm, if you remember,' John reminded her. 'Now go and get the cows in, and stick to your own business. Mine's the farm. Yours is to work under my orders, and nothing else. And you, Ernst, you can let that bull into the fields when you take the cows out. He's all right now. That attack on my father was a one-off. We've had him three years. He's never done anything like that before, and he'll probably never do it again.'

'Probably!' Audrey exclaimed.

'Just get on with what you're here to do,' John said, and walked away.

'I'll bet you any money he never went near that bull this morning,' Audrey said, as they went to get the cows in.

'How much money have you got?'

'Well, if I had any, I'd bet you any amount.'

'I wouldn't take your bet,' Muriel said.

Ernst was smiling at them both, and Muriel guessed he must have understood at least the gist of what they'd said. He disappeared while they were letting the cows out again, and came back when they were washing the equipment.

'He is fed, but he is not tame. I shut him up.'

'So you should keep away from him altogether.'

'He was very thirsty. And hungry.'

Muriel's eyes flashed with indignation. 'Let him be thirsty and hungry, then, rather than you have fifteen broken ribs, and a ruptured spleen!'

'*And* a punctured stomach,' Audrey reminded them.

'He's too dangerous – never mind what John says. Think what happens after the war!' Muriel urged him.

'What happens after the war, Muriel?' Ernst asked.

She felt the intensity of his gaze upon her. 'People who can work can always survive,' she said, 'and people who are crippled by bulls can't work.'

After mucking out they went to join the haymakers again, turning the cut hay with wooden rakes to dry in the wind, and working long after Ernst and Wilhelm had gone. Auntie Elsie and Edie brought scones and cans of cocoa from the farmhouse. One of the farm hands read them the news headlines from the day before yesterday's paper: 'Red Air Force hammer Nazi planes – 160 destroyed –700 Soviet planes carried out the attacks . . .'; 'Flare up in the Med soon? Blow at Italian mainland would isolate garrisons . . .'; 'Heavy damage in great RAF raid on Cologne. Hamburg also bombed . . .'

The tide was turning in the Allies' favour, they all agreed, and then continued turning the hay until it was almost dark.

'No chance of you getting to your favourite chapel today, Audrey,' John said when they were up to get the cows in the following morning. 'No petrol.'

'Can't you take some of the petrol you've got for the generator?' Muriel asked.

'And then the generator wouldn't work, would it, and what happens to the milking machines then, and the lights for the house? Have you ever tried to milk a herd that size by hand? It would take you all day.'

'Never mind,' Audrey said. 'I'm quite happy to sacrifice a sermon to the generator, if it's really necessary. We've all got to do our bit, haven't we?'

'Well, that's one of you showing the right attitude, at least.'

'I don't mind sacrificing my Sunday sermon to the farm, either, John,' Muriel said.

'Not much of a sacrifice for you, is it though, Muriel?' he said. 'You're not the chapel sort. Well, the prisoners won't be here today, so I suppose I'd better go and feed that bloody bull.'

'I wouldn't, if I were you. But don't let it out, will

you?' Muriel said. 'I'm not going into any field that that's in, and I don't care whether it's the right attitude or not.'

His eyebrows twitched upwards for an instant before he turned and went towards the bull house, followed by two of the farm hands.

After milking, they spent their leisure time learning how to cock the hay, setting the dried sheaves into stooks and leaving it to dry further. Then they turned the hay that was still drying again. They went to bed exhausted, but well fed, and content.

Before Ernst and Wilhelm left the following day, the meadow was filled with neat stooks, drying in the sun in long, golden rows.

Muriel found a letter for her in unfamiliar handwriting when they got back to the cottage, postmarked Attlebridge. She ripped it open and read it.

'What is it?' Audrey asked.

'It's Fred! They've sent him back to America. He was in a plane that crashed into a haystack.' Muriel gave a wry smile and shook her head. 'Well, that's just the sort of disaster you'd expect to happen to Fred.'

'You wonder how they manage to fly so low they crash into haystacks,' Audrey said. 'How bad is it?'

'Bad enough. A few broken bones, including his wrist.'

'Oh, well, it got him sent back home. His mother will be pleased about that, I reckon,' Audrey said.

'She will, and I hope she keeps him there, out of harm's way.' Muriel smiled, feeling there would always be a little corner in her heart for Fred. 'Oh, but he was a brilliant dancer. I hope the haystack hasn't put paid to that.'

The sun had not quite set, and they sat outside the cottage to drink their last cup of tea and watch the sun go down, breathing the scent of cut hay and looking over a field of barley, shimmering in the fading light.

'And think,' Audrey said, 'all this could be yours, Muriel. It must be a big temptation. Have you made your mind up about John, yet?'

'I think it'll be made up for me, before I'm much older, especially if I keep harping on about that bull,' she replied.

A letter arrived from Doris the following day. '. . . I went to see Peter on Sunday. He asked one of the nurses on his ward to write to me at the Maypole. She was due a couple of days' leave, and she lives quite near, so she brought it herself. So I went up on the bus, and had an hour with him. He looked terrible. I was shocked to see him and he couldn't talk much, because he was in such a bad way. They say it's a miracle he lived through it, but they think he'll live to fight another day. But not with bulls, I hope. He says John will have got rid of it by now. He said if it hadn't been for those German lads, he'd be shaking hands with the angels. He managed to say that. Isn't that amazing? That the Germans rescued him, I mean? I'm going again, on Thursday afternoon . . .'

Muriel read the letter to Audrey. 'I'd have written to tell her myself, but you know what it's been like here, we haven't had a minute. So Peter's done it, in spite of being half dead. That's what's amazing.' She put the letter aside.

'Old ground for Doris – visiting suitors in hospital,' Audrey said.

John fed and watered the bull the following morning, and came into the cow house to tell Ernst to go and feed it and muck it out before he left in the afternoon. 'No,' Muriel said. 'Don't do it. It's too dangerous.'

John turned on her, furiously. 'Will you stop countermanding my orders?'

'Not if you give orders that might get someone killed. And your dad's expecting you to get rid of it, by the way.'

'How do you know what my father's expecting?'

'Doris told me.'

John started back. 'And how does she know?'

'He told her – when she went to see him.'

He leaned towards her, with his eyes blazing. '*When she went to see him?*' he repeated. 'And how did she know he was there? Was that your doing?'

Ernst came to stand protectively beside her.

She shook her head. 'It was nothing to do with me. He did it himself. He got one of the nurses to write to her at the shop.'

'He did, did he? He could barely breathe when Auntie Elsie left him.'

'Just shows how tough he is, doesn't it? He'll live to fight another day, and he's expecting you to get rid of the bull.'

'I'll have words with you later,' John said, and looked at Ernst. 'You feed and water that bull before you go, Ernst, and muck it out.'

'I'm telling your dad, then,' she called, as John walked away. 'We'll see what he says to it.'

He turned back. 'You've got the cheek of the devil! You must think I'm so besotted with you I'll put up with anything,' he said, 'or that I'm in such straits for workers you can say anything you like, but this is where you get off, lady. So when you go back to the cottage tonight, you pack your things. You'll be leaving in the morning. And you don't bother my father – he's ill.'

'I leave also,' said Ernst.

'All right, you leave also. You can both be replaced.' He looked at Audrey. 'And so can you – if you want to go.'

'I don't want to go,' Audrey said. 'I want to stay, and learn how to work with horses and build a haystack.'

John looked astonished. 'Huh! Not such good friends as I thought, then. Well, that suits me. You're a good worker, Audrey, and you'll get every opportunity to work with the horses – and learn how to build a haystack.' He turned again and strode away.

Muriel contrasted the two men, man for man, without the assets, without the labels. English, German, American – what did they mean? Nothing. They were just words, words that said nothing about what a man really was. Strip a man of everything but the clothes he stands up in and set him against the next, and which is truly the better man? And which man would she rather lie next to in bed for the next fifty years? She watched John go, without regret.

'Do you blame me?' Audrey said, when they were sitting outside the cottage with their beakers of cocoa that evening.

'How can I?' Muriel said, watching the sun do down on Thornhill Farm for the last time. 'I'd have done the same if he'd sacked you, and Ernst had been staying. No, course I don't blame you for hanging on while Wilhelm's here.'

Edie brought a chair out and sat with them. 'The postman gave me his paper when he brought a letter from Robert this morning.' She handed it to them, folded back at the write-up.

FARMER GORED BY BULL

Saved from death by quick-thinking farm workers

Farmer Peter Goodyear is lucky to be alive after being gored and crushed by a bull on his farm near Griswold, doctors say. Mr Goodyear underwent an emergency three-hour operation on Friday. 'I could feel my ribs snapping like twigs. I was gasping for breath, and I could feel the blood running into my lungs,' he said yesterday.

'I thought his time had come,' his sister said. 'If it hadn't been for two lads who risked their lives to drag him away he would not be alive today.'

Mr Goodyear's cowman, Robert Thwaites, said that the family had owned the bull for four years, and although it was sometimes noisy it had never attacked anyone before . . .

'I notice they call the prisoners "farm workers", and "lads",' Muriel said. 'I wonder if that was Auntie Elsie's doing, or the reporter's?'

'Either way, it wouldn't do to give them any credit as Germans, would it?' Audrey said.

'Aye, I noticed that,' Edie said, 'and Robert says in his letter that the boss told them it was the Germans.'

'Well, that's the way it goes,' Muriel said, with a sardonic laugh. 'But if they hadn't rescued him, I bet you any money it would have been "German prisoners stood by and did nothing as farmer gored to death."'

'I bet you it would,' Audrey said.

Muriel slept like the dead that night. When dawn broke he stood in front of her more vivid than life, smiling his little smile, with the grey mist swirling behind him. He moved two or three steps away and held out his hand.

'*Komm.*'

She looked into his blue eyes and breathed his name, knowing she must be dreaming. With a broader smile and a tilt of his chin he beckoned her with the fingers of his outstretched hand. '*Komm mit!*' She laughed in her sleep, and looking directly into his eyes she willingly, wilfully *Komm*ed *mit*, clasped his hand, and felt it tighten round hers, felt him lift her into his arms and carry her away.

She woke up light of heart and laughing, to a glorious dawn chorus outside the open window and the sweet scent of new-mown hay.

Chapter 43

She helped them with the milking until it was almost time for the Land Rover to arrive with the prisoners, and then went to get her suitcase from the cottage.

'I'm sorry it had to end like this, Muriel,' John said, as they stood at the farm gate, 'but you're a wilful, impudent little bugger, and you won't be told. We might have had a future together, but there's a limit to what a man can stand.'

'There's a limit to what a woman can stand, as well, John,' she said. 'Did you see the report in the paper about your dad?'

'Yes,' he said.

'I hope you'll get rid of that bull, then, before it does the same to someone else – or worse.'

The Land Rover drew up and Wilhelm got out with another prisoner. Ernst must have told him about her sacking. 'Thank you, Muriel,' he said.

'*Dankeschön, Wilhelm,*' she replied, and wished both prisoners a cheery '*Guten Morgen!*'

'Can you drop me anywhere near the Land Army hostel in Griswold?' she asked the driver.

'At a bus stop, not far off.'

'That'll do.'

'Jump in, then.'

She got into the Land Rover and sat opposite the only two prisoners remaining: Ernst and the man who had been trying to show them photos of his family the first day she and Audrey had arrived in Griswold. They both smiled at her and tried to make conversation. They had been having English lessons in the camp, the older man said. She sat talking to them and wondering how long it would be before she saw Ernst again, apart from an occasional glimpse of him in Griswold chapel. When they arrived at the last farm on the round the older man got out first.

Ernst looked into her eyes. 'Ernst and Muriel, always,' he said, clasping her hand.

'*Muriel und Ernst, immer,*' she replied.

A brief kiss, and he was gone.

Muriel breakfasted on a cheese and lettuce sandwich, while the warden telephoned the War Ag, and then settled down in the common room for a mammoth letter-writing session. The first was a long letter to Fred, care of his mother in America, hoping he would soon be dancing again, and telling him the tragic news that she had fallen in love with a prisoner of war who – as far as she knew – couldn't dance a step. She hoped he would have better luck and find a nice American girl who could jitterbug, because he should be with his family, and she could never have left England. The next letter was to Doris, to say how glad she was that she had managed to go and see Peter and cheer him up. Finally, she wrote to her mother to say she hoped to be home for the following weekend.

With the letters finished, she took one of the bikes and cycled into Griswold to catch the post. The old warden and her new husband were walking towards her, Miss Hubbard – or rather Mrs Mawson – looking more cheerful than Muriel had ever seen her. The goings-on in the bedroom obviously held no terrors for her – maybe they had even improved her temper. The newlyweds looked quite happy until they saw Muriel, and then their expressions could have turned the milk sour. On the way back to the hostel Muriel rode on the other side of the road, curious to look into Walker's wood-yard to see if she could catch a glimpse of Candlestick. He was there, lifting some floor-boards into a lorry, a nice young lad, she thought – and in looks an unmistakable chip off the old Goodyear block.

The girls were starting to get back from work when she arrived back at the hostel.

'What's up?' Joan joked. 'Has he chucked you off his farm?'

'He has,' Muriel admitted.

Eileen's eyebrows shot up. 'What for did he do that? Did you try to milk the bull or something?'

Muriel gave them a brief report of the proceedings at Thornhill after Mr Goodyear had been gored, without saying too much about Ernst.

'Welcome back,' Joan said. 'We'll put the gramophone on after tea and have a bit of a jig to celebrate.'

'Speaking of which,' Muriel said, 'have you heard about Fred Sears?'

They hadn't, so Muriel gave them the details.

'I'll kill Joyce,' Joan said. 'She knows every GI in Norfolk. She ought to have written and told me.'

Talking about Fred and their one and only party in the hostel took them up to teatime, and food which had gone from bad to mediocre – a step in the right direction, at least.

Miss Fawcett came the following day, far from pleased with Muriel for her failure at the Goodyears' farm. Muriel told her what had happened and made no apology for it. She thought she was justified.

Miss Fawcett took a different view. 'It's not for you to tell farmers how to run their farms,' she said. 'If the prisoner hadn't wanted to look after the bull, it was up to him to say so.'

But Ernst was safe. Muriel had got what she wanted, and for her, further discussion was beside the point. She let Miss Fawcett have her say with no more argument, and was told she would lose a week's wages and be put back to fieldwork. Since she'd learned the art of milking in Norfolk, Joan, much to her disgust, was to be sent to Thornhill to stay in the cottage with Audrey. Miss Fawcett would visit her within the week to see how things were going.

'John's looking for a wife,' Muriel told her after Miss

Fawcett had gone. 'You'd be all right there, Joan. They've got three tractors and a thousand acres, and he gets everything when his old dad's "happed up". Might not be very long, either, judging by the state of him after his bull fight.'

'No, I wouldn't be all right there, and I don't care what he gets,' Joan said. 'I don't want to be stuck on a farm out in the wilds of Yorkshire. That wouldn't be much better than going to America, would it?'

'You could never leave your mum,' Muriel laughed.

'No, I couldn't,' Joan agreed, 'and when this war's over I'm never moving out of Norfolk again.'

Travelling home on a packed train full of young service people and their banter could not be said to be lonely, but Muriel missed Audrey, all the same. She called in to the Maypole on her way up Holderness Road. Miss Chapman asked her about the farm, and John.

'We fell out,' Muriel said. 'I'm not there any more. I'm back at the hostel.'

'You fell out? Whatever for?' Miss Chapman protested. 'He was such a nice young man. I thought marriage was on the cards.'

Muriel shrugged. 'Maybe so, maybe not. Anyway, I went off him, so it won't be happening now.'

Miss Chapman gave her a very penetrating look. 'It's Bill, isn't it?' she said.

'No, it's not Bill. He tried to shove that German prisoner in to feed the bull and muck it out, after seeing what it did to his dad. That's what put me off him, finally.'

'Well, it's a pity. It would have been a wonderful place to bring your children up.'

'Are you going to see Peter tomorrow?'

'Yes. Would you like to come for afternoon visiting?'

'I would.' Muriel nodded. 'I liked him, and I can go back to Griswold from Beverley.'

'I'll come down on the bike and call for you.'

Chapter 44

Muriel walked all the way to Morley Villas with her mind filled with memories, and an awful sadness that the constant companion of her childhood was gone, his ghost alone wandering with her through the familiar streets. Auntie Ivy was having a quiet half an hour knitting and listening to the wireless with her mother when she got home. When Doreen and Betty came in from school Muriel went out to turn the skipping rope for them and a horde of neighbouring children. After tea she had no desire to go out again, but had a peaceful evening with her mother and Arni listening to all the news of Morley Villas and the spiritualist church, and giving them the details of Doris's visit to the farm, Fred's accident, milking cows, haymaking, and the farmer who was gored by his own bull. She thought it better not to mention the fact that she might have been mistress of a thousand acres had she not chosen to sacrifice it all for the love of a penniless German.

She was tired, and went to bed not long after Doreen. She stood at the bedroom window and looked across to

Bill's house, and for one heart-stopping moment she fancied she saw his mischievous little ghost looking back at her and waving, the way he used to do.

Robert's wife Edie and her sister were among the visitors waiting to go in to see the patients. 'I got a lift to Beverley yesterday with the postman to come in and see Robert, but John's coming to see his dad tonight, after milking,' Edie said, 'so he'll take me back. I think it was awful, him giving you the sack like that. Does he know you're here?'

'Not unless he goes in for mental telepathy,' Muriel said. 'I didn't know myself, until I saw Miss Chapman.'

'Well, lucky he's not here until tonight is all I can say, going by some of things he's called you. He's got rid of bull, though. It's gone for slaughter. Come and see Robert for five minutes later on, Miss Chapman; they only allow two visitors to a bed, but my sister won't mind waiting outside, will you, Winnie? He's a bit better now, and I know he'd like to say thank you. He looks a sight, though, now bandages are off. They've shaved all his hair off round where mastoid was – he's half scalped.'

'It'll grow again, and it's a small price to pay, for a life, isn't it?' Winnie said, smiling at Miss Chapman.

'He meant to kill me,' John's father said, 'he intended it. I could see it in his eyes. He threw me feet into air, and when I landed I thought he'd broken my back. If it hadn't been for German lads . . .'

'He gets tired easily,' Doris said. 'He doesn't have to say much before he's worn out. John's coming to see you tonight, Peter!'

'Well, he got rid of the bull, at least,' Muriel said, 'and you look a lot better than you did, Mr Goodyear.'

'Can't get him out of my mind, way he looked at me, coming at me. Can't get him out of my mind,' he gasped.

'It'll take time, Peter. Time, and patience. Time's a great healer,' Doris said.

'I'm not the man I was,' Peter said.

'Time and patience, Peter,' Doris said, and held his hand.

Muriel sat back and looked at her, and realised that Doris was a giver, and couldn't be a taker. First her fiancé, then her mother, and now Peter – and Muriel knew she would stick by Peter as long as he needed her.

'Invasion of Sicily opens Assault on Europe,' the paper said on Monday. 'Many landings reported; operations going according to plan . . . Grim Beach fighting . . . Italians say parachutists were used . . . '

When Muriel went with Eileen, Vera and Laura to the Half Moon the following Saturday the inn was rather depleted of paratroopers and airmen.

'They must be otherwise engaged – being dropped into Sicily, I reckon,' Eileen said, with a worried look that was mirrored in the faces of the other girls.

The landlord was showing some concern as well, and not only for his profits, Muriel suspected.

★ ★ ★

On the last day in July she got a letter from Audrey, giving her the news from Thornhill. '. . . Joan's miserable because she's got nobody to jitterbug with, but the good meals compensate quite a lot. John's got rid of the bull, and he's being very careful how he treats us. I don't think he wants to lose any more workers. I drive a tractor sometimes, now, and go round it with a grease gun to make sure it's kept running smoothly. Everything's going all right on the farm.

'Wilhelm is in a terrible state. He heard about a massive air raid on Hamburg a week ago, and he's worried sick about his family . . .'

The following day Muriel went to chapel with a few of the other girls and gave Ernst as many illicit smiles as she dared. Wilhelm's face looked tight and drawn, and she tried to convey her sympathy with a look. After dinner she sat in the garden with Eileen and a few others who had joined at the same time, all sewing red triangles on the sleeves of their greatcoats, to signify that they'd served six months in the Women's Land Army.

'Just think!' one of the girls said. 'If we stick it another six months, we'll get another triangle, to make a diamond!'

'Whoopee!' groaned Eileen, sounding deeply unimpressed, but she was happy, having had a letter from her young para.

There was a crack of lightning, and a roll of thunder. Soon the girls had to gather up their greatcoats and their sewing tackle, and dash for the house, out of the pelting rain.

Chapter 45

Harvest time found Muriel cycling with Laura and Eileen to the Winters' farm, where she and Audrey had helped with the threshing. Ernst was standing by the Land Rover with two other prisoners when they arrived, while Mr Winter was ranting to the driver about the weather, and complaining about the Land Rover coming for the prisoners at teatime – when the work was only half done.

'I need 'em as long as light lasts, if I'm going to get corn in before weather breaks,' he said.

'They might escape,' said the driver.

'They're left in fields working on their own, most 'o time! They could have escaped a dozen times, if that was in their minds. And where would they escape to?' Mr Winter asked.

'No food, no shelter, miles from anywhere and sticking out like a sore thumb in prisoner of war uniforms!' Muriel added.

'And all the signposts gone,' Eileen chipped in.

'And they don't even speak the language,' Muriel said, with a smile at Ernst.

'There are rules,' the driver said. 'Ever heard of the Geneva Convention?'

'Ever heard of starvation? That's what this country's facing, if we can't produce enough to feed it,' Mr Winter countered, looking pointedly up at the sky. 'It's been unsettled for most of month. Now we've had a few fine days, and Met Office is forecasting rain again. We've got to get harvest in before weather breaks.'

'I'll see what the boss says,' the driver said.

'Come back at ten o'clock,' Mr Winter said. 'We might be done by then. Or don't come at all and leave 'em here all night – they can sleep in barn.'

Mr Winter's two young sons brought the horses from the stables and put them in the shafts, and they set out with the wagons to the fields where the dry corn stood waiting for them, in endless rows of golden stooks.

They set to work, Muriel and the other girls pitching up the sheaves, and the men building up load after load for the straining horses to pull to the stack yard. The work went on until eleven o'clock and a brief rest for sandwiches, fruit pie and cold cider. The sun rose higher in the clear blue sky, and a heat haze shimmered in the air. The work was hot, and the thirsty workers were glad of the extra flagons of cider Mrs Winter had left for them. Muriel felt the sun scorching her skin and the pitchfork blistering her hands and sweat running from every pore, and knew everyone else was the same – but they worked doggedly on until around four, when they stopped for tea and scones. Then work resumed until the sun began to go down and the moon to rise, and Mrs Winter and her daughter brought a picnic supper in one of the returning wagons, plenty for everyone. Then they sat down together to a massive bacon and egg pie and well-buttered sandwiches of ham or cheese, followed by cakes, buns and tarts, and mugs of sweet, hot cocoa. The night was warm, and so was the feeling between farmers and workers, and Muriel thought she had never enjoyed a supper as much in her life.

Mrs Winter and her daughter gathered up the remains of the meal and started the trek back to the farmhouse, and the workers took up their positions again, and worked on until the sun was gone and the harvest moon rose in the sky. Then the last of the corn was loaded and fastened with ropes.

'Land Rover's here for prisoners, but it doesn't matter now. Harvest's in,' Mr Winter told them. 'Do you want to stay on wagon for a ride back?' he called up to Ernst, making his meaning clear as much by gesture as by words.

'No,' Ernst called. 'I walk, with Muriel.'

Mr Winter laughed. 'Heave her up! She can have a ride up there with you!'

So with help from below and above, Muriel clambered up to the top of the last load.

'Just don't fall off, either of you!' Mr Winter warned.

The horses strained forward, and Muriel and Ernst lay back on the warm corn with the cart creaking and rocking beneath them.

'It is nice, *ja*?' he said, pointing upwards at a harvest moon like a big yellow lantern in a sky filled with stars.

'*Ja*, it is nice,' Muriel agreed, and turning towards him, raised her tired arm to stroke his face. Her mother and Arni, Auntie Ivy and Betty, and even Miss Chapman might see him as the enemy, and now she'd thrown her lot in with him they might see her as the enemy too. But he was not the enemy and she saw what they must also come to see in the end: a man is just a man, either a good one or a bad one. No label alters it, and Ernst was the man for Muriel.

The cart moved on with its rocking motion, and a light breeze fanned their faces. He took her hand and squeezed it.

'I was being sensible when I said no more Ernst and Muriel, but love and good sense sometimes pull in opposite directions,' she murmured, half to herself, and not expecting him to understand.

He understood well enough, and turned towards her, gazing into her eyes. 'Love is the strongest.'

'It's not always.'

'It is, or it's not love.'

She was silent, for a moment. 'And what about the children?' she said.

'They have love, enough to make them strong,' he said, and with such confidence, she knew it would be so. The children would have love in abundance; so much it would make them strong enough to face anything life held.

She turned her face to his, and kissed him. 'You are my harvest home,' she said.